Jacqui Rose is a novelist who now lives in London, although she hails from South Yorkshire. She has always written for pleasure but the inspiration for her novels comes from her own experience. Her debut novel, *Taken*, was a Kindle bestseller.

For more information about Jacqui please visit www. jacquirose.com or follow her on Twitter @JacPereirauk

Also by Jacqui Rose

Taken

JACQUI ROSE

Trapped

AVON

AVON
A division of HarperCollins*Publishers*
77–85 Fulham Palace Road,
London W6 8JB

www.harpercollins.co.uk

A Paperback Original 2013
1

First published in Great Britain by
HarperCollins*Publishers* 2013

Copyright © Jacqui Rose 2013

Jacqui Rose asserts the moral right to
be identified as the author of this work

A catalogue record for this book is
available from the British Library

ISBN-13: 978-1-84756-321-7

Set in Sabon LT Std by Palimpsest Book Production Limited,
Falkirk, Stirlingshire

Printed and bound in Great Britain by
Clays Ltd, St Ives plc

MIX
Paper from
responsible sources
FSC
www.fsc.org
FSC C007454

Acknowledgements

The journey I took whilst writing *Trapped* was an altogether different one to anything I'd ever experienced. It was the beginning of a new dawn. A closing of the door on a long, difficult chapter of my life and my children's lives. A time when I had to learn to put my trust wholly in others. A time when it felt I was freefalling though in my heart I knew there'd be someone to catch me this time, and it was for these reasons I wrote this book.

I want to acknowledge the bravery of my children; to thank them for their love and the way they continue to soar and fly. My deepest thanks also to my friends and family for their continuing and unwavering support.

Thank you to my new and amazing editor, Caroline Hogg, whose patience, invaluable help (and steak dinners) guided this story into the finished novel. A big shout out to Keshini for all her help. A massive thanks to Judith Murdoch, the best agent in town, who continues to point me in the right direction and always has my best interest at heart. Thanks to the team at Avon who are, quite simply, wonderful.

Lastly, an everlasting thanks to DS Gavin Popplewell for his professionalism, his sensitivity and for his support in some of the darkest and bleakest of times. Thank you.

I'd also like to thank PC Vicky Siddall for her invaluable support and care when it mattered the most.

To my daughter Georgia, whose courage,
pain and love inspired and embodies the character
of Maggie. This one's for you.

Mummy x

CHAPTER ONE

'Bleedin' hell.' Maggie Donaldson swore loudly as she jumped out of the way, narrowly avoiding being hit by the china teacup which came whizzing past her head as she opened the front door. She watched, slightly bemused, as it smashed against the garish lamp in the corner and tiny fragments of blue china showered down.

Using the back of her red scuffed heel to shut the battered front door, Maggie's confusion slowly turned to anger as she looked around the gloomy hallway, listening to the raised voices. She sighed loudly.

She'd been away for just over a year and somehow during that time she'd convinced herself things would be different. It had been stupid to do so. Violence in her family was like a thirst; as recurrent and necessary as other people's cups of morning tea.

How many times as a child had she cowered in bed listening to the screaming arguments? The crying and the slamming of doors, before she'd made sure the coast was clear to creep downstairs to comfort and tend to her mother's injuries.

The brutality hadn't just stopped there. It had touched everyone with sadistic cruelty, twisting and coiling itself

1

around the heart of her family. Maggie could count on one hand the times she'd been hugged as a kid but she'd lost count of the number of black eyes she and her siblings had received growing up in the Donaldson household.

She'd only managed to survive her mother's visits to casualty, her father's drunken rows and the daily terror she'd seen in her siblings' eyes by having hope; hope that one day it'd all come to an end. But as Maggie Laura Donaldson looked at the discoloured silver cutlery strewn all over the floor with the mismatched tea set thrown about the hall like hand grenades in a battlefield, it told her all she needed to know. Her hopes had once again been as taunting and hollow as ever. Only a miracle could change things – and Maggie knew miracles didn't happen in the Donaldson household: not even small ones.

Standing with weary resignation in the newly painted kitchen doorway, Maggie watched as her father – armed to throw another porcelain bomb at her retreating mother – spat out his venomous words. 'Jaysus fucking Christ, Sheila, if it's the last thing I do, I'll put you in your grave. I'll happily do time for you. Look at me like that again and see what happens. I swear on the Virgin Mary, I'll . . .'

Interrupting her father's furious rant, Maggie spoke. Her voice was filled with the icy, hard edge she'd learnt from him. 'Hello, Dad. This is a nice welcome home ain't it? It's good to see nothing changes. Home sweet home, eh?'

Max Donaldson turned abruptly to stare at his daughter. His bloated red face showed a flicker of surprise before it turned into a familiar veil of scorn.

As he met her gaze, he noticed how much thinner Maggie's face looked from the last time he'd seen her. Her eyes had a distant look about them which hadn't been there before; but however worn out she looked, it could never detract from her beauty.

Her long auburn hair tumbled down in lustrous waves to the middle of her back. Her skin was flawless and pale. Her piercing blue eyes – a throwback from her Irish heritage – were mesmerizing. Where she got her looks from, Max didn't know. He knew he was no Rembrandt and as far as he was concerned his wife's looks were more in keeping with the living dead. Enough to frighten the devil himself.

As startling as Maggie's beauty was though, it didn't blind him as it did others. When he looked at his daughter he saw her for what she was. A cheeky mare who'd always had too much lip and bravado. The hundreds of beatings he'd given her hadn't done anything to curtail her air of arrogance. If anything, with every thrashing, with every bust lip she'd ever had at Max's hand, her sense of superiority and disdain towards him had grown.

Looking back, Max couldn't remember a time he'd seen her cry, in stark contrast to her brothers, who'd done his nut in by wailing for hours on end when he'd raised his fists to them. Maggie had taken the punishments he'd dished out to her in silent martyrdom. There'd been no tears, no screams, just her huge piercing blue eyes sadly gazing up at him; serving only to infuriate and double the severity of her beatings.

There was something about his daughter – though he'd never admit it to anyone, he even struggled to admit it to himself – which made him feel uneasy. He'd almost go as far as saying she made him feel ashamed of who and what he was. And because of these feelings he harboured inside him, that lodged in at the back of his throat like bile, Max Donaldson hated his daughter, Maggie. Putting down the fruit bowl he was about to throw at his wife, Max addressed Maggie with sneering contempt.

'Saints and mothers preserve us, look what the fucking cat's dragged in. I thought there was a nasty smell.'

3

The words slashed out at Maggie and it hurt. It always had. It was all she'd ever known from her father but somehow she'd never learnt to shield herself from his words as she'd done his fists; they continually managed to wound.

Sometimes the pain of his words became so great, it felt as if she was going to pass out, but like Max, when it came to her feelings, Maggie Donaldson was stubborn and proud. She'd rather put her fingers in a vice than ever let her father know that his verbal ill-treatment injured her more than any mouthful of knuckles or black eyes ever could.

Expertly, Maggie pushed the pain to one side, drawing up the protective wall she'd had to build throughout her life.

'Never one to disappoint are you, Dad? God knows what would actually happen if you managed to say "hello" after not seeing me for a year. It'd be like the Second Coming.'

'Oh please, you'll have me running to the bog to shit out the crap you're talking. You expect me to roll out the red carpet when you got yourself into the mess in the first place?'

'No, just a "hello" would do.'

Max snorted. 'You must think you're the Queen of Sheba. Take off that pair of big fucking boots you're wearing before they kick you in the arse.'

Maggie paused and took a deep breath. She was determined her father wouldn't get the rise he was looking for. When she had the fire in her belly not many things would stop her clenching her fists and wading in, even if it meant her coming off worse.

That's what'd partly got her into the latest trouble. Most of her life her anger had gotten the better of her. She'd become resilient to being knocked about and getting into fights with people when her temper rose up. But everything had to be different now. She'd made a promise to herself.

Even though she knew it was going to be hard not to resort to fists and fury, she had to try. Besides, being away this last time had changed her.

After a minute she spoke, narrowing her eyes as she did so. 'You've got the front to stand there and say it was *all* my fault?'

Max grinned menacingly and winked at his daughter, waiting for the usual reaction. But instead, Maggie calmly stepped forward, surprising herself with her control. The surprise was also reflected in Max's eyes. This wasn't the Maggie he knew. The Maggie he knew would have verbally leapt at him without thinking of the consequences, but this tall, beautiful, self-composed woman was a stranger to him. A stranger who unnerved even him.

Maggie was within spitting distance of her father's whiskey-smelling breath, centimetres away from his unshaven face. She stood glaring back at him, struck by a sudden realisation; she wasn't afraid of Max now, not the way she used to be. Wary perhaps, but she'd lost the nauseating fear that used to sit tightly around her chest, stifling the air she breathed, causing her to sometimes wet herself, even as a teenager, when she'd heard his voice.

She felt a light touch on her arm and Maggie became aware of her mother, Sheila, standing fearfully by her side.

'Leave it Maggie, please. For me. No trouble.'

Maggie looked at her mother and smiled softly, wanting to calm the dancing fear she saw in the terrified eyes staring up at her. Feeling the trembling hand on her arm made Maggie's heart almost burst with sadness.

She took in every detail of her mother's face as they stood in the overheated kitchen; the deep furrowed lines, the grey hairs by her temples, the little scar above her lip – the result of a broken bottle thrown in her face – and lastly, her mother's eyes: wide, anxious and blue like her own. Maggie slowly nodded. She would keep the peace – at least for today she would.

Stepping back from her father and facing her mother straight on, she spoke quietly and warmly with love in her eyes.

'For you; I'll do anything for you.'

Maggie touched her mother's cheek then bent down slightly to kiss Sheila on her forehead. 'It's good to see you Mum. I've missed you.'

Max Donaldson watched this exchange scornfully but also acutely conscious of the change in his daughter.

She was no longer afraid of him and he knew it could only spell one thing: trouble.

Still deep in thought, Max took out a small folded wrap from his pocket and emptied the white powder on the table. Leaning over, he pulled a rolled-up twenty pound note from his other pocket and, holding one nostril and placing the note in the other nostril, he expertly snorted up the cocaine in one go.

As it cut the back of his throat and the first tingle of coke hit his bloodstream, he straightened himself up, rubbing his nose between two nicotine stained fingers to wipe off any excess. He stared hard at Maggie who stood defiantly watching him from across the other side of the table.

He chose to ignore her. He had to think. Picking up his car keys, Max walked out of the kitchen, deciding he needed to find a way of putting his tramp of a daughter firmly in her place – and preferably sooner rather than later.

As soon as she heard the front door shut, Maggie threw down her bag and grinned excitedly, giving her mum a huge hug as she spoke.

'Well, where are they? Where am I going to meet them?'

Sheila broke away from the hug and looked down nervously at the red tiled floor, deciding it needed another clean now that most of last night's dinner had been chucked onto it. Not wanting to look at her daughter directly, she spoke softly.

'That's what I was going to tell you love; I didn't like to worry you when I came to visit, but a few things have changed since you were here.'

Maggie squinted her eyes. She always knew when her mum didn't want to tell her something, especially if it was something bad. This was one of those times. Watching her mother shuffle from side to side, Maggie bent her tall, slender frame down to her mother's eye level and spoke firmly but quietly.

'Mum, if you've got something to say, for God's sake, spit it out.'

Shelia stared into her daughter's eyes for a split second but quickly turned away, unable to hold her gaze. Her daughter's big blue eyes always made her feel guilty, reminding her of her kids' rotten childhood.

Maggie had seen so much and heard so much but complained so little. She'd always been a good daughter to her. Even though Maggie had suffered at the hands of her father and had been left for hours on end to look after her siblings when her mum was either in hospital or just couldn't cope, Maggie had always been loyal.

Her daughter was the only one who'd helped around the house, making well-needed brews, helping with the mounds of dirty laundry and the seemingly never-ending piles of washing up. It was only Maggie who'd ever spoken kind words to her and it was only Maggie who'd ever walked through a blizzard of snow to come and visit her in hospital when Max had fractured her pelvis. And closing her eyes at the thought, Sheila knew it'd only ever been Maggie who, even from an early age, had stood terrified but bravely in front of Max, willing to take the punches instead of letting him hurt her mum and siblings. Shamefully she'd let her; Sheila

7

had let her daughter stand there, becoming a human shield for her and for her other children.

Shelia knew by rights it should've been *her* who was there for her daughter, but knowing life would've been even more intolerable than it already was without Maggie, she ignored the gnawing guilt of this role reversal and just continued to be grateful for the care her daughter showed. And now the one time Maggie had *actually* asked her for help and needed some support, she'd let her down and Sheila Donaldson didn't quite know how she was going to tell her.

'Sweetheart, you better sit down. You won't like what I've got to say.'

Max Donaldson hacked a deep chesty cough, releasing sticky yellow mucus from the back of his throat before spitting it out expertly on the step of Ronnie Scott's Jazz Club. He was angry. Not just because Maggie was back home. And not just because the stifling heat of the Soho streets was causing the sweat to drip down his back. And certainly not just because of the run-in he'd had last night at the casino with one of his rivals. He was angry for no other reason because that was who he was and always had been.

Since he was young, Max had felt the presence of anger as he felt the presence of the air he breathed. On some days he'd wake up feeling the slow burn of irritation, and by the time he'd got washed, shaved and was ready for breakfast, he was ready to pummel anyone who got in his way. He didn't fight the feeling – it got things done; made things happen. His temperament had made him a face. It stopped people taking the piss; the sensible ones anyway, the ones who didn't want to wake up in a hospital bed.

Striding to his car and ignoring the 'no littering' signs, Max threw away the contents of his pocket next to the bin. He was heading over to Wembley Park to see a person who hadn't taken what he was saying seriously – but Max was certain once he had paid them a visit, they'd never make such a stupid mistake again.

He'd thought about sending his 'butchers' to deal with it. They were the men who did the chopping – the hurting – but today he'd wanted to do it himself. In fact, he'd go as far as to say he was looking forward to it.

On paper, the Windsor Estate sounded majestic. Anyone who'd read only the name might be forgiven for imagining large white houses surrounded by trees with wildlife roaming in the nearby woods, but in reality Max knew the only wildlife the occupants saw were the cockroaches running up and down the cracked walls. And the closest it got to being majestic was its residents being carted off to do a stretch at Her Majesty's pleasure. There was no other way to describe it but bleak; bleak and harsh. It was, as Max saw it, the arsehole of life.

The estate, also known as Crack Castle, had been forgotten by society, making the tenants living on it easy pickings and often desperate for his services. When they ignored his warnings, there was no one foolish enough to call the police. More tellingly, there were no police officers willing enough to respond to their call.

Max stared at the grey door with peeling paint and indecipherable graffiti. He took a deep breath, preparing himself as if about to go into the ring, then kicked the bottom of the door several times, not wanting to touch it with his hands. The dried red marks looked suspiciously like blood. Receiving no answer after three knocks he booted it hard, taking the door off the top part of its hinges as he did so.

Fired up, Max ran into the front room curling his nose from the stench of urine and ignoring the sounds of a crying baby. He bellowed loudly, banging the wall with his fist and feeling the charge of adrenalin seeping through his body.

'Where the fuck are you?'

A woman in a nightie appeared at the door of the bedroom with a look of shocked recognition. Her thick brown hair was a mass of knots and grease, her skin had an outbreak of angry red spots and her eyes were devoid of any life.

'He ain't here.'

Max snarled, disgusted at the woman's appearance.

'I'll be the judge of who's here or not. Get out of me way.'

Max didn't wait for her to move. He pushed her hard, knocking her to the floor and stepped into the bedroom to see a child no older than six slumped on a dirty mattress which lay on the bare floorboards.

'Where's your Da?'

The boy's eyes were as dead as his mother's and he shrugged fearfully at the angry intruder.

'I said, where's your fucking Da?'

The woman – recovered from her fall – scrambled in front of Max, petrified for her son.

'Leave him alone, he ain't done nothing.'

'That's right, he ain't, but it don't matter to me who I have to knock about to get me money. So cop on to yourself and do your son a favour; tell me where your old man is. He owes me big time.'

The woman's eyes darted from Max to her son.

'Go through to the kitchen, get yourself a drink love, I'll be though in a minute.'

The boy ran out of the room quickly.

'He's paid you; he's already paid you the five hundred quid he borrowed.'

'Yeah, but he was late and as we agreed when you were so eager to borrow the money from me, any late payments means double payments.'

'He was only late by two days.'

'I'm no charity sweetheart. Interest occurs on my loans, just like in a bank. Think of me like a bank.'

'We haven't got anything else to give you; you had your men take the telly last week.'

Max sneered and stepped closer.

'If it makes you feel any better darlin', there's nothing on telly worth watching.'

He sniffed and spat on the floor continuing to talk in a threatening manner, feeling the early summer's heat stifling the already putrid air. 'I want this week's payment *now* or you'll be standing watching your boy becoming my punch bag.'

'You're sick, you know that.'

Max leaned into the woman's face, smelling her early morning breath and stale cigarettes.

'I may be sick babe, but that don't stop me wanting my money. I'm telling you now, I want to feel the greens in my hand by the count of five. Don't underestimate what I'll do.'

The woman's eyes suddenly flashed with terror.

'Look I ain't got your money, I swear.'

Max touched the woman's face and circled his large podgy fingers around her lips.

'Well there lies the problem because I'm not sure if you've got anything I want. Now if you didn't look like an arse end of a rat I might get you to work for me; pay off the money, but I can't imagine many punters willing to pay to shag a hanging bag of bones, can you?'

Max watched the woman's eyes fill up with tears as he walked towards the door.

'Now where is your old man? Or do I have to go and find that son of yours to show you how serious I am? One . . . two . . . three . . .'

As Max counted he produced a small silver headed cosh out of his pocket. The woman's eyes flitted around the room then she nodded her head towards the tall wardrobe in the corner, indicating Max should look there. He opened the doors, then laughed scornfully as he saw a sinewy looking man cowering in the bottom of it.

'Well, well. What have we got here? A coward and a money cheat.'

Without waiting for the man to talk, Max leapt at the trembling figure. His fists pummelled into any part of human flesh he could find. He felt his knuckle knock through front teeth and felt the wet of the blood on his hand. He pushed again with his clenched fist and heard the squelch of the teeth leaving the gum behind.

Max hammered down with the cosh; over and over again, until he felt a twinge in his back. He stood up, panting, still attacking the man with his feet as he kicked him in the side of his head.

'Next time you pay me on time. I don't like having the piss being taken out of me. Next time I won't go as easy on you.'

Max looked down at the man who was silently nodding. He was fairly certain the next time he came for his money it'd probably be wrapped in a big pink bow. Turning to the woman, Max grinned. He walked towards her and started undoing his trouser belt. As he reached her his hand stroked her shoulder.

'Perhaps it's your lucky day after all.'

Outside, Max lit a cigarette. It was only the beginning of summer and already the oppressive city heat was starting to drive him crazy. He unzipped his jacket which made little difference. Walking back to his car he thought of Maggie, hoping that putting the fear back into her would be as easy as it had been with the man.

* * *

The North Circular, the road which would take Max back to central London, had come to a standstill, along with Max's air conditioning. The combination of the two gave way for him to contemplate last night's altercation with a newfound rage.

The altercation had been with Frankie Taylor, a Soho face and successful businessman who'd made his money through strip clubs and peep shows. Max had known him for as long as he could remember. First as a business associate, and then as a rival. As the years passed the rivalry between the two of them had turned to hatred. Then the hatred had turned to a full-scale war between them. There wasn't a person Max loathed as much as the vain, perma-tanned, loud-mouthed Frankie Taylor. And there wasn't a person he didn't want to see in the ground as much as he did Frankie.

He'd bumped into Frankie at the casino and as usual the man had been as arrogant as ever. But the evening had taken a turn for the worse when Frankie had thrown a drink at him in full view of some of the biggest faces in London.

Remembering it, Max touched his chest, almost being able to feel the wet sticky humiliation of last night's drink on his shirt. If it hadn't been for the fact that Frankie had been surrounded by a group of his heavies, he would've taken him out there and then. But he could wait. What was it the priests used to say to him back in Ireland? All good things come to those that wait.

Frankie Taylor had made the ultimate mistake. He'd humiliated him, but Max knew exactly how he was going to pay him back. As the traffic started to move, Max smiled. Frankie had an Achilles heel. An Achilles heel which came in the form of his wife and son.

CHAPTER TWO

Maggie wiped away her tears. She was so unused to them, seeing them as some kind of weakness. She looked at her mother, bewildered by what she'd just been told. Not knowing what else to do, Maggie bent down, holding her head in her hands as she sat at the kitchen table. Not for the first time that day, she took a deep breath to stop her rage getting the better of her.

Prison time had changed her, or at least that's what she wanted to believe. She'd done a number of small stretches a few years ago but then it hadn't mattered. This time it had. She was twenty-five and as she kept telling herself, life had to be different now. She had to keep her temper in check. Stupidly she had thought it was going to be easier than this. She'd only been home a few short hours and already she could feel her resolve being sorely tested.

Her mother poured the tea as she talked.

'I'm sorry love but what other choices were there? We were desperate. Nicky told me Gina offered to help out; it seemed like a good solution at the time. What else could I have done?'

Maggie tried to stop the hysteria coming into her voice

as she watched her mother put down the teapot to open the back door, in a vain attempt to get some air into the stifling room.

'I don't know Mum, but anything; anything would've been better than this. It's the only thing I've ever asked of you.'

'It was hard to get out. I know it sounds like an excuse but . . .'

Sheila Donaldson trailed off. It not only sounded like an excuse, it *was* an excuse. And not until now, looking over at her daughter who was clearly in distress, did she realise how hollow and pathetic it sounded. Sheila tried again, not quite sure what she was going to say, but wanting to say something which might plaster over the damage.

'Mags . . . I . . .'

Maggie put her hand up to stop her mother saying anymore. She loved her mother so much, but the enormity of the situation was starting to sink in. Conflicting emotions were overwhelming her.

'Not now Mum, please. Not now.'

Sheila's agitation stopped her from being able to stay quiet. 'You won't do anything stupid will you Maggie? I don't want you getting into trouble again. I can see you brewing up already. That temper of yours is a Donaldson family trait; a curse running through our veins like bleedin' poison. Before you know it you'll be back inside and we'll all be back at square one.'

Maggie stared over at her mother. She tried to smile the same reassuring smile she'd conjured up even in the darkest of moments since she was a child, but nothing came. It was unprecedented, but for the first time, Maggie found herself unable to give her mother what she needed to make her feel that everything would be fine.

Recognising her mother was about to start talking again, Maggie scraped back her chair on the stone red tiles. Without

15

looking back she stomped out of the house and into the heat of the Soho streets, determined to ignore the words of caution from her mother which she could still hear as she walked down the street. She needed to find her brother.

Nicky Donaldson opened his eyes, wondering where he was. As he began to get his bearings, feeling like he was in a furnace, he realised someone was hammering on the car window. He'd only meant to catch a couple of hours' sleep before driving home. Now he guessed it was the next day, at God knows what time, with God knows who banging on the window.

His lips were stuck together with dry spit and his parched mouth felt as if he hadn't drunk anything for days; which was ironic as only a few hours before, he'd been knocking back double Scotches to take the edge off the effect of the generous amounts of cocaine he'd shoved up his nostrils. He wasn't sure how much he'd spent; only his wallet would know that.

Everyone he knew took coke; Soho was drowning in it. Nicky was certain if NASA took a satellite picture from space it'd look like the area was covered in a white cloud.

For some reason, the cocaine had taken a liking to him and however hard he tried, he wasn't able to kick the habit. Admittedly, he hadn't really tried very hard and taking the coke didn't *really* bother him. What did was the amount he spent on it. More to the point, how much he owed because of it.

The hammering continued and Nicky cursed loudly, before pulling himself up and half falling out of the car as he opened the door.

He was greeted by the amused face of Gary Levitt, Gina Daniels' nephew but more importantly, his coke dealer. Nicky got himself properly onto his feet and stretched, eyeballing Gary hard.

'Do you have to batter on the frigging window like that; you fair gave me a heart attack.'

Ignoring Nicky's annoyance, Gary spoke. He was amused to see Nicky wearing the same clothes he'd been in the night before, which meant he'd probably crashed out on coke and been in the back of the car ever since.

'How long have you been here? You look and smell like crap.'

Nicky Donaldson couldn't answer the first part of the question; he'd no idea what time it was. The second part of the question he agreed with so he didn't say anything, instead attempting to scrape off the encrusted vomit from the collar of his black Chanel shirt.

'I thought I recognised the car. It's your old man's ain't it? A nice bit of motor; shame he'll have to sell it to pay off your debts.'

Nicky shot his head up at Gary. He knew he owed money but he didn't think it was anything near the region of the price of a luxury car.

'Don't look so worried, I'm only having a rib, I ain't going to be too hard on you. Gina tells me you've been sorting her out, I appreciate that. Just do me a favour and clear the money up in the next two weeks. In the meantime, take this.'

Gary Levitt went into his jacket pocket and pulled out a bag of white powder, passing it to Nicky, whose eyes were wide with anticipation.

'Cheers Gal, is this on the house?'

Gary burst out into scornful laughter. 'Is it fuck, I'll just add it to the bill you already owe me.'

As Nicky jumped back into the car and drove off towards Covent Garden, Gary watched and wondered how Nicky could be such a fool for the drugs when he already owed so much. Not that he minded. His clients owing him was a natural part of the business. Eventually they owed him so much he ended up owning them. Hook line and fucking sinker. His to do what he liked with.

More often than not, he'd pimp out the women who owed him money. The men who did? He'd pimp out their girl-friends. They were too scared to object. One way or another he always got his money back and then some. And Nicky Donaldson would be no different – whether Nicky's father, Max, was a face in Soho or not.

Of course he had to be careful, but he doubted Max would give him any trouble. The man didn't seem to give a damn about Nicky. No one did. Apart, he supposed, from Nicky's sister, Maggie, who he hadn't seen in a while. The entire family was messed up and none more so than the oldest Donaldson son, Tommy.

CHAPTER THREE

Tommy Donaldson sat rubbing his eyes on the unmade bed, the only piece of furniture in the whitewashed room apart from the closet. He was enjoying the peaceful solitude as he stared at the blank wall in front of him. This was his private sanctuary. No one really came here and that was just the way Tommy liked it.

There were times he needed to get away, just to think, just to try to get rid of the voice and the vision of the woman he saw and heard so often inside his head. Now was one of those times.

He turned to look at himself in the mirror; he was twenty-eight years old but his blue eyes showed the signs of someone older. A man who hadn't slept for a couple of days. His skin was pallid and pale and Tommy knew he looked as bad as he felt. He was tired; his head was tired and that was a constant.

It seemed as if he'd lived with the voice and the visions most of his life. As a child he'd heard and seen it but there was never anyone to tell. No one to help him understand what it was. No one to trust, except for maybe Maggie. He'd often thought about telling her, but when it actually came down to it, he couldn't. Worried by what she might think. So every night he'd huddled alone in the dark, listening to the voice. Seeing the woman's face which haunted him and made him live in terror. Then on the rare days his head was quiet and still, he'd had to listen to the screaming voices of his mother and drunken father in the room below.

As a child he'd always been too frightened to call out for help in case the woman with her bloodied whispering screeches – which only he could hear or see – became angry with him. Or worse still, in case his father had heard him calling out and had come up the stairs to beat him for making a noise, leaving him struggling to walk the next day.

Over time, the secret fears which had plagued Tommy's mind as a child began to isolate him from his family. He was unable to listen to their raised voices as well as the one in his head.

Sometimes it got lonely being on his own, though he'd never had many friends as a child either. Not after the age of ten, not after Tommy had brought two of his best friends home after school to celebrate his birthday.

He remembered he'd had fun; his mother had secretly made him a cake. Maggie, who was three years younger than him, had given him a cross of St. Christopher, having nicked some of the church collection money off the plate. It had all been going so well, then his father had come home and found them playing with his music collection. Although nothing had been broken or damaged, no excuses were ever needed in the Donaldson household to launch into a violent attack.

His friends had managed to escape with only minor cuts and bruises; too terrified to tell their parents for fear of reprisal from Max. But Tommy had been badly hurt, as well as deeply humiliated at the thought of his home life becoming the subject of his classmates' idle gossip.

After he'd recovered in hospital – telling the medical staff he'd been attacked by a group of boys – Tommy had left friendships for other people. As he got older, the only other people he had around him apart from his family were the almost daily one-night stands. He liked the company of women. If it'd been his choice some of them would've stayed in his life longer than the few midnight hours, but he knew his father would have none of it, seeing women only good for two things; fucking and causing trouble.

On some days like today, shameful, clear and vivid memories came back to Tommy. Things he'd been a part of, things he certainly couldn't tell anyone about. And then he'd find himself drowning in his private sea of despair unable to save himself, seeing himself as a monster; a freak.

It was too late now to tell Maggie, everything had already gone too far.

Tommy stood in the deserted car park behind Lexington Street, wondering if anyone had seen him. It was dark as he stood over the semi-naked woman lying helpless at his feet on the cold wet ground. He saw the fear in her eyes as she looked up at him, wondering what he was going to do now.

His breath formed a hazy mist in the frosty unlit night. He tilted his head to one side watching the woman's chest rise slowly up and down with rasping breaths, blood oozing out from the side of her mouth onto the freezing earth. He put his hand on her mouth but the sound of the horn startled him and Tommy quickly ran off into the dark chill of the night.

The mobile phone rang in his pocket. Tommy's thoughts were immediately broken. He could feel his face covered in perspiration as the adrenalin pumped through his body and the images in his mind started to fade away.

Looking at his watch he saw it was coming up to three.

He needed to get a move on; he was supposed to be meeting his father in Soho later. There was always hell to pay if he wasn't there by the strike of the clock. The last thing he needed today was his father on his case, especially when his father was gunning for the Taylors.

CHAPTER FOUR

Johnny Taylor slowly opened one eye and groaned as the previous night's heavy session of drinking and copious amounts of cocaine finally caught up with him. He could feel the air was heavy with the early summer smog of London and the sound of a saxophone cut through the morning. If he'd been at all capable of moving, Johnny might've been tempted to open the window and throw iced water onto the musically inept busker outside, whose flat rendition of 'Moon River' certainly wasn't helping his hangover.

Carefully he lifted his head, which slammed it into a pulsating throbbing pain. He tried not to move it any more than necessary; afraid of the hangover from the bowels of hell he was certain to awake.

Opening the other eye just as slowly as the first, he was surprised to see the naked body of a sleeping woman, ungainly sprawled with her mouth wide open, snoring discordantly at the end of his bed. Though at least he recognised her, which was a start.

There was no mistaking the harsh bleached blonde with the dark roots and the faded rose tattoo on her thigh who worked in his father's clip joint at the end of Berwick Street.

23

Her name was Lucy; not that Johnny heard many people call her by her real name any more.

She'd turned up looking for a job a few years ago and within a short period of time she'd acquired the nickname, Saucers, thanks to the impressive size of her nipples. Far from being offended however, she'd warmed to the name immediately, proudly telling the punters her new pet name as she licked her heavily glossed lips.

Johnny found Saucers to be a bag of contradictions; a hardened brass who never raised her eyebrows at the often perverse requests asked of her, yet one who spent her spare time devouring books, romantic classical novels being her favourite. On many occasions he'd sat in the back of one of his father's strip clubs, handing her a box of Kleenex as she cried tears over one romantic hero or another.

'Oh I'd like to wring his neck. Pass me another tissue, Johnny.'

'Who is it this time?'

'Prince Stepan Oblonsky, that's who. Not a heart in the man. He's only gone and had an affair with the governess. Chop his balls off, I would.'

As usual he'd look at her blankly, only for Saucers to raise her eyebrows in exasperation at his ignorance. 'Anna Karenina?'

'You've lost me now, babe.'

She'd laughed warmly and stared at him. 'Johnny, a snail would bleeding lose you.'

As Johnny lay on his bed trying to blank out the saxophone, he was thankful that their nakedness was undoubtedly down to the Soho heat, rather than him screwing her. He saw Saucers like he would a sister. Besides, he'd tried to leave all the one-night faceless beauties behind; on the whole he'd managed it. It was really only when he'd had too much to drink – which wasn't that often – that he found himself waking up beside a woman with no name.

He could feel the breeze coming from the open window. He winced as he tried to turn towards it. The pain was now making its way round to the back of his eyes. Even the small movement made his head hurt, though he wasn't surprised. He'd been on one of his 'legendaries'.

They were a joke amongst his friends and family. In the past he'd had to make SOS calls, finding himself stranded in places as far-flung as Hull with no recollection of how he'd got there, or who he'd been with.

He'd always been a lightweight when it came to alcohol; cocaine was more his style. But last night he'd stupidly combined the two and as usual it'd been like poison. He'd had no intention of going on a legendary but then he'd seen Saucers at the club, bubbling with non-stop talk and excitement.

He'd looked at her as she grinned, showing off her gold back teeth; wondering what she was talking about. Then it hit him and it all became clear. Not only had the penny dropped but so had his face. Even in the dim light of the club, Saucers had seen it too and going on one of his legendaries was the only thing he'd wanted to do then.

Johnny heard Saucers stir. He heard her gravelly voice before her face came into view as she leant over him.

'Bleeding hell, the look on your face; anyone would think you'd looked down and your dick had vanished.'

Before Johnny had time to answer, Saucers plonked her head on the pillow next to him, sending shockwaves of pain through his body as the bed jolted.

'Keep it down sweetheart, my head's banging.'

'Your problem, Johnny Taylor, isn't that your head's hurting, it's that you need to sort your life out once and for all.'

'Listen, if it was that simple I'd be the first one to be smiling, but it ain't.'

25

'It's not simple because you don't make it simple Johnny; none of you do. Fuck me, I want to bash your head against something hard; bring you to your senses. It's Anthony and Cleopatra all over again.'

'Oh do me a favour. Spare me your book of the week shit.'

Saucers shrugged, changing tact.

'I've said it before Johnny, but it's that . . .'

He knew what Saucers was about to say. He didn't want to hear it. He turned his back to her, putting his hands over his ears like a child. A few minutes later he felt her hand on his shoulder. He turned round to see Saucers offering him a warm smile.

'I know it's hard Johnny and the last thing I want to do is upset you. I just care, babe. Care and worry about you.'

Johnny felt no malice towards Saucers. She was one of the few people who knew the story; he trusted her. He knew she'd keep her mouth shut.

Johnny closed his eyes, hoping to snatch a bit of extra sleep. This idea was short-lived, however, when a minute later the door was flung open. The booming sound of his father's jovial voice made Johnny's head feel as though it was being stamped on.

'Now this is a sorry fucking sight, son.'

Frankie Taylor stood in the doorway with a wide grin on his handsome suntanned face. He was aware his black Savile Row suit was fitting a bit too snugly around the top of his legs for his liking; a consequence of too many paellas from his recent fortnight at his villa in Marbella.

Pulling at his trousers slightly, hoping to get a bit more slack on the thighs, Frankie took in, as he always did, his son's impressive bedroom. It really was everything Frankie would have wished for as a child – but his mother had been too piss poor to even afford three square meals a day for him, let alone a half-decent house, so it gave him a feeling of satisfaction and immense pride to be able to provide what he'd never had for Johnny.

Most people he knew with sons had already kicked them out or they'd left home on their own accord by the time they reached the age of twenty-five. But with the sixty-inch inbuilt flat screen TV, the custom-built Goldmund chrome music system, the games consoles and the tabletop football with the tasteful drinks bar underneath, he knew there was no reason for his son ever to move out. And Frankie Taylor liked it that way.

It made him feel safe knowing his family were under his roof and as long as he felt safe, Frankie was happy. Family was everything to him. He hadn't known his father and he had a sneaking suspicion his mother hadn't either. He didn't hold that against her. What he did hold against her was her pitiful existence, her acceptance of her surroundings, her inability to provide for her family, and her refusal of ever attempting to raise a smile, even on Christmas Day. These were the things which fuelled Frankie's bitter resentment of his childhood. He could recall her words as if he was hearing them now. 'What's there to bleeding smile about, Frankie? The only time I'll be smiling is when I'm dead and gone from this miserable earth.'

Even though his mother had been the most miserable bleeder he'd ever known and he'd resented his upbringing, it hadn't stopped him loving her. He'd loved her like no one else.

As a child he'd always worried about her, running home from school instead of playing with his friends to make sure she was alright. When his mother had gone on a night out, he hadn't been able to settle until she'd come home. Always staying up waiting for her, making sure she'd got in from wherever it was she'd been. If she hadn't arrived home by

27

eleven, Frankie had gone looking for her. Usually finding her skewed up to the eyeballs on penny lagers, with her knickers round her ankles from one nameless encounter or another.

He was only twelve when the butcher at the end of their street had found his mother keeled over at the bus stop after her heart had had enough of beating. What initially struck Frankie wasn't sorrow but shame at the fact she'd been clutching onto a bag of scrap end meat. They'd needed to break her fingers to remove it from her grip.

When he'd seen her lying on the mortuary slab the first thing he'd looked for was a smile, but all he'd seen was the same tight, pursed expression she'd had when she'd been living and breathing.

He and his eight siblings had been carted off to the local kids' home in Stepney in the East End of London where one by one, they'd been separated. Picked off like cherries from a tree as do-gooders came along looking for a child to complete their own family, not realising or caring they were breaking up one already there.

Fifteen years ago he'd tracked all his siblings down, but besides from his sister, Lorna – who called him every Wednesday evening to moan about everything from her burning haemorrhoids to the miserable skinny fucker she was living with in Belgium – he'd lost touch with all the others again.

The pretence of family unity had been too much for them to keep up. The ties had been severed and damaged a long time ago, and eventually they'd all stopped calling each other, slowly backing away; slinking off to their separate lives. All relieved that they could stop pretending they cared.

As sad as it was and at times painful for Frankie to think about what could've been, he had his own family right here in front of him. He had his own wife, his own son and there was no way history was going to repeat itself. He wasn't losing contact with anyone, because no one was going anywhere, not if he had anything to do with it.

Looking down at his son with a naked Saucers lying next to him, Frankie smiled. Johnny was certainly a chip off the old block. He was proud of him. He couldn't have asked for a better son. Johnny certainly knew how to have fun, but there was a time for fucking about and a time for work.

If they weren't careful they'd be late opening the clubs and as business had been down lately, he didn't want to give any of his regular punters an excuse to go somewhere else. Besides which he didn't want a nag-full from his wife, Gypsy, if she came home and saw him running late.

He smiled again when he thought about his wife. He'd been married to her for thirty-two years, the ceremony being held on the day she'd turned sixteen. And after all this time, she still did it for him. Still gave him a boner when he thought about her – and Frankie knew very few people could say the same about their own missus.

Not that he didn't bang the goods at his clubs on a regular basis. No one in their right mind could expect him to love, care *and* be faithful to his wife. By anyone's standards that would be taking the piss. If he had to do that he may as well cut his balls off now and feed them to the fish in Hyde Park.

He looked at his white platinum Rolex watch; a present from Gypsy for his fiftieth birthday to go with the white gold diamond knuckledusters she'd got him the year before. He really needed to be at the first club by four at the latest, but thinking about his wife had left him feeling horny. Perhaps once he got to his club he'd search out the little blonde with the big tits who'd started work last week. Get her to give him a blow job. Part of the perks of running girls – but for now he and Johnny had things to do.

'Come on son, get up. I'll meet you in the car in ten

minutes. We don't want to be here if your mother comes home. You know what she's like.'

Frankie roared with laughter, then roared even harder as he saw Johnny grimace, putting a pillow firmly over his face. He smacked the pert naked bottom of Saucers who groaned as well. Walking out of the room he whistled, feeling very pleased with himself. Though in particular he felt pleased with himself because the night before he'd managed to rub Max Donaldson up the wrong way. Anything to do with annoying Max always left Frankie feeling good.

CHAPTER FIVE

The ride in the back of the black Mercedes to Holloway Road should've been a comfortable one, but Tommy Donaldson was finding it quite the opposite. Not simply from the broken air conditioning but from having to sit and listen to his father firing off a ranting tirade of abuse, directed at him.

Tommy noticed whenever his father was angry there was a change in his Irish accent. Over the years it'd become watered down from the years he'd lived in Soho. The anger, however, turned it back into a thick guttural growl, making all his words sound more violent and attacking than usual.

Catching his father's eye in the driver's mirror, Tommy continued to listen to the barrage of abuse, hoping desperately to get to their destination as quickly as possible.

'Is it only me who's able to tell the bleeding difference between four and half past four? When did you start to think it's alright to be late? I didn't bring up me kids to make a mug of me. Virgin Mary help me, because I'll beat the shit so hard out of you son, you'll be needing a colostomy bag. Between you and Frankie Taylor you'll have me digging me own grave. What is it with people that think they can get away with disrespect? Well tell me lad, do I have cunt branded into me arse?'

Tommy glanced out of the window, biting his lip; he didn't know if the question was supposed to be rhetorical or not. If he didn't answer when he should've done, he knew when the car stopped he'd get a hard slap. If he answered when he shouldn't; the same rules applied.

Before Tommy had decided what to do, Max swerved the car with blackout windows into the carwash off the traffic-filled Camden Road. The brake was put on too quickly, sending Tommy and one of his father's heavies face first into the back of the leather front seats.

'Well, well, well. Look what we have over there lads. They're right when they say talk of the devil and he'll appear. I'll tell you something, the rats are coming out today in their droves.'

Max Donaldson spoke, staring with hatred at a white Range Rover on the other side of the empty forecourt. As Tommy followed his father's gaze, Max opened the door and got out, giving Tommy a clearer view of the recipient of his father's anger. There, standing larger than life, enjoying a joke together in the late afternoon's sunshine were Frankie and Johnny Taylor.

Watching his father stride over towards them with his face curled up in a vicious snarl, Tommy sighed, preparing himself for trouble.

'You've got a nerve, Taylor, showing your face round here.' Frankie looked up, slightly taken aback but not unduly concerned to see Max Donaldson marching towards him, red-faced. He waited for Max to come closer then spoke, his tone laced with amusement.

'Round here? Now all of a sudden this is *your* turf is it? My, my, how the Donaldsons have an inflated sense of self. You should lay off the coke Max, or is it just your son who sticks the whole of London up his nose? Glad to see you've changed your shirt since last night.'

Max lunged forward but was held back by Tommy. Apoplectic with rage, he turned his anger on his son.

'Get off me boy. I don't need a fecking babysitter. Grab me again and I'll not think twice about slicing you.'

Max shook off Tommy's arm, pushing him out of the way, and stepped a foot closer to Frankie. Squaring up and breathing hard as Frankie stood his ground, thinking about the way Max behaved towards his own son. The man was twisted with anger towards everyone.

Frankie didn't have a problem with fighting usually. However the last thing he needed now was Max Donaldson with a bruised ego, squaring up to him because of a thrown drink and a wet shirt. He was already late to get round all the clubs so he wasn't in the mood for any of Max's crap.

'Listen Max; pick a time and a place. You know I'm happy to have it out with you, but not here, not now.'

'Why not Frankie? Scared you'll not be able to put up when you haven't got your men around you?'

Frankie shook his head. It was clear Max wasn't about to back down and wouldn't be happy if he didn't get at least one swing in. He'd known him for years. Too long to remember. He'd always been a sadistic little bastard. It was common knowledge he'd frequently battered his wife and kids to the point of bones being broken.

Frankie knew the Donaldson boys quite well through his encounters with Max and from the fights Johnny had had with them when they'd been younger. He'd only ever seen Max's wife and daughter in passing, years ago. Though he wasn't complaining – the less he had to do with them the better. The whole family were messed up, or at least the boys were, so it wouldn't surprise him if the girl wasn't far behind.

He glanced at Tommy, who was standing behind his father.

He kept himself to himself but he was known to be a bit of a looney tune. Still, however much of a nut job he was, Frankie had to admit, Tommy Donaldson certainly was a good-looking man. He could have easily graced the cover of any men's magazine with his handsome face and tall, muscular physique.

The other brother, Nicky, whom he saw less of, was almost as handsome as his older brother. Handsome but another space cadet, sniffing up so much coke he hardly knew who he was. Frankie knew Johnny dabbled from time to time. Hell, he often enjoyed a line himself when he'd a late night ahead of him. But there was a difference between social enjoyment and a bang-on junkie.

It astounded Frankie how Max's two boys could look so different from their father, who was short and stocky with a rounded face and beady, sunken eyes. A world apart from the handsome looks of his crystal-blue-eyed boys.

Frankie's thoughts broke off as he felt Tommy's intense stare. As blue and dazzling as they were, there was something unsettling about his eyes. Something that made him seem as if he was not all there. 'Troubled' as his old Nan would say. But then, having a father like Max Donaldson, it was no wonder.

Sighing, Frankie turned his attention back to Max. He could see Max wasn't going to move unless he got a bit of a rumble. What he didn't see was the small knife he was holding in his hand.

Not wanting a stand-off, Frankie took a swing, connecting his diamond knuckledusters to Max Donaldson's lip. The warm blood spurted across both their suits and a tiny bit of bright red flesh landed on the concrete floor. Frankie saw Johnny step forward as Tommy and Donaldson's goon came to wade in.

It didn't take long for the adrenalin to take hold of Frankie, his appetite now wet for the fight. He went to take another swing at Max. Immediately he felt a cold rush go through his body. He touched his side and saw his hand covered in his own blood. Pushing down hard on the wound to try to stop the bleeding, Frankie stumbled forward, grappling to hold onto Johnny for support. He fell to his knees in front of his stunned son and managed to utter a few words.

'He's stabbed me. The fucking cunt's stabbed me. Get hold of your mother.'

Then Frankie Taylor blacked out.

CHAPTER SIX

Gypsy Taylor sat down hard on the marble toilet. She'd been bursting for a wee all afternoon, but hadn't been able to bring herself to use the public ones in Piccadilly. They smelt of stale urine which always reminded her of her beloved Auntie May who'd lived till she was well over a hundred and died with a smile and a fag on her lips. Gypsy was certain she could still smell the foul odour of the public conveniences lingering on her expensive clothes hours later, so she avoided them like the proverbial plague.

She supposed she could've made the short walk home back to Berkeley Square or to one of her husband's Soho clubs to use the bathroom, but going back out to see her friends might have proved tricky. It would've meant explaining to her husband where she was going. And Frankie didn't like her seeing her friends. Frankie didn't like her seeing anyone. Anyone except for him.

Flushing the toilet and washing her hands in the Italian handmade sink, Gypsy wondered where her husband was. His phone was turned off. She'd tried the clubs but they hadn't seen him; no one had. Not that she was worried, quite the opposite. She was going to luxuriate in the peace and quiet without him.

Gypsy loved Frankie with all her heart. She always had done. From the moment she'd seen him at the Reno nightclub on the Mile End Road she knew he was the one. But his possessive nature was starting to become too much. She was no longer the starry-eyed teenager he'd first met in the East End all those years ago. She was her own person now and she wanted her own life. However, trying to tell that to Frankie would be as good as asking him for a divorce.

It wasn't as if she didn't want to be married to him; she did. But him insisting on her having to call him throughout the day to tell him where she was and who she was with, had worn thin a long time ago. At first she'd thought it was sweet, Frankie wanting to know her every movement. However, over time sweet had turned sour; in fact, sweet had turned into a pain in the bleeding hole.

Her best friend was going to Spain soon with some of the other girls from the East End and they wanted her to go with them. 'Come on, Gypsy; just tell your old man you're going. Put your foot down girl.' She'd looked at them and shaken her head. 'You know what he's like; he'll probably think I'll be jumping into bed with every Spaniard in sight. I wouldn't put it past Frankie to turn up disguised as a matador so he can spy on me.' Her friends had laughed hard. So had Gypsy, though her laughter was tinged with sadness. Not going to Spain was another example of Frankie's control she couldn't ignore any longer.

She needed her friends; they were a refreshing tonic. Unlike some women, Gypsy didn't need the constant attention of men. She enjoyed the company of women and saw her friends not just to have a laugh with but also when she needed a shoulder to cry on. Most of all, Gypsy knew they just wanted the best for her.

Frankie, on the other hand didn't see them like that. He saw them as he did anyone who came near her; a threat. A bad influence. 'I don't want you hanging round with those slags, Gypsy. You're better than that.' She knew it was pointless trying to convince Frankie. He was one of the most stubborn men she knew. But she still tried, always living in hope he might be able to see she could still love him *and* have her own life. 'They're alright, Frank. You don't know them like I do. If you let yourself get to know them, perhaps you'd like them.'

The last time she'd said that to him, Frankie had banged his food down on the black cut marble table, and had gone to sulk in the cinema room where Gypsy had found him an hour later. They'd made love and as usual she'd enjoyed it. What she didn't enjoy was her growing dissatisfaction with her princess in the tower lifestyle.

Gypsy sighed, looking at herself in the mirror. She wasn't bad looking. A lot of people told her she looked like Bridget Bardot. Gypsy suspected a lot of her looks were down to the facelifts, along with the expensive weekly facials and that night creams she used religiously. 'Fucking hell Gypsy, do you really have to slap that beauty mask on your face at night? Sometimes I think I'm shagging that geezer, Michael Myers, from *Halloween*.'

Frankie did make her laugh. Apart from his controlling nature he was good to her. And especially good to their son, Johnny, who was the apple of his eye. After Johnny she hadn't been able to have any more children. Frankie had been gutted. Secretly she'd been relieved. Pregnancy hadn't suited her. If she was honest, neither had the first few years of motherhood.

She'd suffered with depression for a long while after the birth of Johnny. She hadn't been able to explain to Frankie what was going on. He couldn't understand why she wasn't on top of the world. He'd wanted her to go to the doctor but she refused, knowing whatever they said or did wouldn't help.

The combination of the way she felt, trapped in the house with a young child, and Frankie's possessiveness had been too restricting for her. She'd had two nannies to help. Although they hadn't really been nannies in the conventional sense. They'd been two ageing strippers who'd worked in one of her husband's clubs but had, according to Frankie, started to put the punters off with their wizened bodies and crinkled fannies.

Frankie was a generous man. A man who, even in the business he was in, was naturally given to looking out for others. Wanting to help and to reward the strippers' loyalty, he'd employed them as home helps. She hadn't minded. They'd been good with Johnny and she'd liked their company. But even with all the help, Gypsy still felt as if her wings had been clipped.

It was only when Johnny had started secondary school that she started to feel more like her old self and taste the freedom again. The more she tasted it, the more her hunger for it grew and with each passing year it got worse.

One way or another she needed to convince Frankie to loosen the rope – or one day he might wake up to find she'd cut the rope herself.

Her white Swarovski iPhone began to ring. Smiling, she saw it was Johnny.

'Hello darling, how's . . .'

Before Gypsy could get the rest of her words out, the colour began to drain from her face as she was interrupted by a hysterical Johnny. Within a moment Gypsy hung up the phone and began to run.

CHAPTER SEVEN

Nicky's face was covered in blood. The water in the men's room turned red as it poured into the clogged sink. For once Nicky's bleeding nose wasn't a result of being hammered by a fist or a foot, but by too much cocaine – which Nicky thought was better than being caused by too little.

It wasn't the first time it'd happened. He knew it wouldn't be the last. Nicky was in no doubt his nose would continue to bleed. Bits of flesh would continue to fall out and the cocaine would continue to erode the cartilage until it caved in completely.

But he couldn't stop. Though at least he had a plan. If, or rather *when,* his nose did fall apart, all was not lost. He'd shoot snowballs or start to smoke more crack. He realised it was more difficult to function once he became heavy on the crack, but if that was the only way, so be it.

After washing his face in the men's room, Nicky went into the main bar of the 'Swag' club; a lap dancing venue off Frith Street. The atmosphere was electric. He liked the place; it was classy, unlike a lot of the bars dotted around the area. Black velvet wallpaper, white leather seating and expensive chandeliers hung from the ceiling. The music was pumping out the latest sounds from New York.

It was a friendly establishment; he'd never seen or heard of any trouble in there. Most of the punters were male but Nicky always noticed a few women scattered around the dimly lit venue, sitting uncomfortably, pushing back into the seating, trying to distance themselves as far as physically possible to what was going on around them. Girlfriends, wives, all being brought along by their partners to join in the voyeuristic fantasies.

The lap dancers were tall, lithe women in their twenties. Good-looking girls who wanted to earn extra money, rather than the girls in the clip joints and peep clubs who *needed* to earn extra money. They gyrated expertly to the music in front of the clients, moving seductively, grinding their semi-naked bodies against the men's laps; tempting them to pay for another dance.

Nicky liked it. But he wasn't really interested in it. Not the drinking nor the women interested him, although he knew most of the girls by name. He wasn't even really interested in the music. What he *was* interested in was the top-grade powder he could score.

He'd driven his father's car back home, then taken the stuff Gary had given him on tick. Now he wanted more; needed more. He hoped Gary would be as obliging as he had been earlier.

Nicky smiled and spoke to the topless blonde Croatian woman sitting in the corner on her break. He raised his voice to be heard over the heavy beat of the music.

'Have you seen Gary?'

She looked up at Nicky and grinned; a stoned glazed grin.

'He's in the back. Oh, Maggie came in; she seemed desperate to see you.'

41

Maggie. He'd forgotten she was coming home. Shit. He'd wanted to explain to her what had happened before other people started talking. He certainly didn't want her to speak to Gina; that might ruin everything.

He was tempted to go and find Maggie and just hope she hadn't seen Gina. Except the draw of getting some powder was too strong, and the grip on Nicky's arm a moment later by the tall wiry black man was even stronger. He was going nowhere.

Gary Levitt was sitting in the back room of the Swag club smoking a cigar. He couldn't abide the taste of them but he thought it looked good and added to his image. He wanted people to see him as sophisticated; not just some toerag dealer from Bermondsey. He glanced up from preening his manicured nails as Nicky Donaldson was marched into the room.

'Nick-Nick. I've been wondering where you'd gone. I wanted to know where my money was.'

Nicky blanched. A look of confusion crossed his face. He'd only seen Gary a few hours ago. He'd told him he'd got a couple of weeks to straighten everything out, but here he was with a cigar longer than his dick hanging out of his mouth, demanding his cash.

'I . . . I . . . I haven't got it.'

'Don't stutter Nicky man, it makes me think of Porky Pig and I always fucking hated that cartoon.'

Nicky could feel beads of sweat forming on his forehead, partly because he needed to score, but mainly because he was eyeing up the cosh that the goon standing behind Gary was holding in his hand.

'I thought I had two weeks, Gary. You said two weeks.'

'Yeah, you're right I did. Now I've changed my mind, a man's entitled.'

'Listen, I can get you some of the money in the next couple of days, not a problem.'

'But it is, Nicky. It's very much a problem. I don't want it in two days; I want it now. I suppose I could always ask your Dad for it. I'm sure Daddy wouldn't want to hear you're in any trouble.'

He chuckled at the deepened fear showing on Nicky's face. Gary could no more approach Max for money than he could the Pope; he wasn't stupid. As much as he knew Max probably wouldn't give a shit about Gary putting the squeeze on his son, he was still as scared as the next man was of Max Donaldson. Though one thing was clear – by the expression on Nicky's face, Gary clearly wasn't as scared of Max as his son was.

It amused Gary to play games with Nicky who was soft by nature. The man had so many beatings and took so much gear that even the changing wind seemed to frighten him.

'Fine Nicky; I'll give you a couple of days to bring me some money, but I don't want you to forget.'

'I won't. I promise.'

'I'm sure you won't, but I want to leave you with a little reminder, a little memo.'

Gary Levitt nodded to one of his henchmen and leaned back in his chair, too uninterested to watch as Nicky's face came into contact with the cosh.

CHAPTER EIGHT

Maggie sat deflated on the steps of the walk-up in Greek Street, waiting for Gina and watching the crowds of people go by. It was getting late and the last of the summer sunshine had disappeared.

She'd been all over Soho looking for Nicky and after making her way round all the bars she'd finally decided to give up, guessing he was probably crashed out in some dive or drug den sleeping off the night before. She'd then taken herself off to Gina's flat in Robert Street on the other side of Euston Road, bracing herself for trouble, but like everywhere she'd gone, there'd been no one in. The frustration of getting no answer had brought her to tears. The second time she'd cried that day. Even though she'd been on her own, she'd quickly wiped them away, feeling embarrassed.

Her next stop had been the sauna on Brewer Street. An old haunt of Gina's, a place Maggie knew she still liked to hang out in. Although Gina's mouth was clamped shut like a good Catholic girl's legs when it came to providing any information about her own business, Gina Daniels did enjoy listening to other people's gossip, especially if it involved their downfall; and in the sauna on Brewer Street gossip overflowed like a blocked toilet.

Another reason Maggie knew Gina enjoyed visiting the sauna was to get herself a bargain from the junkies who went in on a daily basis with their stolen goods, hoping to get enough money to score some brown or a bit of crack.

Perfumes, make-up, watches, even expensive lingerie, made its way to Sonya's Sauna in Brewer Street. All sold for next to nothing – for the price of a hit.

'Hello Maggie love, it's good to see you. Gina ain't here. I saw her earlier though with a big fucking smile on her face. Jammy cow got herself a pair of Gucci shades for twenty quid. She's probably gone to see Joanie in the walk-up on Greek Street to gloat. If I see her I'll tell her you're looking for her shall I?'

Maggie had looked at the Tom behind the reception in the sauna and smiled. She'd known her for years; the last thing she wanted though was Gina to know she was looking for her.

'No, don't say anything. I want to surprise her.'

That'd been at half past six. It was now nearly half past eight. She wasn't sure Gina was even going to turn up at the walk-up, but watching Soho life go by was better than going back home and worrying.

In the two hours she'd been sitting on the stone steps, she'd only had to shuffle over to make way for three punters, eager to make their way up the bare wooden staircase and along the unpainted corridor to be 'serviced' for twenty quid by Joanie. Business was clearly down.

As Maggie saw it, Soho was divided into three different levels and it was down to the individual to see what they wanted to see. The first level was for the tourists, who gazed about with excitement, soaking up the sounds and the smells of the cramped one square mile. Feeling a part of the magic but not getting close enough for it to cast a deadly spell on them.

The second level was the mix of communities; real people trying to live in harmony amongst different cultural and social backgrounds, all attempting to be sympathetic to one another's beliefs. Most of the time everybody managed to be tolerant, but occasionally it kicked off. Then the air would be heavy with tension until the community leaders sorted it out.

And finally there was the deepest level of Soho. The darker level which Maggie had been born into, and doubted she'd ever escape from. The protection rackets, the drugs, the sex trade, and the gangsters. The faces of Soho who ran the areas weren't seen until they wanted or needed to be. That was the part Maggie felt she belonged to. She knew everyone; knew who to avoid and who to take the time to speak to. Soho was in her blood as strong as being a Donaldson was. Whenever she left it she missed it; and whenever she was in it she wanted to get as far away from the place as possible.

'Touting for business, love? I'll give you a quid and even then I'm being generous.'

Maggie looked up and saw the grinning face of Lola Harding who owned and ran a cafe round the corner in Bateman Street. Lola was a good 'un; she'd been a brass most of her life and lived in the area for all of it.

Maggie remembered Lola's kids from when they were little. They'd all played together, though they'd been slightly older than her. One Christmas Eve Lola's kids had been taken into care by social services, and Maggie could still hear the desperate screams as Lola and her kids physically hung onto each other in the street as she tried to stop them being carted off.

When Maggie had seen what'd happened to Lola's kids, she'd envied them. Wishing someone could swoop down and take her away from her childhood. She would've happily traded a place in the Donaldson household for a place in care on any given day.

'Whatever's troubling you babe, it won't help any sitting with your bum jammed to the floor. When you've got an arse full of piles from sitting on that cold step, let me tell you, you'll really have something to cry about. Come on love, why don't you come and have a cup of Rosie Lee with me?'

'No thanks, Lola. I'm waiting for Gina.'

'Well I reckon you'll be waiting a long time. She's probably got her knickers off somewhere.'

Maggie scrunched her forehead into a scowl.

'I thought she only worked as a maid now, thought she was off the game.'

'She says she is, but nobody ever really is.'

'You are.'

'That's because no one will have me. I'd end up having to pay the bleeding punters.' Lola roared out a cackling laugh, making the passing Chinese couple huddle together and quickly cross over to the other side of the street in fright.

'Sure you don't want that brew, Maggie?'

'I'm sure.'

'Okay love, but you know where I am if you change your mind and want a chat. Say hello to your mum won't you, and ask her why she hasn't left that rotten bleeder yet.'

Another roar of laughter left Lola's mouth and Maggie watched her walk away towards Soho Square. She wondered how after such a hard life Lola could still always find a joke; still see the bright side in the darkest of situations.

Maggie sighed, closing her eyes when she lost sight of Lola to the throng of the crowds. It hadn't even been twenty-four hours since she'd been back in Soho, yet sitting waiting in the filthy doorway, surrounded by the smell of piss, made it feel like she'd been back a lifetime. But however bad the homecoming, she was still glad to be home. A year away had been a year away too long.

It'd been her own fault she'd been sent down. When the police had raided the house as they often did, hoping to find something they could pin on her father, she should have let them just get on with it. It was nothing new. Since she could remember the house had been raided. Every six months or so there'd be a hammering on the door, before it was booted in by a dozen or more boys in blue who charged through the house like elephants on crack.

The law knew who Max Donaldson was and he knew the law. He had his fingers in lots of businesses but first and foremost her father was a loan shark and a bag man. He extorted payments off landlords and shop owners. Charging a thousand per cent interest to old ladies who hadn't been able to pay their winter fuel bills. With no strong credit history to take out a loan from a bank, they turned to her father for a hundred pound loan, only to find themselves paying back thousands of pounds from the interest on the interest on the interest. And if they couldn't pay, her father would happily pay someone to break a bone as a warning. A taste of what was to come if they messed him about.

Her brother Tommy had been recruited by her father to join the family business. He hadn't had a choice. And he hadn't been able to drop out of it like Nicky had by default.

Nicky was soft like freshly picked cotton but his drug habit was out of control. It had been since he was twelve. It was this, not his soft kind nature which made him unreliable. Their father had eventually given up with him, giving him only the odd job to do now and again. Therefore it was poor Tommy who took the brunt, forced to work day in day out with their father.

Even though Maggie didn't work for her father, she might as well have done. Everything came from him, whether she liked it or not. Her father owned their house, paid the bills, paid for food, for clothes, for the lot. Everything which was bought had to be run by him before he decided to put his hand in his wallet. She had nothing he didn't own or possess. Including her.

Maggie had never had a job. She'd never been allowed to – a daughter of a face couldn't be seen working outside the family business. Her father however didn't want her working with or by him. Though she wasn't complaining; she'd no desire to be involved in a business which thrived on exploiting the vulnerable.

Consequently, she should have been of use to the police coming into her room, turning it upside down and leaving it a mess. But for some reason, on that day it'd irritated her more than usual. When she'd objected, the copper had just sneered at her. She'd felt her temper swimming through her veins and she'd wanted to clout him, just to take the smug sound out of his voice. But she hadn't, well not until they'd found the bag of pills which she didn't know anything about.

'I've never seen them before.'

'Well then whose are they, Maggie?'

'I don't know. I don't know what they are either and neither do you. They could be Smarties for all you know.'

'I'll need you to come down to the station whilst we check.'

'I can't do that.'

'I'm afraid you've got no choice.'

'You don't understand; I can't.'

Maggie remembered she'd looked over to see her father coming to stand at her bedroom door. There would've been no way she could've talked to the coppers in front of him. To tell them what she needed to say and explain why she

49

couldn't get banged up then. 'Listen, give me an hour and I'll come. I promise.'

They'd grinned at each other, bursting out into laughter. 'This isn't a social engagement. You know the routine, Maggie; you and your family have certainly had enough practice. You'll probably be bailed by tomorrow.'

Tomorrow. Her mind had raced. Wondering where her mother was. Then Maggie had looked over again to her father, and by the look in his eyes she knew he knew something about the pills. She'd stared at him harder, and out of view of the sergeant her father shrugged his shoulders, mouthing a mocking apology.

It was then she'd acted like a fool. And once again he'd managed to wind her up to the point of her behaving stupidly and rashly.

It'd actually been her father she'd flown at, not the Sergeant at the door standing next to him. But her fist didn't differentiate between the two of them. It was a genuine mistake. But a mistake which had made all hell break loose.

A wall of blue uniforms had rushed towards her. For the next ten minutes Maggie Donaldson had kicked and struggled, pushing the men away, surprising them with her force. Then she'd felt a heavy weight on her back as she was forced to the ground by a knee. She'd slammed to the ground, banging her chin on the corner of the open drawer. The blood had sprayed everyone and Maggie had felt a burning pain as her chin split open. She'd howled a deep stomach churning cry, not for the pain, but for what she knew she was about to leave behind.

Maggie stood up from the cold step, rubbing her chin to feel the small scar. A reminder of her stupidity. She should've known better. But her father's mocking scorn had hurt and made her feel humiliated, which always turned into anger.

At the time it'd crossed Maggie's mind her father had

deliberately put the pills – which turned out to be ecstasy tablets – in her drawer. But when she found out the truth, she'd seen it for what it was; a series of unfortunate events which had cost her dearly.

The pills had been confiscated from one of her father's clients, who hadn't been able to pay his weekly instalment.

Nicky had been given the task of picking them up to sell at the clubs. Their father, counting on Nicky to come within the hour hadn't bothered being cautious and had left the pills in the house, which he never usually would've done, putting them in her drawer for an hour's safekeeping. What he hadn't counted on was Nicky's insatiable appetite for drugs, his need for a hit being greater than the fear of the brutal consequences of disobeying their father's orders.

Waiting for Nicky to turn up, Max had snorted some lines of coke, cracked open a bottle of whiskey and drank himself into a stupor. He was oblivious to the fact that Nicky hadn't turned up until he was woken the next morning by the sound of the front door being broken down.

They didn't charge her with possession. Her father had made the pill owner claim he'd left them in her room. The police didn't believe the story, neither did anyone else, but the judge had given the man thirteen months, and Maggie suspected the terrified man had seen being behind bars as a preferable option to owing Max Donaldson money.

Nicky had been inconsolable at playing, as he saw it, a monumental role in putting her behind bars. But when Maggie had seen him in the prison visiting room she hadn't been angry. She'd just hugged him until the prison officers had come over, warning her if there was any more physical contact the visit would be over.

Maggie's heart had gone out to Nicky. Not just because of the engorged black eye and the cuts and bruises he'd received from their father, but because he was a Donaldson

51

and how Maggie saw it, being born into her family was simply part of the series of unfortunate events.

It wasn't in the name of love her father had helped get her off the charges. She'd no doubt if it was purely down to him he'd have let her take the rap for the pills and left her to rot in the cells. The reason her father had done what he did was because it was *the* thing to do; *the* thing expected of him. Max Donaldson couldn't have been seen not to do the right thing.

Reputation was important. It was fundamental in his line of business; to him and to the other faces in London. Reputation got them to where they were. It helped keep them there. If word had got out that Max had left his own daughter to languish between the walls of Highpoint Prison, his reputation wouldn't even be worth the paper he wiped his backside on.

The one thing he couldn't do though was get the charges of attacking a policeman dropped. She, as her father had gladly pointed out, was to blame and 'There's fuck all I can do about you smacking a copper in the mouth, Maggie. There's nobody to blame except yourself. My advice is, pack a decent toothbrush.'

She'd got eighteen months but had served only twelve and a half. Though every second, every minute hand of the clock going round had been akin to a life sentence.

Dusting off her G-star cropped jeans, Maggie started to leave but as she turned the corner into Bateman Street, a small round woman bumped into her. It was Gina Daniels.

Throwing her newly found resolve to the side, Maggie grabbed her, pushing her hard against the wall, slamming her spine into the red bricks and letting her built-up anger spill out. She spoke in a low growl, curling her beautiful lips into a snarl.

'Tell me what is going on Gina, or I swear to God I won't be responsible for my actions.'

Gina stayed silent, clearly shocked by the unexpected

confrontation. The silence infuriated Maggie. She wanted answers.

About to shake the information out of Gina, Maggie remembered why she'd got herself into this predicament in the first place. Her temper. Her damned fiery temper. She closed her eyes, silently beginning to count to ten. Desperate to keep the Donaldson curse under control. As she counted she felt a slight tug on her jacket then heard a tiny voice.

'Mummy!'

Maggie turned. Immediately falling to her knees. Her anger disappeared at once as she gazed into a pair of blue eyes full of warmth and love for her.

'Harley! Oh my God. Oh my God.'

She gently stroked her daughter's face, not quite being able to believe after twelve and a half long months she was finally seeing her again. She hadn't allowed her mother to bring her to the prison. She hadn't wanted Harley to be frightened. She'd been comfortable with that decision, imagining her daughter to be well cared for. Now as she looked at Harley's unwashed face and tangled hair she could see this clearly hadn't been the case.

Maggie scooped Harley into her arms. She'd waited for this moment. Waited to hold her daughter in her arms. To look into the eyes which were identical to her own. She'd been so selfish, so stupid to allow her anger to separate her from being with her little girl. From the one person who needed her the most.

Maggie glared at Gina. She still wanted the full story as to how Gina Daniels, a retired brass who Maggie didn't know well enough to leave her pet goldfish with, let alone her daughter, had ended up caring for Harley. But first things first, they needed to get off the street. The last thing Maggie could afford to do was to let anyone see Harley.

53

CHAPTER NINE

Tommy Donaldson sat in the dark. What his father had done to Frankie Taylor had made him feel edgy. Bringing up memories he didn't want to remember. To try to distract himself he'd come to his private place, to the place where he could think.

'Move along sweetie, I know you'd like to stay up close and personal but we've got to be fair darlin' and let these other passengers on.'

Tommy watched the woman whoop a hearty laugh as she indicated for him to move forward. He hadn't wanted to go and sit in the front, he'd been happy standing and now he was stuck, squashed up against the window by an old woman with all her shopping bags. He hated buses, all the noise and the people; he much preferred being in the car but it was parked at the station.

Gazing out of the window and very much looking forward to getting back to Soho, Tommy heard the woman who'd been ordering everyone about laughing again. She was sitting directly behind him and he could hear her trying to get his attention by making jokes but he didn't bother to look round.

Twenty minutes later they arrived at the bus terminal and as Tommy was walking away he saw a woman from the bus who'd been talking to another passenger about heading back to the West End.

'Hang on, wait up darlin'.'

The woman turned around as she walked towards the main road and Tommy jogged to catch up. He smiled at her, his handsome face lighting up under the street lamps as she smiled back.

'Seeing as though both of us are heading towards Wanstead High Street to catch the bus up West, why don't we take the short cut across Hollow Ponds, it'll save us having to go all the way round or wait God knows how long for another bus. And if the boogie man does come along, I can always jump behind you for protection.'

He listened to her talk and introduce herself and then he smiled at her, his beautiful eyes dazzling brightly.

'Okay, hopefully we can get there before midnight.'

They began to walk as she chatted happily about her friend.

'These big firms think they can treat people how they want to and they always seem to get away with it. My friend lost her job last week, oh, you should have heard the language on her. Still, I say she's best off out of it.'

It was dusk but the path and the woods were still quite visible. She was still talking and Tommy let her go before him along the narrowed path, watching as her head moved whilst she talked.

They got deeper into the woods before he said her name and smashed his skull against her face. The force knocked her to the floor and the moonlight lit up Tommy's face.

As she was about to scream he raised his foot and brought it down hard on her mouth.

'No you don't darlin', no screams. We won't have any

screaming out of your mouth and we certainly won't have any more of your incessant fucking talking.'

He dragged her through the bushes by clumps of her hair, knowing she was still conscious and feeling every scratch from the twisted thorns and twigs as he took her towards the car.

The sound of a distant alarm reminded Tommy he had to be somewhere. He really needed to get back home to see his mother. To make sure she was alright. His father was on the warpath after the fight with Frankie and he didn't want her to be in the firing line.

Thinking about his mother made Tommy smile. He loved her so much but he didn't think she'd ever noticed, or maybe it was just him she didn't notice. Maybe he was as invisible as he felt.

CHAPTER TEN

It was a superficial wound but the police were sniffing around like pigs sniffing on an arsehole and Frankie Taylor watched them scribble down pointless notes.

'Mr Taylor, are you trying to tell us you didn't see who attacked you and neither did your son, even though it was broad daylight?'

'That's exactly right Officer; that's exactly what I'm telling you. Now if you don't mind, I'd like a little time with my wife.'

The police had stayed another hour attempting to glean out any bit of information they could, but Frankie and Johnny had continued to say nothing. In the end the two officers had left somewhat exasperated at the same time as Gypsy pulled back the faded blue hospital curtains with more cups of tea.

'The dirty rotten bleeder. Max Donaldson needs to pay for this.'

Gypsy was on a roll and Frankie loved it. When they'd moved into Berkley Square she'd decided to get elocution lessons. He'd looked at her in amazement. 'Are you off your tits girl?'

'No Frank, I just want to get meself talking proper.'

'Christ almighty Gyps, this ain't my fair lady you know.'

They'd laughed hard but she'd still insisted on taking the lessons, and over time her East End accent had turned softer until it was hardly there at all. Unless of course she was talking about two things. The only two things which brought back the East End girl back into her voice. His sister, and Max Donaldson.

Frank watched Gypsy, her mouth moving ten to the dozen. Thousands of pounds of elocution lessons out of the window. But he didn't mind. The angrier she got about the situation, the happier Frankie felt. He loved that she cared. Loved she'd have no problem rolling up her sleeves to get into a fight to defend him. Not that she'd ever need to – he was more than man enough to look out for himself and his family, but he loved that she was strong.

It was one of the things that had attracted him to Gypsy in the first place. She was beautiful, but so were many other girls down the clubs in the East End. They were all fuckable but they were also unmemorable. Gypsy had been different; her strength had shone out from under the bleached blonde hair and false eyelashes. Her spirit for life had been intoxicating; making him a fool for her. He'd never met a woman like Gypsy. She was so unlike all the other women and so unlike his poor feeble mother.

As he continued to think, Frankie's contentment turned into a scowl. As much as he loved her strength, the problem he had now was her strength was starting to make its way into her overall attitude. A little bit too much for his liking. He could see her starting to want to break away, to do things on her own, when she'd previously only wanted to do things with him.

At first he'd thought she'd some other man boning her but after he'd got some of his men to follow her about for a couple of days he'd realised there *was* no other man. Gypsy's infidelity was freedom. A whole lot harder to deal with than putting a bullet in some lover's head.

Frankie shifted his body on the hospital trolley trying to find a more comfortable position to lie in. The painkillers were wearing off and he was starting to hurt. He'd had to have thirty stitches but the doctors had told him the wound would heal easily. What couldn't be sewn up so easily was the other kind of wound, the one Max Donaldson had opened up. He'd opened a new hatred between them and he was going to wish he hadn't.

He couldn't really believe Max had actually had the front to stab him in broad daylight off the Camden Road. He wasn't going to send his men round for revenge; he would wait until he could do it himself. He would wait to be able to get his hands on Max's scrawny neck. The hatred had grown into a cancer over the years between the two of them and as much as he wasn't quite sure why it'd gone on for so long, he was sure he had Gypsy's support in the vendetta; in fact sometimes he'd got the distinct impression she was egging him on. The few times he'd thought of stopping the feud Gypsy had had more than a few choice words to say about the matter with her voice as thick as the smog that used to be in the East End. 'And why would you want to bleeding do that eh, Frankie? You'll be the laughing stock of Soho if you start waving the white flag. That's not like you to let some no-good bastard get the better of you – or maybe you've lost your bottle and you're scared?'

'Fuck off Gyps, you know it ain't that, I've never been scared of anyone in me bleedin' life, just thought it might make things quieter round here.'

'If I wanted quiet I'd put some frigging ear plugs in. Making peace with that piece of bleeding scum is the coward's way out. Next thing you know you'll be painting yourself yellow and there'll be three white feathers stuck on the fucking front door.'

He'd laughed at her then. Had loved the way her nose always curled up when she got on one, but she'd been right. Looking back he didn't know what he'd been thinking to even contemplate making anything but war with the likes of Max Donaldson.

Years back, before Johnny was born, he and Max had been indirect business associates. Eventually though, Frankie had distanced himself from him when he'd seen the kind of business Max ran and the cruelty he dished out.

Standing back from Max hadn't really caused the rift. What had started it all was Max owing him money from a big poker game and making him wait over six months for it. Even that though, Frankie knew he could've let it go. What he couldn't let go was when Max had picked up one of the girls who worked in his club on Brewer Street.

Max had taken the girl to a hotel, roughing her up and putting the fear of God into her. Turning her from a hardened brass into a quivering wreck. Her face had been messed up and Frankie had taken her to one of the top docs in Harley Street to get her nose and jaw fixed. The girl hadn't stayed in London, deciding to return home to her native Glasgow with a few grand given to her by Frankie.

Frankie had then put the word out for none of his associates or acquaintances to do business with Max again. That had been a lot of people. In essence, Frankie had put the glass ceiling on Max being able to go further in his business and making the money he wanted to, as well as reducing him to a man who people feared but no one respected.

Frankie had then wanted to leave the feud. He'd shown Max that in a way he understood; he'd had his punishment. But the feud had started to grow, leaving him with no control over it. Johnny and the Donaldson boys got into endless fights. Gypsy stoked the flames as if she was building a bonfire, and each time he came across Max the man wasn't ever able to keep his mouth shut and walk away. Leaving Frankie with no other option but to put him in his place, like he'd done last night by throwing the drink over him in the casino.

Frankie sighed, putting his hand out to touch the top of his wife's head gently. The one good thing to come out of being stabbed would be having Gypsy at home with him without excuses. There'd be no sloping off to the shops or to the bars to meet her cronies for a drink, no squeezing half an hour to herself. After all, she could hardly tell a man who'd just been stabbed that she needed to go and get her nails done. He hated to say it but perhaps Max Donaldson had done him a favour after all.

Gypsy touched Frankie's hand in response. She'd had such a fright when Johnny had called. She'd thought the worst but hoped for the best. Thankfully she'd got the latter. And the more she thought about what had happened the more thankful she became. Now Frankie would be laid up for the next few weeks perhaps she'd get some of that longed for freedom quicker than she thought. She'd be able to go to the shops and go to the bars to meet the girls without him popping up from nowhere. She hated to say it but perhaps Max Donaldson had done her a favour after all. Smiling, she looked at Frankie who smiled back just as warmly.

Frankie's phone rang, jarring them both out of their own thoughts and waking Johnny up from his cat nap. Gypsy picked it up in her most eloquent of tones.

'Hello? Gypsy speaking.'

There was a pause and she rolled her eyes as she listened to the caller on the other end, then quickly passed the phone to Frankie. It was his sister. Gypsy watched as Frankie spoke loudly with a big grin on his face.

61

'Lorna! Alright girl, how are tricks?'

Gypsy looked at Johnny who was dropping off to sleep again and pulled a face. She got up to go and find something to eat. She wasn't interested in listening to her husband's conversation with Lorna.

She didn't like Frankie's sister. She was a loud-mouthed meddling bitch who thought she was Lady bleeding Muck because Frankie had a few bob. Before she'd met Lorna, Gypsy had been looking forward to meeting her, wanting to take her shopping and to hear about what her husband had been like as a child, but within an hour of picking her up from the airport she'd hated every bone in the woman's body. From the moment Lorna landed from Belgium, she seemed intent of trying to cause a rift. Instead of being pleased that her brother was happily married to Gypsy, she wanted to cause problems. Bad mouthing her to Frankie behind her back and making constant snide comments. Not only had it irritated her, it'd hurt because all she'd ever wanted was to be friends.

It'd taken some hard negotiation but Frankie had managed to persuade Lorna to get back on a plane to Belgium one week later. She'd kicked up a fuss, wanting to stay another two weeks but they'd waved her off, all breathing a sigh of relief to see the British Airways logo speeding past them on the runway.

That'd been fifteen years ago and Gypsy hadn't seen her since. Apart from occasionally picking up the phone to her, Gypsy had hardly spoken to her either.

Lorna's occupation when she'd lived in London was as a small-time fraudster. Gypsy knew the police had wanted to question her on a number of chequebook scams; apparently one of the reasons she'd run off to Belgium. Her scams hadn't been on any grand scale, though according to Frankie she'd done a couple of short stretches inside.

This was one of the reason's Gypsy had been saved from

any more of Lorna's visits. Lorna couldn't just jump on a plane. She was wanted but had no intention of serving any more time and unless Frankie provided her with a false passport to travel on she was stuck in Belgium.

Gypsy had managed to persuade Frankie not to sort one out, but it was getting harder and harder to do so. Frankie was a good man by nature, so the idea of his sister pining for the streets of London hurt Frankie, to the point of restless nights.

Twenty minutes later Gypsy found her way back to the cubicle. Plonking herself back on the chair next to Frankie her cockney twang was clear to her.

'Well, what did the old witch want? It's unlike her to call on a Tuesday; thought she'd be busy flying about on her bleeding broomstick.'

Frankie scowled at Gypsy. Lorna *was* a witch, a great big interfering one, but she was also his sister. Whatever trouble she had or hadn't tried to cause between him and Gypsy the last time, she'd proved her loyalty to him by the weekly phone calls, the sending of the birthday and Christmas cards and her constant – yet turned down – offers of her coming to pay them a visit.

She was family – and family meant something. Not something, everything, so it didn't feel right Gypsy bad-mouthing her. He'd always felt bad about the way he'd packed her off when she'd come to stay. But if he was honest he'd also been mightily relieved. The bickering between Lorna and Gypsy had done his nut in. If it hadn't been for the company of Johnny, he'd have booked himself into a hotel.

Even though he'd sent her back to Belgium, he'd always shown Lorna respect, and wife or not, Gypsy needed to do the same. If she couldn't, then the least she could do was keep her frigging cake hole shut.

'Don't say that Gypsy, she's my sister.'

63

'Yes, more's the fucking pity.'

'Oh so much for the soft-spoken lady. You'd put the blokes down Smithfield to shame.'

'You know how she takes me, Frank.'

'Is it too hard to hope my missus and my sister can get on?'

'It is when it's bleeding Lorna. Turn it in Frankie, you know what I'm saying's true.'

He did know but he wasn't about to start admitting that to Gypsy.

'I tried to get on with her Frankie, you saw that. I took her shopping, for facials, to the casino. I even got her a pedicure from Marco and you know how long his waiting list is.'

Frankie didn't and couldn't see how having your nails manicured by some queer working in Knightsbridge was any different from getting them done by any of the girls in Chinatown which he on occasion did. But he didn't say anything and listened patiently whilst Gypsy continued to work her jaw overtime about Lorna at the same time as stuffing her face with the grapes she hadn't even bothered giving him.

'Fuck me Frank, we showered money on her and all she did was bleeding moan and criticize. She tried to cause trouble between us. It's no good shrugging your shoulders Frankie Taylor because you know as well as I do that she did. I'm telling you babe, that woman is a nasty piece of work. No matter how hard I tried with her she still acted like an ungrateful cow. What did I ever do to her? It was the longest fucking week of my life Frank, bleedin' . . .'

Frankie had heard enough. He banged his fist on the side of the hospital trolley and immediately regretted the action. A sharp pain tore through his side, making him grit his teeth and throw back his head as he spoke.

'Well now you've got a chance to try again because once I told Lorna what'd happened to me, she wouldn't take no for an answer. I'm sending one of my men over tonight to give her a passport. By the morning she'll be on her way.'

Frankie felt the bag of grapes hit his face before he saw it. Then he proceeded to listen as Gypsy screeched at the top of her lungs at him, before storming out of the Accident and Emergency department.

He looked at his son – who was now fast asleep – and sighed. At first he wasn't really keen himself on his sister coming. But the more he mulled it over the more he thought he might be a good idea, even aside from the guilt he already felt for keeping her away for so long. It struck him he might be able to use Lorna's visit to his advantage. Lorna might be *just* the person he needed.

As much as he'd try to insist on Gypsy being by his side over the next few weeks, he was well aware she'd try her hardest, make all the excuses she could to go out on her little jaunts. And when she did? He'd send Lorna, just to watch her, just to make sure he knew exactly where his pretty little wife was going. Yes, maybe this visit from his interfering, busybody sister was just what he needed.

CHAPTER ELEVEN

Maggie tucked a sleeping Harley into bed as she looked around the tired room. The woodchip wallpaper had been painted several times, yet it did very little to- disguise the damp seeping through the walls, looking like dark angry clouds against a sky of pink. There was a section of the wallpaper which was peeling off completely, and had been patched up by Harley's colourful abstract pictures.

The view from the tiny window looked out onto rows of monolithic grey tower blocks overlooking Tottenham Court Road. And with a heavy heart, Maggie knew this was where Harley had called home for nearly thirteen months. She was past furious.

Kissing her sleeping daughter on her head, Maggie looked once more at her, not quite believing they were finally reunited. She'd washed Harley's hair and now it lay in beautiful blonde ringlets on her pillow rather than the matted hair she'd been greeted with earlier. Her face was tiny with rounded cheeks, though worryingly they were less round than they had been a year ago. Her freckles almost looked painted on, splayed perfect tiny brown dots spread across her tiny button nose. She was nothing short of perfect.

Quietly, Maggie closed the door. Giving up smoking hadn't lasted. She lit up a cigarette, hungrily inhaling the smoke deep inside her lungs, trying to calm herself down. Hoping to stop her head from racing but more importantly, her temper from rising.

The television in the small lounge was on but the sound was turned off and Gina Daniels sat in the tatty burgundy chair in the corner. Maggie pulled a face in revulsion as Gina crammed another bite of the fried egg sandwich into her already full mouth. The egg dribbled out onto her lips, onto her chin and all over her fingers. Unabashed, Gina sucked the runny yellow spillage noisily.

Maggie stared at Gina who seemed deep in thought. She had to find a way to get Harley out of the flat but at the moment she didn't have anywhere to take her. She couldn't take her anywhere near home; even being on the other side of Oxford Street was really too close for Maggie's liking.

In her family only her mum and Nicky knew about Harley and, until her daughter was much older and able to fend for herself, that was the way Maggie was going to keep it.

When she'd first discovered she was pregnant she'd been beside herself with excitement. She hadn't thought she'd feel that way, especially as having children had never been high up on her list of priorities.

Her mother had casually raised her eyebrows when she'd told her, as if to say she didn't expect anything different. Then when she'd told her the full story, the casually raised eyebrows had turned into a worried furrow. 'Maggie, be careful. I'm so scared for you.' Maggie had watched her mum tremble in fear and the surge of hatred towards her father had hit her once again. She'd taken her mother in her arms, trying to comfort her, trying to reassure her it'd be fine. Though she herself hadn't known how it would be. 'It's okay, Mum. I'll make it okay. I promise.'

The next person she'd told had been Nicky. He was the only other member of her family she really trusted. Telling Tommy hadn't even come into the equation. He was lost to himself and over the years her elder brother had become lost to her. She'd tried to reach out but whenever she did, Maggie sensed a dark and powerful rage coming from him which frightened her, not for herself but for him.

When she'd been three months pregnant her mother had come up with a workable idea. She was going to pretend she was looking at a stretch. It hadn't been difficult to convince anyone. Nobody had cared or questioned it. Her father had just sniffed when she'd told him she was looking at ten months inside for handling stolen credit cards. No one else had said anything or had even been concerned. Even though she hadn't really been going away, Maggie had found the reaction painful, but it'd still been the perfect alibi.

She'd rented a poky room in Brighton and far from being lonely, she'd enjoyed the time away. The feeling of Harley growing inside her had been exciting and beautiful. It'd felt fresh and pure, unlike the rest of her life. Of course she'd missed Soho, it was in her blood, but her mother and Nicky had visited. There'd been days when they'd just walked on the beach together, eating fish and chips, enjoying each other's company. Simple but so very rare. A world away from the heaving streets of Soho.

After Harley had been born everything had become slightly trickier. It'd taken a lot of juggling but Maggie had wanted to get back to Soho. Everything she'd ever known was there. It was the tie that bound.

Her mother was there who needed her; had always and would always need her. And though there were times Maggie wanted to run and keep running, taking Harley far away to build another life, she knew she couldn't. Because there was no one else to protect her mother. Maggie was trapped. In a way they all were.

Nicky had found a flat to rent in Holborn for her. Far enough away from Soho, but near enough to be there each day.

Between her, her mother and her mother's cousin, they'd looked after Harley, keeping her safe. At first everyone had found it difficult, paranoid someone would get suspicious, but after a time Maggie had realised once more that nobody gave a damn what she did with her life. They were all too busy not giving a damn about their own to worry about anyone else's.

It'd all been going so well until the day she'd been nicked. Then bucket loads of shit had hit the proverbial fan. Not that she'd known at the time. When she'd been sentenced she'd made a phone call to Harley's father begging him to make it right, and he'd told her he would. 'Between us it'll be fine. Put your head down, do your time. Okay? And Maggie . . . I love you.'

His words however had fallen short of anything remotely resembling the promise made. Nicky's habit decided it was more important than his niece. Her mother's cousin needed to go back to Ireland. Her mother had tried – though Maggie didn't know how hard – but failed to get away from the house enough without raising suspicion. So that'd only left one person. The one person Maggie thought she could rely on. Yet he'd let her down. More to the point, he'd let their daughter down.

Sitting in the drab smoke-filled flat, it became clear to Maggie why Harley's father hadn't helped. It was for one reason and one reason only. He just didn't care. Maggie Donaldson realised like all the other people in her life, Johnny Taylor didn't give a damn.

'I want you to start from the beginning, Gina. I want you

to tell me why my daughter's spent the last year in this dive with you. And why she looked so filthy, with holes in her clothes. And believe me, I'm not in the mood for any of your games.'

'Bleeding charming I'm sure. No *thank you for looking after my child when nobody else wanted her, Gina*. Just abuse. I don't know why I bothered.'

'Don't pretend you're doing this from the good of your heart. I know you. You wouldn't even bother sleeping if you didn't think there was something in it for you. Come on Gina, what are you getting out of it?'

'Nothing apart from bleeding grief. I expected a bunch of flipping Interflora to thank me for what I'd done, not the Spanish bleedin' inquisition. I kept me mouth shut didn't I? Christ alone knows I've looked after her as if she was one of my own.'

'Your kids were put into care, Gina.'

'Well I still say that wasn't my fault. How was I supposed to know they'd knock on the neighbour's door when they ran out of milk. I was only gone for five bleeding days, and anyway that's beside the point. I'm telling you, Maggie, I've done nothing but put your kid first. At times over this past year, I've looked in the mirror and instead of seeing meself I saw bleedin' mother Theresa staring back at me.'

Maggie shook her head, amazed at Gina's audacity. It was clear she hadn't and didn't care about Harley.

'Enough, Gina. I want the truth and I'm only going to ask you one more time. What was in it for you?'

'Well I'll tell you this; I went short for looking after your girl. There were times I . . .'

'Stick to the story Gina.'

Gina looked at Maggie indignantly, then continued.

'From what I gather some soft cow from the sauna had been looking after Harley, you know the sort, thinks taking kids to museums and making cack with them they see on *CBeebies* will do them good.'

Maggie raised her eyebrows but didn't say anything. The woman sounded better than Gina.

'Anyhow, her old man got himself nicked for smuggling in a truck load of tobacco. He's on remand in Maidstone, looking at five years. So of course daft cow decided to move down there. And of course it's not like Johnny could just go to a nanny agency. He could hardly trust a stranger to keep her mouth shut, with all that goes on in his business could he? So he was desperate. And me being me, when Nicky told me the story of the poor little mite, I couldn't not offer to help. What with me loving kids and all.'

Gina noticed Maggie's glare and, realising she may have laid the Mary Poppins part on a bit too thick, changed tack.

'Johnny sorted Nicky out with a few bob. Nicky passed it onto me but that's all it was most of the time. A few bob. I didn't know a kid could cost so much. So you see Maggie, when it boils down to it, it was all from the good of my heart.'

'And you're telling me you didn't slip some in your pocket? That's unlike you, Gina. Goes against the nature of your beast don't it?'

'If anything slipped in me pocket it was a pile full of bills and a packet of headache tablets.'

'Gina, I'm going to check with Nicky and if he tells me something different then you and I will be having more than just a chat.'

'He'll say the same. The only person who probably won't is Johnny. No doubt he'll pretend he was giving us the readies by the handful. But he'll be lying.'

'And why would he do that? Why should I think it's you and not him who'll tell me the truth?'

71

'Then where is he? Where's he been for the last year? I know I haven't seen him. He's been happy to palm Harley off.'

Maggie shifted uncomfortably in her chair. This didn't go unnoticed by Gina. She continued to put the boot in, wanting to put more doubt in Maggie's head.

'I'm sorry Maggie but I don't need to spell it out. You can see for yourself. I've been doing my bleeding best but I won't lie, it's been a struggle. The reason Johnny will probably say he's been giving us more than he has is because he's ashamed. Ashamed he hasn't done enough. If I were you I wouldn't say a word to him. Speak to Nicky instead. The last thing I want is trouble knocking on my door.'

Gina stopped then added slyly, 'And if there's trouble, then maybe I'd have to rethink about having Harley here. And what would you do then eh, Maggie? Who else would keep their mouth shut the way I've done? But of course sometimes it takes a little, how should I say it? A little extra incentive to keep mouths shut. I was only saying to Sonya the other day how I need to get myself a pair of new shoes.'

There was a long silence. Then Maggie leaned forward. She was close enough to smell Gina's foul breath. Her blue eyes darkened as she spoke in a whisper.

'Gina. I hope you're not trying to blackmail me. You'd be very silly to do that.'

'Blackmail! Phew, Maggie Donaldson, what an imagination. Wherever did you get that idea from?'

Gina Daniels wrinkled up her face, pretending to be hurt by the accusations. The last thing she wanted to do was piss Maggie off. She knew Maggie's temper. The whole of Soho did. She'd been silly to say that to Maggie but Gina had a habit of always pushing things further, hoping to see what else she could get out of a situation.

She was onto a good thing. Gina and Nicky had worked

things out nicely between themselves. She didn't need little Miss Maggie May and her spoilt goon of a boyfriend ruining things.

She needed to play things carefully. It was the easiest bit of money she'd made in a long time. The kid was no problem. Most of the times she just sat in her room holding onto her stuffed rabbit or she'd be colouring and cutting up endless pieces of paper.

For a three year old she wasn't any bother, but if she ever did become a bother, she wouldn't hesitate to give Harley a hard slap. Hard enough to show her who's boss, but soft enough for it not to show. One thing Gina wasn't, was stupid.

CHAPTER TWELVE

It was coming into the early hours of the morning and Johnny Taylor looked at his phone. The five texts on his mobile were still unopened, still sitting in his inbox. They were all from Maggie. He couldn't bring himself to read them. He knew what they'd say. He wouldn't blame her. But what was he supposed to do? It was complicated. In fact it was impossible. And now his father had been stabbed by Max, the situation had become hopeless.

Sitting outside Whispers club in Old Compton Street, Johnny pulled his Armani jacket tightly around him. The night air was cool, which he was grateful for. Soho in the summer became oppressive. It was also clearing his head, but he could still feel the excess alcohol in his blood, and he sensed it wouldn't take much for his head to start to ache again.

Johnny continued to sit on the metal chair, enjoying the lights of Soho against the cloudless night sky, aware there was a huge city beyond the other side of the buildings, yet the intimacy of the area made him always feel there was no other place he'd rather be.

He blew out a ring of smoke and slightly choked as it caught the back of his throat. He watched the crowds of people congregating outside the late night opening pubs, smoking their cigarettes, finishing off their beers. Standing around in short sleeved shirts and t-shirts. Feeling the chill of the air, but guarded against the full severity of the cool summer night by the warmth of the alcohol.

It'd been a crazy twenty-four hours. First his father with Max. Then Maggie. The reason he'd gone on his bender in the first place. The woman he loved but was supposed to hate.

If the circumstances had ever been likely to get better, if he'd ever been brave enough to try to broach the subject of their relationship with his parents, it definitely wasn't going to happen now. There'd be all-out war. Once again he and Maggie would be stuck in the middle as they'd always been – and now Harley was stuck in the middle of it too.

Thinking of his daughter made Johnny flinch. After Thelma, the ex-Tom from the sauna, had moved to be near her old man in Maidstone, it'd all gone tit over head. He'd been lucky to find someone like her in the first place and it would be impossible to find anyone to replace her. So then it'd become complicated, and Johnny Taylor didn't like complicated. He wasn't very good at it.

All his life his parents had sorted everything out for him. He'd never needed to make any real decisions. Even when Harley was born he didn't really need to worry, as Maggie had been happy to sort out all the day-to-day care of the baby, and he'd been happy to sort out the cash. Cash was the easy part. But difficult, complicated responsibility, he didn't know how to do.

The problem was Thelma had been perfect. She was like Mary Poppins, taking Harley all over London; to zoos, to parks, to museums. Making cakes, painting pictures and always making sure Harley was beautifully dressed. And his daughter had been happy. The only other person he'd ever

75

seen shower so much love on a child was his own mother when he was a child.

He'd been grateful to Thelma but Thelma had also been grateful to him. She'd gone from being shagged up the arse by strangers and giving ten pound blow jobs to being paid to spend her time going out on day trips in the company of his angelic little girl.

When she'd left he'd panicked. He'd even offered her ten grand to stay, but she'd been adamant she wanted to go to Maidstone. And there was no one else. In Johnny's world strangers weren't to be trusted. There was no way he could bring someone in who didn't have a life like himself, who didn't know the score. It could easily mean having the whistle blown – not only on himself but on his father's businesses as well. There was no way he could've taken the risk.

He'd talked the problem over with Nicky who'd told him not to worry. Within a couple of hours he'd come back to him, telling him he'd sorted it. Sorted it in the shape of Gina Daniels.

Harley had been so upset when he'd taken her to meet Gina, who was a world away from the warm colourful cockney character of Thelma. He hadn't been able to handle it. Didn't know how to make it better for his daughter. So what he'd done, to his shame, was hand a crying Harley over then and there in the street, rather than take her to Gina's to settle her in as planned.

He hadn't bothered going to see her, even though he'd promised Maggie he'd help look after her. Though it wasn't so much that he hadn't been bothered, it was just he couldn't cope with seeing his daughter upset. Begging him to let her go and stay with Auntie Thelma. All he wanted was for her to be happy. But Maggie wouldn't see it like that. Maggie would see it as him palming Harley off to Gina Daniels and pretended she didn't exist.

Johnny was a hard man in the eyes of many. Not a lot of Soho would cross him. He was the next generation of faces. But when it'd come down to standing up for his own, for his then, three year old daughter, he'd been weak. Hell, he'd been pathetic.

'Hiding from someone?'

Johnny turned to see Saucers standing directly behind him. She looked as bad as he felt. Her hair was matted on one side of her head and even though Johnny knew she'd got up with him earlier on in the day, she looked as if she'd just rolled out of bed.

She had the same clothes on as the night before; a short black mini skirt barely skimming the cheeks of her backside, a tight grey top two sizes too small and a cropped white faux leather jacket on. It was clear as day to anyone what she did, as clear as if she'd had it branded on her forehead.

'Who am I supposed to be hiding from?'

'You tell me darling. I'm not the one with the complicated love life. *My only love sprung from my only hate, too early seen unknown and known too late.*'

Johnny shook his head. He didn't need his head filled with Saucer's crap now. 'Do me a favour and keep it closed. I can't be listening to any of your shit now.'

'Shit? Johnny Taylor, go wash your mouth out with soap, you'll have Bill twirling in his bleeding grave. I take it you haven't seen Maggie yet?'

'No, and to tell you the truth it's killing me, but spare me the quotations.'

Saucers cackled and Johnny smiled at her warmly, watching as she took the novel she was carrying from under her arm to squash it into her tatty black bag. As much as he hated anybody knowing his business, he was grateful he could talk about it with Saucers if he needed to.

She'd found out when she'd caught them together after

he'd sneaked Maggie into one of his father's clip joints before opening hours. As he'd been the only one with the keys, he'd naturally presumed they'd be alone there and hadn't counted on Saucers sticking her beak up from nowhere. When she'd walked into the main bar, he'd been shocked and hadn't known what to say but as always, Saucers had made up for that. 'Fuck me, this is a turn up for the books. A pair of star cross'd lovers. *Romeo and Juliet* in case you're wondering Johnny, and standing here seeing the look on your boat race, I'd say you'll be the one playing Juliet.'

He'd opened his mouth to say something but hadn't known quite what, so he'd stood in the middle of the clip joint with his mouth hanging open and staring at Saucers like some fucking simpleton. 'Stop being such a bleeding girl, Johnny. I ain't going to say anything. You know me, I'm all for a little romance.'

'Listen Saucers, I'm telling you, if this ever gets out, I'll . . .'

'Oh there's no need to bring your flipping big guns out and start chomping on your bollocks. I told you, there's no need to worry. I won't say a bleeding thing; you have my word.'

And she'd been true to it. At first he'd kept her under his radar. Keeping close to her, making sure she didn't start talking, but then before long he'd found it was him who'd done the talking. Confiding in her, telling her about Harley when Maggie had been banged up. She'd tried to tell him to do the right thing but he hadn't wanted to listen. 'Johnny, you need to sort out your kid. You can't have that sponge Gina look after her. For fuck's sake, you promised Maggie.'

'I said I didn't want to talk about it.'

'Yeah you might not want to but you have to.'

He'd got mad then and said things he'd regretted.

'Don't fucking push it, Saucers. When I want advice of a

frigging whore, I'll ask for it. Until then, unlike your cunt, keep it shut.'

Saucers had looked devastated. She'd been right in what she'd said but over the year he'd managed to push her words and the hurt in her eyes – as well as his promise to Maggie – out of his head, though she hadn't held it against him and continued to be friends. Worse still, he'd pushed Harley out of it as well, getting on with what he did best; being Johnny Taylor. And that had all been fine until Saucers had reminded him that Maggie was coming home.

Johnny smiled at Saucers as she brought her chair next to him, breaking his thoughts. Without asking she cadged a cigarette out of the box of Camel lying on the table.

'To tell you the truth, I don't know what to do, Saucers.'

'You could try talking to her.'

Before he could answer, Johnny saw the tall handsome figure of Tommy Donaldson walking towards them. He felt Saucers tap him on his knee frantically, as if she was the only one aware of the looming presence of Tommy standing less than a meter away.

Johnny carried on smoking his cigarette as he locked eyes with Tommy; not wanting to break away, careful not to show any weakness. He saw Tommy smile, a dark cold smirk.

'How's Daddy?'

Johnny leapt up, knocking Saucers out of the way as she tried to grab his jacket to hold him back. The two men faced up to each other with Tommy standing slightly smaller at six foot two, though standing just as tall and menacing in stature. They ignored the worried glances of the passers-by and stood motionless, each waiting for the other to make a move.

'What's the problem Johnny? Don't want to take me? Too afraid you'll end up like your old man?'

Johnny curled up his lip in scorn.

'No, Tommy you've got me mixed up with yourself mate. I'm not the one who's afraid. You don't see me pissing myself in a corner when I hear my old man's voice.'

Tommy's face blanched. The humiliation crossed his face and Johnny could've kicked himself. He was fuming with Tommy for taking the rib out of his father being stabbed, but that didn't mean he could throw that in his face. Maggie had told him in confidence when they were having a heart-to-heart. Now like a chump and certainly not for the first time, he'd just broken her trust. He could see Tommy was still reeling from what he'd said and as he was about to say something else, he heard a familiar voice behind him.

'Why don't you just shut your mouth, Johnny?'

Johnny swivelled round to see Maggie Donaldson's beautiful face distorted with anger. She turned away from him and called to her brother as she saw him start to walk away.

'Tommy . . . wait. Tommy I want to talk to you . . . please.'

Johnny saw the hurt appear in Maggie's eyes as Tommy ignored her and disappeared into the Soho night, leaving Maggie to vent her anger on him.

'Maggie, Jesus, it's good to see you. I . . . I was going to call but . . . '

He trailed off, knowing whatever came out of his mouth would sound hollow. He glanced at Saucers for some help who only smiled weakly at both of them, before diplomatically hurrying off down Old Compton Street.

Clearing his throat, Johnny tried again, wanting to apologise for what he'd said to Tommy. 'Listen babe, what I said to Tommy, I wasn't thinking. You know I didn't mean anything by it.'

'Story of your life, Johnny. Always saying stuff you don't mean. Like saying you'd make sure Harley was alright, but you never meant anything by that either did you? Answer me this. Have you even seen her once since she's been with Gina?'

Johnny put his head down, not wanting to admit he hadn't, but not wanting to tell a blatant lie either which he knew Maggie would've known was untrue. So he'd stayed silent.

'I take it from the look on your face you haven't. Then you wouldn't know what a state she's in. She looks a mess, Johnny. What were you thinking, giving her to Gina to look after?'

'She's okay though, ain't she?'

His words sent Maggie into an angry hissing rant.

'Okay? No she ain't okay. How could she be with Gina? Would you want to be stuck with her? Jesus, a fart can't escape from Gina Daniels quick enough. But if you mean, is she alive? Well yeah she is, but okay she ain't. I needed you to help her. She needed you to. I will never forgive you for this.'

'Listen, I don't want to talk here.'

Johnny looked round nervously but Maggie was beyond caring at that point. 'What are you afraid of, Johnny? Someone seeing us together and they rumble your secret life? Then your perfect world comes crashing in on you?'

'It's not just my neck on the block if anyone finds out is it Maggie? It's Harley's too.'

'Don't you dare, Johnny. Don't you dare pretend you're concerned about her.'

Johnny's face darkened and he grabbed her arm as she turned to walk away. 'Think you're so flipping perfect don't you Maggie? Like butter wouldn't melt, the way you look down your nose at me. Well if you're so much better than the rest of us, why didn't you keep that big mouth of yours closed? Keep that temper of yours in check. But oh no, you couldn't do that could you? *You* had to prove a point and lay one out on a copper. So stop judging me, Maggie. Ask yourself instead why you didn't have more self-control. If you love our daughter as much as you say you do, why did you find yourself doing bird for a year?'

His words cut. She knew what Johnny was saying was true. Here she was going round being all high and mighty but *she* was to blame for all this. When Maggie had been in Highpoint she'd opened her eyes every morning, seeing the metal bars on the windows and she'd asked herself the same question: why?

'I hate you Johnny Taylor, you know that?'

He pulled her then, towards Whispers nightclub, looking around anxiously as he did so. Wanting to make sure nobody saw them.

Johnny took her down by the side of the club and firmly – but without hurting her – pushed Maggie against the cold red brick of the wall. Leaning on it with his hands on either side of her he stood inches away, looking down at her, her eye level only coming up to his chest.

Maggie smelt his expensive cologne and felt the heat of his body. He stared at her intently with his beautiful eyes and his raven hair flopping handsomely over his forehead.

'Don't say that to me Maggie. Never say you hate me.'

'I'll say what I want Johnny, especially if I mean it.'

'You don't mean it; it's just that flipping temper of yours talking.'

'Well that's where you're wrong. I do.'

'Then look me in the eyes Maggie and tell me.'

She stared at him and he leaned in to kiss her. For a moment she let him and she forgot. Forgot her anger, her problems, her life – only remembering her love for the man she'd been taught to despise. Then the moment, like the clouds in the sky, passed and everything came flooding back. Maggie pushed him away, locking eyes with him. She spoke angrily.

'Yes Johnny, I do. I do hate you.'

The pain was obvious in his eyes but so was the pain in Harley's when she'd told her she had to stay with Gina for a little bit longer until she worked something out. Thinking about her daughter made Maggie reject any pleading from Johnny. He was a grown man and he'd soon get over it. Harley was a child who needed her. Trusted her.

Harley came first above and beyond anyone else.

'You can't hate me, Maggie.'

'Why can't I, Johnny?'

He gently touched her face again, but this time Maggie pulled away from his touch. She walked away as Johnny continued to talk. 'I'll tell you why you can't hate me, Maggie – because I've never loved anyone the way I love you. And secondly . . . secondly, because you're my wife.'

CHAPTER THIRTEEN

Tommy had felt agitated after the confrontation with Johnny. What he'd said about Max had completely thrown him. Maggie had caught him off guard as well. Seeing her had given him a shock. He'd known she was coming home, but to see her standing behind him, glaring defiantly at Johnny Taylor with her huge blue eyes had taken him back to when they were kids. When it was Maggie, but should've been him, trying to protect them all from their father.

Tommy hadn't wanted to see her. She brought up too many memories, made the noise in his head seem louder. She'd smiled at him, reaching out to put her hand on his arm but as always, he hadn't known how to react. She made him feel confused, so he'd ignored her, giving Johnny a warning look and disappearing into the night-time streets as his head began to spin.

It'd been the second time in less than twenty-four hours a Taylor had made him retreat back to his private space.

Tommy listened and waited. He saw the flickering movements of the woman through the crack as she lay naked on the bed. From the dark of the closet he called her name. He didn't hear her stir so he called again in a whisper. He couldn't see her face but he could imagine the fear on it as he heard her anxious breathing. A moment later he flung open the doors and watched as she screamed.

Tommy heard the muffled tortured screams through her gag as her mouth was taped and her hands bound behind her back. Slow tears trickled down her face, stuffing up her nose, making it harder to breathe as the tape pulled back on her mouth and her eyes bulged with panic. He could see the torturous look on her face and in her eyes, and felt the fear resonating from her as he started to take off his belt.

CHAPTER FOURTEEN

It was Friday morning and Maggie stood in the doorway observing the refurbished ceiling of St. Patrick's Catholic Church in Soho Square. A church she'd been coming to since she was a child and where she'd had her first Holy Communion, watched by her father who'd sat scowling at her with a hangover, with her mother nervously sitting next to him on the front wooden pew, nursing a fresh black eye.

The domed ceiling had been painted and the walls white-washed. The high arched windows sparkled, letting the sunlight beam through the coloured glass, bouncing its rays towards the altar where a large painting of the Virgin Mary stood ten feet tall in judgement and framed in gold.

The refurbishments of St. Patrick's had finished last May and Maggie hadn't seen it since it had been re-opened.

'Maggie Donaldson, why it's good to see you. The sheep returning to its fold.'

Father Maloney greeted her at the church door. She'd never warmed to him, always getting the sense that if it wasn't for her father's large donations of laundered money given to the church in exchange for ten Hail Marys and all his sins forgiven, Father Maloney would never let them near the church – let alone in the continually reserved front row pew.

The other reason why Maggie had no time for Father Maloney was because she felt he'd let her down as a child. And though it might've been petty of her, she could never quite find it in her to forgive him.

Growing up, she and her siblings had been taught never to talk about what went on at home. She'd unbendingly kept to the rule until the day of her eleventh birthday when she'd bunked off school to go to church to ask God for help. Not for herself, but for her mother who, instead of making her a cake, was laid up in bed after having the shit beaten out of her the night before by her enraged father.

She'd sat at the back of the freezing church with her eyes scrunched up, trying to concentrate hard on remembering her prayers. Trying to stop the tears rolling down her face. Father Maloney had come to sit next to her and asked what was wrong. Like a naive fool she'd trusted him, needing to talk. Thinking maybe God had sent the priest to come and sit next to her, Maggie had broken her own family's sacred vow; she'd opened her mouth.

After she'd told him, Maggie had pleaded her concern. 'But Father, you won't tell my Dad I've told you will you? If he ever found out I think he'd kill me.'

He hadn't killed her, but when she'd seen Father Maloney standing in her kitchen with her father that same afternoon laughing and joking about life back in Ireland, Maggie had wished she was dead. She stood rooted to the red tiled floor as her whole body started to tremble; once more the fear of what was to come had almost made her vomit. Her father had spoken to her. 'I understand you paid Father Maloney a visit today Maggie. Gave him a tale.'

Father Maloney had scowled at her then, looking over his

glasses as he spoke. 'You know what they say about liars, Margaret?'

Maggie had looked at her father, then at the priest and had known she was going to get the beating of her life that night. Even at her young age she'd felt her temper rising, incensed by the injustice of the situation. Standing humiliated in the kitchen Maggie had decided she'd nothing to lose. She wanted to make it clear to Father Maloney exactly what she thought of him for breaking her trust. A trust she'd never given to anyone before. 'And you know what they say about cunts like you.'

She'd flown across the room along with a mouthful of blood and landed on a pile of shopping bags. She'd presumed it'd been her father who'd hit her with such almighty force that her front tooth was loose. But when she'd looked up, half dazed, her father was still standing in the same spot. It was Father Maloney who'd stood red-faced, his hand raised in the air. She'd touched her swollen lip and glared at the priest, calmly speaking to him and sounding much older than her eleven years. 'And Father, by the way, it's Maggie – not Margaret.'

The church bells began to ring, bringing Maggie back from her thoughts. She looked at Father Maloney and smiled. 'I've been away, detained as it were Father.'

The priest looked at Maggie, puzzled, and then continued to question her, his strong Irish accent carrying over the ringing church bells as they stood at the door of the church.

'Pastures new, Margaret?'

'I've heard them call it a lot of things but I've never heard them call a year banged up in Highpoint Prison pastures new. Oh and Father, perhaps you're forgetting the discussion we once had. It's Maggie, not Margaret, remember?'

Father Maloney blushed and Maggie saw he'd at least had the decency to look ashamed. With that, she turned on her heel and marched down the aisle into the cool of the church, catching the grin from Nicky and the angry glower from her father.

The regular congregation at St. Patrick's church was an odd sight; made up of locals and tourists, sex workers, gays and lesbians, drunks and the homeless from the melting pot of Soho's community. Then of course there was her own family; the Donaldsons.

Her family were worlds and hearts apart from each other. However, on Friday mornings they'd turn up for the ten o'clock service; sober, drunk, stoned, stressed, whatever state the morning delivered them in, to stand in what was supposed to be the house of God listening to Father Maloney and taking Holy Communion.

It had always been like that; one long hour of hypocrisy. Maggie had turned her back on any belief she'd had in God the day Father Maloney had betrayed her trust and like most things in her family, she only came along because her father told them to. There was no other choice.

Maggie looked down the pew. At the end was her mother, dressed as usual in her beige cashmere coat. She gave Maggie a quick nervous glance and a short smile then looked away. Next to her was her father, who immediately felt Maggie's gaze. He stared at her with disgust before turning away, sticking another piece of gum into his mouth as he did so. Tommy sat next to him, tall and handsome. She hadn't seen him since he'd ran away from her. He stared ahead into the distance, his look blank, cold, frozen. He didn't turn towards Maggie even though she was sure he could feel her looking at him. She loved him so much but she'd no idea how to get through to him anymore.

Nicky stood next to Tommy, his face swollen with bruising, twitching and twisting from one foot to another. Uncomfortable in his own body. Occasionally he leaned his weight on the pew in front for support until it creaked, sending a loud echo through the church.

He looked terrible and as Maggie caught his eye she felt uneasy. This was the first time she'd seen him since she'd got out. She got the distinct impression he was avoiding her. She needed to talk to him but from the manic wide-eyed stare she could see she'd have to wait until he came down from his high. He was sniffing and rubbing his nose restlessly until her mother passed him a handkerchief. He blew his nose and Maggie stared as the white delicate hankie turned scarlet red from his blood.

'Sorry . . . sorry.'

Nicky pushed past them and hurried to the back of the church where he made his way out watched by a worried Maggie, but ignored by his father who couldn't care less what part of Nicky's body was bleeding.

Maggie put her head down and closed her eyes. She'd no idea what she was supposed to do for Nicky, for Tommy, for her mother. They all seemed beyond helping themselves and the way things were going she wasn't far behind them. And then of course there was Harley. Her beautiful daughter who with every breath she took, she missed. She needed to have Harley with her but quite how she was going to do that, she didn't know. She squeezed her eyes shut, not wanting the tears to trickle down her face.

She sighed and opened her eyes, twisting her head slightly, catching her father looking at her with a scowl. Maggie turned away and tried to concentrate on the service but her mind kept bringing her back to Johnny.

For so long Johnny had been everything to her. She'd given him her heart and he had given his to her. But she didn't know if that was enough. Had she really thought that by being with him everything would be alright? Or had she just wished and wanted it to be so much she'd refused to see what was staring her in the face? That it was impossible. Her relationship with Johnny could never go further than their fantasies. He could no longer leave his life than she could leave her mother.

Perhaps Harley would be better off without her. Maybe she was being selfish, thinking she could be what Harley needed. She knew there'd be loving people, good people who didn't have children, who'd take Harley and give her a home and a life she deserved.

Harley was only four; given time and the right family, her daughter would soon forget about her. She'd be able to blossom and grow into a flower, rather than being stunted by the life she had now. But how would Maggie let her go? She loved her daughter so much, the idea of not being part of her life was almost too much to bear. But then if she loved her daughter, truly loved her, wouldn't she let her go? Love her by setting her free.

Father Maloney chanted loudly the holy sacrament in Latin, shocking Maggie out of her thoughts. She stared down at the marbled floor.

The church service was over, much to Tommy's relief. Though he would've rather have done without leaving the cool of the church to walk down the overbearing Soho streets.

During the whole service Maggie had kept her eyes on him, but he'd stared ahead at the altar, listening to Father Maloney's uninspiring sermon. But he'd known. Known she wanted him to look at her. Wanted to give him her warmest smile. He didn't know how to give her what she wanted. Didn't she realise that coming too close would only hurt her? And the worst thing about it was, he probably wouldn't even be able to stop himself.

Tommy continued to walk up Greek Street as the sun beat down on the back of his neck. He didn't want to go straight home, so decided instead to stop off at the coffee shop on the corner of Frith Street and get himself a double espresso.

As he stood in the queue of the overheated and under air-conditioned coffee shop, he watched the waitress struggling to walk about behind the tiny counter.

He watched her in fascination as she leant over the sandwiches on the counter. Rolls of swollen fat hidden under her ill-fitted jumper. Her colossal weight leaning just above the food, passing over it like a solar eclipse.

Tommy looked at her mouth. For all her size she was pretty. Young and pretty. The voice at the back of his head came from nowhere as it always did. Making a noise, until it became louder and louder. The din turning into a scream.

The blood from her nose ran into the back of her mouth. And Tommy watched as it choked her. Her face was covered in dirt whilst she struggled for breath. The gag was still tight. Her eyes wide open, staring directly into his.

'Tommy?'

Maggie stood next to him, a look of concern on her beautiful face. As his thoughts were broken, Tommy realised he'd been clenching his fists so tightly his little fingernail had dug into his palm, drawing blood. He could feel his face covered in perspiration while the adrenalin pumping through his body started to dissipate.

'Tommy, are you okay? I saw you come in here, thought we could have a coffee together.'

Tommy stared at his sister. He was breathing hard and he could feel his chest heaving rapidly but he didn't say anything.

'Tommy, what have you done to your hand, babe? It's bleeding.'

Maggie tried to take hold of Tommy's hand but he pulled it sharply back as he pushed his way out of the coffee shop, his blue eyes narrowing. 'Just leave me alone, Maggie. Do yourself a favour and leave me a-fucking-lone.'

'Tommy! Wait . . . Tommy . . .'

It was too late. He'd gone.

Maggie let herself into the house, her thoughts filled with worry. Worry for Harley. For Tommy. For Nicky. For her mother. So many people to worry about. But anxiety wasn't getting her anywhere. Action, not fear, changed things – yet she didn't know what to do, and this feeling of helplessness made her feel weak; vulnerable. It made Maggie Donaldson feel scared.

Maggie was relieved to find the house was quiet for once, though the cool silence of the Donaldson household also emphasised how void of warmth and love it also was.

Lying on her bed, she looked around her bedroom. Her room had been the only safe haven in the house when she was growing up. As a child she'd tried to leave the chaos on the other side of the white panelled door.

There was a tiny tap on her door and Maggie knew immediately who it was. It was her mother. Since Maggie was a child her mother's knock had never got any louder or softer. To Maggie it was a heartbreaking reminder of her mother's acceptance of her situation. A small, non confrontational – without any strength behind it – knock. Maggie hated the sound of it.

'You holding up, Maggie love? You seemed a bit quiet in church.'

Maggie sat up and took her mother's hand as she came to sit next to her. She smiled warmly.

'Well you know Mum, it's kind of hard to get a word in edgeways with Father Maloney chatting ten to the dozen. Maybe next week I'll tell him to keep it down a bit when he's doing the Holy Communion, give me a chance to have a chat.'

Sheila chuckled, and it warmed Maggie's heart to see her mother genuinely smile, with her eyes lighting up in support.

'How's Harley?'

It touched a raw nerve with Maggie. She physically retreated, letting go of her mother's hands and clasping them in her lap. Her shoulders slumped as her body reflected her feelings.

Sheila Donaldson noticed the change in her daughter and immediately felt uneasy, wishing she hadn't brought the subject up. The hush in the room was too much for Sheila to bear and she blurted out a clunky apology, desperate to see her daughter stop hurting but also desperate for Maggie to forgive her for letting her down.

'I'm sorry to bring Harley up but I can't stand to see you moping around. It ain't worked out the way it should, but she's okay.'

Sheila bit her lip. It wasn't coming out the way she wanted it to. What she really wanted to say she couldn't express. Now she'd lit a fire and Maggie's face had turned hostile. Sheila could see the infamous Donaldson temper boiling under the surface of her beautiful daughter's skin.

'*Moping*, Mum? I haven't lost my brolly on a rainy day. Harley's been shacked up with Gina for the past year and looks like she's stepped out of a bleeding workhouse.'

'Don't exaggerate, Maggie. Nicky's been making sure things are okay.'

'I love him Mum, but I have a feeling the only thing Nicky's been making taking care of are his nostrils. Just leave it. Please.'

Guilt tended to make Sheila say the wrong thing to her daughter. 'Why are you getting so mad at me? I covered up and I've kept my mouth shut all through your pregnancy. I helped you as much as I could.'

Maggie saw the pleading in her mother's eyes, wanting

her not to cause any rows. 'I'm mad at you because I don't know who else to be mad with. None of this is normal, Mum. It isn't normal that I can't have Harley to stay here. It isn't normal that I have to keep her a secret to keep her away from harm. And it isn't normal that I'm thinking of giving her up.'

'What? . . . Maggie, no, listen there must be some other way.'

'Well you tell me what it is then – because I've racked my head and I can't think of a way out. Apart from running away, that is.'

Sheila's face drained of colour. 'Maggie, no. You can't do that. You can't leave me . . . what would I do without you?'

Maggie heard the panic in her mother's voice. She didn't look at her but gave her mother the answer she needed to hear. The answer which she'd been telling her since a child.

'No Mum, I won't leave you. I've always promised you that, but I can't let Harley have the life I had. I love her too much. She deserves so much better. She deserves to have a childhood.'

Sheila stared as the tears rolled down Maggie's cheeks. She was about to lean forward to give her daughter a hug but she stopped herself, unsure how to comfort her. It was rare for Maggie to ever cry and it made Sheila feel very uncomfortable. Not knowing what to do or say, Sheila got up and left the room, leaving Maggie sobbing her heart out.

CHAPTER FIFTEEN

Soho, London. Eight Years Earlier.

'Maggie, get yer fecking arse down here. If I get to the count of one and you're not here there'll be trouble.'

A moment later Maggie stood opposite her father. She smelt the whiskey and saw the remnants of white powder around his nostrils.

'Did you not hear me calling you?'

'I did Dad, but unless I had a firecracker up me bum I wasn't going to make it by the count of one.'

Maggie stared at her Dad, hoping he wouldn't see her knees banging together as they trembled in fright whilst she held his steely gaze.

'But you never tried did you?'

'No.'

'No. Because you're too big for your fucking boots, ain't that right?'

Maggie shifted her gaze and spoke quietly. Mentally bracing herself for what was about to happen. 'No Dad, I never tried because I knew I couldn't get down in time. I also knew whatever I did would be wrong and you'd find a reason to punish me anyway.'

Max Donaldson's face expanded as he blew out his cheeks, enraged by Maggie's front. He disliked his daughter so much. She had an answer for everything. And she looked at him as if he'd just fallen out of a dog's arse.

Raising his hand, Max brought it down on his daughter's face, knocking her over to the side and causing a huge red welt to appear. Maggie scrambled up and headed for the back door. She wasn't going to stay around for trouble. She'd learnt it was best to run.

The back door was jammed, and Maggie had to pull on it hard, giving her father – who rarely ran after her – time to catch up. Maggie felt a clump of her hair being pulled and on opening the door had to motion her head forward to free his grip.

She slammed the door shut behind her as she ran out, leaving her father on the other side of the red door, still able to hear his words.

'You cheeky bleedin' mare. You think you can disobey me and get away with it?'

Her father's voice was loud and penetrating as Maggie ran into the street. She was terrified he'd choose this occasion to run after her. She glanced around just to check he wasn't there, that he hadn't opened the door to follow her out. As she turned back around she abruptly banged into a tall boy roughly of the same age as her. She fell awkwardly onto the pavement as she shouted at the boy.

'Jesus, look where you're going will you?'

'I'm sorry. Are you alright?'

Maggie dusted the dirt off her and stood up to face the boy.

'I'm covered in dirt, my knees are scratched and I've got

a blood blister on me hand. So what do you think, Einstein?'

The boy stood watching her, then gently touched Maggie's face, turning her cheek towards him.

'And you've got a hand mark the size of King Kong's on yer boat race. You didn't get that from falling over just now. What happened?'

Embarrassed by the boy's gentle touch, Maggie pulled away sharply. Annoyed that he expected her to explain herself but more annoyed by the fact it moved her that he could care.

'Didn't your mother tell you not to stick your nose into other people's business?'

'Yeah, but she also told me you don't hit women. I might be a nosey parker but I'd rather be nosey than be the person who did this.'

Maggie opened her mouth, about to give him a piece of her mind, when she heard her name being called.

'Maggie!'

For a moment she'd forgotten about her father. Hearing her name caught her off guard, sending terror jolting through her body. Her body spasmed and she wasn't able to hide her fear from the boy. He looked at her with concern, then at the back door as they both heard it open. Her name was called again, the sound clearer now that the door had been opened.

'What the fuck do you think you're doing?'

Max's voice was low and menacing. Maggie tried to compose herself but she felt her throat become tight and her frown become creased as tears threatened to fall.

'I hope you're not speaking to her, mate?'

The boy's voice cut through the air and Maggie looked at him in shock. She pulled at his arm but he shook her off as he walked closer to her father.

Maggie watched her father, who seemed as much in shock as she was by the boy's involvement. However, in a matter of a split second it turned to anger. A thunderous bellow escaped from Max's lips.

'I'll speak to my daughter any way I want.'

'I'm sorry to be the one to tell you mate, but that ain't the way life works.'

'And who the hell are you to tell me anything?'

'It don't matter who I am. The question is, did you do this to her?'

'Hang on, I know who you are.'

Max stepped forward, beside himself with fury as he recognised the boy. He lowered his voice into a whisper as he stood a foot away from the young man.

'I think you've made a very big mistake today, son.'

'You don't frighten me. I ain't a girl to be smacked about.'

Max had had enough. He clenched his hand into a hard fist, ready to do some damage but from the corner of his eye he saw a policeman approaching and thought it was wiser to back down. No doubt he'd catch up with him, then pigs would have to fly to stop him putting his fist down the boy's throat.

Maggie hadn't bothered to stay around to see what was going to happen because she knew nothing good could come out of it, although there was a part of her which had enjoyed seeing the brief look of shocked surprise on her father's face.

Leaning on the wall at the end of Meard Street, Maggie got out a box of cigarettes from inside her pocket. Lighting one, she closed her eyes. When she opened them again she jumped slightly to see the boy standing opposite her. He spoke with a big grin, lighting up his handsome face.

'Ain't you going to thank me then?'

Maggie blew out the smoke in rings, a trick her brother Nicky had taught her, whilst cocking her head to one side taking in the cheeky smile and the twinkling eyes. Maggie answered, sounding more aggressive than she felt.

'Thank you for what, mate? Flipping making things worse?'

'How I see it, things couldn't get worse.'

'And what would you bleedin' know about anything?'

'Enough to know that your old man's a frigging nutter and he needs a steel bar taking to his head.'

'Oh and that's going to help is it? You're just as bad as he is.'

She turned on her heel and walked down the street, but felt herself being pushed out of the way as the boy ran to get in front of her, blocking her path. Maggie tried to move forward and he continued to face her as he walked backwards, talking to her.

'Get out of me way.'

'I want to talk to you. Listen I'm sorry, I didn't want to fan any shit between you and your Dad, but he shouldn't do that. Nobody should.'

The boy put out his hand and stroked her cheek which was throbbing painfully. The touch, so full of warmth and kindness was the trigger to set Maggie off, lifting the lid on her skilfully controlled emotions. She cried, embarrassed that a stranger, that anyone, would see her tears. But she didn't want to take her eyes off him.

Maggie wanted to see the person who had nothing to gain and no ulterior motive but had stepped in to help her. The realisation that in all her seventeen years this was the first time anyone had looked out for her made her cry all the more.

'Don't let anyone do this to you. Come here.'

Without waiting for an answer he pulled her into him. Maggie didn't resist. She let herself be taken by the moment and allowed herself to be held; wishing it could last forever; until, that was, he spoke and told her his name.

'My name's Johnny. Johnny Taylor.'

She pushed him away feeling like she'd been tricked. He was a Taylor. The scum of the earth, according to her father.

Her family hated them. *She* hated them, though she wasn't really sure why. However, she knew the name, and like she'd been brought up to hate the police, she'd been brought up to despise the Taylors. And here she was, in the middle of Soho, falling into his arms as if he was some kind of hero.

'What did I say?'

He looked hurt. Maggie felt a flicker of shame come over her – nevertheless he was a Taylor, and that's all that mattered.

'It's not what you said. It's who you are.'

Johnny looked at her puzzled.

'I know you ain't some bird I've slept with and done a runner on. Frigging hell I would've remembered you, cos you're too beautiful, not to mention too fiery, to forget.'

Maggie blushed, not wanting to find anything to like about him although she did allow herself to be a little flattered.

'Sleep with you? You should be so lucky. I've got more class than that.'

Johnny laughed out an infectious laugh and Maggie struggled not to join in. Wanting to contain her serious composure to show him how she felt about a Taylor.

She turned away towards the cafe in Bateman Street. As the cafe came into sight Johnny ran up by the side of her.

'I thought I told you to piss off.'

'No, you never said that.'

'Well I'm saying it now, piss off.'

'You don't mean that.'

'I'm not in the habit of saying things I don't mean but if you're in any doubt let me repeat it again for you, Johnny. Piss off.'

'Okay, fine. But before I go why don't you tell me what I'm supposed to have done?'

'I told you, it's *who* you are. You're a Taylor.'

Johnny shrugged his shoulders, still baffled from the sudden turnaround.

'Do I have to spell it out to you? You're a Taylor and I'm a Donaldson. Unless you've been wrapped up all your life in cotton wool then you and I hate each other.'

Johnny stayed silent for a moment. He thought he'd recognised the man back there but he hadn't been able to put a name to the face. Many a time he'd had fights with the oldest Donaldson boy but he had no idea he had a sister. And certainly not such a beautiful one.

'Hate each other. Do we?'

'Yeah we do.'

'Well I prefer to make up my own mind who I hate. You don't strike me as the kind of girl who likes to be told what to do but perhaps I'm wrong.'

Maggie could tell Johnny was goading her but she couldn't help falling for it. 'Are you saying I don't think for myself? Well I do.'

'If that's the case tell me why you hate us.'

'Because . . .'

Johnny stood watching her and grinned. 'Because?'

Maggie was perplexed. She'd never questioned why she had to hate them, she'd just accepted it. Now she was being hauled over the coals about it and she'd no idea. 'Because . . . because you're a Taylor.'

It sounded stupid and it was. Which was why Johnny laughed out loud, causing Maggie to become incensed. 'This is all a joke to you. Well go and find someone else to make fun of.'

Maggie stormed off into Lola's Cafe, plonking herself down in the tiny booth at the end of the steam-filled teashop. As she sat trying to calm herself down she looked around. It wasn't busy. There was a couple holding hands sitting at the window table, another at the next table looking far removed from the early throes of love as they sat stony-faced and as usual, there was a small group of builders poring over the back page of the paper, analysing the football results.

'What can I get you my sweet?'

Lola Harding, the cafe owner came over with a pad to write things down but without the pen, and sat down opposite Maggie.

'I'll have anything, Lo.'

'How about a bit of TLC and advice? Do you want me to get some ice for your face?'

Maggie smiled and touched her face absentmindedly. She could talk to Lola about anything but at the moment she didn't want to. She'd made a fool of herself in front of Johnny Taylor. As much as she knew she shouldn't care what he thought she couldn't help it.

'I'm okay, Lola. You know how life is sometimes.'

'I bleeding well do. I tell you girl, when I'm in front of those pearly gates, first question I'm going to ask the big fella is; what the fuck was that all about?'

Maggie beamed at Lola. She always managed to make her feel better about herself. There'd never been a time when Lola hadn't got her to raise a smile.

'I'll have a tea please and whatever the young lady's having.'

Both Lola and Maggie looked up and saw Johnny Taylor, but it was Lola who spoke.

'Young lady! Bleeding hell, Johnny, I knew my face cream was good but never thought the day would come again when I was mistaken for a young lady.'

'You still do it for me, Lola.'

Lola cackled.

'You've got the charm of your old man. How is he?'

'Good thanks, I'll tell him you were asking after him.'

'You do that but make sure you leave the bit out that you were with Maggie. Don't think he'd much care for you two having a Rosie Lee together.'

Lola laughed again, winking at Maggie before leaving

them to it. She watched Lola with affection as she walked away. Everyone in Soho knew who Lola was and everyone had something good to say about her. Johnny touched her hand lightly over the table.

'Maggie, I'm sorry. I wasn't making fun of you.'

'I don't know how you make that out, because there wasn't anybody else about, so it must've been me.'

'Bloody hell girl, you've got more fire in your belly than St. George's dragon. I ain't looking for an argument.'

'No? Well what are you looking for then?'

'I dunno, but I know I like you.'

'You don't know me and I don't know you. I don't want to either.'

'Just give me a chance. Have a cup of tea with me and if at the end of it you don't want to see me again, I'll piss off and disappear.'

'I dunno. It feels so wrong.'

'What feels wrong, Maggie, is you listening to a person who'll do this to you.'

Johnny touched her face again and looked into her piercing blue eyes.

'Just a cup of tea, that's all I ask.'

Maggie had a cup of tea and when she'd finished it, they ordered another one and another, staying to talk until closing time.

'Let me take you to the fair in Leicester Square, Maggie.'

'I can't.'

'Why not?'

'Because my Dad's going to go crazy.'

'He'll go crazy anyway. So why not enjoy yourself first? I'll get you some candyfloss.'

Johnny winked at Maggie and she laughed. He made her feel alive. Special. And even though she'd known him for less than a few hours, he also made her feel safe. And the feeling of safety was rare in Maggie's life. In fact, it was almost unheard of.

And that was the moment Maggie thought she'd fallen in love. Fallen in love with Johnny Taylor. The first, the last and the only person who'd ever made her feel safe.

CHAPTER SIXTEEN

'Not even a week and she's got her feet so far under the frigging table they're hitting bleeding Australia. Bugger me Frank, can't you book her into a hotel – or better still, into the nearest flippin' morgue?'

Frankie Taylor looked at his wife and wanted to tell her to shut the fuck up. The last thing he needed, however, was another hour and a half of Gypsy screeching at him; it was getting on his nerves. He'd got used to her soft – albeit expensively trained – voice, and had forgotten what it was like to hear the constant presence of the East End girl. But since the arrival of his sister, Lorna, that's all he'd heard coming out of Gypsy's mouth.

What made it worse was the fact he couldn't even go out to get laid to relieve his tension. And by the way Gypsy was pacing about, giving a good impression of a Grenadier Guard, he didn't hold out much hope of getting his dick sucked by her any time soon. He certainly wasn't stupid enough to ask when she was in this sort of mood.

Gypsy poked him hard, knowing he wasn't listening.

'Christ's sake Gyps, you're starting to do me nut in. I

don't want to be worrying about this; I need to start thinking about what I'm going to do with Max Donaldson.'

'Why do you have to mention that man's name in this house, Frank? I told you a long time ago what to do with him. You didn't listen then and look what bleedin' happened. You got cut up the carkers and now you think you know what's best about Lorna staying here. I'm telling you Frank, it'll go arse over bleeding tit.'

'Oh for God's sake Gyps, turn it in or turn it down. Do you think listening to this tripe is helping me? Only just got out of hospital and I'm already getting grief. Would've done better to stay in there. Do yourself and *me* a favour and calm down.

'*Calm down*? How can I when I've got Lorna living under the same hatch as me? I'm telling you, Frank, she's like the witch of the North, South, East and bleeding West all rolled into one.'

Lorna Taylor stood on the other side of the walnut door, listening to her sister-in-law badmouth her, and smiled. From the very first time she'd laid her eyes on Gypsy she'd hated her – and she wasn't going to stop now.

She was certain it'd been Gypsy stopping her from coming across to visit her brother again. Stopping Frankie from sending her a passport to travel on. Lady Muck had as good as made her a prisoner, forcing her to stay in Belgium all this time and Lorna was sure she knew the reason why – Gypsy was greedy and she didn't want to share Frankie with anyone. She certainly didn't want to share his money. She wanted it all to herself, to indulge in the luxury she'd become accustomed to without anyone trying to knock her off her ivory pedestal.

Lorna realised that she and Gypsy weren't so many worlds apart. They were both East End girls with their childhoods being a replica of each other; poverty in their house and on every corner. Now, however, there was one big difference between them – Gypsy had it all and she had nothing. But Lorna knew that was soon going to change. If her sister-in-law thought she'd get rid of her as easily as she did the last time she was in for a shock. Lorna Taylor was here to stay.

She was owed; and owed big time. She wanted exactly what Frankie had and she was going to get it. It hadn't just been her brother who'd been stuck in the kids' home being battered by the workers like a fish in a chip shop. Yet it'd been only her who'd been returned from all those different foster homes because she wasn't pretty enough, smart enough, or she didn't give her new foster father good enough head.

All her life Lorna had been pushed about by men who thought she was something they wiped their feet on, but that was about to stop. She had no intention of going back to Belgium to her excuse of a boyfriend. She belonged here. Here with Frankie. Here with her nephew. Here *without* Gypsy. And whether Gypsy went of her own accord or whether she would have to get rid of her, one way or another, Lady Muck with her stupid pretentious voice was going to lose her crown very soon.

Lorna leant slightly nearer to the door, not wanting to miss a word of the argument between Gypsy and Frankie. As she moved her head to make her ear more comfortable on the hand carved panel, the door was opened and Gypsy appeared red-faced and glowering.

'Oh! Not enough just to be under me roof Lorna; you want to be up in me business too. Flip me, where next? Wouldn't surprise me if I woke up tomorrow morning to find you up me bleeding arse.'

'Is everything alright? I'm sorry Frankie, I didn't mean to interrupt, I just heard a few raised voices when I came to knock. I wasn't wanting to disturb you. You know me, I don't like to pry,' she said sweetly.

Frankie smiled and waved at his sister to come into the room, slightly embarrassed that she might've heard what Gypsy had been saying.

'Don't worry about it, Lorn. I'm sorry you had to hear it babe, especially after you coming all this way to see me.'

Gypsy watched Lorna's sickly smile. She knew she spelled trouble with the letters B.I.T.C.H. Gypsy had been brought up in the East End, she was streetwise. She could smell a rat when she saw one, and Lorna Taylor was one of the biggest ones she'd seen in a long time. Even the Pied Piper of Hamelin would have trouble with her.

Gypsy continued to stare at her sister-in-law. Her bulbous body pushed at the seams of the expensive red Valentino dress which Frankie had sent her one Christmas. Her Harry Winston diamond cluster earrings struggled to stay on her fatty lobes. Her Tiffany necklace – a present from Johnny – almost choked her as it struggled to clasp round her neck and her wrist had ownership of a yellow gold and diamond *Datejust* special edition Rolex watch. Another present from Frankie.

She could hear Lorna breathing heavily from the excess weight pressing onto her lungs and her large breasts hung heavily in an ill-fitting bra. Her face, unlike Frankie's, was rotund and her green beady eyes lay too close to her sharp pointed nose.

Gypsy curled her nose up. Everything about Lorna offended her. As she looked at Frankie and his sister laughing together it felt as if something very nasty had come home to roost.

CHAPTER SEVENTEEN

Gina Daniels was smiling as she looked at her nephew, Gary, on the other side of the room. He was beginning to make a name for himself and once he did, she'd have the name too.

Gina leaned back on the table, stretching out her puffy legs and feeling a twinge of cramp in her calf. She glanced around, noticing how much of a mess Gary's flat was in, but the difference between his mess and other people's was what it was messy *with*.

Lab burners, glass vials, measuring jugs, pans and packets of opened baking powder lay scattered about the room in disarray. Then of course there was the cocaine. The cocaine to make the crack.

Gone were the days of Gary having to buy a few rocks of ready-made crack, earning so little it didn't even pay for a week's grocery shopping. He was moving up in the world. Here he was with his own crack lab in his kitchen, and Gina Daniels couldn't have been prouder.

'Come over and help me. No good just bleedin' sitting there Auntie Gina, you know I was never good at cooking.'

The joke was lost through the white mask Gary wore, guarding his lungs against potent crack fumes. He bent over the pan and watched the combination of water, baking soda and cocaine sizzle and bubble as it started to form white solid lumps. On occasion he'd put white candle wax in the mix to help the crack keep its off-white colour and to help it to form into small solid pieces. Today though, he could tell from the pungent smell – which managed to seep through, even with the mask on – that the coke was already cut with more than enough shit to risk adding anything more. He needed his clients to be able to smoke the stuff, not make a Madame Tussauds waxwork out of it.

He wanted to get the crack cooked and out on the streets. If people were going to take him seriously there needed to be a constant supply. That way no one would get it into their head that it was alright to muscle in on Gary's turf and start serving up to his customers.

He wasn't the biggest coke and crack dealer around by any means, but Gary Levitt reckoned he was the most ambitious. He had a game plan to take over all the clubs in Soho and the West End and he wasn't prepared to settle for anything less. To do that though, he needed to get a certain person on side. Unfortunately that person was none other than Max Donaldson.

Thinking about Max naturally brought Gary's thoughts to Nicky. The roughing up he'd received the other day had sent him underground, no doubt worried about the money he owed. No one had seen him.

He needed teaching a lesson. Gary certainly didn't want people to think he was being soft on Nicky because he was Max Donaldson's son. He couldn't have anyone thinking he was afraid to do what was necessary. Of course, in truth there was a part of him that *was* afraid. He'd have to think about how to handle the situation very carefully, especially if he wanted Max to give him the go ahead to start serving up in the clubs.

Pouring the mix into a muslin cloth to drain away the excess water, Gary suddenly felt tense.

'What's the matter Gal, you look bunged up?'

'Have you seen that junkie mate of yours lately? I want a word with him.'

'Nicky? I'm seeing him later in the cafe, got a little bit of business to sort out. Do you want me to give him a message?'

'Yeah, tell him if I don't have my money by the end of the week the only thing he'll be banging on will be a fucking coffin lid.'

Gina walked along Wardour Street. The early summer sunshine was nowhere to be seen as a dark rain cloud came and stayed over the one square mile of Soho. She thought about the money Nicky owed Gary and it worried her. She liked to get what was owed to her. For two weeks running Nicky had short-changed her, pretending Johnny hadn't paid the amount he usually did for Harley. She wasn't stupid but Johnny was thinking Nicky would be more trustworthy than her when it came to money just because Maggie was his sister. She knew exactly what was going on. Unlike her nephew Gary, she didn't have the ability to beat it out of someone, but what she did have though was more powerful than any clenched knuckle. She had information. Information she knew neither Johnny, Maggie or Nicky would want reaching either Max or Frankie's ears.

As she continued to walk Gina suddenly caught a glimpse of Nicky at the top of the street and immediately broke out into a half-hearted jog, amusing the group of builders standing outside the amusement arcade on the corner of Winette Street with her feeble efforts.

'Nicky! Nicky!'

Finally, Nicky turned around, giving Gina a quick smile whilst his eyes darted back and forth.

'Nicky, I hope you weren't trying to ignore me? We had an arrangement to meet in the cafe, remember?'

'Listen, can we make it later? I have to be somewhere.'

'This ain't got anything to do with the money you owe is it? Not trying to hide away?'

'No.'

Nicky blushed.

'Why am I getting the feeling you're not quite telling me the truth?'

Nicky didn't answer; he found it was always best to do that. Let the other person say what they needed to say and hope they'd be satisfied with that. Gina pulled Nicky into the quiet of St. Anne's court as she continued to walk towards Lola's Cafe.

'Anyway, I've got a message for you; Gary says he wants his money and if you ain't got it, then there'll be ructions.'

This time Nicky swallowed hard.

'Why are you looking worried, Nick? Don't tell me you ain't got his dough?'

'It's fine. I told him I'll sort it and I will.'

'Well then you ain't got anything to worry about. Come on, you can buy me a bacon sandwich, I'm starving.'

Nicky sat opposite Gina Daniels in Lola's Cafe and felt sick. He pushed the toast on the plate away from him. It seemed every week he needed to keep making a new notch on his belt to stop his trousers falling down. The cocaine had taken his craving for food away. It'd taken his craving for everything away – everything but the coke.

He looked at Gina with her knock-off cream Burberry coat done up to the top button and saw she was happy to eat for the both of them. She hungrily grabbed his unwanted

113

toast, stuffing a piece in her mouth and squirreling the other piece onto the blue chipped sideplate.

'Maggie wants to talk to me.'

'Well then, talk. I don't know what you're worried about Nicky; we've got her eating out of our hands like a dog. I don't think Johnny's bothered. He hasn't come to visit Harley in almost nine months, plus he certainly won't want people knowing about her. As for Maggie, well any nonsense from her and I'll just tell her I won't look after Harley. That'll soon shut her up.'

Nicky glared at Gina. He disliked her and always had done but no more so now in the way she was talking about his sister. Then he supposed he was no better. He and Gina were two of a kind when it came to money – albeit for different reasons.

He didn't like the situation he'd found himself in but what could he do? He loved Maggie and never wanted to do anything to hurt her, but he was in debt up to his eyeballs to Gary and he was starting to owe Gina money after spending her cut of the cash Johnny gave him on coke. Not to mention the odd person here and there from in and around Soho. He needed at least a couple of hundred a day to feed his habit but that was nearly impossible to find.

'Perhaps Johnny isn't bothered about Harley – but he will be about his money. What happens when he does find out? He won't be too chuffed when he realises the money went on designer clothes instead of his daughter.'

'Don't try to lay the blame on my bleedin' doorstep. I've got enough dust sitting on it without you adding more. I don't seem to remember you worrying about your niece when you were sticking the money up your nose.'

Nicky stared at Gina. He was feeling hot and anxious and the steamy cafe on Bateman Street wasn't helping. He looked around, seeing a throng of workmen having a laugh with the waitress. He saw a well-dressed couple deep in conversation in the far corner and there was Lola leaning against the greasy counter, seemingly oblivious to the dirty plates piling up behind her as she sang along to the tune being played on the radio. All content in their own worlds. Nicky Donaldson would've happily exchanged his life with any one of them.

'I'm not saying it's all you Gina, but what part of the money did you *actually* spend on Harley?'

Gina turned her head and sniffed loudly. Nicky grabbed her hand hard, making her yelp and bringing them a quick glance of attention from the builders.

'Look Nicky, how much does a three year old need?'

'She's four.'

'Yeah well, whatever.'

Nicky narrowed his eyes and wiped his forehead with the crumpled paper napkin.

'It was her birthday two months ago. You told me you were going to do something for her. Are you now going to tell me you didn't? You were supposed to get her a cake and a present, remember?'

Gina screwed up her face.

'Yeah, well I didn't. What's the point? She's a child, not a fucking calendar. She don't even know what day it is let alone when her birthday is. It's not like she won't have another one is it? It was a bleeding waste of time, so I got myself a new Mulberry handbag off the girls in the sauna. The way I saw it, if I was happy then that little mare would be.'

Nicky shook his head. He wanted to be horrified but it just didn't cut it. He was as much as to blame as Gina, if not more. After all, Harley was his niece, she wasn't Gina's blood.

'Okay, maybe you're right Gina, but we need to be more

careful. At least look like you're buying Harley something. I picked up Johnny's money from one of his men this morning. Apparently he was a little short so it's not as much as usual . . .'

Nicky trailed off, feeling Gina's eyes boring into him. He could tell she didn't believe him and she was absolutely right not to. It was coming to something when he had to rip off the person he was in league with in order to rip someone else off.

He took the cash out of his pocket and discreetly counted it out on the table, feeling the inquisitive eye of Lola Harding looking at him. Gina quickly took the money, wetting her fat finger to separate and count out the notes. She spoke as she mentally counted.

'Nicky, this is the third time in a row now you've pulled me up short. I suggest for your sake this is the last time. I've got two rules. Never trust a junkie and never trust a bloke who'd rip off his family. You, darlin', fall into both them rules. There's a hundred short here and I want it.'

Nicky rubbed his eyes. This wasn't who he was but it certainly was what he'd become. He hated dealing with the likes of Gina, hated avoiding his sister, and most of all, hated not being able to give his niece the life she deserved. It was if his own shitty childhood was happening all over again – only this time it was happening to Harley.

When Maggie had got nicked he'd been inconsolable, blaming himself for her predicament. He knew that if he'd only picked up the pills within the hour like he'd said he would, rather than getting wasted on coke, his sister would've never been nicked in the first place. Maggie had been warm and understanding as always, but the kinder she was to him the more it'd sent him spiralling.

Nicky could deal with cruelty, with hatred, with pain – but he couldn't handle compassion. So he'd taken more and more

116

coke, sometimes for days on end without sleeping. Then one day he'd woken up covered in his own blood after being bang on it for three days and he knew then he was in trouble. Not that he hadn't known it before. He'd been taking the stuff since he was twelve but it was only then he'd realised he wasn't ever going to get out of it alive.

Harley had been a problem after Thelma had left. Johnny had been desperate for her to be looked after but also desperate to distance himself from the whole situation, and not having Maggie around had thrown him. Then Johnny had asked Nicky if he could help out. Apart from having plenty of time for Johnny after seeing the way he made Maggie happy, he'd immediately seen it as a way of earning a quick buck. He'd spoken to Gina about having Harley and the moment she'd known there was something in it for her, she'd been onboard, sticking to it like a whore on a dick.

His mother had been happy to go along with the idea as well; unable to look after Harley on her own, she was more than happy for someone else to take on the responsibility. Everyone was happy to turn a blind eye to what was going on. Everyone, including himself, was happy to let down Maggie. The one person he knew that deserved so much more. So much more than anyone had ever given her.

At first, Johnny had given him two hundred pounds a week for Harley; more than enough for a little girl, though not enough to feed his habit as well as Gina's greed. Nicky had pushed for more, until he'd been getting almost six hundred pounds a week from Johnny.

Most weeks he divided the six hundred pounds equally between Gina and himself but sometimes like today, he'd skim a little bit extra. It'd all been working nicely until he started to get into debt and Gina had started to feed nothing much more than beans on toast to his niece, not bothering to buy any clothes or toys for her either.

117

'She's lucky she's got felt pens, Nicky. When I was a kid I had nothing but me own bleeding shadow to play with and sometimes even that didn't want to play with me,' had been Gina's reply when he'd confronted her for the way she was looking after Harley. He could do nothing else but settle for her answer. Slowly he'd stopped bothering to ask any questions.

Nicky pulled back his head in disgust from the stinking belch Gina let out.

'Nicky, I want me money otherwise I'll have to start opening me mouth. And another thing, I hope you don't think you'll put me at the bottom of the list with the money you owe. Don't think I'll be a soft bleeding touch; I ain't a cashmere jumper. When Gary gets his money, I want mine – or like I said, I'm talking. And the first person I'm opening me mouth about is Maggie.'

Nicky was so angry with himself. How the fuck had he got himself into this mess? He couldn't let Gina serve his sister up on a plate – he'd already done enough damage – but how he was going to stop it, he didn't know.

'Listen Gina, leave Maggie out of things. She's only just come out. I'll sort your money.'

Gina leant over the table and poked Nicky in the chest, feeling how skinny he was when she did so.

'Well that's my point: she's only been out a few days and she's already causing problems. Coming round to me as if she's the bleeding Gestapo.'

'She's just worried about Harley.'

'I like our arrangement and I don't want Maggie spoiling it, but I also want to get what's properly owed to me. Stop playing the dumb fucking blonde Nick, and then there won't be a problem.'

'You're a nasty bitch, Gina Daniels. You can have a problem with me but don't have one with Maggie. She doesn't deserve it, so leave her alone.'

'I don't give a shit what you think about me, Nicky. You were quick enough to come to me before and I'm happy to continue our little set-up. But I won't be ripped off. I'm telling you you've got two choices; either come up with the money quickly, or I'm talking. And to add to your problems I'll set Gary on you like a pack of hungry fucking dogs.'

Nicky could feel the cold sweat running down his back.

'Leave it with me Gina, okay?'

'Fine by me. Anyway I've got to get back. Maggie's with Harley and she asked me to be back by three. Oh and Nicky, no hard feelings eh?'

Gina got up, struggling to remove herself from behind the table. Nicky knew that if he was going to try to save Maggie and stop Gina doing anything stupid he was going to have to come up with a good plan – and quickly.

Nicky felt a hand on his shoulder and saw Lola standing next to him, a look of concern on her ageing face.

'A word of advice, love, from an old brass. There's only one thing you'll get from Gina Daniels and that's trouble.'

Nicky smiled weakly at Lola, her words resonating in his head. He didn't need to hear it because he already knew it.

Trouble was coming at him from all angles, and he didn't know what the hell he was going to do.

CHAPTER EIGHTEEN

Johnny Taylor stood at his bedroom door for a moment, listening to his mother's raised voice and his father's even louder one. Since his Aunt Lorna had arrived there'd been nothing but tension in the house. He wasn't quite sure why his mother had her acrylic claws out for his auntie. Whatever the reason though, almost overnight his mother had become like a deranged ferret with a rat in its mouth.

He could see Lorna liked to have a moan, but then so did all women. She seemed alright to him. He really didn't want to spend time thinking or hearing about it. He'd more important things to think about than two women arguing over fuck all.

He closed the door and the room fell silent. That was the beauty of having soundproof doors. His mother had insisted on it, telling him she didn't want to 'hear her baby shagging the whole of bleeding Soho.' Johnny smiled sadly to himself, knowing the reality wasn't so simple.

Yes, he'd shagged about. Who hadn't? But since Maggie he'd only had the odd indiscretion, mainly caused by going on one of his legendaries. But even if his dick had gone astray now and again, his heart never had. He'd always had it firmly in one place; with Maggie.

The day they got married had been the best day of his life. They'd travelled to Birmingham. The weather had been shit and if he remembered rightly the only way the strangers they'd asked to be witnesses could've been less interested in the wedding ceremony was if they'd been dead, but it hadn't mattered to him or Maggie. Even if immediately after the service they'd both had to go their separate ways. For him, who'd never put himself in the category of being romantic and had always pulled a face when Saucers set off on her romantic bandwagon, it'd been a magical day.

Johnny snorted out loud at the word *magical*. He was being soft and it was pointless reminiscing as if he was Soho's answer to Omar Sharif, *especially* when he'd fucked things up so expertly with Harley.

He could understand how Maggie felt about their daughter being with Gina, but what he *hadn't* understood was when she'd told him about Harley being in rags. He'd been forking out hundreds of pounds a week for her upkeep and even though there was always plenty of money around from the clubs and the hookers his dad ran, Frankie always made him accountable for every penny he took.

It'd started to get harder and harder to get the money past his dad, and even though he hadn't said anything, Johnny had a feeling he was starting to get suspicious. Saucers had even told him Frankie had accused one of the clip joint girls behind the bar of siphoning money. There'd been no fall to take, but if it'd come down to it, Johnny had a feeling he would've let the girl take the blame rather than even attempt to tell his father what he'd needed the money for.

His father was everything to him and he'd always given him everything he wanted. Money and love had all come to him in abundance, so Johnny hated having to keep part of his life a secret. He would've given anything for his parents to embrace the situation, but he knew it was impossible.

There'd been the odd time where he'd brought up the Donaldsons in conversation, steering it towards Maggie, hoping to hear something other than vitriol directed towards the whole family. But he never did. It was always the same. 'Why are you bothering your head over that lot, Johnny?' His mother would say to him.

'No reason. I was just thinking, maybe they're all not bad . . . Perhaps the girl, Maggie I think her name is, perhaps she's different to the rest of them.'

His father would snort scornfully. 'Different? How could she be bleeding different? When you've been brought up by scum Johnny, that's what you are. Scum. They're animals the whole lot of them.'

And that's how it always went. No room, no opportunity to plead his and Maggie's case. His family's mind was made up. The hatred ran fast and deep for the Donaldsons. And it was clear to Johnny that there would be nothing he could say or do to ever change that.

Johnny's phone rang. Although the caller ID was hidden, he decided to answer it anyway.

'Yup.'

Johnny listened to the person on the other end. It was Sheila Donaldson. And he was completely thrown by it. Never before had she called him – never before would she have risked it. So he continued to listen to the voice which was full of anxiety, curious to hear what Maggie's mother had to say.

Putting down the phone, Johnny sat motionless at the end of his bed, letting the information sink in. He couldn't believe what he'd just heard. Maggie was contemplating giving Harley up. And Sheila Donaldson had phoned to tell him he needed to do something because she feared for her daughter. Feared it would break her Maggie's heart.

Johnny looked quickly at the green neon clock on his

122

bedroom wall. He needed to get it sorted. He'd had an idea but he wanted to run it past Saucers before he put it to Maggie. That's if Maggie would speak to him again. He couldn't blame her if she didn't. First, however, he planned to give Gina a little visit to see exactly what she was doing with his money. More importantly, to see what she was doing with his daughter.

CHAPTER NINETEEN

Maggie bent over the sink and washed her face. The cold water felt soothing. She'd spent the last few hours with Harley, just the two of them having fun. They'd been to Hyde Park and Harley had squealed with delight as they'd fed the ducks. Then she'd burst into tears as they'd chased after her, wanting the bread she held in her hand.

They'd gone to the children's park where they'd swung high and low towards the tops of the trees. They'd made themselves dizzy by going on the roundabout too many times and then before all too long, it'd been over. Maggie had had to take Harley back to Gina's so she could come to see her mother. Harley had cried. She had cried. It just wasn't fair. Mainly though, it wasn't fair for Harley. And the more she thought about it, the more Maggie realised that the decision she'd made was the right one.

As Maggie stood up from the sink she let out a gasp. In the mirror, staring blankly at her was Tommy.

'Tommy . . . Jesus. You gave me a fright.'

'Did I, Maggie? I thought you were the brave one.'

Maggie looked at Tommy. He looked pale and she could see sweat dripping down his forehead. He was clenching and unclenching his fist. Maggie took a step towards him but he stepped back quickly.

'Tommy, why don't you come downstairs, babe? Mum's making the tea.'

Tommy sat at the kitchen table with his mother and Maggie. It was the first time he'd seen her properly since she came out. It was nice to see her but he didn't know how to tell her that. He'd wanted to say it when they'd been upstairs in the bathroom, but instead he'd just stared at her.

He watched as his sister laughed, a dimple on her right cheek forming as she did so, her big blue eyes lighting up. All he wanted to do was hold her but all he *could* do was sit and stare. He could see he was making her feel uncomfortable.

'You alright, Tommy?'

Maggie stretched out her hand and touched his arm. It was like an electric shock and she was clearly hurt as he pulled his hand away.

'I'm fine, why shouldn't I be?'

'I dunno; you just don't seem yourself, babe.'

Tommy gave Maggie a tight smile. She was trying to make things better, she'd always done that even as a kid. Fussing around him, desperate to make sure everything was alright, desperate to make him feel loved and safe when nothing ever did and nothing ever could be.

He watched his mother and Maggie gassing away, seeing their mouths moving but not hearing anything they said. Things were getting difficult; muddled. He wanted to stop it but it was like the train had started rolling and he didn't know how to get off it.

The voice in his head was becoming deafening, the sounds getting louder until he wasn't able to think straight. The nightmares had come back and he'd started waking up with his body sweating and his mouth parched dry.

Last night he'd found himself walking through Soho in the early hours, stumbling around as if he was drunk. He'd visited the sauna on Brewer Street where he'd had a massage and then the full works. He'd thought it would've made a difference, releasing some of the energy which was whirling around his body but it'd only added to the feeling. He'd been like a wild dog; he'd fucked the Tom so hard she'd cried out for him to stop and that'd only made things worse. He'd apologised profusely but all he saw was the fear in her eyes as she looked straight at him. A look he'd seen many times before. All he'd been able to do was run; but he knew already there was no running from himself as the memories came back.

He could smell the blood. Her blood. And Tommy closed his eyes for a moment. He was tired. It'd been a long night. Even though it was cold, he could feel the sweat on him. He could see it on her naked body. The room lay silent now. She'd given up screaming. She could see it was pointless. He wasn't going to let her go. It was only going to make things worse.

'Tommy? Tommy?'

His mother was speaking to him with a worried look on her face. He snapped at her, jarred by being brought back to the present.

'Fuck me, where's the bleeding fire.'

'Ain't no fire son, only my words falling on deaf flipping ears. Where've you been? Next time take me with you.'

'Believe me, Mum; you don't want to go where I've been.'

His mother grinned at him and got back up to make another brew. He turned to Maggie who was sitting back in her chair and quietly watching him. They held each other's stare for a moment. Then Maggie spoke quietly and quickly before their mother came back to sit down.

'Tommy, whatever it is; I'm here. It doesn't matter what time of the day or night it is: if you need to talk, I'll listen.'

Tommy stood up and moved around to his mother, placing a kiss on the top of her head.

'I'm off out. Dad wants me to do some bag money with him.'

'Be careful Tom, give me a call on my mobile. Let me know you're alright.'

He smiled at his mother, then looked over at his sister and nodded before turning away with a leaden feeling in his heart.

CHAPTER TWENTY

Gypsy Taylor stood in the hallway and cursed Frankie under her breath for not getting the maintenance guy to fix the squeaking sound on the front door. It was ridiculous, she'd twice tried to open the door to sneak out, and twice the creaking sound had echoed around the hall as if she'd set off a box of Chinese firecrackers.

What was she doing? She hadn't acted like this since she was a teenager, hiding before sneaking out of the house, but she had somewhere to go that she couldn't cancel. She'd an evening appointment. They hadn't had anything else for over a month, so she'd taken it.

She was in two minds whether or not just to go and tell Frankie she needed to go out for an hour. The problem was she knew he'd want to know where she was going; hell, he might even want to drive her there himself. She couldn't tell him and she certainly couldn't have him taking her there.

There'd been enough rowing since Lorna had arrived and as much as Gypsy had a gob on her to rival the firing of the cannons in the Battle of Trafalgar, she hated having cross words with Frankie.

She loved her husband but she wished he could see what

a stirring old cow his sister was. More than that, she wished he could see she also needed her freedom.

There wasn't any part of her inclined to run off with the nearest fella; Frankie satisfied her in every way possible. She just needed to feel she owed her life a bit more and she wasn't just an extension of all his business empire. There'd never been anyone else, well not really. Not anyone who counted.

The clock in the kitchen chimed out. It was eight o'clock. If she stood there any longer she'd miss her appointment and be back late.

Gypsy knew nine thirty was her safety net to be back by. Frankie was as regular as her old Nan's bowels when it came to watching the poker championships on Sky which had already started. Nothing could budge him once he'd tuned in. He'd often joke about it telling her, 'If there's a fire babe, leave me till last, just let me finish watching the game.'

The poker finished at ten fifteen so it gave her plenty of room. She was only popping close to home so there was no panic about having to catch a bus or tube back. It was close enough to walk to and close enough for her hopefully not to be missed.

Bracing herself, Gypsy opened the door, trying to ignore the loud creak. She quickly looked around, making sure nobody had been disturbed within the house and once she saw the coast was clear, she hurried into the street.

After a few minutes Gypsy decided to cut through the backstreets to avoid the throng of people who seemed to be going nowhere fast. She was wearing open-toed Jimmy Choo sandals, so the last thing she wanted was to have her feet trampled on like bunches of grapes at harvest time.

It started to rain and Gypsy swore loudly. She didn't know why because it wasn't as if the British summer did anything *besides* rain. But each time the heavens opened she acted surprised as if bad weather was a new phenomenon in the country.

It began to get heavier and Gypsy ran for cover under the doorway of some newly refurbished apartments. She'd been too busy trying to sneak out without being caught to even think of bringing an umbrella. Now she had a choice of whether to get soaked or spend the rest of the short time she had stuck beneath the building.

Gypsy sighed, and as she did so she thought she heard someone cough. She looked down the deserted street, her eyes darting across the square. Even though she couldn't see anyone, she got the distinct impression she was being watched.

Although it was early summer it was already dark from the stormy sky and she decided to brave the rain rather than stand there. Pulling up her silk jacket she began to walk down the alleyway, quickly turning around to make sure no one was following her. Halfway down she looked back again. Her heart pounded as she suddenly caught a glimpse of someone lurking in the shadows.

Automatically she went into her bag to phone Frankie. Then stopped. What was she doing? She couldn't possibly phone Frankie or any of his men like she normally would've done. Usually if she needed anything, Frankie was the first person she'd call. He was always coming to her rescue if she needed him to. Whether because she'd bought too many clothes in the shops and had loads of bags to get home, or she was caught in a downpour coming back from the beauty salon, or like now, when she felt afraid; Frankie would be there. But for the first time in years Gypsy found herself alone. And she didn't like the feeling at all.

Gypsy quickened her pace, determined not to give way to the panic which was rising within her. She was being silly, she was sure of it, but her imagination was starting to get the better of her.

She didn't want to be conscious of her racing heart, her dry mouth and the sick feeling rising in her stomach. She wanted to run but her fear seemed to be slowing her down. She couldn't think straight but she knew she had to keep walking; keep going towards a place where there'd be people.

It sounded like the footsteps were getting closer, nearer, and any moment she was going to feel a hand grab her by the shoulder. Imagination or not, Gypsy began to run.

She stumbled along the alley, putting her hand against the damp brick wall to hold her balance and stop herself from tottering over in the high shoes. Drips of sweat ran down her back and the sound of Regent Street seemed further away than ever. The tears began to run down her face, misting her eyes and making it harder for her to see ahead as the rain poured down.

She couldn't hear anything apart from the sound of the steps behind her, loud and exaggerated. Gypsy saw the end of the alleyway and to the left of it was a stone flight of stairs. If she could get to them she'd be safe. She started to pick up her pace which was a mistake; her ankle bent to the side and she began to topple over. Reaching out in front of her to try to stop herself from falling, Gypsy's hand touched a stack of disused crates. The moment she touched them they clattered to the floor, blocking her way. As she scrambled over them she felt a pull on her leg and instinctively let out a scream before realising her tights were snagged on the crates. Not caring if she tore them or not Gypsy pulled her leg away and braved a glance around.

There was someone there. She was certain of it. She thought she saw the figure in the shadows not moving but watching. She let out another scream as she began to run, running for all her might to the stone stairs, desperate to get away from whatever lurked in the darkness.

With one big effort, Gypsy reached the stairs, breathing

131

hard from fear and from exertion. At the top of them she saw a throng of people and knowing she was safe now, she looked back.

The alleyway was empty apart from the fallen crates. Had she just been silly? Had it been just the sound of the rain and the darkness of the stormy sky playing tricks with her, bringing back distant memories? She'd been so sure there'd been someone there; someone who was ready to hurt her.

She looked down at her torn tights and saw her leg was bleeding slightly. She hadn't even noticed anything cutting into her, though it was beginning to sting now.

She didn't need a mirror to know she looked a mess. Half-heartedly she brushed herself down as the rain continued to soak into her clothes, drenching her expensive bleached blonde hair. Letting out a loud sigh she made her way up the rest of the stairs wishing she could tell Frankie about the fright she'd had, but wishing more that she was back home curled up in front of the television watching poker.

She walked towards Park Crescent, limping slightly from the cut on her leg and the shoes which were beautiful but certainly impractical. She looked at the address and realised she was standing outside the right place.

It had a large black imposing front door and white coliseum pillars either side, with a small gold plaque on the wall, simply saying, *Clinic*. Taking a deep breath, Gypsy pressed the buzzer and waited to be let in.

Frankie Taylor stood naked apart from a pair of paper pants and a white towelling hair turban. He had his arms stretched out and his legs spread wide as the Chinese woman spray-tanned him in his private tanning room at the top of his house in Berkeley Square.

'Well?'

'Well I saw her. I followed her all the way there, it was

132

like a scene from *Starsky and Hutch*, thought me bleeding heart was going to jump out of me frigging chest. I'm telling you Frank, my ticker ain't what . . .'

Frankie put his hand up in the air as he turned around to get his back sprayed. He interrupted his sister, annoyed and certainly not in the mood for her to recount any tales of her ill health. 'Turn it in Lorn, bleeding hell. Just cut to the frigging chase and tell me what you saw,' he said forcefully.

Lorna looked at her brother, feigning sympathy on her round face as he stepped out of the spray booth wrapping his dressing gown around himself.

'It was just like you feared, Frankie. It was like all yer nightmares had come at once.'

Frankie banged his hand on the handmade walnut dresser, giving the Chinese lady who was packing away her things a fright. He wanted straight facts, not an Elizabethan tragedy played out in front of him.

'Fuck me Lorna, are you trying to torture me? What did you see?'

'Well I hate to be the one to tell you, Frank. You know me, I always want to see a man happy with his wife, but yer old girl's playing away. I saw her with me own eyes. Up close and bleeding personal with some fella. Any closer, and the friction between them would've started a bleedin' fire. They were that entwined anyone passing would've thought they were a pair of conjoined twins.'

Lorna paused, before adding slyly, 'And he was younger than you. Much younger.'

Frankie had heard enough. It was as if his heart was being twisted and shredded into tiny pieces. He felt his chest tightening and a pain so sharp behind his eyes he had to clench his fist from stopping himself from crying out. His mouth had gone dry and he reached over for his glass of whiskey, but his hand was shaking so much he didn't know if he could hold it.

'And where was this?'

'Up near Park Crescent. She went into one of them big buildings. Didn't see which one, but an hour later I saw her coming out. She looked a bit upset and he gave a hug before she jumped in a taxi. But I've never seen a hug like that before. Like I say, any closer . . .'

'Alright, alright I get it Lorn, but you *could* be mistaken, it *could* be innocent.'

'Yeah like the acid bath murderer was.'

Frankie got annoyed.

'You're not helping, Lorn.'

'What do you want me to say?'

'I dunno, but there must be another explanation.'

'Here, look, if you don't believe me. Take a look at this.'

Lorna proceeded to go into her Chloé oversized bag. A moment later she brought out a tiny digital camera and thrust it under Frankie's nose.

'What do you . . .'

'Just look at them, Frankie.'

With a furrowed brow, Frankie Taylor started to scroll through pictures of his wife and a man he'd never seen before in what he'd only describe as a passionate embrace. Lorna had certainly been thorough in the task he'd set her. He didn't know whether to be angry with her or not. But then why would he be? She'd only done what he'd asked her to do. And it showed she cared. He continued to stare at the photos as Lorna spoke to him.

'Okay Frank, let's just say it was an innocent hug. We'll go with the Disney version if it makes you feel better. But what you should ask yourself is; what was she doing there in the first place? If it was so bleeding innocent, why didn't she tell you where she was going? Ask her and see what she says. If she doesn't tell you the truth, then you know she's up to something.'

Frankie listened hard to his sister and then nodded.

'Get out now, Lorn. I want to be on my own. I need to think.'

'Whatever you say, Frankie.'

'And Lorn?'

'Yes, Frankie?'

'Thank you.'

Lorna closed the door behind her leaving her brother with his head in his hands. As she leant on the closed door a wide grin spread over her face. Tonight she'd come a little closer to getting rid of Gypsy and when she had, she, Lorna Taylor, would get exactly what she deserved.

Gypsy sat in her dressing room and sighed. She felt emotionally drained. It'd been a difficult night. First from the fright she'd had, though she could see now she'd overreacted and let her imagination get carried away. And then of course there was the clinic.

She'd got upset when they'd explained things to her and she'd broken down in tears, so much so, one of the staff – a young very flamboyant gay man – had walked her out and helped her hail a taxi. He'd been lovely and had given her a big hug and she'd held onto it, needing every ounce of his concern. When she'd arrived home, she'd popped her head round the door to see Frankie still watching the poker. She'd only spoken to him later to let him know the spray tan lady had arrived but she hadn't bothered saying anything else. After all, what he didn't know about couldn't hurt him.

CHAPTER TWENTY-ONE

It was getting late now and Johnny Taylor eyed the grey tower block up and down for a fourth time. It was a shithole. Nobody needed to tell him that. He hadn't even seen inside but in his gut he knew. Knew he wouldn't make his worst enemy have a piss in the place where he'd put his daughter.

A group of kids tumbled out of the block of flats leaving the steel door open. Their beltless jeans hung almost to their knees, showing off designer underwear and youthful taut stomachs. They stopped pushing and joking with one another when they saw Johnny, nodding their heads in respect for one of Soho's upcoming faces, turning up their own swagger as they did so.

Inside, Johnny decided to walk up the concrete stairwell rather than risk going into the lift which had shit smeared all over the sides. Gina's flat was on the sixteenth floor. He could've easily bounded up the flight of stairs but he chose to walk slowly, taking in the filth, the graffiti walls, the used syringes and general rubbish strewn along the corridors.

He could feel the anger increasing with every flight of stairs he walked up. The fury ran through his body but he wasn't entirely sure if he was more upset about Harley or the money he'd dished out. He knew it was a terrible thing to think. It should've been all about his daughter but the fact that he kept thinking about the money worried him.

He hated the thought he might be a bad father. He'd been given everything in the world; love, money, and apart from the situation with Maggie, he'd had the freedom to enjoy his life as he wished.

He'd always been surrounded by his mum, his doting father or the hookers from the clubs who'd babysat him. All of them giving him truckloads of love. He'd presumed he'd be the same with his own child – and at first he had.

It'd been a shock when Maggie had told him she was pregnant and he'd needed to go on one of his 'legendaries' to get his head round it. When the news had properly sunk in he'd been happy. Not one part of him had wanted her to get rid of it. But then to his shame, when things got tough and complicated, he'd stuck his head in the proverbial. Whilst his wife was banged up he'd palmed his daughter off to Gina Daniels and got on with his life. It was, even by his standards, totally unforgivable.

Gina shuffled to the front door, her hair in yellow Velcro rollers and her feet in brown slippers stained with grease. Her mouth was stuffed full of chocolate and some of it spat out as she swore at the hammering on the door.

'Bleedin' hell, I ain't no frigging racehorse, what's the rush?'

Gina pulled open the front door. She was about to continue spouting off when she came face to face with Johnny Taylor standing there, his face looking like a bulldog chewing a wasp.

'Johnny!'

'Get out me way Gina, I want to see Harley and I want to know what the fuck's going on.'

'I . . . I don't know what you mean.'

'Well ain't that convenient? You didn't think I'd eventually come round to see how you and Nicky were robbing me blind did you?'

Gina Daniels pursed her lips with indignation. She was argumentative whether she was wrong or right but *especially* when she was wrong.

'Jon Jon, I ain't robbing no one. If anybody's being robbed it's me.'

'How do you figure that one out?'

'I'm being sucked dry by your daughter. Every minute of the day she wants some part of me. Some days I worry I'll wake up and I'll just be a pile of bones, she's taken that much of me.'

Johnny wasn't interested in hearing it. He pushed past Gina roughly, walking into the front room, seeing the piled up takeaway trays, the overflowing ashtrays, the crumpled Lotto slips and in the corner, curled up on the mismatched burgundy chair, was his beautiful daughter, Harley.

The shame washed over him once more as he watched her sleep and instead of waking her, he grabbed hold of Gina by the arm who was chattering behind him like a machine gun.

'Kindness of me bleedin' heart and all I've got from it . . . Ow! What's that for, Johnny? Get orf me bleedin' arm.'

'Shut the frig up with your chatter before me head gets wrecked. You and I both know how much money I gave you and Nicky. Coming in here makes me think I've walked in on a scene from *Slumdog* bleeding *Millionaire*. It's disgusting.'

'Charming I'm sure.'

Johnny pushed Gina against the wall with his forearm, so tempted but resisting the urge to hit her; not wanting to raise a hand to a woman even though the woman was Gina Daniels.

'Do *not* take the piss. You need to tell me what's been going on.'

Johnny stared with fury at Gina, who decided perhaps now might be a good time to start talking.

Nicky was twitching. He'd just taken a hit of the pipe and now he needed a bit of smack to help him come down properly from his high, rather than him clucking away in mid-air. Since Gina had spoken to him he'd been worried, so he'd done what he did best when things got too much or things got too painful; he got high.

He couldn't get Gary off his back easily, but the one person he could try to appease was Gina. He knew he needed to stop her talking but so far that was as far as his plan had got.

Gina's front door was ajar and Nicky pushed it open and quietly closed it behind him. He could hear the television on and as he walked into the front room he smiled at the sight of his niece asleep, her corkscrew blonde curls tousled all over her face.

Hearing voices coming from the bedroom, Nicky was about to walk in when he froze, recognising them. It was Johnny Taylor and worse still, Gina, opening her big trap; telling Johnny everything. Everything apart from how much she was in on it all.

'. . . I couldn't believe you'd only give a hundred a week to look after your daughter but Nicky swore blind that's all you gave. Me being me didn't want to turf the poor mite out onto the street. Poor creature ain't got anyone else. That's my trouble, I got too big a heart for my own good. My mother always said that. She said, Gina, people will take advantage of your good nature. I'm shocked, Johnny, I really am. I never thought Nicky would steal from his own, especially when the poor mite's mum was in prison, and with all the secrets surrounding her. That alone would be worth more than a ton wouldn't you say?'

Johnny glared at Gina. She was a sly cow and he didn't believe a word she said about not being any part of it. But at least he knew some of the picture.

'Don't push it darlin', I ain't a muppet. The way I see it you owe me, 'cos I don't buy that you weren't in on it. I'll deal with Nicky later, but I want to tell you how it's going to work from now on.'

Nicky backed away. It couldn't have got any worse if he tried. It didn't take a maths degree to know there wouldn't be any money coming his way now. The only thing which was coming was more trouble. This time in the shape of Johnny. Nicky owed everyone big time, he knew that. What he also knew was that even though he owed money his priorities would still lie in his habit – his habit would come first, whether he or anyone else liked it.

CHAPTER TWENTY-TWO

Maggie opened the curtains in Nicky's room and sighed, wondering what Harley was doing, wondering if she was okay. She was looking forward to seeing her later on. Her thoughts never strayed for long from her daughter; from her smile, from her laughter, from her whole being. Harley was everything to Maggie.

Maggie looked around the room. It wasn't so much of a mess as a disaster. The brown wooden flooring was hardly visible under the mounds of dirty clothes, all stained from vomit and spotted with blood. The furniture tops were covered in empty cans of Pepsi and beer.

Maggie noticed some of them had been cut in half with a hole pierced into them; a sign her brother had been smoking crack. There was a stale smell hanging in the air, partly from the lack of fresh air, partly from tobacco but mainly from whatever drugs her brother had been smoking. She looked up to the ceiling and saw it was stained brown from the nicotine.

Maggie attempted to open the window but it was jammed shut from the dried paint. She doubted it'd been opened since her father had brought round a couple of his mates to repaint the house a few years ago.

Giving up with the window, Maggie looked at the bed. Lying with the cover over his head was Nicky, his black-soled feet visible.

'Nicky, we need to talk.'

Nicky didn't stir. Maggie called her brother's name again, slightly louder which gave way to a small groan and a slight movement, before he turned over to lie motionless once more.

Dragging the cover off him and a stray packet of Rizlas along with it, Maggie exposed her brother – who was still wearing his t-shirt from two days ago – to the chill of the summer's morning.

Nicky sat up quickly with a look of terror on his face, thinking his father had come into the room. Seeing his fear, Maggie's heart sank. The anger which she was ready to fire out machine gun style fell away.

'Fucking hell Mags, I thought . . .'

Nicky didn't finish his sentence. He didn't have to.

'I know, Nick. Sorry, I didn't mean to give you a fright.'

Maggie gave a sad smile, taking in her brother's gaunt appearance. His nails were ingrained with dirt, as was the skin around his eyes and mouth, making him look like he'd been working down the mines rather than living in the heart of Soho. His blue eyes, once sparkling, looked dull and lifeless. His skin had a faint circular rash on it, another sign of Nicky's chronic drug addiction.

Nicky started to cough and reached over to grab the small ashtray which was already overflowing with roach ends. He spat the contents of what was in his mouth in it. Maggie flinched, turning her head quickly, not wanting to feel nauseous.

'Nicky, what's been going on? I know you've been avoiding me since I've come out. Are you in trouble?'

'I've just been busy, Maggie.'

'Don't lie to me Nicky, not you.'

Maggie stopped and looked at her brother, not wanting to admit how much him letting her down had hurt her.

'Things started to get out of hand, Mags.'

'What things, Nick? What could be as important as looking after your niece?'

'We did look after her.'

Maggie shook her head sadly.

'No Nick, no you didn't. She looked a mess.'

Nicky shrugged his shoulders as he lit up a cigarette.

'Kids are expensive. Johnny didn't give us much money to look after her so we had to do our best.'

'*Was* that your best, Nicky? You know I can easily ask Johnny how much he gave to you.'

Nicky's guilt made him snap at Maggie, causing his sister to stand up from the bed in reaction to his verbal attack.

'Okay, I know and I'm sorry. Fucking hell Maggie, she ain't my kid. I did what you wanted, I got her looked after and maybe she ain't in a bleedin' palace but she's certainly not in care is she? We all did what you wanted and if you want to find fault in it that's fine Maggie, but tell me, who else would take her with no questions asked and keep their mouths shut? Yeah, it wasn't ideal but none of it is, not the secrets, not Gina's, not our life; so what else did you expect from me?'

Maggie didn't move and just stood staring at Nicky for a moment, before turning to walk out of the room. Pausing at the door without looking at her brother she spoke in a whisper, trying to keep her voice steady.

'I expected you to care.'

Maggie went back into her bedroom and sat on her bed feeling deflated from the conversation she'd had with Nicky.

She'd been so angry with him but instead of ripping his head off as she'd planned, he'd ripped her heart out.

She threw herself backwards onto the bed and listened to her father ranting at her mother downstairs. Part of her wanted to go and sort it out, the other part of her wanted to bury her head under her pillow.

She felt exhausted by the last few days and more than anything she felt an overwhelming sense of hopelessness. She wanted Harley with her and the ache of not having her made her catch her breath sometimes.

Everyone saw her as a strong woman; invincible even. Maggie, the one who stood up to her father; Maggie, the one who never cried as the fist was brought down on her mouth; Maggie, the one who'll take the fall and the one who would pick up the pieces, both literally and metaphorically. But they never thought of her as Maggie, the one who some-times needed someone.

She sat up and wiped away the tears which had run into her ears. She was feeling sorry for herself. Tears never did anything apart from wet pillows and block noses.

Looking at her phone she saw there was a text from Johnny asking her to call him. There was nothing more to say. She'd made up her mind what she was going to do about Harley. There was simply no other choice and now all she wanted was for Johnny to leave her alone.

They'd been crazy to get married. Crazy to think things could've ever had a happy ever after. Happy endings weren't part of the Donaldsons' make-up.

'Marry me, Maggie?'

'Sorry?'

'Marry me, Maggie.'

'I . . . I . . . we can't.'

'Do you love me?'

144

'Yes, but . . .'

'Then say you'll marry me and we'll worry about everything else tomorrow.'

She stared at him and then a smile spread across her face. It was mirrored by Johnny's, who held his grin as his eyes flicked over Maggie's face to pre-empt her answer.

'So what do you say then?'

'I say you're off your head, Johnny Taylor. Certifiable.'

'Perhaps I am but that don't stop me wanting you to be my wife.'

'No Johnny, it's a bad idea.'

'When did a bad idea ever stop you doing what you wanted?'

'If someone finds out . . .'

Johnny stopped grinning and looked serious. He lowered his voice as he put his hand gently under her chin, lifting Maggie's head up towards his.

'I won't ever let anyone hurt you, Maggie. You got to trust me on that. I don't know what's going to happen in the long term babe, but I swear to you I'll put my life on the line rather than let anyone hurt you again.'

'I don't know.'

'What don't you know?'

'It's just . . .'

'Just what?'

Maggie shrugged her shoulders. 'Okay.'

Johnny turned his ear to her mouth, smiling broadly.

'Say that again.'

Maggie laughed and spoke loudly, drawing stares.

'I said okay. You're crazy Johnny Taylor but yes; yes I'll marry you.'

As Maggie pulled on her coat, she wondered if the danger had added to the attraction. Had they really been in love? Soulmates forever but destined to be apart. Maybe it was simpler than that. Maybe it was just that Johnny had always been kind to her, respectful. Two elements which were hugely missing in her life. Or perhaps, she'd imagined Johnny would save her from her life – when no one else could.

Walking down the stairs she glanced into the kitchen and saw her mother sitting at the table, surrounded by broken pots and a swollen lip. Maggie paused, about to go in and check on her mother, then realised she couldn't do it.

Today Maggie couldn't face wiping the blood off her mum's chin, nor could she face pressing cotton wool on her mother's lip to stop the swelling, hoping it wouldn't sting. Hardest of all, she couldn't face trying to prevent her mother's salty tears pouring into the wound which would never heal.

Closing her eyes for a split second, Maggie braced herself then walked out of the house into the fresh air, knowing there'd always be a tomorrow and a tomorrow and a tomorrow when she'd have the chance to nurse her broken mother.

CHAPTER TWENTY-THREE

Frankie Taylor couldn't sleep. He couldn't eat and he certainly didn't want to look at his wife over the breakfast table this morning. So much of him wanted to think that what Lorna had seen was an innocent mistake.

Gypsy had presumed he'd been watching the poker game but he'd been waiting for her to go out. He'd been on to her after he'd read the ambiguous text on her phone which simply read, *'Eight thirty tonight.'*

The moment she'd gone, he'd sent Lorna to follow her and she'd sped off like a whippet dog with a rocket up its arse.

He was confused. He knew he couldn't ever be with her again if she was seeing somebody else but at the same time he felt like Gypsy belonged to him.

Bottom line though was he loved her. Loved her with all his heart and wanted to give her a chance. A chance to come clean and explain what Lorna had seen was just a mistake. A chance to tell him there was no need for his heart to feel like someone was using it as a football. So he'd spoken to her as they lay in bed and instead of hearing what he was hoping for, it'd just made things worse. The lies had spilled out of her mouth.

'When I was watching the poker Gypsy, where were you? I said to meself, my wife wouldn't go out without telling me, my wife wouldn't sneak about behind me back. Not Gypsy.'

Frankie's eyes had bored into her and Gypsy had swallowed hard. 'Oh, nowhere. I didn't want to disturb you. I saw we'd run out of milk, so I popped to the shop. Sorry Frank, next time I'll say.'

She was lying. Staring right at him and lying. Lying her bleeding tits off.

'We had milk though.'

'Yeah, but not soya milk.'

'Soya? When did you start to drink that crap?'

'Oh I haven't really, it was just something I saw in a magazine and I thought I'd try it . . .'

She'd trailed off and then he'd smiled at her but it'd been a tight smile, the sort of smile his mother gave him when she hadn't wanted to admit she'd been shagging yet another faceless stranger.

Frankie sighed, staring down at his plate and deciding to probe his sister before Gypsy came down for breakfast. Desperate to find answers he could deal with.

'Are you sure it was her?'

'Bleeding hell, Frank, you saw the photos yourself.'

'Yeah but I was thinking, it was hard to see her face properly. It could've been someone else; maybe she did just pop to the shop after all.'

Lorna snorted as she tucked into her fifth piece of bacon. 'If you want to turn a blind eye to it Frank that's down to you, but I wouldn't stand for it – who knows how long it's been going on for or how many others there's been?'

'Alright, Lorn. Christ, drive over a man when he's been knocked over won't you?'

'I'm sorry, Frank. I'm just looking out for you.'

'I know you are, and thank God I've got you, Lorn.'

They stopped talking as Gypsy came into the breakfast room. She smiled at Frankie and cut her eye at Lorna. Gypsy watched her husband push the eggs and bacon around his plate. It was unlike him not to eat his breakfast and even more unlike him not to talk. The one thing, apart from sex, Frankie loved to do was talk. And when he didn't, there was usually something very wrong.

Gypsy had wondered if the incident with Max Donaldson had shaken him up more than he cared to admit. Her husband was a proud man and there was no way Frankie would ever admit he'd had a fright; there was more likelihood of him going on *Question Time* than him talk about his emotions.

She took a sip of her cappuccino and caught Lorna watching. Again she cut her eye at her and her sister-in-law smirked back. Gypsy had given up speaking to Frankie about Lorna; he'd refused to listen and seemed more determined to dig his heels in about it these last couple of days, oblivious to the fact that Lorna was trouble.

The woman seemed to be so welded into the family they'd need a frigging pneumatic drill to get her out. She was clearly up to something but Gypsy didn't know what.

'Are you busy today, Gypsy? I wondered if you wanted some company?'

Lorna's suggestion had Gypsy spitting her coffee out all over Johnny who was leaning over her to reach for some more sausages. She stared at her sister-in-law before answering her in a monotone.

'I'm not sure yet, Lorn, but whatever it is I'll be fine for company, thanks all the same.'

'I don't get you, Gyps. There's me sister reaching out to you and all you do is throw a wet rag back in her face.'

Gypsy looked at her husband incredulously. As a couple they'd never shamed or aired their dirty laundry in public, always waited until they were in private to let rip and sort their differences out. However, here was Frankie, knowing how she felt about his sister, embarrassing her and making Lorna smirk with delight again.

Gypsy was furious and spoke through gritted teeth, making sure Frankie knew exactly what she thought about his tactless comment.

'It ain't no rag, Frank. All I'm saying is, I'm fine on me own.'

'Well what I'm seeing is you not making an effort. Lorna here is doing everything she can do to be nice.'

Open-mouthed, Gypsy looked at her husband, only for Lorna to pipe up first.

'Leave it, Frankie, if she don't want to spend any time with me that's fine. I'll just sit in my room.'

Gypsy turned on Lorna, amazed at the cheek of the woman and feeling upset at being backed into a corner by both her and Frankie. 'Firstly, sweetheart, it ain't your room. Secondly, don't play the martyr; I can see exactly what you're doing.'

Lorna spoke in a slippery tone. 'I don't know what you're talking about, Gypsy.'

'Stop the flipping game playing. You're more clued-up than Hercule Poirot.'

Frankie threw his plate across the newly decorated breakfast room, sending his sunny-side-up eggs, sunny-side-down. They splattered all over the floor, with the Wedgewood plate following a second later. 'This is my house and I'll frigging say whose room it is. Lorna's our guest, bleeding hell she's family, so she'll stay as long as she likes. If you don't like it Gypsy; tough. Because there's fuck all you can do.'

Frankie got up from the table and nodded for Johnny to follow him, who was more than happy to do so.

* * *

This was better than she could've imagined. Lorna held the letter in her hands and let out a loud laugh. She heard the sound of her laughter echoing round the hallway and relished every moment of it. She'd opened Gypsy's letters, as she had been doing the past couple of days. There'd been nothing in them apart from drivel from shops and boutiques inviting Gypsy to see their latest collections.

When she'd opened the nondescript envelope she'd glanced over it quickly, expecting much of the same, but as she took in the words she'd had to reread it again, in case what she was seeing was a mistake. But there was no mistake. As the enormity of the situation sunk in, it felt to Lorna like she'd just won the lottery. She may as well wave goodbye to Gypsy now; get her bags and wish her bon bleeding voyage.

'What have you got there?'

Gypsy's voice cut through her laughter.

'Nothing. Just my rubbish.'

Gypsy's eyes narrowed. It looked like Lorna was up to something; the problem was though, Lorna *always* looked like she was up to something.

'Whatever, Lorn, I'm popping out to get a paper.'

'Well make the most of it.'

'Excuse me?'

'Just make the most out of the beautiful morning. You never know when storm clouds might appear.'

CHAPTER TWENTY-FOUR

Nicky grabbed his bag and headed down the stairs of the Donaldson house. It was still dark outside but that suited him; he didn't want anyone seeing him.

The conversation he'd had with Maggie the other day had sat heavily on his mind. When she'd walked out of the room he knew he couldn't be part of Gina trying to destroy his sister's life. At the same time, he wasn't stupid enough to hang around and wait for the line of people to catch up with him who'd be just as happy to get paid in his blood as they were the money he owed them.

He'd got himself into this mess and now he needed to get out of it, or rather he needed to run the fuck away from it. He wasn't a hero. He certainly wasn't going to start to be one now. The thought of leaving Soho had frightened him however and he wasn't sure how he'd be able to go and leave everything he knew behind, even though it seemed he had no choice.

He'd never been on his own and as much as his family were hardly the Von Trapps, they were all he'd ever known. He'd never done anything for himself. Hell, he'd never even boiled a bleedin' kettle and the more he'd thought about leaving, the more terrified he'd become. That was until he'd run into Saucers the other night. Then things had taken an unexpected turn.

He'd known Saucers before she'd started to work in the Taylor's clubs, when she'd first moved to the area.

He'd first seen her knocking about in Soho just over four years ago, when he'd been eighteen. For a while she'd only acknowledged him with a smile or a wave as he walked past the street corner she was working on. Then one day she'd come up to him sporting a black eye, asking him if he knew where she could get a job.

She'd been fed up of working the streets and she didn't want to have any run-ins with the pimps in Soho, but then she didn't want a pimp either, making it impossible to avoid trouble. The black eye had been a warning from one of the regular pimps who hadn't taken kindly to her working his turf without permission.

Nicky had liked Saucers straight away. She'd made him laugh with her grab-them-by-the-balls attitude to life. Even though she was only three years older than him, she seemed so more worldly wise.

She was well-read, which he'd found strange. Most of her childhood had been spent in care and she'd never really had an education. Yet in between turning tricks, she'd take herself down the library, to take out books which were so thick and dusty the only thing he thought they were good for were doorstops. Nicky had never met anyone who read books for no other reason than they loved to.

A couple of summers ago Saucers had even signed herself up for some sort of literature classes at the City Lit in Stukeley Street. It'd been the first time he'd seen her vulnerability. Gone was the funny, confident hooker who had an opinion about everything, and in her place stood an insecure woman unsure if she belonged amongst the educated of society.

She'd asked him to wait outside for her, confident only in her ability to learn, but not in who and what she was. He'd gone along with her each week, sitting in the bar opposite until her class was over when she'd come out filled with excitement. She'd made him laugh. She devoured books in much the same way he devoured cocaine. Hungrily.

When she'd asked him about jobs he'd said he'd put his ear to the ground and had gone to find Maggie, asking her to pull in a favour from Johnny to get Saucers a job in one of his clubs.

When Johnny had met her it was obvious she was a natural. Saucers wasn't any beauty but her easy manner and willingness to do most things had the punters pecking out of her hand. Saucers had been so grateful to him that she'd offered everything from her body to having a threesome with her and her friends, but Nicky hadn't taken any of it. He'd just been pleased to help and it'd been good to find someone apart from Maggie who he could trust. All he'd wanted was her friendship.

They'd stayed good friends ever since; best friends almost. And when Saucers had seen him looking despondent the other night after he'd heard Johnny and Gina talking, she'd tottered over to talk to him, as always landing a kiss on his cheek. 'Alright, baby. Haven't seen you for a couple of days. I miss you, what's been going on darlin'?'

'I've just been busy man.'

'Busy with that flipping white stuff. It's no good for you, Nicky. Bleeding hell. You're a shadow of your old self.'

'Remind me to come to you when I want cheering up.'

'It's not that, Nick. I'm worried about you. Everyone is and I hear Johnny was baying for you. He's really pissed off, Nicky.'

'Johnny and all the rest of them.'

'Wanna talk about it?'

154

'Talking's not going to sort things out is it, Saucers? If you don't mind I'll keep it to myself.'

'Okay, babe. I'm not one to squeeze secrets out of a man but I'm here if you want to gab. I still owe you one for sorting out that job with Johnny right back when, so if there's anything I can do to help. You know I will.'

Nicky had looked at her. An idea forming in his head. 'Actually, now you come to mention it, perhaps there is.'

Now, opening the back door quietly, Nicky sneaked out of the Donaldson household and breathed in the air. Suddenly he felt a sense of freedom. A freedom he'd never felt before. As much as trouble seemed to be standing on every corner for him – and he owed people more than he could possibly pay back – it actually felt good to be leaving the house behind. The house he'd spent all his miserable life in.

The stairwell stank of every kind of bodily fluid, but Nicky didn't notice. He was used to drug dens and crack houses, where he'd seen and smelt worse. He'd seen babies lying on filthy mattresses in soiled nappies. Young children wandering around hungry and dirty whilst their parents and hangers-on smoked crack in the same room.

The flat at the top of the stairs was number twenty-eight and Nicky knocked on it loudly. After a couple of minutes the door was answered.

'Hey baby, good to see you.'

'Not as much as I am to see you. Thanks again for this.'

Nicky grinned at Saucers who let him in. As she watched him walk into the front room every part of her body knew that letting Nicky Donaldson – the biggest but sweetest drug head since the dawn of time – stay with her was going to be the worst mistake she'd ever made.

CHAPTER TWENTY-FIVE

Max Donaldson sat opposite Gary Levitt. He'd heard a lot about Gary from the other faces in London, hearing how he was trying to work his way up the ranks. He knew Gary was dealing. Starting off small time on the corners of the streets in Soho but gradually getting bigger – both in dealing and also in reputation.

He'd heard Gary was ruthless, his ambition keeping him hungry, and he wasn't afraid to use his fists no matter who he came across. It put Max in mind of Vaughn Sadler, an old-school gangster who once ruled the area before he retired to marry some woman. Vaughn had never been afraid to do what it took, but Max had never been able to respect Vaughn like he should. Vaughn had had a heart and given people chances instead of putting them ten feet under. In Max's book that was nearly as bad as being a grass.

It was important to have people with Gary's focus, but they were becoming harder to find. The young guys today weren't willing to respect the faces like they'd done when he was making the tag. They wanted it all straight away and didn't want to put in for the apprenticeship. Instead of becoming a face or making big money, they got caught up in senseless gun wars, where the winner was only ever a bullet.

It'd been Gary himself who'd put out the message through one of his cronies that he wanted a meeting with Max. Gary had wanted to speak to Max for two reasons. Firstly, a lot of the places where he was starting to deal were on Max's turf and he certainly didn't want to get on the wrong side of him. Being on the wrong side of Max Donaldson usually meant a long visit to the ICU unit – if you were lucky. If you weren't so lucky, an even longer and more permanent one to the morgue.

The other reason Gary wanted to speak to Max was because he wanted to get onboard his bandwagon. There was only so far he could go up the ladder unless he was under the wing of one of London's most ruthless gangsters, and who better than Max Donaldson? Gary could learn from him. He was willing to. Plus, if word got out he was with Donaldson, then it'd take some pair of balls to cross him and Max, and Gary's reputation as a drug dealer could only get bigger.

It'd taken a lot of bottle for him to face Max; there was an unsettling presence about him which made the toughest of men feel uneasy. Gary certainly wasn't the toughest, especially when he didn't have his heavies around as Max had insisted he didn't.

Sitting in the meeting, Gary looked at Max properly for the first time. The man's eyelids hung with excess skin over his heavily bloodshot eyes. His face, puffy and rotund without a trace of softness, was home to an array of tiny purple broken veins. Gary watched him snort lines of cocaine off the desk and noticed the size of his hands, making him shudder and fear creep into his pores.

Gary wiped his hand on his black Evisu jeans. His palms were sweating and felt cold and clammy; it was one of the more unwelcome family traits of the Levitt family. He didn't want to appear nervous. At the same time it was important to Gary he didn't seem too cocksure. He didn't want Max to see him as just a wannabe face, a ten-a-penny guy who had ambitions he'd never be able to meet.

It took something to be a face. It took what most people didn't have; the ability to go that one step further. To take another human being and disregard their right to life. To be able to do whatever it takes to get where you want and, sitting opposite Max Donaldson, Gary knew all those qualities ran through Max like a burst dam. He could almost smell it. He hoped Max might see a trace of the same in him.

As Gary was deep in thought, Max spoke roughly. 'I hope you've got a good fucking reason to call up this meeting. I don't take kindly to people who waste my time.'

'I think you'll be pleased with what I'm bringing to the table.'

'I don't want to think and I don't want anything brought to the table. This ain't a flipping restaurant. You're wasting my time mate.'

Max got up and scraped his chair backwards on the concrete floor of the offices on Duke Street. Gary had pulled a favour from an old mate to use some refurbished offices which were on the market but as yet unsold. He'd passed him a few tasty pieces of crack and six grams of the finest coke in exchange for a few hours of the twelve foot by ten foot room, wanting to meet Max on neutral ground. But as he watched Max reach the door it looked to Gary like the whole venture had been a waste of time and money.

He frowned and sighed, knowing he had to grovel and feel like a boy again rather than a man. Perhaps this was all part of Max's game plan.

'I ain't messing anyone around, Max, I wouldn't do that to you mate.'

Max's whole face seemed to snarl as he curled up his lip in disgust.

'First off, let's get something straight son. No one calls me mate, mainly because I haven't got any. Secondly, you ever call me that again, I swear on the Virgin Mary, as God is my witness, I'll slice your ears off. Do I make myself clear?'

Gary nodded, not saying anything, but felt the wave of humiliation and the rush of blood in his cheeks as they blushed a light red. He saw Max glance at his watch – a huge gaudy gold number but clearly expensive creation – and breathed another sigh, this time one of relief as Max came to sit back down next to him.

'Tell me what you've got, but most importantly what's in it for me.'

'I'm looking to expand,' Gary said quickly. 'I'm dealing a good amount of crack and coke in the clubs but I really want to concentrate more on the crack. There's much more profit in it as well, as the demand is epic. Clubbers, city workers, smack heads, you name it; they all want to start ebbing out on a rock. Thing is, if I expand, I'll be treading on your turf. Obviously I'd have to get the nod from you in the first place to do that, but actually, I want you to come in with me. Or rather me come in with you. I'll be straight with you, Max. I also haven't got the money to expand the way I want to. I'm a big time dealer with a small time wallet. I've got the contacts, the clients and, Christ, I'm willing to do the graft but I need the greens to do it with.'

Max looked thoughtful as he leaned back on the metal chair. He didn't like many people nor did he respect them, but he had to admit he begrudgingly respected Gary for having the belly to face him. Max knew his own reputation and he didn't expect it was easy for Gary to have a face to face without his cronies lifting up his balls for him. However, that didn't mean he was going to make it easy for him. He wiped his mouth and spoke, keeping steely eye contact with Gary.

'So let's get this straight. You want me to provide the readies so you can serve up on my turf which you'd have to pay to do anyway. Don't you think I'd already be serving up myself if I was interested in it?'

'I dunno, it's a lot of hassle and I'm willing to take all the shit so you don't have to. I'll still give you the cut for serving on your turf, but if you give me the backing I'll be doubling your money. I'll make sure after the first layout you won't have to layout again, but you'll always be getting a cut of the profit. Turf money and payback on your initial investment even though you'll already have got that back. My name might not be Richard Branson, but I'd say that's a fucking good deal. Honestly, if it wasn't for the fact I want to learn from you and I ain't got the readies, I certainly wouldn't be giving away offers like that.'

'But I'm a money man. Why shouldn't you have to take out one of my loans like all the rest of them?'

Gary blinked a couple of times before giving a wry smile.

'Because I'm not stupid. There's no way I'd be paying out nearly a grand for borrowing fifty quid no matter how much you're tearing out me bollocks. That ain't a loan Max, that's fucking madness.'

Max stared hard at Gary before opening his mouth, then roared with laughter. He could do business with him. He liked people who showed him respect but also weren't afraid to tell it to him straight.

'Okay, we can sort out details tomorrow. I'll send one of my men to come and pick you up.'

Max got up and straightened his black wool coat and walked to the door. He nodded to his two men who'd been sitting quietly in the corner as they went to stand on either side of Gary. Max looked back at him.

'I'm curious. I'm wondering if your memory's not up to much – or were you deliberately not telling me you've got your dogs out looking for my son?'

Gary swallowed hard. It sounded as if it echoed round the room. His throat was dry but his hands were sweating and by the looks of the goons standing next to him, looking like they were hungry for a bit of action, he needed to be very careful how he answered.

'I'll ask you again, Gary. And I don't have to warn you it wouldn't do for you to start spouting me some blarney. Word gets round. You should know that by now. There's nothing that happens in Soho that I don't know about.'

He wasn't sure if it was a trick. He didn't want to say the wrong thing but realised a bit of honesty – though not too much – at this point was his best policy.

'I'm afraid it's true about Nicky. I didn't want to say anything 'cos the last thing I want is to cause trouble. I thought it was better him getting the stuff from me than some toerag who might rip him off.'

'Or you thought you'd do it yourself. Rip him off, like.'

'No I swear to you, Max. It ain't like that. I thought I was doing him a favour but I can see how it might not look like that. All things considered.'

'So what's the damage?'

'Nothing, let's say we're quits. Whatever he owes me, he can have. He's welcome to it.'

Max stared at him, then walked over to where Gary was sitting. He bent over and Gary tried to crane away but the table behind him didn't give him any leeway to escape the stale alcohol smelling breath.

'And after what you've just said, you expect me to go into business with you?'

'It was just business, Max.'

'And that's my point. Just business. When I consider going

161

into business with someone and they decide it's better not to follow up on what's owed because of sentiment, then I have to think twice about having any dealings with them.'

Gary was stunned. He hadn't expected this, but then, this *was* Max Donaldson. The same Max Donaldson who put so much fear into his kids, even as adults, knowing wherever they went he would always find them.

'I thought that's what you'd want. I thought you'd want me to let Nicky off.'

'Don't try to think for me, Gary. Never try to think for me.'

'What do you want me to do?'

'I want you to sort it.'

'In that case I'll make sure Nicky's my priority. I'll get back what's owed.'

Max straightened himself up, pushing his fingers into his lower back. 'Make sure you do and when you do; tell him his Da sent you.'

When Gary Levitt stepped out of the meeting he'd been in his element. It'd gone better than he could've ever imagined. But as successful as the meeting had been, the shine was starting to wear off now that he was at his flat.

His Auntie Gina hadn't yet bothered to turn up. The new clothes he'd bought to go with his new image were pissing him off. A Dolce & Gabbana black shirt, Vivienne Westwood Gold Label trousers and a pair of shoes from Hobbs which he now knew he shouldn't have bought, especially without trying them on. Because even though they'd looked crisp and the dog's bollocks, they were too small and squeezing the fuck out of his feet.

Annoyed, he threw them to the other side of the kitchen, only for them to drop down, land on the box of baking soda and send clouds of white powder across the room.

Angrily, Gary picked up his mobile, wanting to offload

his annoyance onto someone else. He dialled Gina, hoping she'd pick up so he could give her some verbal for not turning up, but it went straight to voicemail. He cut it off as he heard her request to leave a message, knowing abusing a machine wasn't nearly as fulfilling as it was to her face. Next, and still wanting to let off some steam, Gary dialled Nicky to put the wind up him.

He'd held off with Nicky, extending payment days and not really giving him the full monty of his wrath, because at the back of his mind he knew Nicky was a Donaldson. Now though, everything had changed. Max had given him the nod to send out a warning to everyone who didn't pay their debts by using his son as an example.

Nicky's phone rang but he didn't have a voicemail. Still, he wasn't going to let two people and a pair of shoes spoil his moment. What he'd negotiated with Max was the next step, and it was a big fucking step at that. Everything he did from now on would be backed up by a face. And once people found out, no one would mess with him. Before long he'd be someone. Gary Levitt was finally in business with the big boys.

CHAPTER TWENTY-SIX

'Are you sure there can be no mistake?' Gypsy sat down on the chair; her hand was shaking as she spoke to the lady at the clinic on the phone. The letter lay on her lap.

'I'm sorry, we don't actually send the letters out so we don't know what it says. It comes from somewhere else, but I doubt there's any mistake. I'm sorry if it's not what you wanted.'

Gypsy put the phone down. Putting her head in her hand, she wiped away the tears. Wall to wall of wooden shelves with designer shoes and bags surrounded her as she glanced at the letter again. She'd always thought the not knowing was the worst thing but she could see she'd been mistaken. As the words sunk in, she realised that knowing was worse.

She had to get her head round it. She was due to go to the spa and though it wouldn't make her feel better at least it was time away from the house. A bit of time for her to think.

There was a knock on the door and before she'd managed to put the letter away, Lorna came in, closing it behind her. Gypsy was immediately put out by the invasion of her privacy.

The last thing she wanted to do was miss her massage for Lorna. Gypsy spoke with hostility, bringing back the Bow Road girl again into her voice.

'I don't remember inviting you to come in, Lorn. What's the idea girl?'

'Is everything alright? I was walking past the door and I heard you crying.'

Gypsy straightened herself up. However bad she felt, sharing anything more than the air she breathed with Lorna was sharing too much.

'I'm fine, Lorn.'

Lorna saw the letter crumpled on Gypsy's knee. She struggled not to smile as she spoke.

'You don't look alright. Bad news?'

'Whether it is or isn't, it's got nothing to do with you. So do us a fave, Lorn – open the door and go away.'

'The thing is Gypsy, I don't think you'll want Frankie to hear what I've got to say.'

'What are you talking about? Hear what?'

'I see you've read your letter.'

Lorna gestured her head to the letter.

'I don't know how that's any of your business.'

'Oh but it is. Especially as it concerns my brother.'

Gypsy flushed. She didn't like where this was heading.

'I don't know what you're talking about Lorn, but you may as well turn into the camel you are and spit it bleeding out.'

'I'd watch that mouth of yours, Gyps. You don't want me running back to Frankie telling him how you badmouthed me, as well as hiding things from him.'

'I beg your pardon?'

'Oh you will, Gypsy. You'll be begging my pardon alright and wishing you'd let me come to stay all those times I asked. But I'm here now and there's nothing you can do about it.'

Lorna walked across to Gypsy's vast walk-in wardrobe and pulled an oversized Hermès bag down from the top, grabbing designer clothing off the rails before stuffing them in the bag.

'Have you lost all your marbles? What do you think you're doing?'

'I'm doing you a favour and getting your stuff for you to clear out.'

'Lorna, if you don't want me to put my fist in that gob of yours, you need to get off me bleeding stuff.'

Gypsy pulled her sister-in-law by her cashmere cardigan, astounded at Lorna's front – but she was brought to a halt by what Lorna said next.

'I know what's in the letter.'

Gypsy let go of Lorna's top. She felt the colour draining out of her face.

'Oh don't look so shocked, Gypsy; after all, who's been the one keeping secrets?'

'I'm warning you. Keep out of it.'

'Don't warn me, because I'm warning *you*. If you don't leave, I'm telling Frankie what's in the letter.'

Gypsy moved her mouth to say something but Lorna continued to talk.

'And don't bother saying I wouldn't dare, because you know I will, Gypsy. You know I will.'

After a moment of holding Gypsy's stare, Lorna brushed herself off, straightened her cardigan and shuffled out of the room. As she put her hand on the gold brass handle she stopped and turned to Gypsy. 'A word of advice, don't take too long in going and don't cause a fuss when you go. Just make it as natural as possible.'

'Natural? As if Frankie's going to let me go without any explanation?'

'Don't worry on that score darling; I'm sure you can make something up. You've certainly had practice.'

Lorna winked and opened the door and walked out, leaving Gypsy desperately thinking of a way to try to stop Lorna – before she ruined her life.

CHAPTER TWENTY-SEVEN

'The sly bastard needs his bleeding balls cutting off.' Gina Daniels was mouthing off as she stood in the middle of Sonya's Sauna on Brewer Street. Her mates sat behind the desk of the overheated reception, tutting and shaking their heads in all the right places as they continued to read their magazines. None of them had a clue what Gina was on about and none of them could be bothered to ask her.

'I'm telling you that cunt will get his. He must think he's bleedin' Harry Houdini tying me up in his plans like this. Worst thing is, Sonya, he expects me to do it for nothing. Next thing I know, he'll be having me release a charity single.'

Gina's face was red with fury. Beads of sweat trickled out of her pores as she marched about on the same two foot spot of the budget floor tiles.

'Well what do you think, Sonya, got some nerve ain't he?'

Sonya saw it was her cue to speak. Not having heard or bothered to have listened to Gina's ranting, she was forced to ask a question of her one-time street corner mate.

'Who the fuck are you talking about darlin'?'

'Johnny Taylor that's who. He wants me to look after his kid for nothing. Nothing except the air I bleedin' breathe.'

Johnny whistled as he walked up the stairs to Saucers' flat. It was the first time he'd been there.

He hadn't bothered to call because he knew Saucers hardly went out apart from when she worked, because all she liked to do was sleep and read. He'd never known any other person to sleep as much as Saucers did and to have the ability to be able to sleep through the loudest of sounds and the maddest of situations.

He remembered when there was a ruck at one of the clubs; men breaking bottles, the Toms and the customers screaming like they were extras in a slasher movie and, sound asleep in the corner, getting an extra hour of shut-eye, was Saucers. It was probably all that reading she did. Filling her head with so much crap would put anyone to sleep.

There were four doors on the landing. Three without numbers but one with the number twenty-eight on, along with a large red love heart doorknocker. One of the other Toms had bought it for Saucers for a Christmas present; she'd gone into raptures before bursting into her usual flood of tears.

Johnny rapped on the door, wanting to get into Saucers' flat as soon as he could so he wouldn't have to smell the foul stench anymore. And rather like his mother, he hoped the stench didn't linger on his designer clothes.

Leisurely, the door was opened but the moment Saucers saw who it was, her face drained of its usual rosy colour.

'Johnny! Oh my God, Johnny!'

Johnny looked at Saucers and craned his neck towards her, checking her pupils to see if she was stoned, so strange was her reaction at seeing him.

'Expecting someone?'

'No, it's . . . er . . .'

Saucers turned nervously around at the sound coming from the lounge, then stepped forward to speak to Johnny, closing the door behind her.

'It's not that Johnny, I've . . .'

'Got a visitor? Turning a trick? No worries, I'll wait till you finish him off. I'm guessing you won't take too long. I'll wait in the front room.'

'No.'

Saucers blocked Johnny's way, pushing him back. Johnny scowled, none too happy about Saucers putting her hands on him.

'What the fuck are you playing at?'

'Nothing, Jon Jon. I ain't got no one in there. I'm just not feeling too great. Women's problems.'

'Women's problems? What are you talking about? That's so frigging general it's untrue. Bleeding hell, if it's women's problems that could be one of a zillion things – and if you mean you're on your period, do me a favour Saucers, you've never had problems before. You're *always* telling me how you just stick a sponge up there so you can carry on turning tricks. So what's going on? I *know* you're telling me porkies but I want to know why.'

Saucers wasn't quite sure what to say. She could tell Johnny wasn't going to be fobbed off with bullshit but she had no idea how she was going to get rid of him. He certainly couldn't come into the flat, not with Nicky sprawled on her couch. She knew it'd been a bad idea to invite him to stay but what could she have done? She owed him and besides, there was something about him she was fond of.

Like most people when she'd said to him, 'If there's anything I can do for you,' she'd only half meant it. But he'd gone on to ask to stay and she hadn't been able to refuse. Whatever he'd done, he was still her friend. But now she was going to be right up it once Johnny found out she was letting Nicky stay. No doubt she'd lose her job too.

'Listen Johnny, can we do this tomorrow? I'm really tired. You know how I like my sleep. I'll call you later.'

Johnny pushed Saucers gently out of the way and opened her front door, getting out his hand gun as he walked into the hallway. He didn't mind what she got up to, he wasn't her pimp, but he *was* her friend. He knew when she was lying and he wanted to know why.

If she was in trouble he wanted to sort it. She didn't have many people around her who didn't want to either fuck her or fuck with her. Saucers had been a good friend. She'd kept her mouth shut about him and Maggie so it was the least he could do to try to get her out of the brown stuff if she needed it. He felt her tug on his coat.

'Johnny, no. Don't go in there, please.'

Johnny Taylor couldn't understand why Saucers was so desperate to keep him out, which made him even more determined to go in. With one firm swing of his arm he opened the door of the lounge as Saucers squeezed her eyes shut, not wanting to see what was about to unfold.

Tommy looked round Nicky's room. He'd heard rumours and had wanted to talk to his brother – or at least that was what his plan had been. So often he'd set his mind on wanting to communicate with his siblings, trying to take seriously the role of older brother, but when it actually came down to it, his mind couldn't focus. The visions would come into his head, distracting him from what he was there for, so it was a slight relief to find Nicky wasn't there.

Looking around once more, Tommy sensed something was different. Some of Nicky's things were gone. It was pointless looking in his top drawer to see if he'd taken his passport. Nicky didn't have one. Tommy wasn't sure if his brother had even gone north of Watford; in fact, he wasn't sure where he'd been or what he'd seen. It struck him he didn't know much more about the life of his brother than he did about the lives of the family who lived next door. Of course, like everyone else in Soho, Tommy knew Nicky was involved in drugs but to what extent he didn't know. It seemed to be the habit of his family, not to know and not to care.

The way Tommy was going to judge if it was a permanent departure was by Nicky's statue of the Virgin Mary. If it'd gone he knew his brother had gone too. It was a bizarre thing that his brother, who lived his life in such variance with everything the Catholic Church taught, still clung onto the fact that if he put his faith in the weekly mass and Father Maloney, somehow he'd find redemption.

Tommy kicked back the dirty rolled-up clothes piled in the bottom of Nicky's wardrobe. Jeans, socks, underwear, burnt foil and a home-produced crack pipe made from a miniature Baileys bottle. Everything crammed into the small white wardrobe. Everything apart from the statue. His brother had gone.

A wave of sadness washed over Tommy. He recalled the time he'd gone with Gina Daniels to see Nicky, who'd been banged up on remand in Pentonville for intention to supply. Gina had been happy to smuggle some drugs into prison for Nicky in return for a ton.

He'd sat watching and listening as Nicky had begged Gina to take a photo of the ten pound statue. 'Gina, do me a favour and take a photo of me statue.'

Tommy had stared at Nicky, not quite knowing what he was talking about as he'd watched a smirk spread across Gina's face as she spoke.

'You what?'

'Me statue of the Virgin Mary, I want a picture. I'll pay you a score.'

Gina had thrown her head back and laughed hard and loud. But Nicky had just sat there with his eyes downcast, looking hurt.

'What's with the Bambi look, Nick? You're not telling me you're for real?'

'Forget about it.'

'You're being serious ain't you?'

'It makes me feel better and I can't have it in here, so I thought if I had a photo of it . . .'

He trailed off and Gina looked at him as if he'd lost his mind.

'Most people on bang up would be asking me to bring some bleedin' porn in. I don't get it, Nick.'

Nicky had shrugged his shoulders then, nodding to the passing lags before drawing his attention back to Gina.

'You don't have to get it, I ain't asking you to. I'm asking you to take a photo and bring it to me.'

'You're off yer bonce, Nick.'

He'd stretched over to her and clasped her hands, bringing his voice down to a whisper so she'd had to strain to hear what he was saying. 'I don't get it meself and I can't explain it. I ain't no saint and God knows I ain't got any intention of being one. I'm not saying I feel all that religious stuff that Father Maloney thumps on about. Funny thing is, I don't even say Hail Marys to it or pray to it. It's just something to hold onto. It's all I've got left. So you can say I'm off me bonce and you'll be right, but I need it darling. It's my fucking life raft.'

Tommy had sat in silence as he listened to the conversation and he'd been amazed at Nicky's passion, but more amazed at his tears. It'd cut Tommy to the core but he hadn't said anything; didn't know how to. Instead he'd carried on listening to Gina ripping the piss out of Nicky.

'Cut out the tears right now Nicky. This ain't the place

to be springing tears. Not if you want to be able to sit on your arse tomorrow.'

It was then that Tommy had held Nicky's gaze with his dazzling blue eyes, speaking quietly to his brother. 'I'll do it for you, Nicky. I'll get the photo for you mate.'

When he'd got home he went straight to Nicky's room and found the figurine at the bottom of the wardrobe where his brother had told him it'd be. Tommy had taken the photo like he promised, but instead of giving it to Nicky himself, he'd given it to Maggie to give to him.

The whole situation had made him feel uncomfortable and he didn't want to have to face up to the way it'd left him feeling. The overriding sense was of emptiness and envy; envy that his brother had something aside from chaos to cling onto.

CHAPTER TWENTY-EIGHT

Nicky heard Johnny's voice the moment the door had been opened. It was loud and cheerful, distinct with a lyrical cockney lilt. There was no mistaking it. He'd panicked at first, standing rooted to the spot as if he'd stepped into a can of super glue. Then his survival instincts had stepped in, wanting to escape from trouble. It'd drawn him towards the tallboy cupboard in the corner. Quickly he'd rushed over, still hearing Johnny's voice gently remonstrating with Saucers at the door.

The white cupboard was stacked high with books making it impossible to even contemplate hiding in it. He couldn't go to the bedroom or bathroom; they were by the front door, and impossible to get to without being seen. Greeting Johnny at the door and singing a show tune would be less obvious.

Nicky glanced at the kitchen, his heart doing overtime as fear set in. There was a cooker, fridge and wall cupboards but nowhere to hide. Panic whirled through his body as he heard Saucers' voice on the other side of the door.

'Johnny, no. Don't go in there, please.'

Johnny Taylor flung himself into the front room with almost too much force. He stumbled forward with the gun in his hand, taken by surprise at how quickly the door had opened. The lounge was empty.

There was a cupboard in the corner, its doors wide open, books tumbling out of it. A television, a mismatched winged chair, a large sofa running along the longest wall, and shelves and shelves of books. It slightly disappointed Johnny to find no one. He'd imagined Saucers had been turning a trick who'd become nasty and she needed help to get it sorted.

'What was all the fucking drama about?'

Saucers let out the breath she'd been holding and looked as surprised as Johnny not to see anyone there.

'I . . . er . . . it's a mess Johnny, the place is a total mess,' was all she managed to come out with.

'I'm not the bleeding dirt patrol. Jesus, Saucers, you need to calm down a bit darlin', never seen you so highly strung. I could play the fiddle on you.'

'Ain't a woman allowed to be house-proud Johnny Taylor? I may be a Tom but that don't mean I ain't got standards.'

Johnny looked at Saucers in disbelief. From her face he could see the tension. The lines round her eyes, filled up with foundation, seemed more prominent than usual as she squinted at him. Her lips, stained with baby pink lipstick, pursed in agitation. He'd never seen this side of her and clearly what he'd said had upset her.

'Listen babe, I'm sorry. It's lovely here, really cosy.'

Saucers relaxed slightly, starting to believe her own story and swiftly unconcerned at the whereabouts of Nicky. She continued pushing her face up as she spoke to her clearly bewildered boss. 'Yeah well, I don't like people turning up out of the blue if the place is a mess, it might give the wrong impression.'

Johnny had to check his mouth wasn't hanging open as he gawped at her. The place was clean but unworkable and nothing anyone could do would make it feel cosy – plus, there were too many books for his liking, but he didn't say anything. Instead he threw himself down on the mint green couch, astounded at this house-proud Saucers he'd been confronted with.

Saucers continued to talk; amazed at even herself at how much she had picked up from the daytime DIY programmes that had been on whilst she was disinterestedly being shagged by her punters. Curtains, paint, edging and even voiles were all thrown into the conversation with Johnny. It was only when she saw Nicky's booted foot under the coffee table sticking out from behind the couch she stopped her Stepford wife routine and was brought abruptly back to reality. Getting flustered again, Saucers sat on the end of the couch, wanting to distract Johnny from looking anywhere near the other end of the couch. As she spoke she knew she sounded different. A nuance of high-pitched hysteria edged into her voice.

'So Johnny, what was it you wanted? I ain't got time for chat. Things to do, books to read, cakes to bake and all that.'

Saucers held her feigned grin, feeling the muscles in her jaw twitch and ache as Johnny leant slightly in towards her, checking again to see if she'd been on the foo-foo dust.

'*Cakes*, Saucers? We are talking the same language ain't we? When you say cakes I'm assuming you're talking the ones you smoke in a pipe?'

Saucers' laugh was loud and shrill. Everyone including Nicky – who right then felt like every breath he took was as loud as a clanging bell – knew it was as counterfeit as the money passed between the faces of Soho.

'No, Johnny, I'm talking proper cakes. Muffins, scones, fairy. You name it, I bake it.'

That was the evidence Johnny needed. Saucers was tripping

and tripping hard. What he wanted to do was get the fuck out of the flat before she started banging even harder than she was already.

He would've got up and made his excuses then, but he needed to run his idea past Saucers first. He only hoped she'd be able to fully take in what he was saying.

'I'll make this quick then. I wanted to talk about Maggie. I went to see Gina and I'm telling you Saucers, if I wasn't brought up not to kick the shit out of a woman, I would've battered her black and bleeding blue. Nothing more but a fucking thief; both her and Nicky.'

At the mention of his name Nicky swallowed hard, certain any moment Johnny would realise he was there.

'That's what cuts me up, but it cuts me up more for Maggie. Nicky was one of the few people she trusted and he as good took the bleeding food out of Harley's mouth to shove shit up his nose. I know we all toot but at the price of your own? I expected it from Gina, she ain't nothing more than a cockroach, but Nicky . . .'

Saucers had never felt more uncomfortable in her life, not even when she'd pranced around in a rubber latex suit two sizes too small for a punter who could only come if he saw her sweating.

'Nicky's a good guy underneath, Johnny. He ain't really got a bad bone in his body. It's the frigging stuff, tore out his common sense.'

Johnny hardened his voice, wishing Saucers didn't always see the good in people.

'When I've finished with him, bad bones, good bones, he won't have any bones left in his body. I ain't going to play charity matches with him. He needs to be taught a lesson. He knows I'm after him but he's lying low.'

Saucers tried to divert Johnny off the subject of Nicky.

'And Maggie, you said you wanted to talk about her?'

178

'Did you know she was thinking about giving up Harley?'

Saucers' face whitened. 'No, oh my God. The poor cow, I know how much she loves that girl . . . Christ, Johnny. I'm sorry.'

From behind the couch, Nicky closed his eyes as a new kind of shame washed over him. He listened as Johnny continued.

'I'm not going to let that happen Saucers . . . I can't. I've decided to rent a studio flat. I dunno why I didn't do it before . . . or maybe I just wasn't thinking the way I should've been. It's nothing special, things are a bit tight to squeeze too much from under my old man's nose, but it's alright. God knows it's like a palace compared to the place where Harley is now. It's the new build off Tottenham Street. Monarch Inn. Last one going. I've rented it under the name of Miller and touched the landlord with upfront money so he was happy to have no paper trail. What do you think?'

Saucers was genuine with her answer.

'Good for you, Johnny. Bloody hell, it's about time you got your finger out. I'm made up for you. She ain't had it easy, Johnny, and I know you don't like me saying but everyone bailed on her, including you. It ain't just Nicky.'

'I know. Christ knows do I know. She and Harley belong together; she's a good mum. I'm going to try to make it up, if she'll listen.'

'If I know Maggie she will. How you going to make it work though? Who's going to look after Harley when you're not there? You ain't moving nowhere, your old man will see to that. He won't let you move out and for sure Max won't let Maggie go anywhere either.'

'I was hoping you might.'

'Johnny, I'd love to but . . .'

Saucers stopped. She couldn't say to Johnny what she wanted to say. She wanted to tell him she wouldn't have

179

time because she needed to look out for someone else. She needed to look out for Nicky. Because if she didn't, who else would?

'Johnny . . . I . . .'

'It's fine, you don't need to explain. It was just a thought. Until I find someone else I can trust I've recruited Gina again.'

'Gina? After what she's done? Are you sure, Johnny?'

'It won't be forever and believe me this time I'll be breathing down her neck. If she makes a wrong move, I'll be down on her. She's going to work for me for free. You should've seen the face on her when I told her the new rules. But she owes me babe and the nights I ain't in the clubs, I'll be with Harley. I'm hoping Maggie will be too; even if it's only once a week when we can both get away at the same time, it's once a week where we can be a proper family. I know it sounds stupid but I miss her. Left me spinning when she did some bird.'

Saucers smiled at Johnny. He was a very handsome man but here he was looking like a boy as he blushed as he struggled to explain his feelings for Maggie.

'Have you tried telling her that? She probably thinks you didn't give a rat's arse about her. I'm guessing she thinks you just spent your time shagging the whole of Soho and then some. I can give you a love poem to read to her.'

Johnny spluttered with laughter.

'No thanks doll. I'll give that one a wide berth.'

'I don't know what's so funny. We girls like to hear it, no good bleeding chalking it up in your loaf. We may be a lot of things, but we ain't mind readers.'

'I wouldn't know where to start, Saucers.'

'Stone the crows, you know for an intelligent man you can be very stupid Johnny Taylor. You ain't got no fear when it comes to having a barney with anyone or squaring up against the likes of Max Donaldson when you were a teenager, but a tiny bit of sentiment, you're out and down for the count. Just tell her.'

Johnny's face softened as Saucers spoke about him and Maggie. He shrugged, embarrassed, trying to shake off the awkwardness he felt. Saucers was right; since Maggie had come out of prison all he'd done was act the clown. He hadn't shown her anything but disrespect. Jesus, the day she came out he was shacked up in bed with Saucers – granted he hadn't shagged her or had any intention of doing so, but it was hardly the homecoming she deserved. He cringed openly as he thought about it.

'But for what it's worth, Johnny, I think it's a great idea and once she's stopped being mad at you she will too. Trust me babe.'

Johnny smiled at Saucers, touched by her sincerity.

Saucers smiled back. She was really pleased he was going to try to make it work but she knew the odds were certainly stacked against them. She sighed, feeling a tad wistful, though she didn't have the luxury of indulging in other people's romances at this moment. She needed to get him out of the flat and sharpish. Standing up to encourage Johnny to do the same, Saucers spoke, trying to convey a sense of calmness whilst feeling the opposite.

'Okay, well cheers for coming. I'll see you later in the club.'

As Saucers talked she watched Johnny pull out his phone.

'I ain't going to leave it with Nicky you know. I'm going to keep ringing until he answers. Let's see if he's about now.'

Saucers eyes widened as it struck her what Johnny was doing. He was calling Nicky. As Johnny waited for the phone to connect, panic set in as Saucers realised any second now Nicky's phone would start to vibrate and then ring, the same phone which was lying on top of the coffee table next to where Nicky was hiding.

*   *   *

181

Gina Daniels wondered if blood actually boiled because if it did, hers certainly was. One thing she hated was the idea that someone was taking advantage of her and the idea was not only a thought; it was a fact. She'd heard Nicky had done a runner, leaving her not only short of a few bob, but well and truly in the shit with Johnny.

No doubt Nicky had expected her just to forget about everything now he'd gone, but Gina Daniels had never left anything in her life; apart she supposed from her kids, but they didn't really count – she was best rid of them anyway.

If she couldn't get what she wanted from Nicky, she certainly wasn't going to leave it. She'd do the exact opposite; she'd light a firecracker up the Donaldsons' arse.

Maggie was the cause of everything. If it wasn't for her meddling, things would be running smoothly still. She would be up a few hundred quid a week instead of turning into a skivvy for someone else's daughter and for that Maggie would pay. Yes, Maggie Donaldson was going to pay a heavy price.

CHAPTER TWENTY-NINE

Gypsy stood over Lorna as she lay in a pool of blood. She bent down and touched Lorna's head, watching the blood ooze from her scalp. She stood up, realising she needed to call the ambulance, even though a large part of her didn't want to. But she couldn't let it go that far.

'Gypsy?'

Gypsy jumped, her daze broken by the sound of a familiar voice – though what she saw on her husband's face was far from familiar. Frankie was staring at what she was holding, a look of horror on his face. In Gypsy's right hand was a cosh drenched in Lorna's blood.

'Frank . . . it wasn't . . .'

'What the fuck have you done?'

Tommy Donaldson paced up and down, his shirt feeling stiff from where the summer sweat had dried. He was agitated and couldn't think straight. His thoughts were all blurry. He'd been lucky not to be seen but what he *had* seen had changed everything.

He slumped down on the clean white bed. For the first time in a long time Tommy *needed* to talk. He couldn't get the woman's face out of his head. He'd seen a tiny glimpse of her but that'd been enough. He knew her face, every inch of it, every line, every detail. And now it was as if the walls were closing in on him and the fevered anxiety which had consumed him as a child had flooded back. He felt alone and scared but there was no stopping now, even though the place where he was heading looked dark and frightening.

Tommy lit a cigarette; he wasn't a heavy smoker but occasionally the heavy taste of the smoke circulating in his mouth and the tightness at the back of his throat, for some reason made him feel better.

As Tommy stood at the corner of Berkley Square, Maggie came into his thoughts and he smiled. He liked to think of her. To him she was everything that was good. She was the light to his darkness and when everything started to get too much, it was her face he'd try to picture to stop him falling too far.

Still thinking about Maggie, Tommy leant against the railings and saw a woman in the distance on the other side of the square, frowning and looking concerned as she talked. She wore red patent shoes, smart and expensive, and a black coat with red trim buttoned up to the top.

Tommy walked into the Georgian house quietly. He knew he was taking a risk; it was daylight and he didn't know if someone else was in the house but he wanted to follow his instinct, trust in himself as other people didn't and know it'd be okay.

The back door had been inaccessible, a big iron gate standing between Tommy and what he wanted to do. So he'd pushed the front door and it'd opened with frightening ease.

He stood for a moment and listened to the sound of panting. It was his own. His hands were shaking and for a short while he was mesmerised by them, wondering if it was fear or the adrenalin kicking in.

There were shopping bags left in the hallway and Tommy tried to quieten his breath against the silence of the hall. He moved along the corridor to where a door was slightly ajar. He brushed back his hair with his forearm and took a deep breath and walked into the kitchen.

As she lay in a pool of her own blood, Tommy knew he only had seconds to find an escape route or face whoever he'd just heard coming in. His eyes darted around frantically. At the side end of the kitchen there was another door and Tommy ran to it, his mind loaded with terror, unable to contemplate being caught.

He ran through and exited in another part of the large hallway and then found his way out into the fresh air the same way he had come into the house. As he left, Tommy turned his head – and that's when he saw her. The woman from his dreams.

CHAPTER THIRTY

Frankie's eyes stared at the numerous hospital monitors which beeped out of unison with each other whilst green output lines with sharp jagged points flashed across the small screens in continuous motion. The male nurse, with his rounded sympathetic face, short greying red hair and unfashionable rectangular glasses, silently recorded the data.

Lorna had been brought into ICU at University College Hospital with a head injury and Frankie hadn't left her side, apart from the odd trip to the bathroom and a stay awake coffee run to the ground floor.

She'd been brought in by the ambulance unconscious and had stayed that way ever since. He'd told the hospital staff she must've had a fall. Which couldn't be further from the truth if he tried. He didn't *actually* know what had happened – though he had a damn good idea what had – nothing could get the image of Gypsy holding the cosh out of his mind and once Lorna woke up, he'd make sure she told him the truth. Once he knew that, he was going to sort it out his way. Not a copper's way, not by the laws of the land. He was going to sort it with the rules he'd been brought up with. The rules of the street.

He glanced to the side of him and locked eyes with Gypsy. She'd pleaded her innocence since the attack, imploring him to believe her that she hadn't done it. The problem was he didn't believe her, how could he? She'd proved she was a lying cow by what Lorna had seen and he'd been gutted; devastated.

He loved her. She was his and his alone, though that hadn't been enough for her. She'd been seeing other fellas. The image of his naked wife with her tits out for another man came into his head and it enraged Frankie to the point that he had to hold onto the sides of the uncomfortable red plastic chair to stop exploding in a rage of fury.

For the past couple of days he'd been waiting to decide what to do with the information; perhaps see if he could gather more. But now this'd happened; Lorna had been attacked and he'd walked in to find his wife holding the cosh. It'd messed his head right up. Gypsy had told him she'd just walked in and found Lorna like that, but then she'd also told him she was a faithful wife. It was as if he didn't know who she was anymore. She was so full of hate for Lorna, maybe he should've seen this coming.

What Gypsy needed to do was own up. God knows it was stupid not to, she'd been caught red-handed, but she was denying it. As hard as it would be to hear that his wife had taken leave of her senses by attacking one of her own, he would've preferred to listen to the truth than the running bullshit he'd had to listen to. 'Frankie, you got to believe me babe, I ain't done nothing to Lorna. God bleeding knows the idea hasn't run through me bonce, but actually doing it is another thing.'

He'd looked at her and felt her put her hand between the gaps of the buttons on his shirt. Her touch had turned his stomach and he'd grabbed her hand, squeezing it hard and making her yelp.

Gypsy had brimmed up with tears and seeing her upset had made him start to soften; but as he contemplated comforting her, the image in his head which had been there since the night Lorna had reported back had overwhelmed him. He'd roared in anger at her. 'Stop with the bleeding tears girl. Christ, it'd be easier for us all to stop the frigging charade Gyps and just tell me the truth.'

'I ain't got a flipping clue what's got into you, Frankie. I know you're upset about Lorna but I can tell it's not just that. I've been married to you long enough to know when something's bothering you.'

'You're really pushing it Gypsy. Fuck me, you're really going to stand there and give me a look of bleeding innocence when both of us know what's been going on for a while.'

'Frankie, I don't get it. I know you're upset about Lorna and all this grief won't help you get better either, but I'll be honest darlin', I ain't got a clue what you're talking about.'

'No? Well, let me refresh your memory. I know all . . .'

Frankie had stopped himself mid-sentence. The last thing he'd wanted to do was to let what he knew out of the bag before he was ready. When he'd got his head around it and he didn't feel like someone was driving a stake into his chest, he'd talk to her, keeping his voice cool and hard and emotionless. He'd treat her no different than the way he treated the guys who tried to turn him over.

As Frankie continued to think, the small black monitor nearest to Lorna's bed rang out an alarm, startling both Frankie and Gypsy equally. The nurse sitting at the end of the bed got up and moved around to the flashing machine, calmly pressing buttons and silencing the screeching alarm.

Frankie leapt up anxiously and felt Gypsy put her hand on his leg but he brushed it away, focusing his attention on his sister's wellbeing.

'Is she alright mate?'

The nurse answered in a comforting reassuring voice.

'She will be. The only reason she's still unconscious is that with a lot of brain injuries, for a precaution we keep people in a medically induced coma to help with the swelling. It protects it from getting more damaged by letting the brain sleep and heal. Thankfully your sister hasn't got any swelling and the scan shows her injuries were all superficial. So the good news is the doctors have told us to start waking her up. After the sedatives have worn off hopefully she'll be back to her old self within hours.'

Frankie nodded, relieved now he thought his sister was going to be alright. He turned to Gypsy who was still sitting down and looking at him anxiously. Not wanting the nurse to overhear, he spoke quietly with a definite tone of sarcasm. 'Good news, Gyps? I bet this is what you were praying for hey, babe?'

'Yeah Frank, I'm pleased.'

'Are you, are you really?'

'Course I am. No matter what I thought of the old goat, I wouldn't wish this on her.'

Frankie stared at his wife, trying to ignore all the things about her which made her so attractive to him. He pulled on his Barbour brown leather jacket in angry silence, careful not to bang his stab wound which was healing nicely.

Now he knew Lorna was going to be okay, he could go back to Soho. He needed a stiff drink, a few lines and a God almighty fuck.

He didn't bother saying anything more to Gypsy. Instead he gave an appreciative tap on the nurse's shoulder, pressing a couple of fifty pound notes into his hand before storming off. Gypsy was left wondering exactly what she'd done so wrong for Frankie to believe she was capable of attacking Lorna.

*   *   *

189

The sound of a horn behind the brass made her jump. It was loud and continuous and Frankie saw her nerves wouldn't allow her to ignore it. She turned around and he opened the passenger window, smoothly gliding it down with the gold electric button in his white Range Rover. He grinned boldly, his words loud and punctuated by fake laughter.

'Looking for me, babe?'

A slinky smile spread across the hooker's face, used to the corny chat up lines from punters, but her eyes were dark and guarded.

'That all depends.'

'On what?'

'On what I'll find.'

'How about I jump in, and trust me when I say you won't be disappointed.'

The brass opened the passenger door and slipped herself onto the thick black leather seats, smelling a mix of the burning joint and expensive cologne.

Immediately Frankie reached over and started stroking her leg, making his way up to her thigh before roughly putting his hand between her legs. He grabbed at the crotch of her knickers, ripping them across to one side and slid his fingers into the hooker, licking his lips with his pupils dilating from the cocaine and the thought of sticking his cock into her wet pussy.

The hooker took the joint from the car ashtray, inhaling deeply as Frankie started to drive with one hand on the wheel and the other still roughly inside her. She looked across and saw what looked like tears rolling down the cheeks of Frankie Taylor.

CHAPTER THIRTY-ONE

The phone began to vibrate on the coffee table and Saucers knew in the next beat it'd be all over for her and Nicky when it began to ring, unless . . . It was madness to do it but she knew that's what it was going to take.

She closed her eyes and braced herself before throwing herself onto Johnny. Flinging her body over him, Saucers grabbed the phone out of his hand and sent it flying across the room, causing it to break apart as it came into contact with the wall.

'What the fuck are you doing?'

Johnny roared in shock as Saucers ground her body onto his, pushing him back down on the couch. He struggled with her but he was really too stunned by the strangeness of the situation.

'Oh Johnny baby, I want you, I've wanted you for so long. Fuck me baby, fuck me.'

'Jesus, Saucers, what's got into you? Get off me.'

He pushed her off him; if he wasn't so startled he might've laughed. She was bouncing on top of him, grabbing hold of her boobs and shrieking like a woman possessed.

'Saucers, please, stop for God's sake, you're going to knock me bollocks off. Jesus darlin' I ain't one of your romantic heroes.'

Saucers took a quick look out of the corner of her eye and saw Johnny's phone had come to pieces. She stopped writhing around. However embarrassed she felt, it was a whole sight better than being caught hiding Nicky. She braved a glance at Johnny who looked shell-shocked. She smiled weakly at him and spoke, slightly out of breath from all the exertion.

'Bleeding hell, Johnny, I don't know what came over me. All them books must have gone to me head.'

Johnny scratched his head and knew he needed to be tactful; he didn't want to upset her. She already looked mortified with embarrassment.

'I never knew you felt like that about me sweetheart. I don't want to lead you on and tell you any porkies about how I feel the same. No offence babe, but I ain't seeing you in that light. For a start you'd have me cream-crackered with passion like that girl. I don't think me dick would last longer than a week.'

Saucers cringed inside. She hadn't banked on Johnny wanting to discuss it and felt humiliation in his every word.

'Forget it, Johnny, had myself a few lines of coke before you arrived. It's the reason why I didn't want you to come in; always takes me like that, especially if I'm up to me eyes in swashbuckling tales.'

Saucers straddled Johnny to get off him and went across to his phone, picking up all the pieces.

'Sorry about your phone, I don't think it's broken. I just got a bit carried away.'

Johnny sat up, rubbing his stomach which was now tender from the weight of Saucers' body and still slightly in a state of shock.

'Like I say girl, no worries. I better go.'

Saucers could sense the awkwardness in Johnny as she handed the phone pieces back to him, leading him to the front door. As she let him out, Johnny turned to her and leaned in to give her a kiss on the forehead.

'You know if it wasn't for Maggie, you'd be my girl. There wouldn't be any holding me back then darling.'

Saucers blushed and Johnny grinned. Both knowing but neither caring what he'd just said wasn't the truth. It felt good to both of them; cementing their friendship once more.

'And Saucers, do me a favour will you babe? Lay off the stuff a bit. Next time you have that level of passion you may end up killing some poor geezer.'

The door closed and Johnny let out a gigantic sigh of relief, not quite knowing what had happened in there.

Back inside the flat, Nicky stood up and greeted Saucers with a massive smile.

'Nice one girl, I thought we were goners then but you turned it around. I would've liked to see his face when you jumped on him.'

'I need you to get out.'

Nicky's face dropped and a look of panic spread across it. 'What?'

'I said get out, Nicky. I knew I was taking a risk letting you stay and I was true to my word I'd help you but it's time for you to go.'

'We got away with it though.'

'This time. What about the next? I can't afford to piss Johnny off; I ain't going back to where I came from. I can't be turning the streets. I'm sorry, Nicky.'

Saucers went into her bedroom and picked up Nicky's bag and brought it to him. He was still standing in the same place. She passed the bag, unable to look him in the eye.

'If it could be any other way Nicky.'

Nicky walked past her and a moment passed before

193

Saucers heard the front door open and close. She felt empty, and not for the first time that week, she wondered if she'd just made another big mistake.

Johnny bounded down the busy streets of the West End. The summer always brought the crowds but today he didn't mind. Walking along Tottenham Court Road and then turning into Charlotte Street, he chuckled to himself at the image of Saucers bouncing on top of him, the way she'd leapt on him like a tigress on heat.

He felt happy. Saucers had thought it was a good idea about the flat even if she couldn't look after Harley herself. He'd sorted out Gina and put her in her place. The only other thing now he needed to do was convince Maggie it was a good idea. He wasn't sure if he could persuade her on just his own abilities though, so like all faces in Soho he'd needed to recruit the best – and he reckoned he'd managed to do just that. Johnny smiled as he looked down and gave a wink to Harley.

'What's this about, Johnny? I haven't got anything to say.'

Johnny sighed, exasperated at Maggie's stubbornness on the other end of the phone. He understood why she was behaving like that and, even though he was sure he'd be the same, it didn't help him in trying to persuade her to listen to him.

'Just hear me out babe and then if you don't like what I'm saying you can tell me to do one. I know about Harley. I know you were thinking of giving her up.'

Maggie was stunned. She had no idea he knew and she certainly didn't have any wish to talk about it. The situation was hard enough as it was. She didn't need anyone trying to persuade her otherwise – because then she'd be thinking about herself and not what was best for Harley. And to Maggie, Harley was all that mattered.

'I'm sorry Johnny, I'm not discussing it. Whatever you've got to say, I don't want to hear it. It ain't going to work with me this time. Goodbye.'

'No! Maggie please, hold on. I've got someone here to talk to you.'

Johnny quickly passed the phone to Harley, giving the little girl a big smile and a wink. He could still hear Maggie on the other end of the phone.

'Johnny? Johnny?'

'Hello Mummy.'

Maggie's legs nearly gave way under her as she stood in the open-all-hours shop on Berwick Street. She hadn't been going to answer the phone when she'd seen the I.D. of the caller. But each time she'd pressed it to voicemail, Johnny had rung back. In the end, annoyed and unable to ignore the ringing or the vibration of the phone when she'd put it on silent, she'd answered, snapping harshly down the phone and securing a curious look from the shelf stacker.

Just as she was about to put the phone down she heard her daughter's voice, making her lean against the stacked-up boxes of cereal.

'Harley! Hello sweetheart. What are you doing?'

'Daddy says he's got a surprise for you.'

Maggie could hardly catch her breath. She was talking to Harley who was with Johnny and for the first time ever, she had referred to Johnny as Daddy.

She knew Harley didn't know Johnny really, though in truth Maggie didn't really know her either. The awful thought was the person Harley knew the most was probably Gina Daniels.

Maggie had seen her every day before she went inside, even if it was just for the odd hour. Any time she had spare, she'd give it to Harley. Johnny came and went as he pleased but because she'd been there, as well as Sheila and her auntie, Maggie hadn't cared that Johnny was a loving but fleeting figure.

But that'd been a year ago and one year in a life of a child of Harley's age was an eternity. Thinking back, she'd even been surprised that Harley had recognised her the day she'd got out of prison but she'd run up with a beatific smile, with so much love for her. Maggie would remember that moment for ever.

'Daddy's got a surprise for you. I'm going to be there too.'

'Are you? Well can you put him back on the phone for me please, sweetie?'

After a pause, Johnny came back on the phone.

'What are you playing at, Johnny?'

'Maggie, don't be pissed, it's the only way I could think to get you to listen to me.'

'And what makes you think I still will? You've sunk a long way to get our daughter involved.'

'I thought that's what you wanted? For us to be both involved in Harley's life?'

'It's a bit late now, Johnny.'

'But that's the point, Maggie. It's not too late. I promise you.'

'What is wrong with you to think you can pull a stunt like this and click your fingers and everything will be alright?'

Johnny raised his eyes upwards as he listened to Maggie. She was stubborn. Perhaps it was the Irish blood in her, but whatever it was it infuriated him and captivated him in equal measures.

'I know, I know, I've been an idiot when it comes to you and Harley, but I'm trying to make it up to you. To *both* of you. All I'm asking is that you come and meet Harley and I – will you do that Maggie?'

'What is it?'

'Just come, it's a surprise.'

'Please.'

'I dunno . . .'

'If not for me, for Harley.'

'Okay, Johnny. Tell me where.'

Putting her phone back in her coat jacket and leaving the basket of groceries complete with shopping list on the floor, Maggie walked out of the store empty-handed, unable to concentrate anymore. She didn't know if she should be angry with herself or not at how quickly her resolve to have nothing to do with Johnny had disappeared. How readily she'd agreed to go and meet him. Even though it was Harley she was going for, she could feel a buzz of excitement to see Johnny.

Maggie walked up Berwick Street, feeling the sun on her back. She smiled at the regular market stall holders who she'd known a lifetime, sensing the old feelings come rushing back. Once more Johnny Taylor was beginning to get under her skin. Even more importantly though, for a fleeting moment, her, Johnny and Harley had felt like a family. A normal family. And normality was all Maggie Donaldson had craved her entire life.

CHAPTER THIRTY-TWO

Walking into Nicky's bedroom, Sheila stopped abruptly. Something was different. It was a mess, though that wasn't anything new. Hygiene had never been high on her son's list of priorities, not since he'd been involved in drugs, which was as far back as she could remember. But what was different was that the plate of sandwiches which she always left for him lay untouched, still covered in cling film on the window sill. Her heart did a double beat as a deep but familiar fear hit her; the dread of being told her son was dead, overdosed with the drugs he'd been encouraged to take by Max when he was barely more than a child.

The sandwiches had always been an unspoken code between them. A code for Sheila to let her know he was alright. A code for her son to let him know that however much she didn't or hadn't shown it, she still cared. Sheila would leave the white double buttered bread sandwiches, only ever consisting of cheese and ham, for Nicky on the window. He'd either eat them or if not, he'd put them in the fridge, an indication he'd slunk back in the small hours of the morning. Sometimes it was the only indication she had for days to know her youngest child was still alive.

Sheila looked around the room but couldn't decipher through all the mess if anything else was different. Turning quickly, she ran to the only person she had to go to; Max.

Eyes closed and mouth open, Max Donaldson lay in a contented sleep. Seeing her husband's bloated body spread across the large red winged chair made Sheila have her doubts at disturbing him. But it was too late; five seconds later his left eye opened, revealing a bloodshot gaze.

'This better be good.'

'I'm . . . I'm not looking to disturb you Max, go back to sleep.'

Max shot up in his chair, rubbing his tired eyes and snorting phlegm into the back of his throat.

'You've fair got some cheek woman, telling me what to do. First you come in here sounding like a heard of charging nellies and then you tell me to go back to sleep.'

'I never meant anything by it, Max.'

'Now you've woken me up, you may as well tell me what you wanted and don't try giving me the bullshit about not wanting anything, I know you better than that Sheila. You wouldn't have put one foot inside this room if you didn't have to.'

Sheila had never been great at lying and no more so than when Max stared at her with unflinching hostility. She was uncomfortable from the summer heat and her anxiety was only making it worse.

'I'm waiting, Sheila.'

'I was wondering if you wanted any tea?'

'Bullshit.'

'I . . . I wanted you to lend me some money; I'm a bit short this week.'

'Bullshit.'

'I . . . I . . .'

'The smell of bullshit is hurting me nose Sheila, it's hanging

199

in the air. So I'll ask you again and I'd think very carefully about serving me up porkies. Look at me Sheila. Do not tell me any lies.'

Max got up and walked towards Sheila. He raised his fist and Sheila cowered, closing her eyes. She kept them closed for a few moments, but nothing happened. Cautiously she opened them to see Max standing with his fist lowered, a sinister grin on his face.

'Boo.' The roar of laughter from Max was loud and cruel, making Sheila well up in tears.

'Behave, Sheila; I haven't got time for you. Just tell me what I want to know then I'll let you go.'

Max caressed Sheila's cheek before pinching it hard. Bringing up a red welt. Sheila Donaldson's fear of her husband strangled the truth out of her and she spoke quickly and quietly, playing with the tissue she had in her hand.

'It's Nicky. I think something's happened to him.'

She looked up when there wasn't a reply. Sheila saw her husband's expression and she knew she needed to carry on.

'I'm worried something's happened to him. He hasn't been back to the house.'

'And what's so unusual about our waste of a space son not coming back home?'

'Nothing, it's probably just me. Forget I said anything.'

Max clenched his fist and placed it on Sheila's temple, turning one of his knuckles gently into it as he spoke.

'Sheila, I'm running out of patience.'

'I . . . I . . . I usually leave some sandwiches for him . . .'

Before Sheila had managed to finish her sentence, Max slapped his hand under her chin, clamping her mouth closed and banging her teeth together. It wasn't a hard slap but it caught Sheila's tongue. She tasted the blood in her mouth.

'And how long has this bum-wiping been going on? You've

been going behind me back and feeding him up like a stuffed goose. No wonder we have useless kids, with you treating them like royalty.'

'It was only a few sandwiches, Max. I worried about him not eating.'

Max laughed scornfully.

'You're pathetic. Serving Nicky food stops right here but I'm curious how sandwiches fits in with you thinking something's happened to him.'

'He hasn't touched them or put them back in the fridge like he always does. I'm afraid Max. Like he's overdosed or something.'

Max roughly pushed past his wife and barged into Nicky's room, closely followed by Sheila. His face was red from his sudden exertion and fury. He marched into the room, flinging clothes, shoes, magazines and anything within his reach out of his way. Using his feet, Max opened Nicky's wardrobe, turning his nose up at the stench of stale clothes and yellowing crack pipes.

Max looked on the top shelf of Nicky's wardrobe which seemed to serve as an extra waste bin. Dried orange peel, foil, burnt out matches and damp paper filled the shelf which then filled the floor as Max threw his son's belongings around.

Sheila watched the back of her husband's head as she gnawed on her lip. He suddenly stopped, and turned around to face her, holding an envelope with the word, 'Mum' written on it. Immediately he tore it open, reading it silently. Sheila knew better than to ask what it said. She watched her husband screw the letter tightly up in his hand then throw it in the middle of the room. 'Nothing's happened to him woman, not yet anyway. Your precious Nicky has done a fucking runner and when I lay me hands on him, he's going to wish he never had legs to move.'

Max marched towards the bedroom door past where Sheila was standing. Without thinking she instinctively reached for Max's arm, afraid for her son. She grasped hold of her husband for only a fleeting moment before she realised what she'd done, then locked eyes with her husband as fear and dread hit her, along with Max's clenched fist.

Max Donaldson felt sick. He always did when he stared at his wife's face. Pulled up in a tight scrunch, always looking out for trouble, it was making him sicker than usual.

He could hardly see her eyes. They were hidden in deep red and purple swollen flesh. The bridge of her nose was bulging out with puffy tenderness and her bottom lip hung to the left with the weight of a painful engorgement.

He'd been looking forward to eating his bacon sandwich but Sheila was turning him right off it. What pissed him off even more was how much ketchup she'd put in the butty. It'd dripped out and run down his fingers, getting into the cut caused by his knuckle coming into contact with Sheila's front tooth and now it was stinging like mad.

'Turn yer fucking face away woman, unless of course yer sticking yer face out for another walloping.'

Max spoke as he shoved his sandwich away to one side. The force skated the green plate along the table until it came to the edge, then didn't stop until it crashed to the tiled kitchen floor.

He was annoyed with himself, or rather with Sheila for making him do that to her face but he'd been so enraged by her grabbing him that he didn't stop to think. To plan where he was going to lay his fists. Over the years, the do-gooders brigade had started to stick their noses into other people's business when they turned up in casualty. Gone were the days of him being able to teach his family a lesson in the way he saw fit. Now some stuck-up doctor always wanted to know exactly how the injuries occurred.

Of course, his family knew not to talk, but he'd got more cautious, sticking to body blows with his wife. Apart from keeping unwanted people out of his business, it had the added bonus of him not having to look at her swollen face which always made him feel sick, as it was doing now.

The other reason he felt annoyed was Frankie Taylor. He'd been on his mind and any time Frankie came into his mind, Max felt angry. Angrier than usual. If Max had had his way he'd have an all out war; but wars cost money, and although he didn't want to admit it, Frankie with his fake tan and whitened teeth was popular amongst the other faces. Max wasn't certain it was a good idea to go to battle, knowing most of London would be siding with Frankie.

No, Max would go about it another way. The way he knew would hurt. He'd already had his men watching Frankie's family, reporting back the movements of his wife and son. But he was going to have to do something big, if Frankie was going to take real notice. And it needed to hurt. Frankie had stopped him from being able to make the money he should've done years ago, but when he'd thrown the drink at him, he'd also humiliated him. Frankie would pay for that; or rather, his family would.

Sheila turned away from her husband. The whole of her face was aching and she didn't know how she was going to face the kids. The shame she felt when she looked at her children from behind swollen features hurt more than the injury could.

She saw what they thought, it was written in their eyes as clear as if she was reading a book. Their incomprehension at why she stayed, why she still continued to put up with the violence and abuse with each passing year and why she'd brought them into the world only for them to join her in the torturous chaos.

But she was trapped, imprisoned by an invisible wall, stopping her from freeing herself and her children – and she hated herself for it. Hated herself more than she did Max.

CHAPTER THIRTY-THREE

Gypsy pulled a face as she watched Frankie from across the table. He was tucking into a plate of fried egg, chips and jellied eels bought from Eddie's in Brewer Street. For the past twenty years it was always the same order but today it turned Gypsy's stomach. Everything about her husband at the moment had started to annoy her.

It'd been Frankie ignoring her which had done it. At first, she'd tried to make amends for whatever she was supposed to have done, had wriggled up in bed with him but he'd pushed her away as if he'd found some vermin crawling up his leg. She'd made him his favourite dinner; rib roast with Yorkshires and all the trimmings but he'd told her he wasn't hungry and had gone to make a cheese sandwich instead. She'd even run him a bubble bath, offering to watch porn with him – her pet hate – on the large bathroom television whilst they lay in the tub together. He'd looked at her, his face full of derision and quietly told her he'd already had a shower before storming off to one of his clubs, not returning until the next morning.

It was after that she'd started to feel annoyed, bristled by her husband's attitude and treatment of her. Unless he gave her an almighty apology for thinking she'd bashed Lorna over the head and an even bigger one for making her feel so bleeding lousy about herself, she wasn't going to make any effort either.

Frankie watched Gypsy who was deep in thought. As usual she was done up to the nines. She was a classy East End girl and always had been. Her make-up was always immaculate. Her hair was beautifully coiffed within an inch of its life and her clothes, a grey Vivienne Westwood ensemble, looked stunning. The more beautiful she looked to him the more furious Frankie felt about her betrayal.

He thought about the Tom he'd picked up the other day from Wardour Street. He'd needed it, after spending the last few days by Lorna's bedside. However, his thoughts had gone straight back to Gypsy. Instead of taking the girl to his club, he'd brought her back to the house, hoping Gypsy would've caught them. He'd wanted to see the hurt in his wife's eyes as he revenge-fucked some silly bit of nothing in the bed and in the house which Gypsy and he had made together and been so proud of.

His wife knew he tasted all kinds of goods at the club; white ones, black ones, oriental ones, but she'd never actually *seen* it. He'd been discreet because he knew how women were, so he'd never rubbed it under her nose like she'd done to him. He wanted to tarnish everything that was good about their lives like the way she'd tarnished his heart.

Gypsy hadn't come back to the house and he'd been disappointed. In actual fact he'd been disappointed in a lot of things. The fuck, the way the tart had looked like she wasn't enjoying herself, and strangely enough, he'd been mostly disappointed in himself.

'Are we going to get going Frank or what?'

Gypsy's voice was loud and aggressive and her cockney accent cut through the words all the more.

'I ain't stopping you getting in the bleeding car woman. I don't need to be Zimmer-framed to it. You may not have noticed but I'm on the mend.'

'Oh too right I've bleeding noticed, Frankie Taylor. Only men on the mend leave other people's stuff lying around.'

Frankie looked puzzled.

'Don't talk in bleeding riddles Gypsy, this ain't an episode of *Countdown*.'

'No? I beg to differ, because what's been happening in this house lately is nothing but one big fucking conundrum. Next time, Frank, tell yer tart not to leave her knickers in me bed, I dunno where they've been.'

And with that, Gypsy marched out of their breakfast room, leaving Frankie with egg on his face, both literal and proverbial.

The white-washed ward on the twelfth floor was a women's only ward and the private room paid for by Frankie at the end of the corridor was where Lorna had been taken after her stay in ICU.

Frankie made his way down the corridor, walking carefully along the overzealously polished floor. Gypsy walked a few steps behind him, taking the trouble to smile at the old ladies sitting up in their beds, wrapped up in what looked like uniform pink crocheted shawls and waving to anyone who passed.

At the door, Frankie waited for Gypsy to catch up and noticed how she avoided his gaze. He tapped on the door; lightly at first and then harder when there was no answer. He heard a muffled, 'come in' from the other side.

Frankie opened the door widely, booming loudly, rather too loudly. Knowing her husband as she did, Gypsy sensed he was covering up his unhappiness.

'Alright girl? How are you doing? You had us worried

there for a moment. Bleeding hell, I thought you were brown bread. Spoke to the doc and he says your CT scan was fine. He said you were good to go almost, you can be shot of this place if you feel up to coming home soon.'

Lorna smiled at her brother, touched by his concern but more touched about her surroundings. She was in a private room which meant she wasn't going to take any shit from anyone, especially the nurses who wiggled around in their uniforms like a poor man's Marilyn Monroe. Even though the doctors had said she could go home soon, she was enjoying being waited upon; perhaps she could squeeze out another few days before she went home.

She was starting to enjoy and appreciate what money could buy and it certainly bought people being at her beck and call, whether they bleeding liked it or not.

From behind her brother she saw Gypsy, done up to the back teeth in designer gear, trying to look younger than she was. The last person she wanted to think about at the moment was Gypsy, but seeing her walk in as if she didn't have a care in the world made her impossible to ignore.

Lorna scowled at the sight of her, surprised Frankie hadn't given her the big heave-ho but even more surprised she hadn't taken her warning seriously.

She'd assumed Frank would've kicked her out by now with his toe up the crack of her arse but it was clear he was struggling to do that. Before her attack, he'd told her he needed to think about the best way to deal with it all. From the looks of him, Lorna guessed he was caught up in sentiment and no doubt with what was between Gypsy's legs.

Maybe she was going to have to put a bit more pressure on Gypsy to show her she wasn't playing games. The only reason she'd hesitated in saying anything to Frank about the letter was that she wasn't quite sure how he'd take it. Yes, he'd get shot of Gypsy alright, but what she didn't know was if he'd shoot the messenger as well.

'I hope the room's alright for you, Lorn; they didn't have any on the top floor in the private wing, so I sorted this one out instead. Couldn't have me favourite sister roughing it with that lot out there.'

'Thanks Frank, you know I appreciate it. I ain't one to be impressed by splendour, unlike some.'

Lorna paused dramatically and stared at Gypsy, making it clear who she was talking about. 'I don't want much, you know that Frank. Simple pleasures is all I ask for, though sometimes I didn't even have them. But I don't like to moan, so it's nice to be treated with some care for once.'

Gypsy couldn't believe what she was hearing; she'd seen Frankie's bank accounts and knew her husband sent Lorna a couple of grand each month without fail, let alone all the extra birthday and Christmas money. Lorna Taylor was an ungrateful cow and she'd shown her true colours to her. Of course she was nervous about what Lorna had over her but she wanted to at least get one thing straight.

'Gucci, Dolce & Gabbana, Chloé – call them simple pleasures? Do me a favour. Stop the bleeding quacking, Lorn. Let's just get this sorted shall we, Frank?'

Frankie glared at his wife, amazed after everything that she still had the cheek to front up.

'When I need you to butt into my business, Gyps, I'll frigging well call.'

'But it *is* my business when you go accusing me of nutting your sister over her bonce.'

Lorna sat herself up. It was the first time she was hearing this. The old bill had come to talk to her but she'd told them nothing and hadn't wanted to until she ran it by Frankie. She'd told them she didn't remember a thing, but the face of the intruder was as clear as the face on her Rolex watch

209

and it certainly wasn't Gypsy. But now she was hearing something else and she wanted to hear more.

'I'm sorry, Lorn, I never wanted to bring it up like this but Gypsy here obviously thinks otherwise.'

'I only want to get it sorted Frank because believe it or not I'm pig sick of it. You and your frigging accusations.'

'*You're* pig sick of it? What about Lorna? Bleeding hell, she comes over and next thing she's laid up in hospital thanks to you. Lucky she ain't no grass, otherwise you'd be sewing bags at Her Majesty's.'

Gypsy shouted, infuriated with the accusations.

'Are you out of your mind? How many times do I have to tell you I ain't done nothing. Tell him, Lorn; for God's sake tune us out of our misery and let your brother know he needs to be looking somewhere else – and then we can all get back to normal.'

All eyes turned to Lorna. She looked at Frankie first and then at Gypsy. It'd only just become clear what they were saying. Frankie, for some reason thought Gypsy had attacked her. She didn't know how and why but she could always ask questions later. What was apparent though was the need to get this sorted; clear up anyone's confusion, any misunderstanding, so everyone knew exactly where they stood.

'Well, Lorna?'

Frankie's voice urged her on.

'Well Frankie, it's like you say. It was Gypsy.'

A howl was let out – Frankie wasn't sure if it was his wife or Lorna, as Gypsy flew across the room onto Lorna's bed.

'Get her off me, Frankie. Get her off me.'

Frankie leapt in trying to pull Gypsy away as her red nails scratched in the air.

'Piss off, Frankie. Let go of me, I'll bleeding strangle the truth out of her.'

The door was swung wide open and three horrified nurses,

alerted by the noise, came rushing in with a security guard. The guard leapt in and grappled Frankie, assuming it was him attacking both Gypsy and Lorna.

Lorna let out a fishwife's screech as she saw her brother being pushed around. Gypsy clung onto the covers, and they pulled away with her as she was pulled back by Frankie. He in turn was pulled back by the Indian security guard. Lorna's high pitched shriek cut through the air. 'It's her not him, let go of him yer bleeding moron.'

Gypsy snarled back as her perfect hair fell over her eyes. She panted as she struggled to get away from Frankie who was effing and blinding at the guard and the nurses, who didn't know what was happening.

'Shut up, Lorn, you've been nothing but trouble from the first day you came. Tell him the truth; tell him I ain't the one who did it.'

'You did it, like you did it when you were copping off with that fella in the street. I followed you Gyps. Frankie told me to. I saw you.'

'What fella? You lying cow!'

Lorna, eyeing up Gypsy's hair and seeing it was in her reach, pulled it, bringing Gypsy's head up to her own face. She hissed in her ear, making sure no one else heard.

'Make your mind up, Gypsy, you can take this as a way out. Say it was you or I'll tell him *now* about the letter.'

All fight fell away from Gypsy. She froze and blinked several times, then sadly shook her head at Lorna. Her action seemed to be a cue for the others to stop. Everyone stilled themselves in the room, craning to hear what Gypsy was saying as she whispered hoarsely and tears came to her eyes.

'Okay, okay . . . I . . .'

Lorna's eyes were wide in anticipation as Gypsy recomposed herself to be able to continue.

'Lorna's right. If that's what you want to hear and want

211

to believe I did it, but as for filling your head with poisonous lies that I was cheating on you, that ain't true Frankie. You have to believe me, it's always been you babe.'

Gypsy turned to her husband. The nurses and the guard stayed silent, hooked by the conversation they didn't understand, only that the woman had just admitted to doing something.

Frankie faltered. Shocked by Gypsy admitting she'd attacked Lorna. For a second he turned away as he heard the plea in his wife's voice. So much of him had wanted to believe otherwise.

She'd been so convincing telling him she hadn't done it. He'd as good as believed her and had only gone on about it because he was angry. Angry and hurt but mainly jealous. Now here she was saying it was true; but she still expected him to believe she *hadn't* been shagging the cock off other men?

He looked at her and he saw something in her eyes which made him doubt it for a minute, then an image of Gypsy romping naked with some stranger came into his mind. It was all too much for Frankie Taylor to bear.

'Do you really expect me to believe anything which comes out of your mouth now, Gyps? If you never cheated on me, why did you sneak out of the house? You disgust me.'

'You really think I'd cheat on you? I'm not like that Frank, you should know that.'

Lorna chipped in, angry at not seeing any fury on Frankie's face. The only thing she saw was weakness and she certainly wasn't going to stand for that. Lorna laughed coldly, full of scorn. 'You wouldn't cheat on him? Do me a favour. I'm guessing you don't want me to jog your memory.'

Gypsy's face turned red and she pointed a finger.

'Don't you dare, Lorn, don't you frigging dare. You've no idea what you're talking about and you better leave it well alone. I said I'd done it, so you can leave it at that.'

Frankie stared at his wife not understanding what was going on. 'I'd like to know what you're talking about. Am I missing something here? Is something else going on that I need to know about?'

It was Lorna who answered.

'I'll tell you what it is. Your wife here would do anything to save her neck. She's been rolling you for years.'

It was another cue. Gypsy once again flew at her sister-in-law, followed closely by the security guard and Frankie.

'I'll flipping do you in if it's the last thing I do.'

Through flying arms, and hair Lorna screeched.

'You see Frank, you see. She's a bleeding animal.'

A stampede of uniformed hospital security officers came rushing in and between the chaos Gypsy managed to strike out at Lorna, hitting her across her face.

'I'm not playing your games no more, Lorna. I've done like you said and I see what you want. You're nothing but a money-grabbing bitch and as for you Frankie, I expected more from you. Yeah I sneaked out of the house, I bleeding had to. Your grip on me was tighter than a frigging cobra on heat, but unlike you, my idea of a good time isn't sleeping with strangers. I'd never do that because asides from the fact that I love you, I know how much it'd hurt you. I could never hurt you. If you don't know that by now, our marriage isn't worth the paper it's written on.'

'What would you know about marriage, Gypsy?'

'Maybe nothing Frankie, but I do know when it's time for me to leave.'

Gypsy shook off the security guard who was lightly holding onto her arm and picked up her red Mulberry bag from the floor. She pushed past the rest of the people in the room, turning as Frankie grabbed her.

'And where the fuck do you think you're going? You're my wife don't forget.'

213

'I know Frankie, and I always will be, but I'm going home to pack my stuff.'

Frankie's face flushed red.

'You ain't got no stuff Gypsy, everything you have, I bought, remember? It all belongs to me.'

Gypsy looked at Frankie sadly, taking in his rugged handsome face, his piercing eyes and the way his mouth curled up at the sides. She lightly touched his chest as she spoke very quietly.

'Okay Frankie, if after everything we've done and gone through together the most important aspect of it all is who bought bleeding what, then I ain't going to fight you.'

She went into her bag and pulled out her house keys and wallet, taking hold of her husband's hand and placing them in it. 'Have it all Frank, if that's what makes you happy, have it all darlin'.'

With that, Gypsy turned and walked away, watched by the guards and the three female nurses.

'Gypsy, wait!'

'Bleeding hell. Let her go, Frank. How the bleeding hell can you be calling her back, it's beyond me.'

Frankie Taylor turned and stared at his sister with a furious look on his face; the one Lorna had been hoping to see all afternoon, but not directed her way. He walked towards the bed and leaned into his sister, speaking through gritted teeth.

'Lorna, do us all a fucking favour girl and shut yer bleeding pie hole.'

Leaving his sister aghast, Frankie stormed off out of the room. He marched along the corridor, ignoring the waves from the old women and wishing he had a cosh to finish off the job himself.

CHAPTER THIRTY-FOUR

Gary Levitt was anxious. There was no mistaking it and no pretending to himself he wasn't. He could tell by the drip of sweat which was slowly making its way down his back. The ticking of the grandfather clock didn't help with his nerves either; seemingly synchronising itself with his beating heart, emphasising the agony of having to stand in front of Max Donaldson as he stared at him with dark sunken eyes from beneath wiry overgrown eyebrows.

'You were late, Gary. I don't like people that keep me waiting. Makes me unhappy son.'

Max's Irish voice was brimming with anger and once again Gary admitted something to himself that he wasn't really keen to; he was afraid.

'I'm sorry about that Max, you know how it is.'

As Max kept his voice low, Gary's fear of him rose.

'No son, I don't know. Tell me.'

'I was doing a deal when your call came in.'

'So I'm the fool who pays your wages but some crack head comes before me, is that what you're saying boy?'

'No, no of course not, it's . . .'

Gary decided it was wiser not to say anything more; it could only get him into trouble.

Max got up from his chair and walked over to the small cherry table near the fireplace. On it were some cut lines of cocaine and Max leant over and snorted them up noisily, reminding Gary of a baying mule.

'I want you to find Nicky.'

'Has something happened to him?'

Max scornfully faced Gary, wiping the excess cocaine off his nose.

'You sound like me wife. Why all of a sudden is everyone concerned about that low life?'

'I just thought . . .'

'That's why I decided to work with you Gary, I assumed you wouldn't think.'

'No, it's . . .'

'Still talking, Gal? If you've trouble keeping it shut, how about I put yer face through the fucking wall.'

Gary straightened himself up and consciously gave a check to make sure his mouth was closed as Max continued to pace round the room and talk.

'I told you I wanted him sorted – I expected you to do it straight away. I don't understand why nobody's concerned about the money he owes. You see, the way I figure it Gary, now you're working for me, anyone who owes you money ultimately owes *me* money. So I want it back. I want you to find Nicky and teach him a lesson he won't forget. No one walks away without my say so. And when you find him, I want you to call me. Understand?'

Gary nodded and as he did, Max walked over to him. He could smell the sickly sweet smell of stale coffee on Max's breath and the bitter residue of cocaine.

The punch in his stomach was low and hard and took Gary by surprise. Immediately winded, he fell forward onto the floor, clutching his middle, rolling into a foetal position and trying to get some air into his lungs as the excruciating pain took hold of his belly. Through his agony he heard Max speaking in no certain terms.

'And if you don't find him, Gary, next time I won't be so easy on you. Do I make myself clear son?'

Gary could barely nod, but that didn't stop him understanding exactly what Max had just said very clearly indeed.

CHAPTER THIRTY-FIVE

This was the fifth time Maggie had been to the flat but she still couldn't help smiling. She didn't think she ever would. It was tiny, but it was everything Maggie could've ever wished for; clean and bright and high enough for the view from the sitting room window to soar over the red and grey roofs of the West End. In the distance Maggie could see Soho; it seemed so far away and it felt so refreshing to get away from the madness which circulated through the tiny streets.

'You still like it, babe?'

Johnny came up behind her but didn't touch her. He didn't want to push it and scare Maggie into retreating into herself again. He knew her better than that. He needed to give her time, then eventually she'd come to him. Johnny could see she was genuinely still taken aback by it.

'I love it. It's perfect.'

Johnny smiled, out of relief as much as happiness. He knew how hard it was to please women. Maggie was beautiful but stubborn with it. Over the years he'd known her, he'd been baffled by her as much as he'd loved her.

'And Gina, is she alright with the arrangement until we

find someone else? She knows we're going to keep a close eye on her.'

'Yes she knows that but she wasn't happy. She nearly swallowed her arm when I told her, but what choice has she got? She ripped me off good and proper like I was a bleedin' piece of paper on a notebook, but then so did . . .'

Johnny stopped, not wanting to sour the air talking about Nicky. He knew how much Maggie loved her brother, for all his faults. She'd been more hurt than angry with Nicky; though she'd given it a good shot trying she hadn't been able to hold the anger for long. Like always, she defaulted to defending and feeling sorry for him.

'I know what you were about to say, Johnny – I know what Nicky did but it's really not him that's doing it.'

Johnny raised his eyebrows. If it wasn't Nicky doing it, he didn't know who was. Nicky was a druggie first and foremost and no matter how much Maggie loved him, drugs would always come first. There was no saving to be done, because the only person who could fish himself out of the deep hole he was in was Nicky. Unfortunately he'd been in the dark for so long he was blind to it and as far as Johnny was concerned, Nicky just didn't care.

Of course he wasn't stupid enough to verbalise this, and merely raised his eyebrows, letting Maggie continue to pour on metric units of sympathy to Nicky.

'He's had it hard, Johnny. He was the youngest one and perhaps even the weakest one of us all. I dunno. By the time he came along Mum was tired. She'd almost given up and if she hadn't protected us before from Dad, she certainly didn't have the strength to protect Nicky when he came along.'

'Don't give me all that Mags. I know it was you who put yourself out there. You were the punch bag, not them.'

'We all were, Johnny. Nicky might not have been battered as much as the rest of us when he was older, but he had more than his fair share of crap. He was the only one who Dad fed the gear to. My own father, feeding him that crap. First the speed, then the coke, Johnny. He never had a choice or a chance, so if you're going to blame anyone for ripping you off, go back to the beginning. You'll see where the blame lies. So lay off him alright, or you'll have me to answer to.'

Maggie smiled and Johnny walked across to the couch. Nicky had got away with a lot. He was always skanking around Soho, ripping dealers and Toms off, sniffing out anything which would give him a fix, but Maggie couldn't see that. All she saw was her baby brother.

Nicky owed him big time but for Maggie's sake he'd leave it. Well, he would for now. He'd sit back and see what was going to happen. He'd heard through the Soho grapevine that Nicky was wanted; wanted by a lot of people and he was happy to wait his turn in what seemed like an almighty queue.

'Let's see if she's asleep.'

Maggie put out her hand for Johnny to take as she spoke and he gladly took it with a smile, letting Maggie lead him into the bedroom. He noticed that whenever anything was about Harley, Maggie's defences went down. The tough street-wise woman who'd roll up her sleeves in a fight softened and melted. It was if he was getting a glimpse of the woman she would've been if she hadn't been born into the chaos of the Donaldson family.

A double bed was squeezed into the single bedroom. The whole room needed to be a few feet larger on either side but it was fresh and pretty, with sun yellow walls, and white linen curtains with tiny daisies, matching the covers and lampshade. Simple white shelves with newly bought dolls and cuddly toys on them complimented the small white wardrobe on the newly laid laminate floor. The window was slightly open, and the warmth of the summer blew in.

In the middle of the bed, curled up fast asleep, was Harley.

Her soft blonde corkscrew curls almost covered her face and the sense of her fragility struck Maggie as she watched her daughter breathing.

Johnny and Maggie stood at the end of the bed, aware they were still holding hands but worried to say anything in case their words spoilt the moment. For Maggie, this was what it all came down to. She'd been waiting for this ever since Harley had been born.

'Does this mean you'll put that silly idea out of your head about giving her up?' Johnny said, gently.

Maggie looked at Johnny, her face soft as she talked.

'It wasn't a silly idea, Johnny. It was about giving Harley what she deserved. Look at her. How did you ever think having her as a prisoner at Gina's was okay?'

Johnny bent his head in shame but lifted it up to look at Maggie as she touched his cheek. 'I'm not having a go at you Johnny. We're all to blame. But I love her, I love her more than I thought was possible. And that's why I was going to let her go. I couldn't leave her at Gina's and there was no one else. What was I supposed to do, Johnny?'

'I've let you down Maggie and I'm sorry. I'm not very good at all this.'

He shrugged, not knowing what else to say.

'You were my hero, Johnny. You came riding in to save me when no one else had and perhaps I would never have fallen for you if it wasn't for that. But I did. I fell for you and I fell in love with you. I still love you, but it's difficult Johnny. Sometimes I get so tired.'

'But I'm here now Maggie, you don't have to be tired anymore. I'll fight your battles for you. I promise things will be different this time. I know I've said it before but we can be a proper family. Once I find someone I can trust, we can get rid of Gina. She'll be fine to look after Harley until then; she won't do anything stupid. She wouldn't dare.'

As much as Maggie hated the idea of Gina having her daughter, at least she'd be policed by Johnny, and it would be here in this flat rather than the squalor of Gina's grotty place. Her daughter would at least be able to have somewhere she could call home, a place of safety and care.

When she could be here, this was where Maggie would spend her time; with her daughter, getting to know her like she should've always been, loving her like any little girl deserved.

Taking in the room again, Maggie turned to smile at Johnny. He'd done well. What he'd done to Harley had been wrong, so wrong, but Johnny knew that and she admired the fact that he'd tried to turn it around. And like all those years ago when he'd been the first one to ever stand up for her, he was now the first one who'd bothered to try to make a difference in her life.

'Thank you Johnny.'

'You're welcome babe. After all, you *are* my wife.'

'How could I forget eh? What with our idyllic, picket fence lives.'

She winked at Johnny, who noticed how sparkling her piercing blue eyes were. 'I'm happy to give it to you Maggie. It's what you and Harley deserve. My only regret is that I never did it for you sooner. Despite what I did, I never for a moment stopped loving you.'

Johnny was about to say more but he found himself shrugging his shoulders again, ill at ease with opening himself up to Maggie. He felt her squeeze his hand and he smiled, wondering if it was safe for him to lean in for a kiss or if it would trigger Maggie's walls going back up. Husband or not, she'd probably just see it as his way of trying to get laid.

The shrill ring of his phone put paid to him deciding. He saw the caller I.D. on his screen flash up; it was his mother. He pulled away from Maggie and clicked the phone to answer. He couldn't remember a time he'd ever ignored his mum's call. They spoke each day on the phone in the evening if they'd missed seeing each other at the house, but he knew she only called in the daytime if there was a reason, otherwise on the whole she'd leave him alone to get on with his life.

'Alright girl, how's it going darlin'?'

Johnny addressed his mum as he would anybody, but with the added warmth he saved for people close to him. He'd never been the clingy type as far as he knew, though his mother begged to differ, telling him stories of him holding onto her skirt when she and the women from his dad's club dropped him off at school in the mornings, but whatever the truth, Johnny was always glad to hear from her.

He expected to hear the usual banter coming down the phone followed by the reason for the call, but what he got pulled on his brakes. His mother was sobbing, a new and uncomfortable phenomenon for him.

He could count in single figures the times he'd seen his mother cry. Mostly they'd been caused by his actions as a teenager when he'd gone missing as he partied with his friends. Or when he'd been on one of his legendaries. She'd be out of her mind with worry and when he eventually turned up, so relieved was she to see him, that she'd burst into tears at the same time as giving him verbals. Hearing her deep sobs down the phone completely threw him.

'Mum? Calm down girl. I ain't hearing what you're saying, Mum. Stop, please. You're doing me nut in 'cos I can't hear you and I'm worried. What's happened? Is it me old man? Has something happened to him?'

Between sniffs, hesitations and deep breaths on the other end of the phone, Gypsy managed to get some of her words out.

'He's kicked me out . . . bastard's gone and given me a do one.'

Johnny was stunned. He walked through to the front room looking out of the window, not really comprehending the situation but feeling an instant anger towards his father.

'What do you mean he's kicked you out?'

'Well he didn't exactly kick me out, I walked – but he would've done babe. The words were hanging on his tongue, you could almost bleeding see them.'

'Why though? What's he done? If he's been boning too many Toms, Mum, I can talk to him, but you know what he's like and it's never bothered you before.'

Johnny heard his mother's voice change as she snapped down the phone at him. 'It ain't that, Johnny; bleedin' hell, if I was going to care about that I would never have got married, he was knobbing the bleedin' bridesmaids before I even managed to say "I do". It's that witch of a sister.'

Johnny sighed. Since Lorna had come there'd been tension in the house and, unlike most of his friends, where tension had been part of their daily outlook, he'd never had that problem. When he'd been growing up it'd been a house full of raucous laughter, his parents loving each other in an overtly sexual manner. Parties and big, big celebrations yes, but tension; never.

'What's she done?'

'What hasn't she frigging done is more the question, Johnny.'

'But she's been in hospital. How much harm can she do from her sick bed?'

'Well if we were talking about most people babe you'd be right but we're talking about your father's sister.'

'Okay but what? I know you and Dad have been at each other's throat. It's been a war zone.'

'I know sweetheart and I'm sorry. I never wanted to upset you.'

'I know but what I don't get is why you walked out. Jesus Mum, that's a bit radical.'

'No it ain't – not when you're accused of shagging some bloke and attempted murder.'

'What? I don't understand.'

'It's a long story, Johnny. Can you come and see me babe? I'm staying at the Hilton, but God knows how long for, I ain't got more than the clothes I'm stood up in and all I can say is thank God it's a Vivienne Westwood.'

Johnny smiled to himself.

'But Johnny listen, I'm worried because you know how your Dad is when he gets hurt, he starts behaving like a spoilt kid. I reckon he'll stop me cards and then I'll have nothing.'

'But you'll go back, won't you?'

'No Johnny, I ain't. I ain't ever going back.'

After Johnny had put down the phone to his mother, he couldn't help reeling. For one, he was surprised his dad had let her go. There was no doubt how much his father loved his mother, so it surprised him how it'd ever come to this. He didn't know the full story but he guessed between his father's possessiveness, love and no doubt an element of fear in losing her, his father had allowed himself to wind himself up and be manipulated by his sister's stirring.

One thing Johnny Taylor *was* certain of was that his mother was no cheat. He'd bank his life on it and if his father had any sense, which he clearly didn't at the present, he'd bank his own life on it too.

Maggie came over to sit next to Johnny, bringing a sleepy Harley with her. He smiled at them both before touching his daughter's cheek softly as Maggie placed her on his knee. He rocked her gently as he stared out of the window feeling his daughter's warm breath on his face as he held her tightly.

He glimpsed a look at Maggie and as he did an idea began to form in Johnny's head. It was a long shot but if his mother

225

really wasn't going to go back to his father she'd have nowhere to live and like she'd said, her days in the Hilton were certainly numbered.

Most of her friends were long-term mutual friends so they'd be too anxious to let her stay, worried about what his dad might do, though he doubted his mother would even ask them; she wouldn't want to put them in such a position. He knew she was well aware of her husband's wrath and reputation.

She had friends like Molly from the East End but she'd be no match for his father and one whiff of his mother staying with *'a cheap whore in expensive clothing'* would send his father into an apoplectic fit. No, his mother had to have somewhere permanent; somewhere she could call her own and where better than here, with her granddaughter?

It was mad, crazy, and he doubted his mother would be too keen at first to hear about his secret child and wife who happened to be the enemy, but he was sure she'd come around, especially now.

No one could look at Harley and not fall in love with her. Yes his mother would be pissed off, but with him, not Harley. When she saw how much love Harley had, his mother wouldn't see a Donaldson, she'd see her granddaughter – and then how angry could she really be?

CHAPTER THIRTY-SIX

Gina Daniels was stoned. So stoned she couldn't remember where she was. That was until Gary stormed in – then there was no escaping where she was, but that didn't stop her being pleased about what she'd discovered.

'Look at the fucking state of you.'

Gary used his foot to move his auntie from the position she had been lying in for longer than she cared to remember. Sitting up from the floor and needing the support of the edge of Gary's couch to pull herself up, she groaned quietly as the room came into focus.

She stared at Gary whose face was scrunched up angrily as he paced around the kitchen.

'What's up baby? Had a bad day?'

Gary stopped and his face contorted into an expression of amazement.

'No Auntie Gina, me boat race always looks like this when things are going well . . . of course I've had a bad fucking day and if I don't find that brother of Maggie's soon . . .'

'Who, Nicky?'

'No, Barack Obama. Of course fucking Nicky. If I don't find him it's going to get a whole lot worse, especially for me.'

'We *are* talking about Nicky?'

'Are you stupid? How many other Nickys do you know who are stealing, junkie runts?'

Gina's face reddened. She spoke, sounding as stoned as she felt. 'I need to see him as well. Proper took the piss, did Nicky.'

Gary spoke impatiently, unconcerned at Gina's petty quarrels. 'Yeah, well this ain't about you Auntie Gina; how come you always want the world to revolve around you?'

'I don't, all I . . .'

'Just shut it. Just shut the fuck up. If you don't know where he is, I don't want to hear it.'

'But that's the point Gal, I know exactly where he is.'

Saucers couldn't sleep. She hadn't slept all night, and now it was near lunchtime and she felt exhausted. It was an unusual predicament she found herself in. Since she'd been little, she'd been able to sleep in all sorts of circumstances. The day her old man had topped himself and the Old Bill had stomped through the house questioning her drug-addicted mother, she'd slept. The day she'd been carted off to care after the neighbour had called in social services, she'd slept. When she'd been given a six month stretch for soliciting she'd slept, and even last year when Eddie Austen, one of the market store owners from Berwick Street had shagged her, giving her his best shot, she'd slept. But now as she lay on her bed, Saucers was wide awake.

Not even her latest novel had been able to send her off and the only explanation she could come up with was that she was worried. Worried about Nicky. It was stupid; he was a grown man but yet so much of a young boy as well. She knew her allegiance should lie with Johnny and to a certain extent it did, but there was a vulnerability about Nicky. And he was her friend.

Granted, he was a junkie but he was a person first, as were all junkies. Underneath the coke and crack, the meth and the smack, was a boy who'd been hurt and broken from the day he'd been born.

She couldn't get the picture of his eyes out of her head when he left. They were full of fear and panic but what'd struck her the most had been the loneliness in them. Shit. She hated herself now, and lying staring at the wall wasn't going to make her feel any better.

She might as well get up and washed. Perhaps she'd go and speak to some of the street girls to see if they'd seen him. Most of them were bang on it as well and frequented the crack dens nearby. So if anyone had seen Nicky they would have done.

Junkies were creatures of habit and Saucers doubted very much he would've gone far, though a huge part of her wished he would. Far away from Soho and to a new life, but she knew perfectly well that wasn't reality as she knew it.

A hammering on the front door had Saucers getting up off her bed a few minutes before she was planning to do so. She looked at the clock, but it was pointless, the battery had gone a few weeks ago and she'd never got around to buying a new one.

Pulling her silk kimono on, which she'd been given by one of her punters as a present, Saucers shouted loudly as the hammering persisted.

'Alright, alright. Anyone would think you needed to talk to me.'

Part of her hoped it might be Nicky but as she opened the door she was pushed to the side aggressively, hitting her head against the cream coloured walls. Used to fighting and having her door kicked in over the years, Saucers didn't feel fear, only anger. Quickly she hauled herself up to see who the intruder was, not having had a proper glimpse of them.

229

'Oi! What the hell do you think you're doing?'

As Saucers spoke the man turned around, and she got a face full of Gary Levitt. Gary snarled as he slammed into the front door with his boot.

'Where is he?'

She'd known Gary for a while; only as an acquaintance, never as a friend. He was low life scum; the runt of the pack who thought he was something to be reckoned with. She'd come up against worse in her life; much worse. Hard, sadistic men who made Gary look like Snow White. All he was, was a violent bull and she'd recently heard he was now hiding under the shirt tails of Max Donaldson to sell his crap.

'Am I supposed to say, 'where's who?' because you're wasting your time darlin'; whoever you're looking for ain't here. Besides, you know me well enough to know I ain't telling you jack shit sweetheart.'

'Is that right? We'll see. I want to know where Nicky is.'

'Oh we're talking about Nicky are we?'

'Make this easy on yourself; people talk, one of the girls in the club said you had him staying with you.'

Saucers stared at him saying nothing. It never stopped amazing her how much people gossiped. Even when people were turning tricks and smoking rock there was still tittle tattle.

'You won't find him here, but you're welcome to take a look. Then you were always going to, weren't you Gal?'

Gary marched back out of the room to kick open Saucers' bedroom and bathroom doors, leaving her standing with her arms crossed in the hallway.

'He ain't there.'

'Jesus, we've got a genius in our midst. I told you he wasn't, Gary.'

'Yeah, you did but *now* I want to know *where* he is.'

230

'I don't know, but you're not going to believe that are you Gary, so I might as well pack my hospital bag now.'

Gary sneered at Saucers.

'You better believe it darlin'.'

With one swing of his fist, Gary Levitt knocked Saucers unconscious, cutting her eye with the sovereign ring he was wearing as he did so.

CHAPTER THIRTY-SEVEN

The Hilton hotel near Warren Street was chic and stylish, decorated in contemporary cool, calm colours, in stark contrast to the way Johnny was feeling. It was stupid, he felt like a school kid going to tell his parents he'd been caught doing something he shouldn't.

He'd kept the secret about Maggie for so long now that he was nervous. He hadn't told Maggie that he was going to tell his mum but once it was all sorted, he knew she'd be fine. Thinking of it in those terms gave Johnny a little boost of confidence as the lift door opened to the air-conditioned sixth floor.

Room 403 was at the end of the thick carpeted corridor. Johnny gave the door a slight tap, knowing his mother was waiting for him.

When Gypsy opened the door her face lit up with a beaming smile. 'Alright my darlin', I'm so pleased to see you. Come in baby.'

Johnny kissed his mum as she squeezed him in a loving embrace. 'Alright mum, Jesus, you'll break me bleedin' ribs.' Gypsy let go and smacked him playfully. 'Give over, you sound like Lorna; one theatrical queen in the family is enough. How is the scheming witch?'

Johnny shrugged his shoulders, not really wanting to get into a conversation with his mum about his auntie but not really knowing either. After the phone call this afternoon from his mum, his father had called immediately after, wanting Johnny to sort out the clubs because he didn't feel up to it.

He'd probably stay at the flat for the next couple of nights with Harley; the last thing he wanted to do was make an appearance at home. He hated gloom at the best of times and the last thing he wanted to do was to get in the middle of his mum and dad. He didn't want to be seen to be taking sides. Even though it seemed to him his Dad was being a prime arsehole, he loved them both in equal measures.

Yes, he was going to help his mum out by offering her the flat to stay in, but that would help him as much as it did her. He knew his father would be mightily pissed off with him when he found out, but at the same time Johnny also knew his dad – though he would never admit it – would be relieved that she wasn't shacked up with some fella, which no doubt his imagination and Lorna had convinced him she would. He also knew his father's pride would stop him going round to see his mother at the flat, so until he was ready to tell his dad about Harley, his secret would still be safe.

'I ain't seen her Mum. Dad says she's coming home from hospital tomorrow apparently, but I'll be keeping a low profile.'

'How was your Dad when you talked to him?'

Johnny noticed how his mum's voice softened and her eyes looked sad as she spoke. It was clear they both loved each other but they were equally as stubborn when it came to backing down on something.

'I think he's in a bad way, Mum. He asked me to sort out the clubs for now. Why don't you just go back?'

Gypsy put her hand up. 'If you've come here to try and

persuade me to go back, you can forget it darlin'. I know he's your dad but the man drives me over the edge. Staying here will be the first bit of peace I've had from him since I've been married.'

'All I want is for you to be happy.'

'I know you do, but if he's sent you to talk to me, do me a favour sweetheart; don't.'

Gypsy got up and walked across to finish off the coffee she'd ordered from room service. It was true what she said about it being the first bit of peace she'd had from Frankie, but even though it'd been only a few hours, she was hating every moment. She'd wanted the freedom but she'd also wanted her husband too. Was that so much to ask?

'That's not what I came here for, Mum. If you really don't want to go back, I might be able to help you, but first I've got something to tell you.'

'Good news I hope son. I could do with some.'

'Yeah, it is. Well I think so.'

'Go on babe. I'm all ears.'

Johnny watched his mother sit down eagerly. He took a deep breath, noticing he didn't feel as anxious as he did before. Maybe this was going to be easier than he thought.

'You're a grandmother.'

'Sorry?'

'I've got a kid.'

Johnny watched his mother's face and then saw a grin appear.

'When? Crikey son, you kept that quiet.'

'She's four.'

'Four! How come you're only saying now? Have you only just found out?'

'No, I've known all the time.'

Gypsy's face dropped and she looked serious.

'So why didn't you tell me, Johnny? Why keep it schtum? Why didn't you come to me? You know me better than that; I would've been there for you, for both of you. Are you still with her?'

'Yeah, but it's complicated.'

'Nothing can be complicated about me being a grandmother.'

Gypsy roared with laughter as she heard herself.

'Hear that? Grandmother. Makes me sound old. And does your dad know about this?'

'No.'

'What's up with you, Johnny? Is this why you've kept yourself to yourself a bit more these last few years? I was worried but I just thought it was you turning into a man; needing your space. It makes sense now. Though I don't understand why there's all this secrecy. For what?'

'I guessed I thought you and Dad would . . .'

'Would what? Disapprove? Have you lost your nut? Your Dad earns his living from Toms and I've been chasing women out of your bedroom since you were fourteen. So a beautiful baby ain't going to matter to us is it?'

'It's who the mother is.'

'Oh what! Go on tell me; she's only a few years younger than me.'

'No.'

'Is she black? Because Johnny, don't insult me by saying you thought I'd mind, I ain't having that. You know I'm not like that at all . . .'

Johnny stood up, agitated.

'No, she's not older, she's not black, she's not even in a flipping wheelchair.'

'Well what then? What's so bad you ain't telling me? I'm not following you babe. What you getting upset about?'

'She's a Donaldson, okay? That's what she is. Through and through, a Donaldson.'

Gypsy's face drained. She sat back on the bed, her whole body beginning to shake.

Johnny watched his mother's reaction, slightly disturbed by seeing her in shock.

'I know it's a bit of a surprise, but . . .'

Gypsy looked up, her face rigid with tension, mouth drawn back into a grimace. Spitting her words, she shook as she spoke to Johnny.

'A surprise? A surprise is a gift at Christmas time or a special holiday, even coming home to find the washing machine's flooded is a surprise. *They're* surprises, Johnny, not this.'

'I don't get it.'

'I don't want to talk to you; just get out of my room.'

Johnny had never seen his mother like this; he knew she might be upset but the hatred which was spewing out of her genuinely shocked him.

'What?'

'You heard me, get out of my sight.'

'What's wrong with you?'

Gypsy stood up and faced her son, her eyes glaring with anger as she raised her voice and threw her magazine at him.

'You never fucking listened did you? Why couldn't you just stay away like I told you? Why go there, Johnny? God knows there are enough whores in Soho to dip your dick in.'

Johnny was angry now. 'Maggie ain't a whore, you know that. I never planned it, it just happened.'

'It never just fucking happened, you stupid, stupid boy; nothing ever *just happens*. Now get out, Johnny. Now!'

'No. Stop it Mum! I know Dad hates them because of business, but you, what's your problem? You've always wound Dad up about the Donaldsons; pushing and pushing so he won't let his barrier down. Always wanting him to

236

continue the fight. It was you who stirred up the hatred. He would've let things drop a long time ago if it wasn't for you. You gave him so much grief, but he always thought you were backing him up but you weren't, were you? This is about you.'

'That's right, Johnny. About me, is that so bleeding hard to get into your cranial? It's about how I feel about them.'

'Oh yeah that's right, Mum, all about you. Sod the rest of us because otherwise it'd stop being about you.'

Gypsy was beside herself. 'Accept it, Johnny; you've fucked up. Fucked up so big, that *big* ain't coming into it anymore. Now for the last time; GET OUT!'

'And for the last time, Mum; no. Not until you tell me what's going on.'

Gypsy lashed out at her son, smacking him across his cheek. Her face was red and tears streamed down as she screamed whilst Johnny held onto her wrists, wanting to avoid getting another smack.

'Please, just go.'

'Harley, that's her name. She's your granddaughter. Don't that mean anything to you?'

'Don't mention her name to me. Do you understand? I don't want to hear her fucking name.'

'Well too bad, because you know what I'm going to do, I'm going to bring her to you, and then try telling me you don't feel anything.'

'I will *never* feel anything apart from hate towards the Donaldsons, Johnny. Why ain't that sinking in?'

Johnny let go of his mother's wrists.

'Why, Mum? Just tell me why.'

'Ain't no reason when it comes to hate. That's reason enough. So from now on, you stay away from that girlfriend of yours and her daughter. Do you understand?'

Johnny laughed out painfully. 'You ain't putting rules on

me mum. I'm a bit old for that now. I feel sorry for you because your hatred is going to make you miss out on such a special girl. God knows I've missed out on her long enough because of all this shit. Me and Mags have hidden away for years like a pair of flipping fugitives because of your feuds. But no more, Mum. From today, there ain't going to be no more hiding. Oh and you can stop calling her my girlfriend because she ain't; she's my wife.'

Gypsy, who was already reeling, staggered to the side to lean against the wall.

'You kill me, Mum, you know that. I thought you'd be different but you're as twisted as the rest of them. Decay in your own self-pity because I'm going to go home to Maggie.'

'You ain't, Johnny! You ain't.'

Gypsy flew at Johnny, catching the back of his neck with her nails. He flinched from the scratch and turned round, his eyes matching the flames of anger in his mother's, his voice as loud and raging as hers. 'That's where you're wrong, Mum. Me and Maggie are going to make a real start of it, become a family.'

'You can't. You just can't.'

'Why the fuck are you so against me and Maggie being together?'

Gypsy ran over to grab her bag and pulled out the letter, shoving it into Johnny's chest. 'Because he raped me. Max Donaldson raped me, and I've just found out he's your father.'

CHAPTER THIRTY-EIGHT

Gina Daniels was too hot and she was in pain. Her leg was hurting, her back was hurting, and as far as she was concerned her body might as well have had a forklift truck roll back and forth over her.

In truth, all Gina Daniels' symptoms were, was a flight of stairs. A flight of stairs she had to climb to get to Johnny's flat.

'No poxy lift, Sonya, can you believe it? What's that about, hey? Flats without a lift. Think I was living in some third world country rather than in bleedin' Soho. Johnny Taylor has some front.'

Sonya lifted her eyes away from the magazine she was reading to look at her friend who was shooting off her mouth, clad head to toe in knock off designer gear.

The sauna was always hot but the air conditioning had packed in making it hotter than usual and Gina's face was bathed in sweat. Her hair had lost any volume it ever once had as it lay sticking to her forehead.

'I don't know what I'm going to do, Sonya, but when I do, believe me it'll be so big, it'll make the Big Bang look like a bleedin' fart. I woke up this morning and I was aching all over, I could hardly move. I had to double-check to make sure I wasn't dead, my legs were that stiff I thought bleedin' rigor mortis had set in.'

Sonya yawned but didn't bother looking up again from her magazine. 'You'll live.'

'Yes but for how long, son, that's the bleedin' question ain't it? I might well take meself down Whitechapel later, have a look in the funeral parlour on the Mile End Road; pick myself out a decent coffin, because if this goes on any longer the only stairs I'll be climbing will be heaven's.'

After having a moan with her friend Sonya, Gina felt slightly better. She'd had a call from Gary, letting her know he hadn't been able to find Nicky. He also wanted her to go round to the flat to start cooking up some more crack, but she wasn't in the mood to be anyone else's errand boy, so she'd given him excuses.

The sun was high up in the sky as she walked slowly down Wardour Street towards Shaftsbury Avenue and Chinatown. She was going to buy herself some special fried rice and roast mixed meat. The summer always made her feel hungry. In fact, most times she felt hungry. She was almost able to taste it and she quickly crossed the road, taking her chances with a red double-decker bus.

At the corner of Leicester Square, she leant on the black railings to take off her coat, surveying the area; it'd changed so much over the years and was hardly recognisable from when she'd first come up West.

As she continued to watch the people pass her, she caught a quick glimpse of a familiar face in the crowd which made her forget any aching parts.

Hunched over and pestering some tourists, looking skinnier

than ever with greying skin and filthy clothes, was Nicky Donaldson.

'Nicky!'

Gina shouted loudly and she saw Nicky look to see where the voice was coming from before he quickly scuttled off. Gina wasn't sure if Nicky had seen her but he'd certainly heard his name being called and from the look on his face it'd made him very uncomfortable.

Bracing herself, Gina set off after him, banging into people and barging her way through the crowds whilst still keeping a good eye on the top of Nicky's head.

'Lord don't take me now.'

Gina spoke out loud as her heart raced and she struggled to catch her breath. She didn't want to lose sight of Nicky because whilst she was going to have to wear the soles of her shoes out going up and down the stairs to look after Harley, Nicky had got away with everything scot-free. And there was no way he was going to get away with ripping her off *and* making her into Johnny's scullery maid.

They were already in Irving Street and Gina could still see Nicky ahead of her. She wasn't sure how long she'd be able to keep up. Just as she thought it was hopeless, she saw Nicky glance around, prior to knocking on a brown door near the end of the street. Gina hung back not wanting to be seen, grateful to be able to stop and catch her breath.

The man who opened the door looked as bad as Nicky did. It was clear he was a junkie and clear it was a crack house. Gina had known there were a couple off Leicester Square but had never known for certain where they were. She wasn't going to bother knocking on the door; they weren't going to let her in; plus, she'd no wish to go in either. *She* wasn't that desperate to speak to Nicky, but she did know who was.

Getting out her phone from her oversized Chloé bag, Gina dialled someone who was not only desperate but who'd pay her to know where they could have a word in Nicky's ear.

'Hello Max, it's Gina.'

CHAPTER THIRTY-NINE

'No, Lorna, I ain't spending me pennies to make it Fort bleeding Knox. You're doing me head in. Gypsy's hardly going to be shunting up the drain pipes now is she?'

'I ain't saying she is, but don't you think we should add a few extra bits of security, just in case?'

'Just in case of what? There ain't no just-in-cases. So give it a hibernation will you?'

Lorna sat next to her brother in the car as he drove her home from the hospital. She'd liked it in there, not only because of the nurses running around after her, but because she felt safe. Going back to Frankie's, knowing he hadn't and wouldn't put anymore security in frightened her. But she couldn't say anything. As far as her brother was concerned Gypsy had attacked her, but Lorna knew different. She knew the real attacker was still out there, and all she could do was keep her mouth shut and pray he didn't come back.

Tommy Donaldson stood against the lamp post. Just standing. Just watching. The wooden blinds and curtains were shut and there was no lights on. Nobody had come in or out of the house since the Range Rover had pulled up and two people had gone in. He hadn't seen who they were though; the rain had been beating down too hard and blurred his vision.

He'd been standing there most of the day but he hadn't seen the woman and he needed to. He needed to see her face again. The face that'd haunted him since he was a child, the face he'd always thought had only been in his imagination.

It'd tortured him every time he'd closed his eyes and every time he'd opened them. Visions of childhood merged into nightmarish dreams. The voice, the face, all from his dreams – but now he knew it was real.

The rain began again, and Tommy pulled the collar up on his Boss navy trench coat. It'd gone cold and he was certain it must be quite late. He looked at his Rolex but couldn't manage to make out the time in the dark. As tired and cold as he was, he was prepared to stay. If it meant seeing her one more time, nothing else mattered.

Frankie and Lorna Taylor sat in the dark. Lorna muttered under her breath angrily; loud enough for Frankie to hear her annoyance but not loud enough for him to decipher the words.

Since they'd got home from the hospital her brother had hardly spoken a word and gloom had descendeed over the household. The curtains were shut and the light switch not used. This was certainly *not* how she imagined it would be.

She'd unceremoniously been brought home, bundled into the car with no care. She'd wanted to stay in the hospital but Frankie had just ignored her. She'd presumed she was going to have a home nurse to look after her, but Frankie had been on one since Gypsy had walked out and the only person he was caring about was himself. And he wasn't doing a very good job at that; by the looks of him, it didn't seem as if he was going to snap out of his misery anytime soon.

'Bleedin' hell Frank, look at the state of you. All you need now is a wedding gown and you'll have Miss Haversham down to a tee.'

Frankie only grunted and went to get changed, coming back to sit morosely in his silk Ralph Lauren pyjamas and dressing gown, ignoring most of the phone calls apart from one from Johnny.

'Frankie, it ain't going to do you or me any good having those blinds closed. We'll end up chalk white with bleeding rickets at this rate if we don't get any sun. The whole day's gone.'

'If you don't like it, Lorn, you know where your plane ticket is.'

Lorna bristled. She couldn't have Frankie seeing her as disposable. She needed to keep him on firm ground until he'd worked Gypsy out of his system and then by that time, it'd be too late; he'd be so used to having Lorna around he wouldn't want to see her go. Until that happened though, she'd have to try to keep her trap shut and humour him as best she could. Which she knew wouldn't be easy.

'Shall I get you a drink, Frank?'

'No.'

'What about something to eat? You can't sit about here and starve yourself to death.'

'So what do you propose I do then, Lorna, because it's like a steam train has hit me.'

At this point in the proceedings, Lorna Taylor was more than relieved that it was dark, so she could roll her eyes and pull a face without being seen. He was acting like a soppy maid and it was grinding on her nerves.

Gypsy was a greedy cow and she'd had it easy all these years, but now the shoe was on the other bleeding foot, and what a foot it was because she was going to kick Gypsy's arse with it. 'It's all well and good crying tears over your wife, Frank, but seems to me you've forgotten two things here. First, she was camel-humping some fella behind your back and the other thing is, though God knows I seem to have been overlooked in all this, your wife nearly done me in. If I wasn't lucky I might not have been sitting here now.'

Frankie let out a bellow. 'And bleeding hell, Lorn, wouldn't that be a pity. Imagine, if you weren't sitting here doing me nut in and I could sit here in peace. They'd be some tears I'd have shed.'

Lorna heard Frankie stand up, bang into some furniture and curse loudly before he switched on the light. When she looked at him, his face was red with anger as he growled out his words. 'I'll tell you some home truths darling, shall I? The *reason* I don't want to have the lights on is because I can't bear to see this place without me wife in it. I loved her, *do* love her, and maybe that sounds strange to you because as you *keep* reminding me Lorn, for some reason, she nearly had you six foot under. And as much as I tell my head I should hate her, my heart's not having it. It's telling me something else. So I'm *sorry* I ain't grinning and doing an impression of Billy Smart's travelling circus for you, but I'm fucked, darlin'; well and truly, and it's killing me . . .'

Frankie stopped. His words sticking in his throat as he welled up with emotion. When he'd composed himself again, he continued, trying to convince himself what he was saying was true. 'But don't worry, Lorn, it doesn't mean I'd even consider having her back. I know what she's done. If she came back banging down the front door and begging for forgiveness, I'd turn her away.'

'Well there's no need to worry on that score is there, Frank? We ain't seen hide nor hair of her and I doubt you will. She's probably out there having fun.'

Frankie glared at his sister. 'You can be an insensitive cow.'

Lorna curled her top lip and suddenly felt rather peckish. 'Only stating facts, Frankie. One of us has to be strong. It's no good us both drowning in a sea of tears is it?'

Frankie picked up his phone from the side, remembering from years gone by what it felt like to want to cry. He rubbed his eyes, cutting off the tears which were threatening to come. 'I'm going to get changed, then I'm off out.'

'Where?'

'Where? I'll tell you fucking where shall I, Lorn? As far away from here, and you, as possible. Don't worry – all the alarms are on, so there ain't no one breaking in but if they do, Lorn, just open your bleeding mouth and start talking. You'll soon get rid of them.'

Lorna looked at her brother and decided perhaps now wasn't the best time to ask him to bring home a Big Mac meal.

About to give it up for a lost cause and come back tomorrow, Tommy saw the light come on and felt his heart skip a beat. A few minutes later he saw the front door open and there, arranging his jacket, stood Frankie Taylor.

The sight of him made Tommy baulk. It didn't make sense. What was Frankie doing there? He'd always thought the Taylors lived off Carnaby street. If this is where they *did* live, who was the woman he'd seen coming into the kitchen? His wife? None of it made sense to Tommy but as he watched Frankie jump into his white Ranger Rover, he knew there was only one way to find out. Putting his head down and crossing the square, Tommy went towards the house.

Tommy was good at breaking into houses. In fact, he was one of the best in the game. His father had taught him at an early age how to break locks and as anything in life, practice made perfect.

The hall was exactly as he remembered it, and stepping into the dark kitchen brought back the memories of the attack. He pictured the woman lying on the floor in a pool of blood and then he recalled the sound of the other woman coming in, oblivious to his presence. But he hadn't been oblivious to her. He'd seen her.

The house was dark and Tommy carefully went up the grand curving staircase. He wasn't sure if the house was empty or not, so he needed to be careful. He walked along the landing, and stopped halfway to look at the framed photographs. He could just make them out thanks to the moonlight from the domed glass ceiling and there was no mistaking where he was; the Taylors'.

Tommy sneered at the photo of Frankie Taylor standing by a swimming pool somewhere, deeply tanned with so much bling around his neck he was surprised he didn't fall over. The next photo was of Johnny holding a snooker cue in one hand and a silver cup in the other. Then Tommy saw what he'd been looking for. Her picture. He was drawn to her eyes. They were the same as he remembered them from all those years ago. And as he thought back, his head started to hurt and the voice came loud and clear. But it was no longer just a voice in his mind. He knew the voice had been real.

Putting the photo in his pocket, Tommy glanced around before quietly making his way back downstairs, ignoring a sleeping Lorna in the front room, and made his way out back into Berkeley Square.

CHAPTER FORTY

Saucers had been knocked unconscious before. Many times before. But with each time she found it took longer for her to recover from it. Back in the day, once she'd come round she'd been able to get straight up and carry on with whatever she'd been doing. Maybe it was her age, or just Gary's fist had hit the bullseye. But regardless of whatever the reasons were behind it, Saucers was hurting, and as she leaned over the tiny sink in her bathroom the cut on her eye refused to stop bleeding.

Looking in the mirror, her face was puffy and her eye was slowly closing. She knew she needed to get her thoughts straight. Nicky was in trouble and she had to find him before Gary did. She hadn't been able to do anything last night. She'd laid on the floor most of the night and had only just been able to drag herself up onto the couch in the early hours of the morning where she'd slept until now.

The pounding of her head didn't stop as she went to get her phone. Whether she got into trouble with Johnny or not, she didn't care. All that mattered was Nicky. Johnny's phone went straight to voicemail but she left a message.

'Babe, it's Saucers. You need to call me straight back . . . it's important.'

The next person Saucers tried answered. 'Maggie, it's Saucers. Nicky's in trouble.'

Maggie listened to Saucers talk as they both hurried along Greek Street. She'd had to call Gina to come and look after Harley when she'd received Saucers' call.

Johnny's phone had been off and there was nobody else to look out for Harley. She didn't want to bring her mother into it; she knew if her father came home and found her mother not in at night there'd be trouble.

Johnny had told her to call Gina any time she needed to, and Maggie had presumed when she'd demanded her to come to the flat to look after Harley, there'd be the usual groans and melodrama as to why it was too much for her. However, when Gina had arrived at the flat she'd been inexplicably cordial to Maggie. 'You know the score Gina, if you need to leave the flat; don't. Me or Johnny will be in touch. I'm on my phone if you need me.'

'You got it sweetheart.'

Maggie had looked at Gina suspiciously. This was not the Gina Daniels she knew – or anyone knew for that matter. Gina Daniels was a mean person, but as she stood in the kitchen opposite her, she oozed amiability.

'What are you up to, Gina?'

'Can't think what you mean.'

'You know exactly what I mean. All these smiles, it isn't like you. You're up to something.'

'Can't a person be happy without being accused of being undercover?'

'If I find out you've done something, Gina, it won't just be Johnny you're worrying about; it'll be me too.'

'Charming.'

Maggie had just nodded and turned to leave, unaware of the money deal Gina had just made with Max Donaldson.

Saucers rushed up the stairs in front of Maggie as she finished telling her the story.

'I tried Johnny but his phone was turned off.'

'I appreciate you calling me, Saucers. I wish he'd told me how much trouble he was in.'

'He was worried about what he'd done to you and Harley. He was ashamed of it.'

'But I'm his sister. I know I've got a big mouth and my temper goes off like a spring but Nicky could've come to me.'

Saucers smiled but didn't say anything as she headed up the stairs and past the walk-ups to the top floor where she knew there was a small crack den, one which Nicky hung out in.

When they were on the landing, Saucers turned to Maggie.

'You know, I'm not sure if I should tell you this but Nicky told me Gina's been putting pressure on him to give her the money she owes him. Threatening that if he didn't, she'd tell Max about you and Johnny.'

Maggie's face drained of colour and she grasped Saucers' hand. 'Oh my God.'

'Listen, try not to worry. It'll be okay Maggie.'

Maggie smiled weakly at Saucers and spoke, her voice small and frightened. 'What about Nicky? Do you think we'll find him before Gary does?'

'I don't know, but we'll have a damn good try.'

'Hello son. Didn't think you'd see me again, did you? You look fucking pitiful. A little bird's been telling me a few things. What you've been up to and how you've been using my name to get stuff and not pay for it, but then we all know how much you like the gear. Whole of bleeding Soho knows it.'

'I'm sorry Dad . . . I . . .'

Max looked across at his son in disgust, as Gary bundled him into the car. He'd got a call from Gina telling him where he was and he'd been straight round to the crack den to collect him. Gary had dragged him out of the place, and now here was his son sitting in his car blubbering away, when nothing had even happened to him yet.

'Stop the whimpering, Nicky, or in a minute I'll have to stop the car to check and see if you've got a pair.'

His father craned his neck slightly backwards as Gary drove back to his flat. 'Let me out Dad, I'll get your money. I promise.'

'Son, you're one big joker ain't you? You must think I'm the bleeding clown.'

Nicky implored more to his father; his eyes wide from the pipe he'd been smoking and from the terror he felt.

'What do you want me to do?'

'I don't want anything, Nicky. Not that you can give me anyway. It's out of me hands now; I'm leaving it to Gary.'

'What if I were to tell you something. Would you let me out then?'

'There's nothing I want to hear.'

'There is, but then if I tell you, will you let me out?'

'You're starting to do me head in son. If you don't want me to brain you here and now, shut it.'

'It's about Maggie.'

Hearing his daughter's name was always of interest to Max, especially if it was something he didn't know about. Looking at his son with drips of sweat running down his pallid face, it was clear to Max the terror that his son was feeling would make him sell-out his beloved sister.

252

Max watched the traffic go by as Gary weaved expertly through it. He didn't look at his son as he spoke. 'Go on then, because I'm sensing the only thing I'll hear coming from your North and South is bullshit. But I'm listening, and this better be good. Then we can see about letting you out.'

Nicky swallowed and talked in a whisper, not wanting to hear the words which would betray Maggie, but ones which hopefully would get him out of the mess he was in.

'Maggie. She's seeing Johnny.'

Max's fists clenched. He bit down on his lip to try to stop himself smashing the passenger window. He turned to Nicky and spoke through gritted teeth, spitting fine droplets of stale saliva as he did so.

'Go on Nicky, carry on.'

'There's nothing else . . .'

Max bellowed, startling Gary who hadn't heard any of the conversation. 'I said, carry on.'

Nicky closed his eyes and Max saw Nicky's lips move. As Max watched him, he thought he caught what he was saying. He could be wrong, but Max had a strange suspicion he'd heard his son say some of the words from the prayer of contrition, the prayer of forgiveness.

After a moment Nicky opened his eyes. With a blank stare he turned to Max and spoke slowly and painfully as he pictured his sister's sad blue eyes. 'They're married. Maggie's no longer a Donaldson; she got away, Dad. They've got a flat together, off Tottenham Street, the new build . . . Now will you let me out?'

Max couldn't believe what he was hearing. Johnny and Maggie. His daughter. The liar. She'd gone behind his back. All this time she'd been sneaking behind his back with a Taylor, and clearly she was ready to leave. Well, she wasn't going to go anywhere. He would put a stop to Maggie's

253

plans and as he and his men had been watching the Taylors for the past couple of weeks, he knew exactly how.

Ignoring Nicky's pleading to get out of the car he spoke to Gary. 'Stop the car, Gary. Take Nicky to your flat. I'll catch you up, but there's something I need to go and do.'

CHAPTER FORTY-ONE

Johnny Taylor was messed up. Messed up to the extent that he couldn't remember where he lived, but something in the back of his mind told him he didn't want to know.

His phone had rung several times. From Maggie, from Saucers, but mostly from his mother. What she'd said to him, he remembered only too well. He didn't think he'd ever forget that.

Johnny sat in one of his father's clubs, a bottle of Jack Daniels in one hand and a double Rizla joint in the other.

'On one of your legendaries babe?'

Johnny tried to focus his eyes on the person who was talking to him, but between the darkness of the club and the flashing lights on the strip show stage it was impossible. So he just raised his bottle in hazy acknowledgement.

The room started to spin and Johnny lay back on the sofa in the club feeling the loud beat of the bass going through his body. But no matter how drunk, he couldn't stop thinking. As he took a swig of Jack Daniels out of the bottle – half of it spilling over his face – he knew no amount of whiskey would blank it out.

It all made sense now. Why his mother had never allowed

his father to drop the fight with Max. All this time she'd had to carry the pain on her own. And the first person she'd told was him – and what'd he done? He'd looked at her like scum before walking out of the room and out of the hotel without saying a word.

He wanted to kill Max for what he'd done. But that of course was the easy part. What wasn't easy was what it meant by Max being his father. It meant Maggie was his . . . He couldn't think about it. Fuck. Fuck. Fuck. He refused to. His head wouldn't get around it. It was too awful, too shocking to think what he and Maggie had done. What they'd produced together, albeit without knowing.

But what gave him the most enormous amount of pain was the fact that he and Maggie, the woman he'd loved from the very first day they'd met, the woman he'd held in his arms and the woman he'd die for, could never be together again. He could never be Harley's father anymore, never be Maggie's husband. It was over before it'd had the chance to begin.

He curled himself around the bottle of Jack Daniels and openly let the tears fall. As he stared up to the ceiling, he suddenly felt the need to go and see Harley. He didn't know if he'd be able to see her again. He didn't know what was going to happen and before he gave Maggie the news, he wanted to see his daughter in the innocent light she was. He wanted to remember her the way she should be remembered.

He staggered up, still holding the whiskey and walked towards the exit. The hostess on the door purred at Johnny.

'Going somewhere? Sure you should be walking about in that state? If you're looking for company, I can sort you out sweetie.'

Johnny took another swig of the JDs and grinned as he swayed unsteadily on his feet, slurring his words as he spoke.

'Thanks for the offer darling, but I'm off home to see my baby.'

And with that, Johnny Taylor stumbled out of the club, trying to remember how to get back to his flat.

'He ain't answering darlin'. Saucers smiled softly at Maggie who looked like she was going to drop.

'Where could he be?'

'You know Johnny. He's always doing his disappearing acts.'

'I need to speak to him, put some boys on the lookout for Nicky. Christ, Saucers, I'm worried.'

'I know babe. But listen, maybe you should get back home. I don't know where else we can look. We've been to all the crack dens, all the clubs he hung around in. None of the girls have seen him. He'll turn up.'

Saucers hoped her voice sounded more confident than she felt. She'd thought they'd have a hope of finding him, presuming someone must have seen him but no one had, and to Saucers it was a bad sign. A very bad one.

Her face was still hurting and she didn't doubt Nicky would have some of the same but a whole lot more of it.

'Maybe we should go back to Gary's? See if he's come back. I ain't scared of the likes of him. Not once my temper's up. Honest to God Saucers, I've been keeping it under wraps. It deserves a bit of airing.'

Saucers grinned. There were very few people Maggie Donaldson was scared of but she was no bully. She was a loving friend, a loyal, caring woman who'd had to deal with more shit in her life than the London sewers. And even after all Nicky had done to Maggie – betraying her by sniffing Harley's wellbeing up his nose – she was still running around London wanting to save him.

As they walked past one of Frankie's clubs, Saucers waved to the hostess on the door, whose name was Jenny.

'Alright girl, how's tricks?'

'It's a bit quiet tonight but I'm not complaining. Frankie's not in and I saw Johnny go off a while ago; he's on one of his legendaries.'

Maggie spoke up. 'When? Do you know where he was going?'

Jenny eyed Maggie suspiciously. She was aware who she was and knew her reputation of being a hard bird but it still didn't make it alright for her to butt into the conversation she was having with Saucers. She answered, wanting to make sure Maggie knew she was annoyed with her, but not too much that Maggie would take offence. She'd no wish to be on the other side of a Donaldson. Especially one whose temper preceded them.

'I might do.'

Maggie stepped forward narrowing her eyes, remembering to count to ten as she spoke. 'Don't play games with me. Do you or don't you? I won't ask you again.'

Saucers, seeing the confrontation and not wanting it to escalate even more, jumped in quickly. 'It's alright Jen, you can tell her.'

Jenny pouted her lips and checked her chipped nails, purposely making Maggie wait for the answer. 'He was on one of his legendaries – clinging onto a bottle of whiskey like it was a flipping life raft. Anyhow, he said he was off home to see his baby. Lucky girl is all I can say. I wouldn't mind having a piece of it. Some of the girls who've been with hi—'

'Alright Jen, that's all.'

Saucers stopped Jenny, not wanting her to say anymore. Johnny was like all the other men she'd known; though in fairness, his indiscretions only happened when he was on one of his legendaries. Unlike any other man she'd known, however, his heart was only with Maggie.

Saucers pushed Maggie away as she spoke, cutting her

eye at Jenny who shrugged, not quite knowing what she'd done wrong.

'Okay, well that's good. At least we know Johnny's gone to the flat to see Harley. You go back there and see him. I'll go and see if Gary's back.'

'No, I think I should go with you Saucers.'

'Listen, I'll be fine. I ain't stupid. He's done all he wants to do to me and, besides, it's not as if I'm going to advertise I'm there. I'll keep me head down and if I see he's in, I'll give you and Johnny a call.'

'Okay, if you're sure. And Saucers; thank you.'

Maggie watched Saucers walk away until she could no longer see her, then made her way quickly through the streets of Soho towards the flat. As she turned the corner from Tottenham Street into Scala Street, Maggie froze, and then let out a piercing scream which would stay with the onlookers for a long time after.

Saucers ran up the stairs two at a time. So much for her keeping her head down. But she'd heard shouting as she stood in the stairwell and there was no mistaking the voices. Gary's and Nicky's. And by the sound of Nicky's cry, there wasn't any time to make a phone call to Maggie. She wasn't going to wait. She already had enough guilt from kicking Nicky out. Perhaps none of this would be happening if it hadn't been for her.

'Get up, Nicky. Get up, you skanky motherfucker. Where did you think you were going, hiding out in a crack den like that? Did you think you could just run away without paying? People talk.'

'Leave him. Leave him alone, Gary.' Saucers ran in, speaking as she entered the flat and seeing the scene in front of her. Surprised by the intrusion, Gary turned to Saucers and hesitated for a moment to snarl at her, before lifting her off her feet with a hard backhand. The smack to her face split open her lip and she tumbled to the floor.

Not caring for herself, only concerned for Nicky, Saucers called his name as she attempted to crawl over to help her friend, who looked in a bad way. As she reached out her hand to him, Gary used all his strength to kick Nicky to the other side of the room. He rolled in agony, helpless and pathetic as Gary put his boot out, stopping Saucers getting nearer as he placed his foot on her head.

'Don't make it harder darlin'. He's going to get what he deserves.'

'Stop it please, Gary, please.'

Gary looked at Saucers as he pulled Nicky up by his hair to a kneeling position. 'What did you think was going to happen when I caught up with him? Thought we'd all be having a tea party?'

'Please, Gary. I'll get you the money. I'll work the streets for you. Do anything you want to me but leave him alone.'

'I don't *want* to do anything to you because I don't give a fuck about *you*. Never have, never will. So save the heroics babe.'

Saucers looked at Nicky. His face was distorted in pain. One of his eyes had swollen up so much he couldn't see out of it. The other eye was bloodied and his lid was torn. His bottom lip had doubled in size and blood dripped from it, down his chin and onto the floor.

'Nicky, I'm sorry. Nicky, please listen to me. I know you can hear me. I'm *so* sorry.'

'What's all this fecking commotion?'

Saucers felt sick as she saw Nicky's head jolt towards the sound of Max's voice coming into the room, along with an overpowering smell of petrol. She couldn't do anything besides watch as he walked over to Nicky.

Max held up Nicky's face towards him as he spoke, and Saucers saw his body trembling.

'Remember when you heard the stories of kids being caught smoking? Their parents would make them smoke the whole packet to make them sick. Try to deter them from doing it again. Well here's the thing, Nicky. You owe a lot of money because of the stuff you take, and I don't think anything will deter you. Not me, not Gary, so you need something to stop you son. You need to get sick to stop you doing it again.'

Max let go of Nicky's chin and went into his coat pocket, pulling out a paper package the size of half a bag of flour. Taking out his penknife, he cut it open and placed it on the table. The paper bag fell apart easily, spilling out its contents onto the wooden coffee table. Cocaine.

Max turned to Nicky. 'There you go boy. Take it. I'm going to stand here and watch you take the whole fucking lot. And you can be sure of one thing son, you won't be doing it again after that.'

Saucers screamed and without thinking ran over to Max and clutched his arm. 'Max, please no, you'll kill him. Nicky, don't let them do this.'

Max grabbed hold of Saucers, pulling her hair and putting her in a headlock. He banged her face with his forearm and shook her neck hard, painfully clicking one of her vertebra.

'You think you can challenge me? You think you can tell me what to do?'

A hoarse voice was heard. It was Nicky. 'Leave her alone, you bully.'

Max's fury turned back towards his son, letting go of Saucers who fell to the floor, crying. It was the first time Nicky had ever spoken back to him. Max scooped up a handful of cocaine, stuffing it into Nicky's face; making him splutter whilst he tried to turn his face away as Max roared with

261

anger. 'Say it again son, I dare you. Say it to me bleedin' face.'

Saliva, tears and cocaine spread across Nicky's face as he yelled back. 'Don't call me son; you've never been a father. We were your kids and all you did was terrify us. Look at me, Dad, I'm a junkie. That's all I've ever been, a junkie, and you were the one who did this to me. Look at Maggie, at Tommy, at Mum. You hurt us all. I'm not surprised Maggie ran off with Johnny Taylor. So fuck you and I hope you rot in hell, 'cos that's where we've been living all this time.'

Such was the strength behind Max's slap to his son's face, that it made Gary's arm judder as he held onto Nicky's hair. 'Very moving son. You should be a bleeding poet. Oh and don't you worry; I'll be sorting out Maggie and Loverboy. But until then, let's get on with why we're here. Take it.'

Max pushed Nicky towards the cocaine but it was all too much for Saucers; she ran out of the flat, down the stairs and into the street, searching the passing strangers, looking for someone to help her. She ran blindly, panicked and afraid, crossing roads without looking and as she ran across the junction of Soho Square, screeching brakes sounded in the deserted streets.

'What the fuck? I could've killed you.'

The driver got out of the car and walked towards her. It was Frankie.

'Frankie, Frankie, you've got to help me, please.'

Frankie Taylor stared in amazement at Saucers. He'd only seen her a couple of days ago laughing and joking in her usual manner, but now here she was in hysterics, her lip bust, dried blood covering her chin.

He put his arm around Saucers' shoulders and led her to his car, wondering if there was any woman on earth who didn't want something from him.

* * *

262

Max looked down at his son, who lay motionless and face down on the floor of Gary's flat. Max went into his pocket to see if his cigarettes were there; they weren't. He walked over to the drawn curtains and looked out, he had to get going. He had something very important he needed to do. He stretched and let out a loud fart before turning to Gary who talked in an excited manner.

'We did well.'

Max strolled across to where Gary was standing, bending over to put some coke on his finger, rubbing it onto his gums, feeling the tingle on them as he spoke.

'Well? My son's lying dead on the floor and you're calling that something good?'

Gary Levitt's excitement dropped into an enormous sense of apprehension. 'No . . . er . . . I didn't mean it like that.'

'Well what then?'

'I just thought . . .'

'There you go again, Gary; thinking. And that's going to be your downfall.'

'I won't do it again.'

Max let out a roar of laughter. 'What? *Think*? You're a fecking sheep, Gary, but maybe that's not such a bad thing. What is a bad thing, is that you'd do this.'

Max pointed at Nicky.

'Me?'

'Yeah, you were happy to watch me kill my son. Stood back and did nothing. What sort of person does that?'

Max walked closer to a red-faced Gary and hissed through gritted teeth as he continued to talk. 'I'll tell you, shall I Gary? A man who'd be prepared to do anything to get ahead. A man who if I didn't watch my own back would top me off.'

'I wouldn't do that to you.'

'Wouldn't you? Well we'll never know now, will we?'

Gary's voice was panicked. 'What . . . what are you going to do?'

'Let me worry about that. You've nothing to worry about; not any more.'

They were the last words Gary Levitt ever heard, as Max Donaldson expertly fired the bullet between his eyes.

The moment Frankie Taylor saw him he recognised him. Nicky Donaldson looking well and truly croaked, almost blue. As for the other one, he couldn't tell who that was. He was lying face down but he could see from the side he'd had a bullet through his head. It was pointless even checking him. He was a total goner. Frankie looked at Nicky again and saw Saucer's terrified expression.

'Is he alive? Frankie please, is he breathing?'

'I dunno darlin' but I'm out of here. Donaldsons aren't my territory.'

Frankie turned and walked out of the flat but within a minute of leaving, Saucers ran up to him, tugging on his coat.

'You can't leave, you can't.'

'Try stopping me sweetheart. Don't take me for a mug. You know I can't get involved and we've got a conversation to have; I don't take kindly to anyone I know having contact with this sort of scum. Makes me wonder about their loyalties.'

Frankie tried to move away but Saucers stayed holding onto him.

'Whatever you think of me is fine, Frankie, but I need your help. Yes, I know him. He's my friend but then so is Johnny, and I thought you were my friend too.

Frankie grabbed hold of Saucers' face.

'Playing games with dangerous men babe will get you into trouble. And no Saucers, we ain't friends; you're just some two-bit whore who works in one of my clubs.'

'Think what you like, Frankie. Say what you like, but please help Nicky.'

Frankie pushed Saucers away and marched down the stairs, but Saucers was relentless in her pursuit and manoeuvred herself in front of Frankie as he was opening the communal front door downstairs.

'What if that was your son up there? What if that was Johnny?'

'It wouldn't be, because he ain't bang on it.'

Walking out of the door Frankie heard Saucers cry out to him but he didn't turn round, only listened.

'No, and you know why that is? Because Johnny's lucky. He's lucky he's got you. I know you love Johnny and Johnny loves you, there ain't no denying that, but Nicky's had no one. Who do you think did this to him eh, Frankie? It was Max. That's what his dad does. So you see there's never been anyone to look out for Nicky the way you looked out for Johnny; nothing's ever come close. So I'm begging you Frankie, help me; help Nicky. Give him the chance he never had. Please, Frankie, I'm begging you . . . I'm begging you for him, but I'm also begging you for me . . . because I love him and I've never had anyone to look out for me either. I've never loved anyone before.'

Without looking back, Frankie Taylor walked to his car, trying to shut out Saucers' cries.

CHAPTER FORTY-TWO

Gypsy Taylor had a bad feeling; more than a bad feeling, and it wasn't helping not being able to get through to Johnny. She was angry with herself. Why had she told him – or at least why had she told him that way? After all these years of keeping it a secret, she'd blurted it out like that, but she'd been scared, terrified by what he'd told her.

The years of Johnny growing up had been so difficult and with each passing birthday her fear had grown as she hoped and prayed for her son to turn into the image of Frankie.

Johnny had grown, tall and charming, with dazzling eyes and a thick head of hair. Handsome to the point of turning heads, but Gypsy hadn't been able to see either Frankie or Max in him and over time she'd tried to push it to the back of her mind.

She'd known to keep it to herself. There was no way she'd ever contemplated telling her friends, though there'd been times when she'd looked at Frankie and longed to talk to him. Wanting to share her fears and heartache instead of carrying the secret on her own. But Frankie was old school; there'd be no small talk, he would've put Max at the bottom of the Thames – which hadn't been particularly her worry

– but the love between Frankie and Johnny was so strong. After being brought up in care, having a family of his own was central to who Frankie was, so the truth would've destroyed him. For all he loved Johnny, if he'd found out he wasn't his real son, the pain of that would've made Frankie reject him and drive him away.

She'd kept quiet for all these years because she'd wanted to protect Frankie and not lose him. But now because of Lorna having read the test results it'd all been pointless – she'd lost him anyway.

But when you keep a secret it starts to consume you, so Gypsy had decided that knowing couldn't be worse than not knowing. And in a way she'd convinced herself it was all alright. It'd taken her just over three years to work up to doing it and when she had, it'd been relatively easy to get the samples she needed.

She'd taken a swab of Frankie and Johnny's saliva off to the clinic in Park Crescent; it'd been simple to get it, pretending she wanted to test out a new toothbrush she discovered on them. They hadn't thought it strange, they were used to her making them her guinea pigs; bringing home new creams, new hair products, new scents she'd bought from the shops. Frankie was nearly as vain as she was, even though he pretended he wasn't.

'Alright Gypsy, I look like a right poof with this face cream on. Get it off me.'

'The lady in Harrods says it works as well as Botox. Says it's great for men too.'

'They saw you coming, Gyps, and they saw me wallet next to you. One hundred and fifty big ones on a pot of cream no bigger than a packet of tartare sauce in Eddie's.'

'Stop moaning and keep still.'

Even discovering that Frankie wasn't Johnny's father, she might've been able to live with once she'd got her head around it all, but once Lorna, Maggie and Harley were dropped into the equation, it turned into a nuclear bomb.

She'd escalated the feud with Max and Frankie into a monster, not allowing Frankie to put his guard down at any time, to the point where Frankie couldn't set eyes on Max without some sort of argument. Even after Frankie had been stabbed; a direct consequence of the drink throwing in the casino, she still hadn't been able to let it lie. She'd always tried to stir the hatred and sow the same seed of distrust into Johnny, only it hadn't worked. In fact, it had done the opposite, attracting her son to the forbidden beauty of Maggie Donaldson.

Maybe if Gypsy hadn't pushed quite so hard, Johnny would've left the Donaldsons alone. But it was too late to worry about that now. She needed to find her son. Speak to him and make sure he was alright. Then she'd sit down and think what to do next, but until then, the only person that mattered was Johnny.

Grabbing her coat, Gypsy walked out of the hotel and into the night deciding the first place she'd try to find her son was back at home. It'd mean having to see Lorna and Frankie but however much she didn't want to see either of them, Johnny was her main priority. They could give her all the grief they wanted to. Whether they liked it or not, she was going to walk inside her own house to see her son.

CHAPTER FORTY-THREE

Saucers was trembling. She tried to wipe away her tears and calm herself but seeing both Nicky and Gary lying face down, Nicky in a pool of vomit and Gary in a pool of blood, only made her tears come faster. She was afraid to go over to see if Nicky was breathing, which was stupid, but she was terrified he'd be dead. She couldn't face that; it felt like it was her fault that her Nicky had ended up like this. If she hadn't made him move out perhaps things might be different.

Knowing that she needed to at least try, she put her hands over her eyes then slowly moved towards Nicky, peeping through her fingers as she walked.

'I'll sort it.'

Saucers jumped round to see Frankie standing behind her. He smiled and gently touched her shoulder, moving her slightly out of the way, then leaned down to Nicky and turned him over. There was vomit coming out of his mouth, but when he put his face close to his, he felt the faintest breath.

'Is he breathing, Frank?'

'Just.'

Saucers got out her phone and Frankie looked at her incredulously. 'What are you doing?'

'Calling an ambulance.'

'Have you lost it girl? Firstly, he probably won't last that long if we wait, and secondly, in case you haven't noticed we've got a bullet in the head over there. The Old Bill will be crawling all over the place if we call the ambulance. I don't want that, and I'm sure you don't either.'

Saucers nodded. She knew the score.

'Here, hold this.'

Frankie passed Saucers his car keys, then effortlessly scooped Nicky up into his arms, carrying him quickly down to his waiting Range Rover. Saucers followed and couldn't stop herself from starting to weep again.

Frankie didn't say anything as he sped through the traffic towards Euston Road and the University College Hospital. He never thought he'd give the time of day to a Donaldson, but Saucer's desperation and love for Nicky had touched him.

He hadn't been able to do it; hadn't been able to ignore the pain and hurt in her voice. He was going soft, but what she'd said had struck a chord in him. When he'd got into his Range Rover and driven off, all he'd done was driven around the block and come straight back.

Maybe the way he was feeling was why he felt a connection with what Saucers had said. She was desperate and so was he. His heart was breaking for Gypsy and Saucers' heart was breaking for Nicky.

When he'd seen Nicky lying in the flat the second time, he'd seen just what a kid he really was. He didn't have to stretch his imagination very far to know what sort of life he would've had living in the Donaldson household. Jesus, he was getting soppy. Lorna was right; he was losing it.

As Frankie pulled into Accident and Emergency, Saucers touched his arm.

'Thank you. I owe you, Frankie; I owe you big time.'

Frankie looked at Saucers as he scrambled to undo his seatbelt. He didn't know whether he should laugh or cry. Of all the things he thought he'd be doing tonight, having a Donaldson at death's door in the back and an overly grateful hooker in the front wasn't one of them. A second later Frankie jumped out of the car, shouting for help.

'I think he's still breathing. He was when I put him in the car.'

Nicky was quickly put onto a stretcher and rushed to a cubicle, his face covered in a green breathing mask as monitors were placed on him. The junior doctor called out.

'There's no heartbeat. He's stopped breathing.'

A rush of doctors and nurses started to administer CPR, shouting orders to each other as Saucers and Frankie stood back and watched. A breathing tube was pushed down Nicky's throat whilst emergency drugs were pumped through his veins, and Frankie and Saucers held hands tightly as they watched the monitor continue to flatline whilst the doctor tried to shock Nicky's heart into beating. His body writhed up from the shock of the CPR but the monitor's output stayed the same. Then the registrar in charge made a judgement call.

'I think there's no point in continuing. I'm sorry.'

Saucers just stood there unable to say anything but found herself shaking Frankie's arm violently, wanting him to do something, and for all his hatred of the Donaldsons, Frankie Taylor stepped up to the mark.

'I ain't hearing you right, pal. You stop when I say you stop.'

'Sir, I don't think you understand.'

'Don't I? I think I do, it's written all over your face mate.'

'I'm sorry, but it's pointless continuing on someone like that.'

Frankie stepped forward, towering over the small Asian doctor, and spoke quickly. 'Try telling his friend it's pointless. When did saving someone's life become pointless? Or are you making judgements on people's lives, Doc? You might not like what you see lying there but to the people that love him, he's a person. Their friend, their brother, their son, their child. So you need to keep on going.'

'We've been doing that, we've tried, but . . .'

Interrupting, Frankie raised his voice and took hold of the doctor's starched white lapels. 'Then fucking try harder. I ain't leaving here until you show me you've done everything you can. You're going to treat him as if you were trying to save the fucking Queen, otherwise your colleagues here will be performing CPR on you. Do I make myself clear?'

The doctor looked around nervously, then nodded his head to the other casualty staff to continue to work on Nicky.

'200 joules. Charging . . . Stand clear. Oxygen away.'

The doctor put the defibulator pads on Nicky again. Frankie wasn't hopeful. He looked at Nicky and saw what a state he was in. His skin was almost blue. Track marks covered his arms. He was painfully thin and his face was badly swollen from the beating he'd had.

Frankie was about to turn to Saucers to say something but the sound of the monitor beginning to beep stopped him. A look of relief spread over the doctor's face as he spoke.

'He's back in sinus rhythm.'

For the first time Saucers was able to find her voice.

'He's going to be okay, Doc?'

'We'll take him straight up to the ICU. He's very weak and there's no guarantee his heart won't stop again, but he'll be in good hands up there.'

*   *   *

272

Saucers and Frankie sat in the Range Rover in the car park of the hospital. Neither of them spoke. Both of them were drained. It'd been an emotionally exhausting couple of hours. Eventually Saucers turned to Frankie and smiled. 'What changed your mind, Frankie?'

Frankie looked at Saucers and shrugged his shoulders.

'Who knows? Maybe I'm just getting soft in me old age babe. Maybe all that romance stuff you read is rubbing off on me.'

With that, Frankie drove them out of the car park into Gower Street looking for somewhere to eat, wondering why all the fire engines were suddenly crowding the streets.

CHAPTER FORTY-FOUR

Maggie ran towards the flats, her scream carrying with her. The fire raged from the top flat and the billows of black smoke flew out of the shattered windows, blackening the already darkened skies.

She cried out to anyone who'd listen.

'Help me . . . please! Harley's in there, my daughter's in there!'

She lurched forward to where the police and the fire marshals were standing, wanting to get nearer to the building, but finding herself held back. As she struggled to push through the human barrier they'd formed she shouted to no one in particular. 'Let me through, I've got to get through, you don't understand – my daughter's in there.'

'I'm sorry, madam; we can't let you go in. It's not safe.'

'She needs me, please, I've got to get to her,' she shrieked.

'I know and I'm hearing what you're saying, but we've got the best people in there working to stop the fire so we can get her out.'

Panic-stricken, Maggie turned to the stranger standing next to her who looked at Maggie with sympathy.

'What am I going to do? I can't lose her. I can't. I should've been there. I should never have left her. What was I thinking?'

'The fire brigade seem to know what they're doing. I'm sure—'

Maggie, not really listening, cut the woman off. 'Oh my God, Johnny's in there too. 'Oh my God!'

Maggie bolted forward again, this time managing to break through the small throng of people as she took them by surprise.

'Madam, no!'

Ignoring the shouts she raced into the flats, and into the deserted corridor. Even though the fire only seemed to be on the top floor the whole building was filled with toxic smoke.

Coughing, she covered her face with her jumper and attempted to climb the stairs, but the higher she went the thicker the smoke became. Her chest was tight and she wheezed with each breath she took, struggling to pull clean air into her lungs. She felt a searing pain in her eyes from the intensity of the smoke but the thought of her daughter trapped inside the flat pushed Maggie forward.

Through her clothes Maggie could feel the heat. It felt like the material was melting against her skin but she continued to climb the stairs, hearing the firemen above her on the next landing.

Each step was becoming more of an effort as the air became denser. She tried to shout but her throat tightened, making it impossible for her to speak. As she reached the top landing her arm was pulled back and through the black smoke it took a moment for her to see that it was a fire officer gesturing at her to go back down.

When she looked at him her jumper slipped from her mouth and Maggie inhaled the fumes, sending her into a painful coughing fit. She held onto the banister feeling herself being led back down the stairs. Dizzy, barely able to stay standing, Maggie was unable to put up a fight and was grateful for the supporting arm around her waist.

The fresh air hit her lungs and she fell to the ground as the fire officer let her go before turning to go back into the building. Maggie lay on the floor, pain cutting into her lungs and throat. She couldn't open her eyes; they were too painful, feeling as if glass was in them. She was hauled up by strong arms either side of her.

'I think we need to take you to hospital, get you checked out.'

Maggie strained to speak to the police officer but the words wouldn't come out. She just shook her head and attempted to open her eyes once more. The pain began to lessen as she blinked several times, managing to open them to face the policeman.

Maggie was led to the other side of the barrier and it was there that she noticed the film of black soot covering her clothing, triggering off the enormity of the situation inside her. She burst into tears, hoarse cries of pain between coughing fits. Shaking, she watched as the fire continued to rage, knowing every minute that passed was a minute less likely that anyone would get out alive.

Gypsy walked along the well-lit street and attempted to get through to Johnny on his mobile. She'd tried several times already but it was still going to voicemail. This time she left a message asking him to call but she didn't hold out much hope; she'd just have to wait until she saw him and then hopefully he'd listen to her. Saying sorry wouldn't be enough, but at least it was a start.

Walking through to Gower Street, Gypsy saw the fire engines rush past and in the distance she could see the smoke billowing high into the sky, coming from one of the buildings on Scala Street. Not wanting to get caught up in the commotion, she decided to walk home a different way.

The route around Great Portland Street was much longer, but it gave her time to think. She didn't quite know what she was going to say to Johnny when she saw him. He'd be in shock. She'd had the last twenty-five years to think about it and *she* was still in shock. There was no doubt in Gypsy's mind the way she'd blurted it out had done a lot of damage. It'd destroyed everything Johnny had known, and everything he thought he had.

Crossing the road, Gypsy had to stand back quickly as a car sped past, showering her clothes with the muddy remains of the rainwater from the night before.

'Oi! Thanks a lot mate,' Gypsy shouted loudly after the car. It was totally pointless but it made her feel better. There was a large stain on the white Armani trousers she'd bought only yesterday and now they were wet, the balmy evening felt chilly.

Gypsy quickened her pace, wanting to get to her house and see if Johnny was in, if he wasn't she'd go back to the hotel to change into some dry, clean clothes before she decided what to do from there.

When she'd walked out of the hospital the clothes she was wearing were the only ones she'd had to stand up in, but she'd gone down to some of the saunas in Whitechapel and bought some designer bits and pieces from the crack heads who came around daily.

She'd handed her house keys to Frankie in a grand gesture but she wasn't that stupid, she'd had a spare pair in her bag. It was important she'd done that though – if she hadn't, Gypsy knew that Frankie would've changed the locks, trying to make a statement. This way, as long as there was no one home, it allowed her to still be able to access the house to get her things, not that she'd make a habit of it.

The strange thing was she'd agreed to own up to hitting Lorna over the head because of the letter, but she'd never until now stopped to think who'd *actually* hurt Lorna.

Everything had been so mad, so chaotic, and then the added shock of Johnny and Maggie hadn't given her a moment to think about it. But now, it was actually terrifying to think that a stranger had come into their home and attacked Lorna.

The house was dark and Gypsy could see the blinds and curtains were all closed. It was unusual, but the top floor shutters were closed as well. In all the time they'd lived there they'd never bothered closing them. The house was tall and regal and from the top two floors you could see above the trees and most of the surrounding shops and houses, but no one could see in. Gypsy scowled. It was probably Lorna putting her touches on the place already.

Sighing, Gypsy pulled herself back from being upset. She had to remember that whatever Lorna chose to do in the house was her business; Gypsy no longer lived there, so what her husband and Lorna did or didn't do was no concern of hers anymore.

Striding across the residential square, Gypsy braced herself for what she knew could be make or break with Johnny. She hadn't been this scared in a long time.

Five minutes later and there was no answer. She'd rung the doorbell but she couldn't even hear it, it didn't seem like it was working, which also meant the alarms would be off as they were all connected.

The house looked too dark for anyone to be in, though there was a possibility that Lorna was in bed asleep. It was too early for Frankie or Johnny to sleep. The last time either of them had found themselves in bed before three in the morning was when Johnny was fifteen, and Frankie had got sunburned out in their villa in Marbella when he'd had too much red wine at lunchtime, dozing off in the heat of the midday sun.

Gypsy wasn't sure if she was relieved or not that Johnny wasn't in. She'd really wanted to get it over and done with, even though she was terrified of his reaction.

Popping in a piece of gum, Gypsy wondered if it was worth the risk of using her keys to let herself in and take some bits and pieces. Then, what did she actually have to lose? If she was caught she was caught. And as much as Frankie had said everything was his, she'd been the one to support him as he built up his club empire. If Lorna saw her and didn't like it, then she'd be more than happy to tell her where to stick her witch's fingers.

Unlocking the front door, Gypsy walked into the dark hallway. It wasn't pitch black due to the light coming in from the domed glass ceiling, but it was dark enough to have to step carefully. She went to turn on the small table lamp sitting on the hand-carved marble table. It wasn't working. She tried the main light. That didn't come on either. Power cut. Well, she'd have to get her things in the dark, though there was probably enough light to make her way up the stairs and to her bedroom.

Stepping forward further into the hallway Gypsy heard a familiar voice and a moment later, Lorna walked into the hall. 'Is that you, Frankie? Bleeding hell I was off to the land of nod in there. Dozed right off. With these blinds shut I don't know whether it's day or night. Frig me, if this carries on I'll end up like a flipping vampire . . .'

Lorna stopped as she saw Gypsy and even through the dark, Gypsy could see the hostility on her face.

'What you doing here, Gypsy? Does Frankie know you're here?'

'No, he doesn't. Like he doesn't know what a lying scheming cow *you* are.'

Lorna sniffed and folded her arms, pushing up her large breasts. 'You got what was coming and I got mine. Ain't no point in playing sourpuss. Maybe if you hadn't been so greedy for all these years, then it wouldn't have come to this.'

'Me? Greedy? We all know who's greedy here and I'm sure it won't be too long before Frankie finds out what you really are.'

'And who's going to tell him, eh? I ain't the one with the DNA test saying Frankie's not the father.'

'You keep your mouth shut on that.'

'Ain't that what I'm doing, Gyps? You stay away and keep your side of the bargain, and in return I'll keep my mouth shut.'

'You're something else, Lorna. How could you even think about doing it to Frankie and Johnny?'

'I'm doing nothing. You're the one who is – or rather *has*.'

'But you would. If I didn't falsely 'fess up to bashing you over the head, you would've told him. Do they mean nothing to you? You know what Frankie's pride's like? As much as he adores Johnny, if he thought for a second he wasn't his father his hurt would be so much he'd push Johnny away. It'd destroy two lives.'

'Like I say, *I* never cheated on no one.'

Anger flashed in Gypsy's eyes. 'You don't know anything about it, Lorn; it's not what you think.'

'No? Well I see what I see. And Johnny being another immaculate conception ain't going to wash with me.'

'One day, Lorna, maybe you'll realise what you're doing girl.'

'My heart bleeds. I ain't going to—'

The house phone rang and interrupted the terse conversation. Gypsy moved over to get it but Lorna barged past her and grabbed the phone. 'I think you've forgotten you don't live here any more. I'll get the phone if it's all the same to you. Hello?'

'Hello.'

'Hello?'

'Hello.'

'Bleedin' hell, I ain't saying it again and going round like a merry-go-round. Who is this?'

'Am I speaking to Gypsy?'

Lorna looked slyly at her sister in law, who was standing a few feet away. It didn't seem Gypsy had heard the caller's request. Lorna, curious as ever, moved away slightly before she began her pretence.

'Yes, speaking.'

'It's been a long time, Gypsy. Too long.'

'Who is this?'

'Surely I don't need to tell you that. Don't you recognise my voice – or perhaps you need to see me. Would you like that, Gypsy? I know I would.'

Lorna swallowed. She wasn't enjoying this. There was something about the caller which made her feel uncomfortable. Something about the way his voice lulled and hung in the air with a threatening tone. Lorna hardened her voice, hoping not to give away clues to either the caller or Gypsy that she was beginning to feel afraid.

'Enough with the games. I don't remember you, and if I'm honest I don't want to neither.'

Lorna slammed down the phone but within a moment it rang again, cutting shrilly through the air. She hesitated and then quickly picked it up. 'Didn't I make meself clear?'

'Oh perfectly, but the thing is I didn't make myself clear. I don't think you quite understand. You can't get rid of me that quickly, Gypsy. Did you really think you could? I came looking for you before, thought you'd be in but you weren't, so I had to make do with that fat friend of yours.

281

How is she, anyway? She put up one hell of a fight in your kitchen.'

Lorna was beyond frightened.

'Listen, I think you should do one.'

'You'd like that wouldn't you? Well, sorry. No can do. I'm coming to see you. In fact I'm just across the street, any second now I'll be at your door, and then we'll see if you remember me, Gypsy. And if you can't then I'll make you scream to remember. One . . . two . . .'

The line went dead and Lorna looked at Gypsy, her face taut. Gypsy was startled to see genuine fear on Lorna's face.

'What's the matter, Lorn? Lorna what's wrong?'

Lorna started to tremble, her face creasing as she began to cry with terrified tears. She ran to the front door and started to bolt it, hands trembling as she turned the key. Sweat dripped down her face and into her eyes, preventing her from seeing clearly in the already-dark hall. Lorna leant on the door, trembling and still unable to get out her words and Gypsy shook her hard, picking up on Lorna's terror.

'What's wrong?'

Lorna's words came spilling out in an incomprehensible jumble. 'He said he was . . .was . . . he said he was coming . . . We've got to lock the windows, Gyps. Oh my Christ.'

Gypsy still didn't understand what was happening but something was clearly very wrong, and she wasn't going to stand around waiting for questions to be answered when the fear was etched into Lorna's face and body. She ran to the front room and barred the windows, pulling the wooden shutters closed. Next she ran into the kitchen and did the same thing, hearing Lorna in the other rooms.

Once all the windows in the kitchen were done it was significantly darker and Gypsy took hold of Lorna's hand, leading her up the stairs. 'Come on, it's lighter up here. I'll phone Frankie.'

The phone rang again as they got to the landing and in the moonlight Gypsy saw Lorna's face change. The phone seemed so much louder than normal echoing around the hall and up to where they were standing on the first floor landing. Gypsy felt Lorna squeeze her arm tightly and as she began to walk over to the upstairs phone, Lorna pulled on her and whispered.

'Are you sure you should get that, Gypsy? Leave it.'

'It might be Frankie.'

Gypsy walked over to the phone.

'Hello?'

'Nine . . . ten. Coming, ready or not.'

CHAPTER FORTY-FIVE

'Pull over! Pull over!'

Saucers' sudden shrill voice made Frankie swerve. The Range Rover hit the bump of the kerb and before he'd fully stopped, Saucers had opened the passenger door and jumped out, running into the throng of people watching the building on Scala Street in flames.

Frankie watched as he saw Saucers speaking to a beautiful, but distressed looking woman. He was going to stay in the car; he wasn't interested in watching buildings burn or listening to more hysterical women. The last few hours had been draining enough.

Jesus. What was wrong with him? He was Frankie Taylor and here he was feeling *drained*. Gypsy had a lot to answer for. It was almost like his fucking balls had been cut off and he'd been emasculated the day she'd walked out.

Frankie looked at his watch. The doctor had told them to come back and see Nicky in a couple of hours, though he wouldn't, he'd just drop Saucers off. He'd done his good deed, gone against the grain in helping. He'd even called a favour in from his old buddy, Alfie Jennings, to use his 'cleaners' to get rid of Gary and the mess. And now he had, he was going to fuck off. Nicky was a Donaldson. Simple as. Helping didn't change anything between their families or how he felt about them.

Frankie was about to turn his head away when he caught a glimpse of Saucers beginning to cry hysterically and start pointing towards his car. What the hell was going on? Something was happening and it looked like he had no other choice but to find out exactly what it was.

'Oh my God.'

Saucers spoke half to herself and half to Maggie, clearly in a state of shock. She turned away from the firefighters who were still battling with the fire but were slowly getting it under control.

Maggie couldn't take her eyes off the entrance to the flats, praying that at any moment she'd see Harley being brought down safely. Saucers was telling her something but she couldn't answer; she could hardly think, let alone talk.

'Nicky, we found him. He's in hospital, but he's okay. The doctors think he'll be okay. I'm so sorry, I tried to stop it, I swear. Oh God, Maggie, he must have done it; I didn't think even he was capable of something like this.'

Maggie battled back the tears. She couldn't cope with any more; she didn't want to hear about Nicky or listen to Saucers, much as she loved her. All she needed to know was that her daughter and Johnny were alright. Everything was spinning around in her mind. She'd have to think about Nicky later, deal with it all another time. At least he was in hospital; it wasn't much comfort, though it was better than not knowing where he was, and for the time being he'd be safe.

A few seconds later, as Maggie watched the dying flames, a thought struck her. What had Saucers said? What did she mean by *he must have done it*? She turned to face her friend, her heart pounding as she looked at her, scared to know that what she was thinking was right. 'Saucers – say that again. Who were you talking about? Tell me who you think must have done it?'

Saucers saw the pain in Maggie's eyes and answered in a whisper. 'Max. I think it was Max who did this.'

Maggie screamed, letting go of any control she'd been trying to hold onto.

'He found out about you and Johnny, I heard him say something to Nicky about it. When I saw Max earlier he stank of petrol. Oh my God, it all makes sense now.'

Frankie stepped into the conversation as he approached them. 'You and Johnny what? Who is this? Can someone tell me what the fuck is going on?'

Maggie ignored Frankie but he grabbed hold of Saucers' arm. 'What's she talking about Johnny for?'

Saucers only hesitated a moment before speaking. 'They were together. Maggie is Nicky's sister. She and Johnny were together.'

Maggie stood and shook her head, speaking in anguished tones, ignoring the look of horror on Frankie's face. 'Why would he do that to me? He's my father and he's done this. Our daughter's in there.'

Frankie spoke, hoping that what he was thinking wasn't true. 'Whose daughter?'

Maggie snapped, tired and scared. 'My daughter. Johnny's and mine.'

Frankie's face blanched. 'Dau . . . dau . . . daughter? You've got a daughter?'

'Yes, and they're in there.'

'They?'

'They? Who's they?'

'Johnny's in there as well.'

Frankie couldn't speak. At first he'd not really comprehended quite what was going on, but then his head clicked into gear and it all started to make sense. His face didn't move, his expression didn't alter, and his eyes just flickered once. He turned to Maggie and spoke coldly.

'Are you trying to tell me my son is in there?'

Maggie nodded.

'With our daughter; your grandchild.'

Frankie's head was spinning now. What was happening to him? He couldn't get his thoughts straight. He felt a pain shooting down his arm. If Gypsy was here she'd know what to do, but he didn't know how to react; it felt like he'd gone into shock. His default position was to get angry but he couldn't. And Frankie Taylor knew why. He couldn't get angry because for the first time in his life he was scared, really scared; terrified that he was standing outside a building where inside his son was being burnt alive.

That thought was all it took. The adrenalin kicked in and Frankie ran forward, bellowing and waving his arms around as if he was going into battle. No one was quite sure what was happening when they turned to look at Frankie, and anybody looking on might have laughed at the sight of Frankie Taylor charging towards the building, flaying his arms like an extra in *Braveheart*.

Maggie and Saucers ran forward to Frankie, hoping to stop him, but they were all brought to a standstill as the doors of the building opened. The moment came which everybody had been dreading. Coming out of the building were two firemen carrying a stretcher – on it, a body bag. The scream was louder than most of the bystanders had ever heard. It only came to an end after Maggie Donaldson passed out after she watched Frankie Taylor clutching his heart and dropping to the ground.

CHAPTER FORTY-SIX

Frankie Taylor lay in a hospital cubicle alive and fully conscious, with only one thing on his mind. Nobody had told him anything yet but then they said they didn't know themselves. They'd have to wait until the morning to get clear answers. The body was too charred, too blackened with the fire to tell who it was and so they'd told him he'd have to wait. That's *all* he had to do. Wait and see if his son was alive or dead.

He'd come around in the back of the ambulance. Like the paramedics, he'd thought he was having a heart attack. When he'd seen the stretcher coming out of the building pains had shot down his arm, and his chest had become so tight it was as if a ten ton weight was crushing him, preventing him from breathing. Then he'd heard the scream and that was the last thing Frankie could remember.

They'd run check after check and had come to the conclusion it hadn't been his heart giving up on him, it had been stress, and now he felt like a bit of a fool.

He'd tried to call Lorna but her phone had gone onto voicemail and the home phone seemed permanently engaged. He'd given up and turned off his phone. In a way he was relieved not to have to speak to her; he wouldn't know where to start or how to begin.

Frankie's thoughts were broken by Saucers putting her head around the curtain. She gave a weak smile.

'I know it's a stupid question but are you alright, Frank? You had a bit of a shock tonight.'

Frankie narrowed his eyes. 'How much did you know?'

'What about?'

'Fuck me, not you as well. I need someone round here who'll give me the bones of things; the truth. Between Gypsy and Johnny . . .'

Frankie trailed off as he said his son's name and sucked in air. It was a head spin – he needed to call Gypsy, she would know what to do, but he was too furious with her right now. And even though he needed her more than ever and Johnny was her son too, his stubbornness and hurt wouldn't allow him to call her. She'd let him down but he was struggling to cope without her and the idea of that only fuelled his dismay at her absence. He was angry, hurt and confused. Most of all though, he was scared and the last time Frankie Taylor had felt like that was the day he'd been marched into the kids' home all those years ago.

'All I know Frank is Johnny and Maggie loved each other. They didn't want to hurt you, but sometimes these things happen. Ain't you read the books? Love happens. Surely that's enough for you?'

'Are you taking the piss girl? How can that be enough for me? If it wasn't for a Donaldson getting her claws into my son, none of this would have happened and I wouldn't be lying here wired up like a muppet.'

Saucers had heard enough. 'Listen to yourself, Frank. You've made it all about you. Well, let me tell you something which might come as a bit of a surprise. The whole world don't revolve around you. So get off your bleeding high horse and think of someone else.'

'Have a word with yourself darling; if it wasn't for me none of you would be sitting pretty. Everything you earn is thanks to me.'

Saucers looked at Frankie with scorn. 'Well, as Albert Einstein said, 'Try not to become a man of success, try to become a man of value.'

As Saucers began to storm off she heard a furious Frankie shouting after her. 'Yeah well, you can tell that Einstein from me, if he's got any sense he'll keep his nose out of my bleeding business.'

Saucers made her way up to the fourth floor and braced herself, knowing when the lift doors opened she had to be strong. She felt shaken by all the events, not least admitting to Frankie that she was in love with Nicky. Especially when for all the romantic novels she read, she hadn't even recognised it herself, not until that moment. She would go up and see Nicky later but for now, she had to go and check on Maggie and Harley.

The paediatric ICU unit was more depressing for the fact that the hospital had tried to make it cheerful. The ceilings were beautifully hand painted with favourite Disney characters and cheerful scenes of the outdoors, but to Saucers it was almost if they were trying too hard to make the visitors forget where they were – if they felt anything like she did, there was certainly no chance of that.

The nurse pointed Saucers in the right direction and as she walked to the end of the ward, she avoided looking to either side of her. She could cope with a lot of things but sick children whose lives hung in the balance was not one of them.

'Alright babe? How's she doing?'

Maggie looked up, relieved to see Saucers, and was unable

to hold back her emotions any longer. She burst into tears and gratefully accepted the shoulder to cry on. 'She's not good. Doctors were talking about her having respiratory failure; smoke burns in her lungs or something. To tell you the truth, Saucers, it just goes over me head. Can't take it in. She hasn't come round yet, but to see her lying there.'

'Don't beat yourself up. She's alive, that's the main thing.'

'What about Nicky, have you seen him again?'

'Not yet, but I'll go there after to see if there's any change.'

Maggie took a deep breath. She was scared to say the next sentence. 'What about Johnny? Have they found . . . do they know if it was . . .'

Saucers spoke very quietly and stroked Maggie's auburn hair as she stared at Harley. 'No, they won't know until morning, according to Frankie.'

'How is Frankie? Jesus, we need to take shares out in the hospital. It's like we've taken over the asylum.'

Maggie tried a smile but it waned and she put her head down again as Saucers answered her.

'Frankie's okay, he's sounding off, only because he's worried. It's all a mess though.'

'I know . . .'

'Maggie?'

Sheila Donaldson interrupted and looked at her daughter as she stood at the end of the bed staring at her granddaughter. Maggie turned to Saucers and spoke angrily.

'What's she doing here? Get her away from me.'

Saucers looked uncomfortable. She knew Maggie loved her mother and was just lashing out.

'Maybe it's better you come back another time, Sheila.'

'I'm not going anywhere till Maggie listens to me.'

'I don't want you anywhere near here.'

'Why are you angry with me, Maggie? What have I done?'

'You haven't done anything, Mum. That's the problem,

it's always been the problem, and now Nicky's lying in a hospital bed and so is Harley. Somehow you seem to have got away with it all scot-free.'

'That's not fair, Maggie; you know it's not like that.'

Maggie also knew she wasn't being fair, but she was hurting so much she needed to lash out at someone; as much as it was breaking her heart to do it, her mother was the perfect target.

The ICU nurse, sensing trouble, came around the bed to speak to the women cautiously but with the authority of someone who'd seen it all before. 'Is everything alright? Because this is not really the place to work out any disputes.'

The nurse didn't wait for an answer, she'd made her point, Immediately the women lowered their voices, as well as relaxing their body language.

'Maggie, please.'

'I can't do this, Mum; I'm going to get a coffee.'

Maggie walked out of the ward leaving Saucers with Harley. She needed to get some fresh air. Behind her she heard footsteps and turned to see her mother close behind. Not wanting to wait for the lift which would allow her mum to catch up with her, she headed for the emergency stairs.

'Maggie, wait! Maggie.'

'Leave me alone, Mum, please. I've told you, I don't want to speak to you at the moment.'

'Give me five minutes, that's all I ask.'

The women continued to run down the empty stairwell as they spoke.

'What is it about the word "no" that you don't get, Mum?'

'Please.'

Maggie halted and turned abruptly to face her mother who took a few seconds to catch up, then she spat her words out, anger pouring from her.

'All those times as a kid when I was getting the crap

beaten out of me, did I ask for your help? No, not once. In fact it was you who asked for mine. Calling out my name to come and help you as Dad hurt you. Wanting me to tend to your injuries. I was only a kid. Do you know how that made me feel, to see you like that? I prayed every night for you just to take us away to somewhere safe. Did it never occur to you that all we wanted was to feel safe? And when after all these years, Mum, I finally ask for your help; once, just once, you couldn't do it could you? You couldn't help me; you couldn't help Harley. Yet another generation of the Donaldsons messed up by violence.'

'I didn't know he'd do anything like that.'

Maggie laughed bitterly. 'Why not? How is starting a fire any different to anything else he's done? But then, it wouldn't have mattered if you did know, because it wouldn't have made a bit of difference. You would've still stood back and done nothing.'

'No, Maggie, no, that's not true . . . I'm so sorry.'

Maggie closed the distance between them as she stepped forward. 'I don't want your sorrys, Mum. They ain't going to make anyone better, and even though I love you so very much, I don't care you about you at the moment.'

Sheila's eyes filled with tears. 'Don't say that Maggie, please.'

Maggie walked off but Sheila caught hold of her sleeve. 'Maggie . . .'

'Don't. Don't make me think you're as bad as him.'

Sheila raised her voice but it was full of pain. 'I'm not.'

'The way I feel at the moment, doing nothing is as bad as doing what he did. So please, Mum, I'm begging you, just let me go.'

Sheila covered her ears like a small child and Maggie had to turn away to prevent seeing her mother in such pain.

'Don't say that, Maggie, please don't say that.'

Maggie was on a roll, letting all her pent-up despair out and she shouted venomously. 'I *will* say it because it's true.'

'No, no, no.'

Sheila still held her ears and shook her head and body. The tears were coming fast and the hurt in her voice was clear but Maggie carried on regardless. 'I trusted you, Mum – you were my mum but you were my friend as well. My best friend; I would've laid me life down for you and I got nothing in return. None of us did. And I've had enough.'

Sheila let go of her ears and shrieked, startling Maggie who'd never heard her mother raise her voice. She fell into a stunned silence as she watched her mother breakdown in front of her.

'I know Maggie, I know what I've done – and not a day goes by without me knowing how much I failed you. But I always thought you'd be alright because you were the strong one. You were the one who said no. You stood up to him and he could see your strength but I never had that, none of us did, only you. There was such strength within you. You were such a spirited child. My big blue-eyed girl; strong and unbreakable and there I was, your mother, unable to help any of you. I was so scared Maggie. I swear I wanted to help with Harley, I swear I did, but once you were gone, I . . . I was terrified. I could cope with the beatings, Mags, but it was what was inside my head I couldn't cope with; the fear he put inside me head.'

Sheila paused for a moment and looked at Maggie before she carried on talking. 'I know none of what I said will make any of it better but I never meant to hurt you, Maggie, and it's not that I didn't want to help; I just couldn't. I couldn't even help myself. Can you ever forgive me Maggie for bringing you into the world? I wouldn't blame you if you couldn't, because I can't forgive myself. I'm so, so sorry.'

'Oh God, Mum . . .'

'I'm so sorry, Maggie.'

Sheila tightened her body and shook her head, wiping her nose on her sleeve as Maggie opened her arms and held her mother, before grabbing hold of her mother's shoulders and gently shaking her.

'You listen to me, Sheila Donaldson. None of this is your fault. You hear me? What he's done to you, to us, is not your fault. Do you trust me?'

Sheila nodded.

'Then you *have* to believe what I'm saying – and believe this, he will never do it again. You understand me? I will never let him come near you or hurt you again.'

Maggie pulled her mother back into her and held her tight. Her father wouldn't get away with causing pain and terror to the people she loved. For the first time in her life, Maggie Donaldson wanted something from her father; revenge.

The humid night brought light showers of rain and the news everyone had been waiting for. Frankie – who'd discharged himself – Saucers and Maggie stood in a tiny room with an oversized window, all feeling no relief from the heat. A tall man dressed in a starched suit with a London fire brigade motif on his top pocket spoke to them. 'It looks like there was nobody else in the flat and although there'll still have to be lots of tests, it looks like the deceased person was a woman; but we can't be sure until we get dental records back. The person certainly wasn't six foot odd, like your son, nowhere near it in fact.'

Maggie nodded, her face strained. 'Gina. Oh my God, I forgot about Gina. Gina Daniels – that would make sense, she was helping to look after Harley.'

Frankie spoke up, uninterested in hearing or talking about anything apart from his son. 'When you say it doesn't look like anyone else was there, could it be possible . . .'

He took a deep breath, not wanting to say the words, but needing to know the answer. He looked at the three women in the room, all with the same expression of concern. Saucers gave him an encouraging smile and he was touched by her support, enabling him to say the next few words. 'Is it possible you can't find another body in the flat because he was burnt so badly his –'

The fire officer picked up on what Frankie was trying to say. 'His body disintegrated from the heat? No sir, it does of course happen but the fire was nowhere near hot enough to do that. I'm not sure where your son is, but it's certainly looking less and less likely that he was there.'

When the fire officer had gone, Frankie and the women were left standing in the room all quietly lost in their own thoughts. The overall feeling was one of relief. It was Frankie who spoke first. 'I'll wring his bleeding neck.'

Saucers burst into laughter, grateful she was able to let out some of her pent-up emotions. 'A minute ago, Frank, you would've done anything to make sure he was alright and now you want to bury him yourself.'

'Well I would've done anything when I thought he was dead; now I know he's not, I want to kill him.'

Saucers looked at Maggie who was still standing quietly, her face not moving. 'You alright babe? Maybe you should go home and have some rest.'

'No, I'm not leaving Harley or Nicky, and I'm certainly not going home. Saucers, I want you to do me a favour, find out if my mum's left the hospital. The only other place she'll be is back at home. Can you take her to your flat? I want her out of the way.'

Maggie turned her head and spoke to Frankie. 'I need your help, Frankie. Max started the fire and he needs stopping.'

Saucers spoke up as Frankie began to turn away. 'Please,

Frankie. If it wasn't for you, Nicky would be dead, and if Johnny had been in the flat Max would've killed him. You can't let him get away with it.'

This was the first Maggie was hearing about Frankie saving her brother; everything had happened so quickly and nothing had really sunk in. She looked at Frankie, not quite knowing what to say but then simply said 'thank you', hoping he'd hear the sincerity in her voice.

Frankie walked to the door and kept his back to them as he spoke. 'Now we know everyone's sorted we can stop this pretence. You're Donaldsons and I'm a Taylor – and some things just aren't supposed to be together. I'll deal with Max in my own way once I speak to Johnny, but I ain't teaming up with you; this ain't *Family Fortunes*.'

Maggie ran to the door where Frankie was standing.

'What about your granddaughter?

He turned to her with a dark look on her face. 'Like I say, some things aren't meant to be sweetheart. Now I've been very good about this whole thing, I've kept me mouth shut, but don't push it. To know you and Johnny were bed mates don't sit right at the back of my throat but I can just about handle it. What I can't stomach is you and him having a kid. It churns my stomach to know somehow my boy's got part of his genes in your freak of a daughter.'

The slap echoed round the room and Frankie gripped his own face, feeling the sting on his cheek. He snarled at Maggie.

'Once. I let you slap me once. Next time I won't be a gentleman, next time you'll be through that wall.'

Frankie swung open the door and marched out of the room as Saucers came up to Maggie, putting her arm around her shoulder as she spoke. 'I ain't one to split hairs but slapping Frankie; not sure if that was one of your better moves.'

CHAPTER FORTY-SEVEN

Lorna tried Frankie's mobile again. It was still switched off. Her hand was shaking and she could feel the drips of perspiration running down her face.

'It's turned off.'

'Keep trying, Lorn.'

'We're going to be murdered.'

Gypsy turned to Lorna angrily. 'This is what happens, Lorna, when you tell lies. Maybe now you'll tell him the truth, that it wasn't me.'

Even in the dark and under pressure, Gypsy could feel Lorna tensing up in defensiveness. 'This doesn't change anything, Gypsy Taylor.'

The phone rang again and both women froze. Gypsy took a deep breath as she heard Lorna start to whimper in the dark. She hissed at her, 'Shut up.'

They let the phone ring, hoping it'd cut off but it continued to ring. It was too much for Lorna to bear and she ran to pick it up, her voice loud and hysterical.

'What do you want?'

'Nine . . . ten, a fat dead hen.'

'What?'

Laughter came down the other end of the phone.

'Did you really think I'd let you lock me out? You've just locked us in. Surprise.'

The phone fell out of Lorna's hand and the words froze in the air. 'He's in the house.'

The bang behind them made Lorna and Gypsy jump in fright. They turned around and saw a shadowed figure in the dark. As they both opened their mouths to scream, Max Donaldson stepped into the moonlight. 'I wouldn't do that ladies.'

He turned to Gypsy and smiled. Lorna screamed, running for the top of the stairs, but Max stood in front of her, blocking her way. She ran towards the back of the house, shrieking as she ran.

'Nowhere to go darlin'.'

Max followed Lorna in long strides as she attempted to run, waddling from side to side towards the back room. She went to open the door but it wouldn't open.

'I don't think so, do you?'

Max laughed and swung his fist into Lorna's face, knocking her out cold. He turned and ran along the landing hearing Gypsy downstairs trying to undo the front door. It was dark but he could see her outline as she attempted to quickly undo the bolts. 'Do you think I'm going to let you go again, Gypsy?'

Max Donaldson sneered as he approached her, cornering her in the darkness against the hall table. He reached and stroked her face. 'It's been a long time.'

Gypsy spat in Max's face and waited for the inevitable hard slap which sent her reeling backwards. 'You ain't going to get away with whatever you're planning, Max. Frankie ain't going to just let you walk in here and do this.'

Max looked around and chuckled nastily. 'Oh yeah, I can see the cavalry coming.'

Gypsy scrambled up, frightened but defiant. 'You don't frighten me, not now Max, because I've got your number marked. I see what you are. And there's nothing you can do to me that you haven't done before. You can't hurt me more than you have already.'

'There's few things I hate more than women with a mouth on them. I'm surprised Frankie lasted this long with you. I don't suppose you ever told him about our little adventure did you?'

'If I had, Max, you wouldn't be standing here now.'

'So why didn't you tell him?'

Max walked closer to Gypsy and for the first time he saw hesitation in her eyes. He licked his lips and moved his finger down Gypsy's neck, stopping at the top of her blouse. She flinched and for some reason smelt petrol on him.

Max grinned. 'Do you know what I think? I think someone didn't tell him because they were afraid of what he'd say. Worried he wouldn't believe you. Worried he'd think it was *you* leading *me* on.'

'You . . . you, you don't know what you're talking about.'

'Don't I? I think I do.'

Gypsy stared into Max's eyes and she knew what he'd said was right. Max smirked and started to undo the belt on his trousers. 'I tell you what, how about you and me, for old-time's sake. What do you say, Gyps?'

Johnny Taylor woke up – or he hoped he had. He couldn't actually tell what was real and what wasn't any longer. He felt as if he was on death's door or perhaps he'd even gone through it. His head was the worst it'd ever been on one of his legendaries and it felt as if his throat had swollen, not allowing him to breathe properly. The amount of alcohol he'd consumed and the lines of gear had made him hallucinate to the point of becoming frightened, which wasn't an easy admission for the likes of Johnny Taylor to admit.

He was cold and sore and it wasn't helping that he was lying on his back, staring up into the darkness. He could see a crack of light a few centimetres away and he supposed it was the door which led somewhere, but even the thought of having to move exhausted him.

As he lay there he heard a loud scream and raised voices. It was the motivation he needed to sit up. His head felt like a lead weight and the pain shot through his brain. He winced and was about to give up and lie back down again when he heard another scream.

Looking around, his eyes began to adjust to the darkness and he suddenly realised where he was. There were the boxes, the skylight, the tool kit which was never used and never would be. The neatly packed away toys and the red racer bicycle. He was at home. He was in the attic. How the hell he'd got there and why, he didn't know; and trying to think about it was like looking into a black hole.

But if he *was* at home, who the hell was screaming like that? Johnny got up quietly and went to the door, still feeling slightly drunk. Cautiously he opened it and saw the house was in total darkness. Slowly and silently he felt his way down the stairs to the second floor of the house. The voices were getting louder but he couldn't see anyone. The stairwell twisted down to the first floor landing and Johnny opened the door. He had to pull it hard, it always jammed.

Pulling it open, he saw someone at the far end of the landing.

The pain was almost too much to bear as she crept along, but no pain in the world was going to stop her trying to get the hell out of there. She must have blacked out for a few minutes and in that time, they'd gone downstairs. She could hear Gypsy's voice and Lorna stood listening in the darkness, feeling more frightened than she had ever been in her life.

Stepping back, Lorna's body froze as she banged into something behind her which hadn't been there before. A hand spread its way around her face, pulling her backwards, clamping onto her mouth and cutting off her scream. Lorna struggled but the hold on her was too tight; her knees gave way and she sank to the ground as the person pulled her down. Her nose felt as if it was going to explode from the pressure of the hand on it – she could feel the blood coming down the back of her throat.

Shaking violently from pain and fear, Lorna felt her head being turned to face whoever was there. She squeezed her eyes shut, not wanting to see the intruder. A dim phone light shone in her face and blue eyes stared, piercing and fixed on her. It was Johnny. He whispered in her ear.

'I'm going to take my hand off your mouth Auntie Lorna, but don't make a sound. Are you okay? Just nod your head.'

Lorna nodded. The moment the hand was lifted Lorna broke down quietly and Johnny noticed her face was covered in blood. Her nose had been broken. In a whisper he spoke.

'What the hell's going on?'

Lorna blinked her eyes, so relieved to see her nephew.

'The man in the house, he's . . .'

Lorna's words were cut off as a loud scream came from downstairs. Straight away Johnny recognised it as Gypsy. He spoke urgently to Lorna. 'Is there anyone else here? My dad?'

'I don't know where he is. No one's answering their phone.'

'Stay here, do *not* move, and whatever you hear don't make a sound.'

Lorna's eyes filled up with tears as she nodded and watched Johnny stealthily make his way along the corridor.

*   *   *

Johnny got to the top of the stairs, pressing himself against the wall. He tried to put the fact he was feeling dizzy to the back of his mind; he didn't want to dwell on the knowledge he was still pissed and not as sharp as he'd liked to have been.

Even though it was dark it was hard not to be seen coming down the stairs. He wanted to surprise whoever it was; he'd have a better chance that way. He didn't have the gun he usually carried on him and he had no idea where he'd left it so he'd have to risk going without it.

Gypsy scratched Max's face, pushing him away as he pulled off his belt. He laughed and grabbed her as she tried to run. She was no match for him.

'Playing hard to get?'

He pulled at her hard, ripping her top and exposing the top of her black bra.

'Don't make this any harder on yourself, Gypsy; you know how it's going to end.'

Grabbing a fist of hair he pulled her to him and tried to force a kiss on her, but as he did he felt an arm lock around his throat. He instinctively let go of Gypsy and twisted around, getting the better of the person. Johnny stumbled back, struggling to keep on his feet as the alcohol whirled in his body. Gypsy screamed.

'Johnny!'

Seeing his mother with her dress torn drove him on. He threw a punch at Max, catching his chin and unbalancing him. As Max fell to the right, Johnny saw him pull something out of his pocket.

The knife glinted in the moonlight, the jagged teeth of it slashing the air. Johnny jumped back as Max lurched forward, swinging the weapon.

'Take me on, will you?'

Gypsy screamed and tried to grab Max.

'Leave him alone.'

'No, Mum, no!'

Johnny came forward to Gypsy as she grabbed Max's arm, but he easily flung her off, sending her spinning across the hall. The step Johnny had taken towards Max had put him in reaching distance of the steel blade, and a cold pain followed by a rush of warmth along Johnny's stomach followed. Immediately he fell to his knees clutching his stomach as the blood poured over his arm.

'Johnny!'

Gypsy's voice punctured the air as she watched Max grab her son by a clump of hair, rocking forward on his knees. Max brought the knife back again and again, stabbing and twisting the knife into Johnny's flesh, accompanied by Gypsy's screams. Max let go and Johnny fell to the side in a pool of dark blood.

'Now then, Gypsy, where were we?'

As Max came towards her a loud police siren was heard from outside, making him freeze for a second. He turned and started to head for the front door, but paused before he disappeared, sneering as he spoke. 'Don't think this is over yet Gypsy, we've still got unfinished business. This is only the start.'

Gypsy scrambled on all fours towards her son. She lifted his head and cradled him in her arms, crying.

'Johnny, please, please don't leave me.'

She could see she needed to get help and got up to run towards the front door which was still open from Max leaving, but as she stepped out her exit was blocked. She screamed and staggered back. The stranger walked into the hall and saw Johnny lying on the floor. He bent down and took a deep breath as he lifted him up, carrying him to the door. He stopped and turned to Gypsy. 'Where's your car?'

Without waiting for an answer, Tommy Donaldson walked out into the night, carrying Johnny in his arms.

Gypsy and Lorna clung to the headrest of the backseat as Tommy weaved in and out of the Soho traffic, taking a no left turn to tear right into the main entrance of the hospital.

Tommy drove towards the high red hoarding boards with the words 'emergency' written in reflective letters. In front of him was a barrier and, putting his foot down, he careered Gypsy's Porsche Cayenne 4x4 through it, snapping part of it off and scraping the serrated end of the pole down the side of her brand new car.

Screeching to a halt on the 'ambulance only' parking spot, the Accident and Emergency doors opened, triggered by the Porsche on the sensors.

As Tommy jumped out of the car covered in Johnny's blood, nursing staff swarmed around and like a well-oiled machine, had Johnny out of the car and onto the trolley within minutes.

Frankie, who'd got lost trying to find a place to have a smoke, turned the corner of the corridor. His mouth fell open as he saw Tommy and Gypsy covered in blood with a shell-shocked Lorna behind them.

'Holy Christ.'

Then he saw who was lying on the trolley. He let out an animalistic cry. 'No!'

As they ran he turned to Gypsy. 'What happened, Gypsy, what the hell happened?'

There was no answer as they watched the staff with organised urgency slide Johnny onto the waiting bed. Pink plastic needles were forced into veins on the back of Johnny's limp hand.

'Stand back.'

Frankie listened to the same words he'd heard only a few hours ago as the nurses attempted resuscitation by hand, but with every compression more blood pumped out from the abdominal gashes.

'Cut the clothes.'

The nurse cut away at Johnny's clothes and threw them to the side, beyond the pool of red which was spreading across the floor. The grey rubber wheels of the trolley were set in a shallow pool of coagulating blood. Tiny rivers of fresh blood haemorrhaged off the edge of the bed and ran in streams towards Frankie.

'We've got an output.'

CHAPTER FORTY-EIGHT

Nobody really knew how long they'd been waiting. It could've been a few minutes but it could've been a few hours. Everyone was in shock.

'You really should let a doctor see to you.'

The staff nurse looked at Gypsy kindly.

'I'm fine.'

'Well at least let me get you a top to wear.'

Gypsy nodded and became conscious of her torn dress coming off her shoulder with Johnny's dried blood all over her bra. Frankie, who hadn't said anything since they'd been brought into the family waiting room on the ICU turned to Gypsy with angry concern.

'What happened? It looked like a fucking blood bath down there. Look at you, Gyps.'

Lorna spoke up. 'Leave it Frank, not now eh?'

'Don't tell me not now, Lorn. Johnny's in theatre with his life in the balance and my wife looks like she's been on some hedonistic adventure.'

Gypsy stared with so much scorn at Frankie that he looked away, embarrassed at his crass comment. She stormed out of the room and headed for the stairs, leaving Lorna staring hard at Frankie. 'What did you bleeding say that for?' she shouted at her brother.

Lorna slapped him on his back as she marched out of the room, hoping to see if she could catch up with Gypsy.

'Gypsy, wait. I'm Tommy. Tommy Donaldson.'

Tommy stood in the dim corner of the fifth floor stairwell and put out his hand, his shirt still wet with Johnny's blood. Hearing his name she flinched back but she managed to answer him. 'Thank you for what you did.'

'You don't remember me?'

Gypsy studied his face and saw how handsome he was. Crystal blue eyes, a strong angular face and raven black hair but she didn't think she knew him. The name; yes, without a doubt. But him; no.

'I don't think we've met babe.'

Gypsy began to head down the stairs again, needing to get some fresh air and wanting to get away from this extraordinarily handsome but strange man.

'I heard you scream.'

Gypsy hesitated and spoke tightly.

'I know, and I'm grateful Tommy, really I am, but if you don't mind I want to go for a walk. Johnny's still in surgery, he'll probably be in there for a while yet.'

She got further down the stairs and she heard Tommy speak again. 'I knew my dad was planning something but I didn't know what. Ever since he stabbed Frankie, he's been more on edge than usual. So a few days ago I decided to follow him, to see what he was up to, and he led me to your house. Although I didn't know it was your house at the time. I hung around a bit and saw him talking to Lorna in the square. I didn't think much of it so I went to get some cigarettes, but when I walked back through the square to go home, I saw Dad coming out of your house and I knew. I just knew something bad had happened. I let myself into your house and that's when I saw Lorna in a pool of blood on the floor. But it was probably you he was after. All that fucking shit with Frankie had got right under his skin. I guess he knew the only real way to hurt Frankie was through his family – but I didn't know *you* were his family.'

Gypsy looked at Tommy strangely, feeling more and more uncomfortable with the conversation. 'So why were *you* at the house tonight as well?'

'Because I knew he'd eventually come back to finish it off. I didn't know when but I couldn't let him, not when I knew you were real. I couldn't let you scream again, Gypsy.'

Gypsy, not understanding, tensed up again. 'I don't know what you're talking about. I'm sorry but I really have to go.'

'I was there. I was there when he did it. When Max hurt you. I was only a boy at the time.'

Gypsy stopped and held onto the railings for support as Tommy gently walked towards her, taking off his jacket and putting it around her shoulders. She heard herself breathing heavily as she looked into Tommy's eyes and began to recognise him.

He was the boy with Max. The beautiful boy who couldn't have been older than five or six. She felt as if she was going to faint as she listened to Tommy speak again. He tilted his head and stared at Gypsy warmly, continuing to talk.

'It was your voice, your scream I heard. You're the woman in my dreams. The woman who's haunted my waking hours. I remember everything. But what I didn't realise was that you were real until I saw you on the day Lorna was attacked. It's you I see in the woods. It's you I see being dragged into the cottage before he left you in the car park. I see it and hear it all the time in my head and in my dreams, but what I see most of all Gypsy, what I see so clearly and so vividly is not being able to help you

309

when you screamed out. I couldn't stop it then but I can now – and I promise I will.'

Gypsy searched Tommy's face and the memories came flooding back as if it was only yesterday. They'd all been on the bus.

'Move along sweetie, I know you'd like to stay up close and personal but we've got to be fair darlin' and let these other passengers on.'

A passenger had taken it upon herself to shuffle everyone down the bus and Gypsy was squashed along with all the other people, including the little boy, pressed up against the window.

It was crowded and Gypsy was relieved to get off. Why she'd bothered going all the way to Essex she didn't know but Frankie was away and she'd got lonely in the house, so she'd thought she'd take a trip to the shops and see some of her mates who'd moved out of the East End and up to Essex.

It'd seemed like a good idea at the time but the car Frankie had bought her had packed in on her on the outskirts of Buckhurst Hill and now she was trying to make her way back to Soho. If Frankie knew she was out late, he'd have a fit. She wouldn't tell him and just make out she'd lent her car to her friend Molly.

'Hang on, wait up darlin'.'

Gypsy turned around as she walked towards the main road and saw a man she vaguely recognised from Soho, accompanied by a little boy no older than five or six. He smiled at her, his handsome face lighting up under the street lamps; he was one of the most angelic children Gypsy had seen.

'I recognise you, aren't you Frankie's missus? Long way from home. I'm Max by the way and this is my boy Tommy.'

'Well nice to meet you Max and Tommy. I'm Gypsy. I've been a bit of a clump really and took it upon meself to go

310

shopping and then the car broke down, found myself stranded. Good job Frankie's away; he'd go mad if he knew.'

'Well I won't tell him, if you don't.'

Max grinned at her.

'Seeing as though both of us are heading towards Wanstead High Street to get the bus up West, why don't we take the short cut across Hollow Ponds, it'll save us having to go all the way around or wait God knows how long for another bus. And if the boogie man does come along, I can always jump behind you for protection.'

Gypsy looked at the little boy who smiled at her, his beautiful eyes dazzling brightly. It couldn't do any harm; it wasn't as if anything would happen, he had his little boy with him.

'Okay, hopefully we can get there before midnight.'

Gypsy started to walk and to tell Max about her friend who'd just lost her job, hardly stopping to catch her breath as she did so.

The path into the woods was dark but the sky was clear, allowing the moonlight to cast shadows along the ground. When they got further into the woods she heard Max say her name.

'Gypsy?'

She turned to see if the little boy was alright; it must be difficult for him to keep up and it was getting late, but as she did a fist smashed against her face. The force knocked her to the floor and in the moonlight she saw the little boy's eyes wide in terror.

In her haze she felt herself being dragged along the ground as branches and stones scratched her. Semi-conscious, she heard a car engine and the cry of the little boy and she realised she was being driven somewhere.

*　*　*

She woke up on a bed naked and as she moved her head, she heard her name being called out. She heard it again, in a tiny whisper and then the closet door flung open and the little boy stood there watching her. He looked like he was going to say something, but the sound of Max coming through made him run into the corner, making her scream.

'Hello, Gypsy.' The grin on Max's face was like a demonic clown; his eyes were dark and vacant. She began to scream and she saw the boy cover his ears. Max taped her mouth and bound her hands. Slow tears trickled down her face, stuffing up her nose, making it harder to breathe. As the tape pulled back on her mouth, her eyes bulged with panic.

'Now we're going to have some fun.'

Gypsy's screams stopped. There was no one to hear her as she watched in horror as Max began to undo his belt.

The car park opposite Lexington Street was deserted. Gypsy sat next to Max, her hands still bound, terrified but with a small hope she might get out of it alive.

'Not a word; if I find out you've breathed a word of this I'm coming for you. Do you understand?'

Gypsy nodded her head and from the back she heard the little boy crying. Max shouted gruffly.

'Keep that fecking noise down.'

The crying didn't stop and Max got out of the car and grabbed his son.

'Stand there and shut up, if you don't want to feel me fist lad.'

Gypsy watched the boy stand shaking under the street light as Max got back into the car. He started to grope her, his hands everywhere as he grunted and groaned.

Ten minutes later he leant over and untied her hands.

'Remember, not a word.'

With that warning, he opened the passenger door, kicking Gypsy out onto the cold floor.

'Come on son, get in the fecking car.'

Max started up the engine and reversed, pulling to a stop as he waited for Tommy to run to the car. Gypsy watched as the little boy ran past but he paused for a moment standing above her, not knowing what to do as she lay at his feet, his eyes fearfully watching his father's car at all times. He gently reached down and put his small hand out, touching Gypsy's face. The boy opened his mouth and went to move towards her again but the beep of the horn was sounded and he ran off, leaving Gypsy alone.

Gypsy looked at Tommy who was staring at her. She spoke through her tears. 'I said nothing to anyone – when Frankie came home a few days later my face and body was so battered and bruised I ended up telling him I'd been hit by a car.'

'I'm sorry . . . I'm sorry I didn't . . .'

Gypsy smiled at him and spoke in the warmest voice Tommy had ever heard. 'Tommy, it wasn't you. If you hadn't been there, he probably would've killed me. You saved my life.'

Tommy put out his hand and touched Gypsy's face. Together they both closed their eyes, trying to shut away their shared secret memories.

At the top of the stairwell, Lorna backed away. She'd heard everything and for the first time in her life, she felt ashamed; ashamed at what she'd done to Gypsy.

CHAPTER FORTY-NINE

'He's lost a lot of blood in theatre but thankfully we managed to stop the bleeding and stitch him up before we exhausted the hospital supply – we've had to send off to Colindale for some more, but he should be alright for now, although we'll monitor him closely. He's critical, so the first twenty-four hours are what we need to get through.'

The doctor spoke as Johnny lay in the ICU ward, almost obscured by the amount of equipment around him. Gypsy, still in Tommy's jacket, and Lorna, Frankie and Maggie stood in the office, staring through the glass window at him.

Frankie turned to Maggie.

'You happy now? None of this would have happened if it wasn't for you. If something happens to him . . .'

Gypsy interrupted Frankie angrily.

'Leave her be, Frankie, it ain't her fault, none of this is. We're more to blame than her, the whole lot of us.'

Maggie shook her head but was grateful for the surprise support from Gypsy.

'I ain't going to stand here and listen to you lot at each other's throats,' Gypsy continued. 'Hasn't there been enough damage already?'

She turned to the doctor, fighting back the tears.

'Doctor, do you think it'll be okay if I go and get myself a coffee?'

'Of course, he'll be unconscious for quite some time.'

The ventilator rhythmically hissed in the side room where Johnny lay unconscious, gentle bleeping from the monitors and flashing from the five syringe driver pumps surrounding him in the dim lighting. From under the crisp white sheet which covered Johnny, drips and abdominal drains left in to catch and draw off any internal bleeding snaked out and hung visibly down the side of the bed.

The nurse, a large Chinese woman who was monitoring Johnny, checked the charts. She began to frown as she saw his heart rate begin to speed up. The monitor alarms started to beep as his blood pressure dropped; slowly at first, then quickly.

It was clear to Frankie and the others that she was getting increasingly anxious. They saw her speak but were unable to hear what she said to the sister in charge.

Frankie, unable to watch without knowing what was happening took it upon himself to go and speak to the nurse, closely followed by the others.

'Is everything alright?'

'Yes, it's fine sir.'

The nurse didn't look at Frankie and she continued to monitor the drains which were filling up quickly. Within only a minute, the nurse started to empty the blood from the drains into a cardboard bed pan. As the second pan started to fill up with red blood, another doctor and the sister in charge rushed across to the bed space, looking concerned.

'We need to do an arterial blood gas and if . . .'

Frankie grabbed hold of the doctor's arm, interrupting his conversation with the sister.

'What's going on with my son?'

'That's what we're trying to find out; it looks like he's having another internal bleed.'

The doctor looked down at Frankie's hand which still held onto his sleeve. 'And if you'd let us get on with our job, it'd be much easier.'

Frankie let go and stepped back, feeling Lorna's arm on his as they all watched the flurry of activity. The nurse hurriedly took a blood sample from the drainage pipes but within a couple of minutes came back ashen-faced, speaking to the doctor in medical jargon which Frankie or the others didn't understand. However, the urgency in the nurse's voice told them all they needed to know. Johnny was in trouble.

'His HB is 5.5.'

'Call the surgeons, get three units of blood, four pools of platelets and two units of FFP.'

'I will, but I think they ran out of O negative earlier: I don't know if there is any. I know a call was put in to Colindale.'

'Well bleep haematology and call the blood bank, try to find out what's happening. Tell them it's urgent.'

The activity within the ICU was driven by silent tension and to Frankie it was almost like watching a movie; watching but not being a part of it, unable to do anything to help.

The buzzing on the ICU unit security entrance made everyone turn their heads. The surgeon stood bleary-eyed, waiting to be let in. Once inside he walked straight up to the family and Frankie could almost smell the sleep on him. He spoke to the surgeon aggressively.

'I hope you're not going to fob me off and not tell me the score.'

'No, I'm here to explain. What we really need to do is take Johnny back down to theatre because he's bleeding again, but we can't because I've been told there's no more

316

of his blood match to use, and it's going to be at least two hours before it gets here. And his HB is . . .'

The nurse answered quickly. '5.5'

'With a HB of 5.5 there's a serious chance of his heart failing, so it's certainly not safe to operate.'

'Where the fuck am I? In a toy hospital? How can you tell me you ain't got any blood? What sort of place are you running? Just take him down to theatre and save him, ain't that what you're trained to do?'

'If he bleeds anymore, which he will in theatre, there won't be anything we can do to save his life. The situation is life-threatening so we need to keep him here until the blood comes – we'll do everything we can but I can't promise. I'm so sorry to have to tell you this.'

Maggie, who'd looked stunned throughout the whole of the conversation, spoke.

'So what you're telling us is if you had the blood you'd be able to operate?'

'Yes, but we can't take that risk; without blood we've lost him.'

Frankie had started to pace up and down, his face red with anger and his eyes wide with fear. 'Fuck that; fuck that for a reason for my son to die in front of my eyes. Because you didn't have the resources ain't going to be on his headstone.'

'I'm sorry; it's got to come all the way over from Colindale.'

'I'll go and get it from Colindale, I'll send one of my men; just tell me how to help save my son.'

The pain dominated Frankie's voice and he didn't bother wiping the tears away as they fell and listened to the doctor's reply. 'You going to get it wouldn't be any quicker. I've got one of my consultants to bleep Moorlands Blood Bank to see if they've got just one more unit of blood to push up his HB a bit. If they have, as long as he doesn't bleed again until the blood arrives, we could get him to theatre. Then he might have a fighting chance.'

'What about me, why can't I give blood? I'm his dad.'

'It's not as simple as that sir. It's a sensible idea but in practice not the way it works.'

'You're not hearing what I'm saying. Surely if I'm his dad I can help. It don't get simpler than that.'

'Yes, but you're not necessarily the same blood group, I didn't have a chance to look at his notes to see what blood type he is and if he gets the wrong blood we'll kill him and then there are no second chances.'

'If you don't know what blood group he is, then how the fuck can you tell me there ain't any?'

'Obviously my consultant knows; he's the one doing the checking. He bleeped me to advise me of the blood situation.'

'This can't be the end. I can't get me head round the fact you're telling me my son's not going to make it.'

As Frankie angrily pushed Lorna away who was trying her best to placate him, another doctor quietly thumbed through Johnny's notes. Almost under his breath he spoke.

'Actually Johnny's blood group is AB+ so he could receive his father's blood.'

Frankie grasping for any hope jumped onto what the other doctor had just said. 'What? Is that good?'

Frankie started to pull up his jacket sleeve. 'If there's something you can do, then do it. Take my blood.'

'We can't just take your blood and put it into him just like that.'

'Why not? You've just said I've got to be AB whatever it is, so what's the problem? Would it save him?'

'Well, there'd be no guarantees, but we shouldn't even be having this discussion.'

318

'But would it improve his chances?'

'In principle, yes. But as I say, we can't; there's screening procedures, HIV and other reasons.'

'What the fuck are you on about? I don't have bleeding AIDS. Do I look like some nancy boy to you mate?'

'I'm not suggesting anything sir, apart from we can't do what you're asking us to do.'

'You'd rather see my son die?'

'Of course not, it's just that it's not the correct procedure; we could get into trouble.'

Frankie defaulted to bellowing and in the quiet of the ICU it sounded as if a bomb had exploded. 'Trouble? You're worried about getting into trouble? You'll let my son die because of trouble? If that happens you will wish you were in trouble because what I'll put you in will make trouble look like thanks-fucking-giving. I will ask you once again. If you take my blood and put it into him, so long as he doesn't have anymore internal bleeding, it might save him?'

'Yes it might, but equally it might not.'

'Then you better try.'

The doctor, who'd been standing silently spoke up. 'Okay, we'll give it a shot.'

The surgeon whisked around in amazement. 'We can't do this.'

'Then I'll take responsibility for it as his doctor.'

The doctor looked at Frankie with the same calm manner and spoke to him. 'I'm putting my neck on the line but I want to help your son.'

The nurse who'd been monitoring Johnny and was anxious about the falling numbers on the monitor, helpfully interrupted the doctor. 'We've got veno-puncture sets on ICU, so we can just drain a unit of blood and transfuse Johnny straight away.'

*　　*　　*

319

In the side room the doctor ceremoniously washed his hands and put on his gloves whilst Frankie stretched out his arm preparing for his skin to be wiped with the alcohol swab.

'Ready?'

Frankie was more than ready and he just wished the doctor would hurry up, but he nodded, realising the doctor wanted some sort of response.

A surgical glove was tied around Frankie's arm and a pink cannula was put into his arm. He caught Maggie's eye and they exchanged glances, both at that moment calling an unspoken truce. The tape was strapped over the needle and expertly a two foot tube with a flat blood bag at the end was connected. With a quick check the doctor released the tourniquet on Frankie's arm. Immediately, dark red blood started to drain into the bag.

Everyone in the room stayed in silence as the bag filled up and Frankie began to feel slightly lightheaded. Within what seemed a few minutes, the doctor painlessly pulled the cannula out of his hand and capped off the bag.

With the solemnity of a funeral procession everyone followed the doctor with their heads bowed down and stopped by Johnny's bed as the bag of blood was placed on the drip stand. Everyone looked at each other knowing what they saw on each other's faces, was a mirror of their own.

'Bleeding hell all this drama has got me fit to bursting. I'm going for a wee, if I leave it any longer we'll be swimming in it.'

Frankie scowled at his sister, wishing that one day she'd learn just to keep it buttoned. He was rewarded by a scowl back as she threw her head in the air and walked off, waiting to be buzzed out of the ICU ward.

* * *

Gypsy threw water on her face in the toilets, trying to pull herself together. Her head didn't seem to be able to process the conversation she'd had with Tommy, nor what was happening with Johnny. Then of course there was the situation with Maggie, Harley and Johnny, and of course not forgetting the events of the night with Max. It was too vast, too high and too horrendous to cope with. The worst part about it all was she had no one to confide in.

Throwing more freezing cold water on her face, the toilet door was opened and Lorna waddled in.

'Okay, Gyps?'

Gypsy stared at her sister-in-law. The last thing she wanted was a ruck; there'd been enough to last a lifetime. Almost as if Lorna was reading her thoughts, she smiled at Gypsy.

'I ain't looking for trouble . . . I'm . . .'

The words wouldn't come out for Lorna, so unused to apologising or exchanging pleasantries was she. Instead she changed tack, reporting on the last half an hour's proceedings which Gypsy had missed.

'Friggin' hell, not sure if me nerves can keep being stretched over the edge like that. Johnny began to bleed again whilst you were gone.'

Gypsy threw the paper towel on the floor and began to run for the door.

'Don't panic babe, it's alright; for now anyway. Cut a long tale, they didn't have any blood but because Frankie's automatically the same blood type, he's giving him some, it'll . . .'

Gypsy didn't stop to listen to the rest. She ran faster than she ever had in her life, heading down the corridor, knocking the tea trolley out of the way. Almost skidding around the corner in her speed, she reached the ICU security door and began banging on it.

'Let me in. Open the door. Open the fucking door.'

From outside the unit Gypsy could see the others standing around the bed and the nurse turning on the roller clamp of the drip. The red drops of blood splashed down into the gelofusion, mixing together prior to slowly crawling down the giving set.

'No! Stop, you can't. Open the door.'

From behind her Lorna came up flustered and sweating as the ICU doors were buzzed open by a worried nurse before Lorna had managed to speak.

Gypsy ran in and across to where everyone was standing.

'Turn it off, you can't give it him, turn it off. Stop! You'll kill him.'

Frankie stood up and blocked Gypsy's way. 'What the hell is wrong with you woman?'

'Get out of me way, Frankie. Stop it. You've got to stop it going in. The blood. Stop it, it'll kill him, it's the wrong blood.'

Frankie shook Gypsy, horrified at the hysteria.

'For God's sake, pull yourself together; it's fine. They said it's alright because I'm his father.'

It took only a blink of a moment for Gypsy to screech her confession.

'But that's the thing, Frankie; you're not. You're not his father.'

Frankie dropped hold of her arms, frozen to the spot.

Gypsy pushed around him to where one nurse was racing to shut off the roller clamp, with the other one ripping the drip out of Johnny's hand before any of the blood entered his veins to poison him.

'Will he be alright? Will he be alright?'

The nurses ignored Gypsy as they continued to work and Lorna shouted above the chaos at the nurses.

'It's fine. It's fine.'

Gypsy turned, her eyes blazing. 'Have you lost your flipping mind? It ain't bleeding fine and you know it ain't. You saw the letter, didn't you just? You relished knowing the fact that Frankie ain't his dad. Are you happy now, Lorn? Feel good does it?'

'You don't understand.'

'I understand. I understand so well it's engraved on me head. I left because of it, because you told me to, so I understand all too well.'

'But you don't see. You don't.'

With tears in her eyes Gypsy screamed at Lorna. 'Enough. Enough already. You've done what you came here for. I get it.'

'You don't . . . you don't, because I lied. I lied, Gyps. Frankie *is* Johnny's father. I tampered with the letter, I changed the results.'

It took a few seconds for Gypsy to comprehend the enormity of Lorna's confession. And as it sank in, her face darkened and she lowered her voice. 'You did what?'

'I . . . I . . . I lied.'

Lorna flew backwards as Gypsy's fist came into contact with her face. She lay sprawled on the ground as Gypsy stood over her; anger, tears and pain etched into her face and in her voice.

'You evil bitch. What did you get out of it, eh? All this time I was out my mind, sick with it, and all this time it was a lie. For what, Lorn? An extra designer bag? Well you could've had it. You could've had it all. I wanted to be your mate all those years ago, I wanted you to like me, be the sister I never had, but all you did was make life difficult for me. But that wasn't enough was it? This time you came across with the sole intention of destroying me and Frankie. Well congratulations darling because you managed it. You know the last time I saw Johnny I was screaming at him. He told me about Harley. He came to look for my support and all I did was scream at him because I thought he'd been

323

shagging his own sister, because I thought Max was Johnny's father. And that's what he thinks. He left me at the hotel believing that and if he dies . . . if he dies . . .'

'I'm sorry . . . I know, I know what happened, I heard you talking to Tommy. I . . . Gypsy . . . I'm . . .'

Maggie looked dumbstruck. She glanced up at Frankie who was by the ICU unit doors waiting to be let out. She didn't know how much he'd heard but from the look on his face he was a man in turmoil. Maggie spoke to Gypsy.

'Gypsy, about me dad, what did you mean he . . .'

Gypsy snapped at Maggie as she ran after Frankie.

'Not now, Maggie. I'm sorry.'

The doors opened and Gypsy ran to follow Frankie as he walked out. Her voice was full of pain.

'I'm sorry, Frankie. I never wanted you to . . .'

'Find out? I bet you didn't. Max Donaldson, of all people. It makes sense now. I can see what a mug you were making of me. I bet you were laughing behind my back; you and him. Pretending you hated each other, making me have my own war with him when really you were like rabbits behind me back.'

'It wasn't like that, Frank.'

'Save it, Gypsy, save the fucking tears.'

'You have to listen to me.'

'No I don't darling, no I don't.'

'Frankie . . .'

He grabbed hold of Gypsy tightly, squeezing her arms hard. His distress ignited his words.

'Any other man would blow your fucking head off for what you've done but I ain't doing that, Gyps, I ain't going to go down to that level. I loved you babe, I know I never said it much, but I loved you.'

'I loved you too – I ain't stopped.'

Frankie raised his voice up another level. 'Don't insult me;

don't talk about loving me with the same mouth you've kissed him with.'

The image of Gypsy with Max flashed through Frankie. He smashed his hand on the wall, drawing pain, blood and relief all at the same time.

'Why won't you listen to me, Frankie?'

''Cos you've got nothing to say worth hearing. Now piss off out of my way, otherwise I won't be responsible for me actions.'

'Where are you going?'

'Where do you think? I'm going to do what I should've done a long time ago. I'm going to kill Max.'

CHAPTER FIFTY

Lorna leaned her weight against the white door of Frankie's Range Rover as he tried to push her away.

'You *will* listen to me, Frankie Taylor – whether you want to or not – and once you have, you don't have to see me again, if you don't want to.'

'Are you having a laugh darlin'? Which part of, *get the fuck out of my life* don't you understand?'

'Whatever you think of me Frank, that's okay. I reckon I deserve it.'

'You reckon?'

'Alright, I do. I deserve it for trying to make out Gypsy was the one who done me in.'

'You blackmailed her Lorn; my own sister blackmailing my wife. I just want to know why, Lorna? Why did you do it? You've left a hurricane of disaster behind you, so at least tell me why.'

Lorna hung her head but still kept her body firmly against the door. 'I know Frank, it's a bloody mess. I just wanted what you had.'

'Don't give me that, Lorn. I fed you the money *every* month. Everytime you called me up for something, I sorted it. I paid your rent while the muppet of a boyfriend you had did fuck all. I looked after you girl, so don't tell me otherwise and don't you dare try to tell me you wanted what I had. You got it.'

Lorna's eyes filled with tears but she controlled them and continued to look down at the gravelled car park floor.

'What you had Frankie, no money could buy. You had a family. A family who adored you and who you adored. I never had that, Frank. I ain't ever known what it was like for someone to look me in the eye the way Gypsy looks at you.'

'You've had boyfriends.'

'Yes, but they never gave me a look which said anything more than sex, anger, disgust or *what's for tea*? None of it said love. I want to have someone look at me like that, I want to know I'm worth enough for someone to love me.'

Frankie kicked the gravel hard, trying not to be moved by his sister's tears.

'So you thought, because you don't have it, you're going to mess it up for everyone else?'

'That's about the size of it . . . I'm sorry.'

Frankie looked at his sister and as much as he was angry at himself for doing it, his voice softened slightly. 'You say you've never had a family who loved you, but when you were a kid we had Mum.'

'Mum? Do me one Frank, she never loved us. Christ, she never loved herself. She lived unhappily and she died with the same sour expression on her face.'

Frankie bristled, not wanting to hear anything negative about his beloved mother. 'How many more people do you want to trash, Lorn? Why stop there? Why not trash Johnny as well while you're at it?'

'You know what I'm saying is true, Frank. Take those rose-tinted bifocals off and see our childhood for what it was.'

'The only thing I see is what you did, Lorn. But then again, who am I kidding? If Gypsy wasn't giving off behind me back, you couldn't have spread your poison like flipping manure.'

'She wasn't though, it wasn't like that. Gypsy didn't cheat or have an affair.'

'No? Tune me in. Let me guess, Lorn, it was a mistake and it happens.'

'Yeah it does, but it shouldn't – rape should never happen.'

CHAPTER FIFTY-ONE

Max Donaldson knew when it was time to lay low. And now was one of those times. Frankie was already on his tail no doubt and he wasn't going to wait around for it to be chopped off.

He started to throw some stuff into his bag; trousers, shirts, a few pairs of shoes. He wasn't too worried. He had enough money to last him a long time and once he got out of London, he'd head up to Manchester and call the big boys in to get rid of Frankie Taylor once and for all. He hoped it'd all be sorted within a couple of weeks; the last thing he wanted to do was to have to spend his time in some God-forsaken green field.

He stopped packing, sensing someone behind him. It was Sheila.

'Going somewhere?'

'What the hell has it got to do with you woman?'

Sheila didn't say anything; just walked into the room and opened the drawer of the white dresser, pulling out socks and underwear and putting them in Max's bag without fuss.

'I need you to drive me up to the place in Epping Forest Sheila, and then drop me off.'

'Won't you want the car?'

'If I wanted the fucking car, I'd take it wouldn't I? Jaysus woman, if you don't want a slap, stop asking me fecking questions.'

Shelia nodded and Max was pleased that after all these years she still remained subservient. But as she walked away, he failed to see the change in her eyes.

'I don't know where they're gone.'

Saucers stood in the front room of the Donaldsons' house whilst on the phone to Maggie. 'The place doesn't look like it's been cleared out. There's still dishes in the sink, washing on the table; the usual domestic bliss. It looks more like they've gone to the shops.'

On the other end of the phone Maggie chewed on her lip. She was worried about her mother, but she needed to catch up with her father. The one thing no one could afford was for Max to go underground. He'd be more dangerous than he was now and there was no telling what he'd do once he was under pressure.

She didn't want to leave the hospital. It seemed her whole family was in there. Nicky, Johnny, Harley; all hurt by Max, but if she wanted to stop it happening again, then she'd no choice. 'Listen, Saucers, I'll meet you in an hour. I think I know someone who'll know where he's gone.'

Maggie walked into Lola's Cafe on Bateman Street.

'Alright darlings, what do I owe this honour of having more than one Donaldson in me cafe? Tommy's been sitting over there waiting for you; says he's arranged to meet you, but I reckon word's got out that I'm doing my coronation chicken today.'

Maggie smiled as Lola cackled.

'Listen, Maggie, joking aside. I heard a bit of what

330

happened. Nicky, Johnny and a young lady going by the name of Harley; you kept that part quiet.'

'I know; I'm sorry.'

'Hey, don't apologise, keep what you like to yourself, but always know I'm here if you need to chew off an ear to chat about something.'

'Thank you.'

Maggie kissed Lola on the cheek, who blushed as she continued to talk. 'God forgive me but I can't say I'm sorry to hear about Gina Daniels. Nasty piece of work. But I bet we haven't got away that lightly – miserable cow will no doubt come back and haunt us all. We'll see her ghost on the corner of Berwick Street still touting for business if I know her.'

Lola chuckled, then pottered off to serve a customer who'd just walked in, leaving Maggie to go and speak to Tommy.

Her older brother greeted her with a nod. It was the first time they'd sat down together properly for a long time, and Maggie couldn't remember having a conversation with him since they'd been small.

'Thanks for meeting me, Tommy.'

It was a greeting which didn't require an answer and Maggie got straight to the point. 'I need you to help me find Dad. He can't get away with what he's done, not to any of us. He'll probably be more dangerous if he goes underground.'

Tommy said nothing and just stared at Maggie with his piercing blue eyes, not unkindly, but with a look she didn't really understand. Maggie called it his 'somewhere stare', and not for the first time she wished he'd let her in.

'And there's one other thing Tommy, I don't know where Mum is. She's not answering her phone.'

Tommy, already sitting up straight in his chair, seemed to sit up even higher. 'What do you mean?'

'It's probably nothing but it's unlike her not to be

contactable. The washing's still on the table and dishes in the sink and you know as well as I do, there's no way on earth she'd go out without doing them because of what Dad would do if she did. So my bet is she's probably with him, and the idea of that worries me.'

'Who've you spoken to?'

'I've had a word with the Winterson brothers, Tony Cragwell and the guys from south-east, as well as the Albanians who were more than willing to help me if they could; they've got their own beef with Dad. But no one's seen him, Tommy. Delanco and the men are still doing Dad's bag money rounds, but of course I can't speak to them. That leaves you; you did a lot of his rounds with him.'

Tommy bristled and sounded defensive. 'That ain't my fault, Maggie; I never asked to do those things with him.'

Maggie put her hand on Tommy's. 'I know Tommy; I'm not saying that. I just hoped you might be able to think of somewhere apart from the usual turf that he might be.'

'If he's really gone to ground and he's not in London, I know exactly where he'll be.'

It was only the second time Sheila Donaldson had been in the tiny property, but her shiver of disgust was no different from the first time she'd been taken there all those years ago, on what was supposed to be her honeymoon.

Max had driven her along the long deserted roads, and even though she'd already met with his fists before and even on their wedding day, foolishly there was a part of her which had hoped he was going to surprise her with something worthy of a new bride.

When she'd walked in, she'd seen the bare whitewashed rooms; the only pieces of furniture a bed in the middle of the small bedroom and a closet. The place had seemed inoffensive but on closer inspection she'd seen the handcuffs, the chains and hooks hanging discreetly from the corners of the room, and immediately she'd known what was going to happen.

There was plenty about those twenty-four hours that Sheila couldn't recall, but not being able to remember it was, as she saw it, the only light in a lot of darkness. The images she did have in her head were depraved, grotesque and humiliating, and over the years she'd disconnected from them, shut down a part of herself; forever locked away so that she could carry on breathing and carry on putting one foot in front of another. And even though over the years he'd abused her, nothing had come close to the horrors of those twenty-four hours.

She couldn't feel the terror or the pain anymore – and now, when she thought about the parts she *could* remember, it was as if she was watching someone else through a glass wall, seeing a person who was screaming for help, but she couldn't hear her cries.

All these years Sheila knew she'd been waiting for this moment, waiting for something to happen so her invisible cage could be unlocked, allowing her to escape. At times she'd thought it would never happen. The times she'd been beaten and raped, and the times she'd failed her children by allowing them to suffer at the hands of her husband; all those times she'd only been an observer in her own life and she'd felt worthless. But something inside her had kept her going, something had told her, one day; one day she'd be free. Now at last the waiting was over. Sheila Donaldson could finally unlock the door.

'Max.'

Max turned to look at his wife – and as he did so, he came face to face with the barrel end of a gun.

CHAPTER FIFTY-TWO

The convoy of Range Rovers drove with speed along the deserted roads to the north-east of Epping Forest. It was rural and sparsely populated for an area which was so close to London.

Frankie was in the lead Range Rover with a sullen-looking Lorna sitting next to him. They drove in silence, neither knowing what to say – it almost felt to both of them as if words weren't quite enough. Too many things had already been said.

Frankie had received the call from Maggie insisting she meet him, and as usual he'd dug his heels in far enough down to plant the summer bulbs; but Lorna had stopped him slamming the phone down, coming up to him when she'd heard him getting upset. She'd put her hand gently on him and spoken with an understanding he didn't know she had.

'Frank, we need to go and help sort this out.'

He'd let her take the phone from him to speak to Maggie, and when she was finished, she'd come to find him. 'You're in shock, Frank, but we need to go and do this and you need to talk to Gypsy.'

'I can't. I can't get me head round it.'

He'd been thrown a spiked curve ball by what Lorna had said to him, especially as he'd already been planning in his mind how to finish off Max. It was going to be easy; imagining Max Donaldson and his wife happily frolicking away had meant he was going to make him suffer until the last breath was pummelled out of his body, but when Lorna had said the word which seemed so short but held so much meaning, the word which explained what had happened to Gypsy all those years ago, it'd changed everything. It'd made him worse than bleeding useless.

'If it makes you feel like this, how do you think Gypsy's feeling? She's had to carry it around for all these years and then just as she's trying to get answers, I come along and destroy everything. I know you're hurting, Frank, and you do need to lick your wounds, but not now. You need to rise above how you feel darlin' and think of your wife. You can't just leave her on her own. She needs you more than ever.'

'I don't know, Lorn.'

His sister had got annoyed with him then which had surprised him. 'Well I do, even if you don't. Put down your dummy and grow up, this ain't about you.'

'Talk about a turnaround; a waltz has nothing on you. When did you become best friends with Gypsy?'

'Listen, I doubt Gypsy will ever talk to me again but that don't mean she has to stop speaking to you. None of this means the end, Frank. She needs caring for, not judging.'

'But she's been . . . I can't help it, but when I think of her and . . .'

'No, Frankie boy, I ain't listening; I don't want to hear it. She's the same woman you loved and you need to shovel that macho bullshit out of your head. Being raped is not the same as her sleeping with another man.'

He'd just nodded his head and then Lorna had given him

a hug and gently chivvied him along. 'Now get your keys and let's go and meet Maggie, we've got to help. After all, we're family now.'

The middle Range Rover was driven by Tommy, and next to him sat Gypsy. She hadn't wanted to go in the same car as Frankie, even though Lorna had texted her to say he now knew the truth about the situation. So when Tommy had suggested she jumped in his car, she'd leapt at the chance.

Frankie had been so quick to believe she was lying, which had hurt her but she'd put that to one side in her concern about Frankie and how he felt. But when she'd got the text from Frankie saying, *'I'm not angry now'* it'd only served to annoy her.

How lucky it was for Frankie Taylor not to be angry, well bully for him – because she was. It was her turn now, her turn to be angry about everything that had happened. So she'd ignored him. When Frankie didn't know what to say or was sorry about something he'd been caught out doing, like his numerous indiscretions or getting drunk and obnoxious at Christmas or at their villa in Spain, a pitiful, boyish look appeared on his face. And at times like that, Gypsy supposed it had a place. But for this? For what they were talking about, she needed more than soppy eyes and a hangdog expression; much more, but sadly, she wasn't sure that Frankie was capable of it.

The last Range Rover held Maggie. She'd almost lost faith in her family and any hope they could be mended, but here they were, albeit in the most difficult and extraordinary of circumstances, coming together as one. And no matter what happened in the future, she was going to hold onto this unique moment of unity for the rest of her life.

* * *

The cottage at the end of the path looked deserted but Tommy noticed the padlocks were open. Apart from the strong black metal door with three sturdy-looking locks, the rest of the place was rundown; although he came here on numerous occasions, he noticed it never more so than now.

Tommy was about to stride in, but Frankie, more cautious and worried that someone might be in there, held him back, then signalled to the others he was going in. Kicking open the door, Frankie looked around. It was empty, though an unpacked suitcase and a woman's handbag lay in the hallway. Always mindful, he checked every room, checking under the bed to be extra vigilant, with Tommy following behind him.

After they finished checking, Tommy spoke. 'Ain't no one here.'

Frankie eyeballed Tommy. Although he was undeniably grateful to him for saving his nearest and dearest there was still something about him which made him feel very uncomfortable, although he was trying not to show it. Frankie spoke to Tommy with as much politeness as he could muster. 'You're right there, son. Any ideas?'

'Plenty, but not any that will help.'

'Why don't we go into the forest? They can't be very far, their car's still there so they haven't left. We can split up, Frankie can go with Gypsy and Lorna, and I'll come with you.'

'Sounds like a good idea to me. Is that alright with you, Frankie?'

Tommy got an absentminded nod in return and then an enquiry from Frankie.

'You got your own tool, Tommy?'

Tommy pulled out a gun from underneath his jacket. Silver and gleaming to match the one Frankie held in his hand.

'Yeah, I'm more than ready; I've been waiting for this for a long time. In fact, I've wanted to do this for most of my life.'

CHAPTER FIFTY-THREE

Max laughed out loudly, his voice full of scorn as Sheila pointed the gun at him. She'd led him through the woodland, to a deserted clearing within Epping Forest, the gun pointed to his head, all the while. Now she was looking at him, and even though it was *her* who had the gun in her hand he could see the look of terror on her paler-than-usual face. He growled at her. 'Jaysus woman, yer a fecking mess. You can't even kill me properly without shaking like a stinking fecking rat caught in a trap. Do yourself a favour and turn the gun on yourself – because if you can't kill me, yer going to wish you had, because your life won't be worth living.'

Max started to walk towards her, dragging his feet through the fallen leaves. Sheila shouted at him. 'Stay there, stay where you are or I'll shoot.'

Max roared with laughter. 'You've been watching too much *C.S.I. Miami* sweetheart.'

He chuckled menacingly, ignoring her threat and continued to walk forward, watching as her hand shook and the tears rolled down her face. He was about to reach out and grab hold of the gun until he heard the quiet, but definite sound of the trigger of the gun being drawn back. He froze. For the first time, it crossed Max Donaldson's mind that his wife might be serious.

'No more, Max, no more, it comes to an end here. I should've done this a long time ago. You've hurt too many people for too long. You did everything you could to break us and you almost managed it, Max; almost, but not quite. I'll go to my grave knowing I failed my children but you Max – you'll go to yours knowing I put you in there. I finally put a full stop to it.'

'Do it then, come on, I dare you. Put the bullet through my brain because words don't stand for much, it's actions darling.'

Max's eyes were blazing and he screamed at Sheila, pressing his forehead on the gun.

'Do it, do it then! Come on, what are you waiting for woman? You can't, you can't fucking do it can you?'

'No, but I can.'

The voice was loud and came from the thicket of trees. It belonged to Tommy.

'Hello, Dad.'

Max was clearly shocked but he regained his composure as he spoke. 'What the frig are you doing son? Put the gun down.'

'Why? So you can blow my brains out? I don't think so.'

'I said put it down, Tommy.'

'And I say fuck you. Fuck you for everything you've ever done.'

Max looked at Sheila then back at Tommy and roared with laughter. Taking his chances he quickly brought up his fist; backhanding Sheila. She flew backwards holding the gun which went off as she landed on the hard ground, then she dropped it.

Max raced over to pick it up and was about to point it at Tommy when he saw Frankie Taylor running through the thicket, brandishing a gun in his direction.

Deciding he didn't want to be outnumbered, Max quickly decided to head in the other direction and disappeared into the forest.

'He's been shot.'

Sheila's voice was as worried as the look on her face. Frankie, Maggie and Lorna hurried over to Tommy, trying their best not to slip down the steep bank.

'I'm fine, it's just my leg, the bullet's just skimmed it.'

Frankie spoke to Sheila and Tommy. 'Will you be alright here for a bit? I don't want him getting away.'

'We'll be fine.'

Maggie, crouching down with Tommy, looked up at Frankie.

'Where's Gypsy?'

'She didn't want to come with me. She's in the car back at the cottage.'

'Which is probably where my dad's heading.'

Frankie's face fell before he started to run, quickly followed by Maggie. 'Frankie, you go along the path, I'll go this way back to where he's parked his car, it might be quicker.'

Breathing heavily, Frankie watched Maggie dart ahead in the other direction. As he ran, he mouthed a silent and unseen thank you.

Gypsy hadn't wanted to sit in the car any longer, she hadn't wanted to go into the forest – or rather she couldn't cope with it. The moment she'd arrived, she knew exactly where she was. She knew this was where it'd happened. And knowing that, she hadn't wanted to go and revisit any part of it, and she certainly hadn't wanted to go with Frankie.

'You ain't sitting in the car, Gyps.'

'Oh? And who says I can't, Frankie?'

'I do.'

'Well you can tell 'I do' to keep his nose out of me business, and whilst you're at it, you can also tell 'I do' to shove it where the sun don't shine.'

She'd stormed off and sat in the car, listening to the radio until the songs had got too emotive and she'd needed to turn it off and go for a walk.

Now as she looked down the track of Epping Forest and recalled the memories she felt very ill at ease. She'd walked quite far from the car and now she wished she hadn't. It was a beautiful place but the memories cast ugly shadows, making her nervous of even the trees. The wind was getting up and Gypsy thought it was best to head back to the car.

A sea of buttercups covered the ground and Gypsy bent down to pick a bunch to take to Johnny and Harley.

'Hello, Gypsy.'

Max's hand covered her mouth and he forced her backwards into the woody undergrowth. Her legs scrambled to support her as she toppled to one side as Max spoke. 'So finally the cavalry's turned up.'

Max's laughter made her burst into tears fearing she'd used up her cat's lives with this man. His hand was heavy and hard on her mouth and she bit down on it, managing to pull her mouth up enough to let out a scream.

Frankie turned at the sound. Gypsy was in trouble.

'This way.'

He shouted loudly as he ran, not knowing if Maggie or the others would hear, but he wasn't going to wait and find out; his gut instinct told him to wait would be fatal.

Frankie couldn't hear anything now as the wind caught the branches of the trees, and he didn't know which way to turn. He ran to the left seeing only a voluminous mass of trees and bracken and turned back to the right, again only seeing a mass of identical foliage.

'Clever girl.' Frankie spoke out loud as he saw a shoe ten metres in front of him. He was certain Gypsy had purposely done that, as the only way she'd part with her Jimmy Choos was if it was a matter of life or death.

Max dragged Gypsy through the trees and out onto the road which he knew would be empty, pushing her forward, one hand still gripped hard over her mouth and the other one twisting her arm behind her back. He didn't know the forest well enough to hurtle through it with Gypsy in tow. He'd stick to the road and make it back to the car.

'Gypsy? Gypsy?'

Gypsy could hear Frankie calling her name some way behind, but nevertheless it was his voice. It gave her strength and she tried to wriggle away from Max's grip, but the sound of Frankie's voice seemed to have the same effect on Max as his grip became harder, driving her on faster.

Max could see the car ahead and he quickly took a look around. He couldn't hear them anymore; hopefully he'd lost them. He let go of Gypsy but pointed the gun at her.

'Get in.'

Gypsy didn't hesitate; she could see she had no other choice. A second later Max got in and started up the car, putting it in reverse. As Max looked in the driver's mirror he saw a pair of blue eyes staring back at him – and a moment later he felt a gun in the back of his head, as Maggie sat up properly from the backseat of the car.

'Hello, Dad. Ain't this a nice surprise?'

A few moments later the driver's door opened and Frankie stood glaring at Max. 'Get out.'

Max didn't object; it was pointless. He got out slowly with two guns aimed at him. He saw Sheila coming up the road and blew her a kiss, followed by a cruel laugh. He looked at Lorna who was red in the face and smirked, then back to his wife who was supporting Tommy – Max sneered at them all, then turned to Frankie and spoke with a quiet, menacing calm.

'Come on then, let's get this over and done with.'

He turned away without giving his family another glance as he was marched into the forest by Frankie.

The single gunshot was heard a mile away, scattering the birds from the trees. Max Donaldson's reign of terror had finally come to an end.

Two months later

'About bleeding time too, you've got a daughter to look after.'

The words came from Gypsy's mouth as her son finally regained consciousness; the tears came from her eyes as she looked at his injured body, and the gentle embrace she gave him, which made Johnny wince with pain but smile at the same time, came from her heart.

'There's someone to see you.'

Johnny shifted his gaze to the end of the bed and saw Maggie holding Harley. He looked at Gypsy with a puzzled look; she put her hand on his.

'It's fine, I was wrong. A lot's happened since the last time we spoke. And Johnny; I'm sorry.'

Gypsy got up and kissed Johnny gently on his forehead.

'I'll leave you three to it. You've got a lot of catching up to do.'

Maggie approached Johnny and smiled as she spoke.

'Hello you.'

'Maggie, I'm sorry . . .'

'Don't tire yourself out trying to talk babe, just listen. I love you, Johnny Taylor, I always have – and I don't want you to have to say sorry anymore. None of us are without blame. I don't want to look back now, only forward. I want us to have a future together, all three of us to be a proper family . . . if, of course, that's what you want.'

Johnny gave Maggie a dazzling smile.

'*If* it's what I want? That's all I've ever wanted, Mags. I just messed up a bit trying to show it . . . but what about . . .'

Maggie shook her head.

'Like your mum said, you've got a lot of catching up to do.'

Johnny reached out to touch Maggie and Harley who both took his hand and squeezed it.

'Maggie? Marry me.'

'I'm already married to you silly.'

'No, I want to marry you again, only this time let's do it properly. With both our families there. Give you the wedding you deserve. Harley can be bridesmaid. What do you say?'

Maggie's blue eyes sparkled as she answered.

'I say yes. Yes, Johnny. Yes.'

'You help her, I can't. She won't listen to anything I have to say, she's driving me potty.'

Tommy raised his arms in the air in exasperation and grinned at Frankie, tapping him on his back encouragingly as he left the room.

'Bleeding hell, Frank, where've you been? Have you seen the time? It's pointless you wearing that fancy watch of yours for all the good it does. A man running backwards would be quicker than you.'

'Lorn, I've things to do you know, clubs to run, money to make.'

'Stop your moaning, Frank, and give us a hand. Any more of your chatter and we'll have to add another month to the year. I don't know why you bothered employing that Tommy, he's worse than useless in putting up curtains. Careful of my wallpaper with that bed, I don't want it marking. It's a bedroom not a homework book.'

With a deep breath, Frankie helped Lorna move the bed for what must have been the tenth time that day as she searched for the perfect position for it in her new room – and it'd all been Gypsy's idea.

'Ask her to move in, Frank.'

He'd looked at his wife incredulously. 'Even after everything she did to you? To us?'

'Even after everything she did, Frank, you should still ask her.'

'But . . . ?'

'There's been enough hurt, Frank; I ain't going to cause more by sending Lorna away. I ain't doing that to her. We've all had our lessons to learn and I reckon she's learnt hers. We all need someone to love us. We all need our family.'

'So does that mean you'll be coming back home? You can't leave me on my own with her, she'll have me tearing me bleeding hair out and not only that . . . I miss you.'

'You'll be fine Frank.'

Gypsy had taken a lot of her clothes, going to stay in a hotel and keeping her distance ever since. Frankie felt lost. Without Gypsy by his side it was as if some part of him was missing.

In the past two months a lot of things had changed. The doctors had said Johnny would make a full recovery and when he'd heard the news, he'd cried and hadn't been ashamed to. He'd also employed Tommy Donaldson to be his right hand man, as a favour to Gypsy.

Tommy no longer wanted to continue with Max's business, unhappy at screwing people over for money, but wanted to support his family. The way Frankie saw it, the Donaldsons had in a way become his family as well so he'd been happy to help Tommy, always indebted for what he did for Gypsy and Johnny. He respected a man who wanted to look after his family and in a way saw some of himself in Tommy.

They'd both gone around to all the people who owed Max money and explained that their debts were written off. Strangely, seeing the relief on the people's faces had made Frankie feel good.

Tommy had surprised him. Almost overnight, he'd begun to come out of his shell, showing himself to be a funny, sensitive, caring man. Frankie liked him. He also liked the way Tommy not only spent time with his mother each day, but how he also popped in daily to see Gypsy at the hotel as well. It was clear that family meant everything to the lad but he'd just never been given the opportunity to demonstrate it before.

The best bit of all to come out of all the chaos was Harley, his granddaughter. From the first time Maggie had brought her round and Harley had cautiously climbed up to sit on his knee, he'd fallen in love with her. Almost there and then he'd ordered his men to sort out getting one of the bedrooms in the house turned into a pink palace so that Harley could have her own room and stay as often as she liked. And when the little girl wasn't staying at his house with Maggie, he missed her like she'd always been a part of his life.

The business with Max was sorted and it'd been relatively easy. He'd taken him into the forest but had made Maggie turn back. She didn't need to see her father's brains blown out; she'd been through enough. Before he'd pulled the trigger Max had shown no remorse.

'Gypsy. She squealed like a pig, Frank, when I . . .'

He'd put the bullet in Max's head then. He hadn't wanted to hear anymore. He hadn't wanted to know how his wife had suffered, not from him anyway. Not from the man who'd caused the pain.

He'd called his men, who'd disposed of the body in Epping Forest, ironically alongside the other gangland faces that Max had buried in the past.

'A penny for them, no let's make it a monkey. A monkey for your thoughts?'

Frankie turned around and saw Gypsy standing behind him. He grinned as he saw the suitcase next to her, but he spoke cautiously.

'Hello, Gyps.'

'Alright, Frank.'

'Are . . . are you here to stay?'

Gypsy smiled and watched Lorna muttering away as she fussed over the position of the pillows on the bed. She gestured with her head towards her sister-in-law.

'Well how can I leave you on your own with her? We can't have you pulling your hair out; bald men ain't really my thing.'

Sheila Donaldson sat in her front room, enjoying the peaceful stillness. Frankie had sent some decorators around to do the whole house up. Now it no longer held the yellowing gloom of yesteryear and memories of Max. It was light and bright and, for the first time, it felt like a proper home.

She smiled to herself as she looked at the photo of Tommy, Nicky, Harley and Maggie sitting on top of the television. She'd insisted on getting one done and they'd had it taken last week. It was the first family photo she'd ever had of her kids and when she looked at it she didn't look at their faces, she looked at their eyes. And in their eyes she could see what had always been missing in them; happiness.

*   *   *

'You want me to read to you, Nick?' Saucers smiled at Nicky as she held his hand in the day room and he nodded. He'd been out of hospital for a month but had gone straight from hospital into rehab, paid for by Frankie. Nicky hadn't objected; he wanted to get better.

The rehab centre was in a tiny village in Oxfordshire. Frankie had got Saucers a hotel to stay in for the whole of Nicky's treatment programme so she could visit him every day. She'd been so grateful and hadn't quite known how to thank Frankie, but he'd just waved his hand at her and winked.

Each weekend the whole Donaldson and Taylor families descended on the small village in Oxfordshire; taking family photos and bringing tales of Soho for Nicky and Saucers. Rallying around in support.

The bond of love running through the two families touched Saucers. It was the first time she'd been part of something so special. And the Donaldsons and the Taylors were certainly special.

Saucers, about to read to Nicky, smiled to herself as she looked down at the book, catching a glimpse of the tinfoil engagement ring Nicky had given her last week when he'd proposed.

'Ready?'

Nicky nodded and kept hold of Saucers' hand as he closed his eyes and listened to her read.

'A glooming peace this morning with it brings;*
The sun for sorrow will not show his head.
Go hence to have more talk of these sad things
For never was a story of more woe
Than this of Juliet and her Romeo.'

Read on for an exclusive extract from Jacqui's next novel, *Dishonour*, published by Avon in August 2013 . . .

Laila Khan opened her mouth and screamed, although it wasn't the sound of her cry which echoed around the room, it was the sound of the slap against her cheek. For Laila, the burning pain on the side of her face was a welcome distraction to what her uncle had just angrily told her.

This was a moment she knew she'd never forget. Unlike so many other experiences in her life which blurred and faded with the passage of time, Laila was certain only death would erase today.

Exhausted, she sat down, looking around her tiny bedroom, taking in every detail. Acutely aware she was making a mental picture for herself, knowing nothing would ever look the same to her again.

The yellow flowered wallpaper she'd hated from the start. The red wall clock her brother had given her last year. The vast array of thimbles she'd been collecting since she was a child, lined up neatly as usual on the shelf above her bed, and the box of aluminium cooking pots her mother insisted on storing in her room. Everything she knew was in this room; was in this house. This was where she came from. A small red-bricked terraced house in a nondescript street in the Horton area of Bradford.

But as Laila looked at her family, standing watching in reproachful silence with her mother's face lined with disapproval and her uncle rubbing his hand, it was as if Laila could see a door opening, leading her out of the life she knew to take her into another, darker, more foreboding one.

Laila's eyes darted around the room in panic before they were drawn to a large black fly landing on the maths homework she was supposed to have handed in last week. She watched, fascinated, as it seemed to stare back at her as intently as she was staring at it. The sudden movement of the curtain swaying in the warm summer breeze was enough for the fly to abandon the red tattered textbooks, but Laila continued to stare. Unable to move. Unable to fly away.

Trance-like she sat on her bed until her vision was clouded by the welling of her pricking tears. She bowed her head, wanting to keep her composure now. Closing her eyes, she sat motionless, almost forgetting to breathe.

The aromatic smells from the palak chicken and rice cooking downstairs began to overwhelm her senses as the pungent spices wafted into the stifling room. Snapping open her eyes, Laila jerked her body up as a wave of nausea hit her. She managed to reach as far as the door before she hunched over to empty the contents of her stomach into the overflowing paper bin in the corner of her room.

It was a couple of minutes before she straightened herself up, not trusting that she wouldn't be hit again by another wave of sickness. Wiping her mouth with the back of her hand, Laila quickly turned away as she noticed the fly land on the foul-smelling vomit.

She felt a scratch on the palm of her hand and realised she was still clutching onto the reason for the sudden onset of illness. It was a photograph. Loosening her grip on it to stop it digging into her hand, Laila allowed herself to look at it. It was a picture of a man. A man she'd never seen before, yet Laila Khan had just been informed in a week's time she was going to become his wife.

* * *

Half an hour later Tariq Khan sat across from his sister at the dinner table noticing how her eyes were red, blotchy and swollen. Reminding him of a bullfrog he'd seen last year in Pakistan.

He'd come in from work to hear screaming upstairs and when he'd gone to investigate, he'd seen Laila kneeling on the floor at their uncle's feet, begging and pleading with him not to force her to marry.

He'd watched as their uncle had called his sister names. Accusing her of being nothing short of a disgrace. Spitting at her in disgust. She'd then turned to Tariq. Pulling at his trouser leg and looking up with her big almond shaped eyes. Begging him to do something to help.

Why did Laila have to make such a fuss? She knew what their uncle was like. Didn't she understand that everything would be easier for her if she didn't put up such a fight? She was making it harder. She knew she had a duty. A duty to their uncle. A duty to their family.

What did she think her uncle was going to let her do? Run around like the other slags in her class? Laila was sixteen, almost seventeen. Old enough, their uncle had told her, too old nearly.

How was he supposed to feel sorry for his sister when she'd brought it on herself? Word had got back to them that she'd been cosying up with some English boy at school. Flaunting herself and making dirt out of their family name. And of course, the moment the rumours had hit their uncle's ears, he'd straight away put what needed to be done into action.

Laila should be thankful. Her life wasn't over, though it would've been if their uncle and the family had had their way. Tariq had had to beg with them, pleading for leniency on Laila's behalf and eventually they'd backed down, on the condition that she marry.

She'd been lucky. A lot of girls he knew who'd behaved like Laila had didn't get away with it so lightly.

'Is everything in order?'

Tariq's thoughts were broken as his uncle spoke to him in a gruff tone of voice.

'Yes, everything's sorted; just like you arranged.'

Mahmood Khan looked at his nephew. There was a lot to do before tomorrow. He was feeling tired but he prayed that he would be given the strength to deal with the next few hours.

He glanced quickly at Laila as he reached for another helping of rice. Girls were a curse. Especially beautiful ones. The more beautiful, the more of a curse.

Quite frankly he wasn't sure what wrongs he'd done to deserve to be blighted with three nieces. But then, he knew he shouldn't question what he'd been given. Only make the best of it, which, if he were to be honest, was very hard to do.

Laila had always been spirited. Her two sisters, who were older than her and already married, had been different. They'd been quiet and willing to please. Understanding what it was to be a woman. Neither of them had the brains nor the dazzling beauty of Laila; they'd been blessed with simplicity and plainness.

From the moment Laila was born, Mahmood knew his youngest niece was trouble. As a baby she'd had the cry of a lion; roaring with discontent. When she was little she'd suffered with stomach problems. No doubt caused by the fire of the warrior in her belly, fighting to get out. She absorbed knowledge like the jacaranda tree absorbed the water and her spirit whirled and glided like a Middle Eastern Sufi dancer.

It was all too much. She was nothing like her mother who'd been a good wife to his brother, although admittedly

354

he'd needed to show her his word was final in the beginning. Nevertheless, his sister-in-law was silent and attentive. Two traits a woman should possess, but two traits his niece didn't come close to holding. Thankfully though, by this time next week, Laila would be someone else's problem.

It felt to Mahmood that all he'd done for the past few years was battle with his niece to keep her in her place. With each passing year it became more of a struggle as he fought against her curiousity about the world she lived in.

When his brother, their father, had died, the responsibility of looking after the family had fallen on his shoulders. And the adjustment had taken some doing for both he and them.

His brother had been soft; far too soft for a man who carried the Khan name. Often Mahmood had disapproved of the freedom his brother offered his wife and children. Giving them leave to argue, question and be educated. He'd often chastised his brother but the admonishment had been wasted and fallen onto deaf ears. But then his brother had passed away and everything had changed.

Under his guidance everyone had been shown the error of their ways. And though the changes had come up against long faces and the occasional question, they'd all eventually accepted the way it was going to be under his rule. All except Laila.

Mahmood looked at his watch 'We better go, Tariq, time is short.'

Mahmood pushed his chair away and looked once more at Laila. Her face was marked not only from her tears but also from the bruise now forming on her cheek. Tomorrow when they went out, he'd make her wear her burka. It would hide it. By next week it'd be gone, and then maybe for the first time in his life he could be proud of her. Proud to give her away.

Laila's eyes widened as she watched her older brother and uncle. She was terrified, but she had a rising suspicion that something worse was about to happen. Her uncle rarely ventured out at this time of night, preferring instead to have his friends come to him.

Mustering up some courage, Laila directed her question at her brother which she almost always did. 'Is everything alright, Tariq?'

Before Tariq had a chance to say anything, Mahmood snarled at her, his strong Pakistani accent punctuating the words.

'You bring dishonour on this family then you ask if everything's alright?'

Laila sat up in her chair. Her face reflecting the puzzlement in her tone. 'Dishonour? Tariq, what's he talking about? I don't know what he's talking about.'

Tariq banged his fist on the table as Mahmood Khan stood back, admiring the forcefulness of his nephew. 'Laila, don't play the innocent with me. I've heard the talk. Uncle's right, you've brought shame on us. On me. Well, it stops right here.'

Laila's face was drawn and her fear was apparent. The look on her face made Tariq feel uncomfortable and he turned away, not wanting to see the terror in his sister's eyes.

'Tariq, please. I . . . I really don't know what you're talking about.'

Tariq's arm shot out, sweeping the supper dishes off the table, sending Laila's untouched plate of palak chicken to stain the beige carpet rug.

'Don't make a fool of me, not when I've tried to help you . . . I know all about you and the English boy.'

'English boy?'

Tariq clenched his fist. Why was she doing this? Why was she lying to him when all he needed her to do was quietly get married so there'd be a stop to all of this? He didn't want any harm to come to her but there was only so much he could do to help if she wouldn't help herself.

Tariq leant forward, his arms on the table; ignoring the fact that he'd just put his hand in a pile of cold rice. 'Raymond Thompson. Ring any bells, Laila?'

Laila Khan swallowed hard. She knew the name. She knew the boy. But not in the way her brother was trying to imply.

He sat next to her in class and that's all it was. Yes, she'd talked to him. He made her laugh. She'd even given him a CD of her favourite song, covering the case with pink smiley stickers. But it'd all been innocent.

He hadn't been at the school long, moving up North from London to come to live with his mother on the south side of Bradford. He was popular and handsome, his cockney twang adding to his appeal, though it wasn't just the girls who flitted around him and swooned over his six-foot frame. The boys wanted to be his friend too. They seemed to respect him, getting the feeling he could handle himself. That he wasn't going to be messed with. Even Mrs Rigby, the sixth form maths teacher, blushed when he went to talk to her.

So she'd been surprised when Raymond had moved his desk next to hers. Though quietly pleased. At first she'd ignored him. But slowly she'd started to smile when she'd heard his jokes. Then the smiles had turned into laughter and they'd become friends.

Laila didn't know why he'd chosen to be her friend but she'd cautiously welcomed it. She loved it when he teased her as his blue eyes twinkled back at her. But that's all it was. A smile. A laugh. A tease. That's all it *could* be. She knew that more than anybody.

Apart from that one time. That once. The day she'd decided to forget she was Laila Khan, respectful and dutiful daughter of the late Zarin Khan and niece of the ever-present Mahmood Khan. That day she'd chosen to walk to the bus stop with him instead of with her friends.

'Laila, your uncle will kill you if he sees you.'

'He won't though, will he?'

She could hear the conversation now between her and her best friend and she'd been right, her uncle hadn't seen them. Nobody had. But words don't need to have eyes; only tongues.

As Laila sat at the table, trying to ignore her uncle's cutting stare, she knew her friend had talked. Not intentionally, but talked all the same. And it didn't take a whole vine for it to reach her uncle's ears.

'Tariq . . . it was nothing. Nothing happened . . . I was . . .'

The look on her brother's face made Laila stop talking. The rage which was already there in his eyes had turned into something else. Hatred. And she couldn't bear it. She couldn't bear to have her brother, who she loved more than anyone in the world, hate her.

She watched as her uncle nodded his head to her mother – who'd sat silently throughout – gesturing to her to leave the room. Laila could feel her legs trembling as Mahmood walked around the table towards her. He pulled her up as he grabbed her arm, painfully squeezing it as he did so. She saw Tariq step forward, then stop. Her uncle's face almost pressed onto hers as he spoke in a whisper. 'Understand this. If it wasn't for your brother pleading your case, Laila, you might not have had a tomorrow.'

Laila pulled back. Terrified by what her uncle was insinuating. Though it wasn't an insinuation, was it? It was an outright threat. Clear for her to understand. She knew her family respected the cultural teachings and traditions as she did. But this? This wasn't a part of it; this was just some twisted misinterpretation of it.

She'd heard time and time again about what happened to girls in the community who brought shame and dishonour on their family. But *she* hadn't brought shame. She'd walked less than the length of a high street with Raymond. Refusing his requests to go to McDonald's. Refusing his requests for him to walk her all the way home. It'd been innocent.

Mahmood dropped her arm and walked towards the door, deciding not to bother with a jacket. He turned to Laila as Tariq opened the dining room door.

'*You* might have been lucky, but your boyfriend's not going to have such an easy ride.'

Laila ran to her uncle, grabbing at his sleeve. 'What are you going to do? Uncle, please. He's done nothing wrong.'

'For someone who's so innocent you seem to care an awful lot about what happens to him. You're a disgrace.'

'I don't care . . . I mean, I do care but not like that, I care because he's done nothing . . . Uncle, please, don't touch him.'

Mahmood grabbed Laila's hair, pulling her head back. 'Try stopping me.'

He let go of her hair and started for the front door, but Laila refused to let him walk away. She grasped hold of him, trying to pull him back. She was beside herself with anguish and the tears rolled down her face as she cried. Her uncle sneered. She was out of control and he was going to enjoy seeing Raymond Thompson squeal. '*Izzat*, Laila. Honour. Doesn't it mean anything?'

'It means everything to me, Uncle, you know it does. But not like this. It isn't about this.'

She let go of her uncle and ran to Tariq, pulling on him and hearing his shirt tear as he tugged it away from her grip. 'Tariq . . . no, stop. You can't do this. Leave him alone.'

'What do you want me to do, Laila? I've got no choice.'

'For me, please, Tariq. Do what you want with me but leave him alone.'

Tariq didn't want to listen to her any more. He didn't want to hear his sister like this. Couldn't she see what harm she was doing by acting like this? It was just making their uncle more determined. Pushing Laila to one side, he followed his uncle out of the door.

'Tariq, no!' She shouted after her brother. She needed to stop them but she didn't know how. No one would help her. No one would get involved. This was family business, family *honour*, and most people she knew would think her uncle was doing the right thing.

She didn't even have Raymond's telephone number to warn him but she couldn't let them hurt him. Not because of her. Without thinking, she picked up the phone.

'Police, please.'

The phone went dead. Laila turned round. The first thing she saw was Mahmood with the telephone wire in his hand. The second thing she saw was his fist coming towards her. A moment later Laila Khan blacked out.